EDWARD MARSTON was born and brought up in South Wales. A full-time writer for over thirty years, he has worked in radio, film, television and the theatre and is a former chairman of the Crime Writers' Association. Prolific and highly successful, he is equally at home writing children's books or literary criticism, plays or biographies. *Fire and Sword* is the third book in the Daniel Rawson series.

www.edwardmarston.com

a&b

Fire and Sword

EDWARD MARSTON

Allison & Busby Limited
12 Fitzroy Mews
London W1T 6DW
www.allisonandbusby.com

First published in Great Britain by Allison & Busby in 2009.
This paperback edition published by Allison & Busby in 2010.

Copyright © 2009 by EDWARD MARSTON

A CIP catalogue record for this book is available from
the British Library.

10 9 8 7 6 5 4

ISBN 978-0-7490-0895-6

Typeset in 11.5/17 pt Adobe Garamond Pro by
Allison & Busby Ltd.

The paper used for this Allison & Busby publication
has been produced from trees that have been legally sourced
from well-managed and credibly certified forests.

Printed and bound by
CPI Group (UK) Ltd, Croydon, CR0 4YY

Fire and Sword

CHAPTER ONE

Flanders, 1707

Daniel Rawson rode at a steady canter along a winding track. It was late afternoon and autumn was already chasing some of the light from the sky. He was resigned to the fact that he wouldn't reach the camp until well after midnight. Daniel was a captain in the 24th Foot and his regiment had gone into winter quarters. But he was not in uniform now. Instead, he was dressed in the civilian clothing that allowed him to slip through enemy lines so that he could act as a spy in Paris. The forged papers he was carrying bore the name of Marcel Daron, a wine merchant, a pose that was reinforced by his ability to speak French like a native and by his knowledge of certain vineyards in the country.

As on previous occasions, the disguise had served him

well. During his stay in the French capital, he'd garnered some crucial intelligence. Most of it had been committed to memory so that he was not caught with sensitive documents in his possession. However, a couple of dispatches he'd managed to intercept were concealed in the lining of his coat. He smiled as he recalled how he'd got hold of them. The messenger had been left with a bad headache and had faced the ordeal of making an embarrassing confession to superiors in the French army. Severe punishment must have followed. Daniel had no sympathy for him. The messenger had been careless.

He was still musing on his encounter with the man when a noise brought him out of his reverie. A French patrol had suddenly appeared on the crest of the hill to his left. A dozen or so in all, they paused for a moment then kicked their horses into a gallop and came surging down the incline with predatory zeal. When he saw one of them draw a pistol, Daniel didn't hesitate. He knew that Marcel Daron wouldn't be able to talk his way out of an awkward situation this time. The soldiers were likely to kill him first and identify him afterwards. Digging in his heels and urging his mount on, Daniel fled, riding hell for leather and sending up small clouds of dust in his wake. The blue uniforms kept up hot pursuit. They were clearly gaining on him. His assignment was in danger of ending abruptly. The thunder of hooves behind him could be the sound of his death knell.

There was no chance of outrunning them. Daniel

accepted that. Their horses had been chosen for speed and stamina. His, by contrast, was the kind of serviceable but willing animal that a wine merchant might be expected to own. It was only a question of minutes before he was overhauled. Since there was no hope of winning a race, Daniel's sole means of escape was to elude them somehow. The wood ahead of him offered that vague possibility. Coaxing the last ounce of speed from his horse, he pounded towards it then veered off to the right, heading for the point where the trees and undergrowth seemed at their most dense. He was just in time. The moment he changed direction, a bullet from the pistol whistled harmlessly past him. Had he stayed on the track, it would have hit him squarely between the shoulder blades.

Unaware of his good fortune, Daniel rode on. Plunging into the wood, he had to slow his horse down so that he could pick a way through the trees and bushes with a degree of safety. He finally had something in his favour. Though most of the leaves had been shed, there was still a thick fretwork of branches above his head, darkening the interior of the wood and limiting visibility. It was like riding through a huge cavern with a timber roof. The deeper he penetrated, the murkier it got. When he stole a glance over his shoulder, he could barely make out the shadowy figures hunting him. Confident that their quarry could not escape, the soldiers had fanned out and were moving at a trot. Some of them taunted him, ignoring the scratch of bushes and the jab of low branches. Nothing would stop them. They were lusting for a kill.

Most people in that predicament would quail but fear was unknown to Daniel. What drove him on was an instinct for survival, sharpened by years in combat against French armies. Fear only induced panic and he always remained cool. As he zigzagged his way through the wood, his eyes were alert as he searched for ways to shake off the patrol. The half-dark that enfolded him had come to his aid but it now proved treacherous. Unable to see it properly, his horse misjudged the size of a fallen tree trunk. Instead of hopping easily over it, the animal caught its front hooves against the timber and pitched helplessly forward. Daniel was thrown from the saddle, hitting the ground hard and somersaulting twice before he came to a halt.

The horse was the first to get up. Momentarily dazed, Daniel scrambled to his feet but he was too late to stop his frightened mount from careering off into the undergrowth in the direction from which they'd just come. It was eventually caught by one of the soldiers.

'I have his horse!' he cried in triumph. 'He's on foot.'

The announcement produced a round of cruel laughter.

Daniel didn't stay to listen to it. He was already running at full speed through the trees, dodging bushes, jumping logs, looking to left then right in a desperate search for a hiding place. His heart was pounding and his lungs were on fire. Any second he could be ridden down and hacked to death with a sabre. He came at last to a small clearing and clambered up a tree. Then he deliberately dropped his hat onto the ground below. Nestling against a thick branch, Daniel waited, trying to muffle the sound of his heavy breathing. He was no French wine merchant now but an experienced British soldier who'd been cornered by the enemy before. There had always been a way out in the past. The trick, he'd discovered, was to find it.

He could hear their voices, calling out to each other, placing bets on who would catch their prey first, boasting about what they'd do to him with their sharp blades. The only consolation was that they sounded a little distance away. Much nearer, however, were the jingle of harness and the rustle of hooves in the undergrowth. Somebody was coming towards him. Daniel had two weapons. One was the dagger he pulled out and the other was the element of surprise. What the soldier was looking for was a terrified fugitive, cowering under a hedge. He never thought to look up. When he saw the hat lying on the ground, he dismounted at once and drew his sword, remaining silent so that he didn't lose the wager by rousing the others.

Daniel was ready. The moment the man bent down to retrieve the hat, Daniel hurled himself from the tree with a vengeance and hit him with his full weight. Stunned by the attack, the soldier had no time to resist. One hand over the man's mouth, Daniel used the other to slit his throat. The soldier twitched and flailed impotently as his lifeblood drained inexorably away. Daniel kept him in an iron grip, squeezing him tight and waiting until he went limp before letting him drop slowly to the ground. Sheathing his dagger, Daniel recovered his hat, seized the discarded sabre and mounted the horse.

He then rode on again with renewed urgency. After a few minutes, he came to a path that meandered through the wood. It enabled him to pick up speed but he was not the first rider to find the path. One of the soldiers lurched out ahead of him on his horse to block his way. It was a direct challenge. Though he was in a regiment of foot, Daniel had also taken part in cavalry charges. He'd felt that soaring exhilaration before. Blood racing and sabre held aloft, he galloped towards the man and swung his arm with murderous force. Though the soldier parried the blow with his own sword, the sheer power of the strike snapped his wrist and he dropped the weapon with a howl of pain. Without even looking back, Daniel sped off into the darkness.

The farmer was short, stocky and round-shouldered. He used a wooden bucket to tip the mixture into the trough. The pig was on it immediately, grunting contentedly and dipping his nose to smell his food before gobbling it up. The animal was kept in a ramshackle pen with a small, low hut to protect it from bad weather. When winter came, it would be slaughtered and used to feed the family. A drumming sound made the farmer turn and he saw horsemen being conjured out of the gloom. They were French soldiers. Most of them sat tall in the saddle but one of them was hunched up as he nursed his broken wrist. Another man was slumped lifelessly across his mount. Towed along behind the cavalcade was a riderless horse.

Removing his hat, the farmer adopted a deferential tone.

'Good day to you, good sirs,' he said. 'Can I help you?'

'We're looking for a fugitive,' explained the sergeant. 'He's a man in a brown coat and has something of my build.'

'We've seen nobody like that, sir.'

'Are you sure?'

'The only person to go past all day was a carter.'

'Be warned,' said the sergeant, pointing a finger. 'If we discover that you're hiding the villain, you'll die alongside him. He killed one of my men and wounded another. We *want* him.'

'I'm sorry, sir. He's not here.'

'He must be. He abandoned a horse a mile or so away, hoping that we'd keep chasing it all evening but we soon caught up with it. He couldn't have got far. I think he came this way.'

'You're welcome to search.'

'We don't need your permission to do that,' snarled the sergeant. 'Right,' he went on, nodding to some of the men, 'look *everywhere*. Turn the place upside down.'

'Do as you wish,' said the farmer, spreading his arms

in a gesture of welcome. 'We've nothing to hide.' As the men dismounted, he walked over to the sergeant. 'Is there anything I can get you while you wait, sir – a cup of wine, perhaps?'

'I don't drink that Flemish piss.'

'We have beer.'

The sergeant spat contemptuously. 'That's even worse.'

The farm was small so the search was short-lived. The soldiers didn't stand on ceremony. Barging into the house, they began to look in every room. Outraged at the sudden invasion, the farmer's wife and son came hurrying out to protest. He waved them into silence. While their home was being subjected to a rigorous search, the barn was also inspected along with the outbuildings. The hens were disturbed in their coop and the cows complained bitterly when soldiers burst into their byre. The old horse, munching hay in the stable, was offended when two men poked into every corner of its domain. Only the pig remained unruffled, head still deep in its trough.

'Don't you ever clean that sty out?' asked the sergeant, wrinkling his nose. 'It stinks to high heaven.'

'You get used to it,' said the farmer.

'How can anyone get used to that stench?'

The question hung unanswered in the air because soldiers came out of the house and shook their heads. Those who'd searched the barn and the outbuildings had also done so in vain. Remounting their horses, they waited for orders. The sergeant was angry and frustrated.

'He must have come this way,' he insisted. 'Spread out and make for the river. He might have made it that far. And whoever catches him,' he added, curling a lip, 'keep him alive until I get *my* hands on him. I want to make him suffer.'

The patrol galloped off and the farmer's wife was able to give vent to her fury. She swore at the departing horsemen then told her husband what they'd done. Her husband went into the house and saw the mess. Chairs had been overturned, cupboard doors wrenched open and cooking pots swept aside so that someone could peer up the chimney. It was the same story upstairs. In all three of the tiny rooms, beds had been propped against the wall, chest lids had been lifted and their contents had been scattered everywhere. The trapdoor to the attic had been left dangling. Everything stored up there had been ruthlessly trampled on.

When her rage was exhausted, the farmer's wife gave way to tears. It took him minutes to console her. Their son, meanwhile, was trying to tidy the place up. He noticed that some apples had been stolen from the table. Leaving the two of them in the house, the farmer ambled across to the sty. The pig had just finished the meal.

'You can come out now,' he said. 'They've gone.'

Covered in muck and reeking of excrement, Daniel emerged warily from his hiding place. Nobody would take him for a wine merchant now. His clothes were soiled and his face filthy.

'How did you know I was in there?' he asked.

'It was the way the pig behaved. You're a brave man. He has a vile temper. If he'd been upset, he could've bitten clean through your leg.'

'I was born and brought up on a farm,' said Daniel, giving the pig a friendly pat. 'I know how to handle animals.' He grinned. 'And that was the one place where they wouldn't have searched. I'm indebted to you, my friend. You could easily have given me away.'

'We hate the French.'

'What if they'd found me?'

The farmer chuckled. 'Then they'd have smelt almost as bad as you,' he said. 'Let's find some water to clean you up. My wife won't let you into her kitchen like that.'

It was two days before Daniel was able to return to the farm and he took the precaution of riding with a detachment of cavalry at his back. He was in full uniform now. Seated astride a black stallion, he used a lead rein to tow along the old horse he'd borrowed from the farmer. It had done good service and been well fed in camp. Daniel enjoyed the ride but his companion was a reluctant horseman.

'I joined the infantry,' argued Welbeck, 'not the cavalry.'

'Even you wouldn't have wanted to walk all the way, Henry,' said Daniel. 'Apart from anything else, we're on French territory.'

'I'd sooner have my feet on the ground, Dan. All that

horses ever do is to upset my stomach and give me a sore arse.'

'I thought you'd like a chance to escape from the camp.'

'Nobody told me we'd have so far to ride. Why bother to take that old nag back? You could have sent someone else.'

'The farmer saved my life. The least he deserves is to see how grateful I am. I'm deeply obliged to him.'

Welbeck snorted. 'I don't know why,' he said. 'I wouldn't be grateful to anyone who sent me back to my regiment, riding a flea-bitten old jade and stinking like a latrine during a hot summer. Do you realise what you *looked* like, Dan?'

'You should have seen me when I got out of the pigsty.'

'I could smell you from twenty yards away.'

Sergeant Henry Welbeck of the 24th Foot was Daniel's best friend in the regiment, and rank disappeared when they were alone together. The sergeant was a solid man of medium height with an ugly face decorated with a long battle scar. He had the greatest respect for his friend but even he had joined in the laughter when Daniel came back to camp in such an appalling state. Welbeck had continued to poke fun at him until Captain Rawson had bathed naked in the river, put on his scarlet uniform and at last looked like someone who deserved to be a member of the British army. In spite of his dislike of horses, the sergeant had agreed to accompany Daniel to the farm.

'How much farther is it, Dan?' he asked.

'We'll be there soon – it's on the other side of that hill.'

'At least we'll get a warm welcome.'

'What do you mean?'

'Use your eyes, man. Can't you see that smoke up ahead of us? My guess is that they're roasting that pig for you.'

Daniel made no reply. He'd only glanced at the hilltop before. Now that he looked properly, he could see dark smoke curling up into the air. No chimney would produce such billows. Handing the rein of the farmer's horse to Welbeck, he kicked his own mount into action and galloped up the hill. As he neared the top, he could hear the distant crackle of flames and the sound filled him with alarm. Cresting the hill, he saw that his fears were justified. Down below him, blazing merrily in the sunshine, was the little farmhouse, the barn and the various outbuildings. It was a calamity. Everything that the farmer had stored against the winter had been destroyed.

When the others joined him, Daniel barked an order.

'Come on!' he yelled. 'We may still be able to save someone.'

But he could see that it was a futile hope. As he led the charge down the hill, he watched the barn collapse and send up an enormous shower of sparks into the air. The roof of the house had already gone and the stable was a mass of charred timbers. There was no sign of the animals. Somewhere in the middle of the grotesque firework display was a family who'd come to Daniel's aid in a crisis. He prayed that they were still alive. As the riders got closer, however, they were confronted by a hideous sight. Staggering out of the house was the farmer, a human inferno, engulfed in flames, his clothes, his boots and even his hair and beard alight. Yelling in agony, he still had the strength to raise a defiant fist at the approaching redcoats.

Reaching him first, Daniel leapt from his horse, pushed the farmer to the ground then rolled him over in an attempt to put out the blaze. He used his gloves to smother the flames on the farmer's head and face. Instead of being thankful, however, all that the man could do was to curse and strike out at him.

'It's me,' said Daniel, whisking off his hat. 'Don't you recognise me? I'm the man in the pigsty. I came to return your horse.'

The farmer stopped struggling and stared in amazement.

'Is it really you?'

'What happened here?'

'They stole everything,' said the farmer, coughing badly. 'They killed my son. I was tied up and made to watch while they took it in turns with my wife. They were *animals*. I only got free when the fire burnt through the ropes holding me.' Writhing in torment, he peered up at Daniel. 'I thought we were friends.'

'We are, we are.'

'Then why did you let them do it?'

'What do you mean?'

'Why did you let them burn us alive?'

'This was nothing to do with me,' said Daniel, mystified. 'I swear it. I came here in good faith to thank you. We brought your horse and some provisions for you. Why should you blame me?' He indicated the house. 'This was the work of French soldiers, surely.'

'No,' said the farmer, eyelids fluttering and voice dying to a hoarse whisper. 'They were British. They wore red.'

CHAPTER TWO

January, 1708

Amsterdam was carpeted by a heavy frost that obliged its citizens to wrap up in warm clothing and walk along its streets with careful feet. Traffic adjusted its normal hectic pace. Coaches and carriages no longer hurtled along so wildly and few horsemen moved at anything above a trot on the slippery surface. It was a cold and dangerous start to a new year. Gazing out of the window, Beatrix Udderzook was glad that she was in a warm house on such a cold day. She was a plump woman in her thirties with a podgy face and a nervous manner. When she saw a man slip on the icy pavement and fall to the ground, she let out a gasp of horror and brought both hands up to her mouth. The next moment, her anxious face was lit by a broad grin as she spotted someone crossing the road towards the house. Beatrix ran out of the room as fast as her chubby legs would allow her.

'Miss Amalia! Miss Amalia!' she called up the stairs. 'You have a visitor, Miss Amalia.'

'Who is it?' asked Amalia Janssen, appearing on the landing.

'Captain Rawson.'

'That's wonderful! I'll come at once.'

'I'll let him in,' said Beatrix, determined not to be robbed of the pleasure. 'I saw him first.'

While Amalia descended the stairs, the servant rushed to fling open the door at the very moment when Daniel was about to ring the bell. Beatrix beamed at him and ignored the cold blast of air coming in from the street. After exchanging a few pleasantries with her, Daniel stepped into the house and doffed his hat. While the door was being closed behind him, he gave Amalia a welcoming kiss then stood back to appraise her. Beatrix, meanwhile, was goggling at him.

'That will be all, Beatrix,' said Amalia, tolerantly. 'I'm sure that you have plenty to do.'

'Yes, yes,' agreed the servant, taking Daniel's hat from him and reluctantly backing away. 'But it's so good to see the captain again. I must tell your father.'

'Don't disturb him just yet.'

'But he'll want to know.'

'Father can wait ten minutes.'

Amalia wanted some time alone with Daniel first. He wiped his feet on the doormat so that his boots would leave no marks on the spotless tiles of the *voorhuis* then he followed her into the parlour. It was a large, low room with exquisite tapestries woven by Emanuel Janssen on three walls. A fire blazed in the grate. Away from the watchful eyes of the servant, they were able to embrace each other properly before sitting down side by side.

'I was beginning to forget what you looked like,' teased Amalia.

'That's a problem I've never had,' he said, feasting his gaze on her. 'I can always remember exactly what you look like. I'm just sorry that we've been apart so long this time.'

'Your last letter said that you'd been to France.'

'Yes, I was back in Paris once more.'

'I'm not sure that I'd ever want to go there again,' she said with feeling. 'I don't have happy memories of our time there.'

'But that's where you met *me*,' he pointed out, feigning dismay. 'I'd hoped that that might qualify as a happy memory.'

She squeezed his hand. 'It does, Daniel. You know that. I'm just sad that we met in such unfortunate circumstances.'

It was well over two years since Daniel had been sent to Paris to find out what had happened to Emanuel Janssen. Braving the accusations of betrayal, the tapestry maker had accepted an invitation to work for Louis XIV at Versailles in order to gather intelligence for the Allies while in such a unique position. Daniel had arrived in the French capital to learn that Janssen was imprisoned in the Bastille and that, even if he managed to rescue him, he would then have to spirit him, his daughter, his assistant and Beatrix out of the closely guarded city and back to the safety of their own country. Though the seemingly impossible feat was finally accomplished, it had been beset by recurring perils.

In the course of their adventures, he and Amalia had been drawn together into something more meaningful than a friendship. Since he was constantly on the move, he could maintain only a fitful correspondence with her. Whenever he was able to visit Amsterdam, however, he always made straight for her house. Seeing her again was a joy. Amalia was short, slight and fair with a delicate beauty that had captivated him. Having been a soldier all his adult life, Daniel was used to taking his pleasures where he found them before moving on. In Amalia Janssen, he'd at last found a woman who was much more than a passing conquest.

'Tell me where you've been since we last met,' she pressed.

'It would take far too long.'

'I want to know *everything*, Daniel.'

'You'd only be bored,' he said. 'Let me just tell you about my time in France and about my brush with death on the way back.'

'With death?' she cried in alarm.

'Don't look so worried, Amalia. As you see, I survived.'

24

He reassured her with a smile then gave a brief account of his weeks in Paris, describing how he'd contrived to acquire secret information, though revealing none of its actual content. It was when he talked about his encounter with the French patrol that he went into more detail. She was horrified to hear about the grisly fate of the farmer and his family.

'British soldiers killed them?' she said in disbelief.

He nodded grimly. 'That's what I find hard to accept. It's so untypical. There were no foraging parties out. His Grace, the Duke of Marlborough, always makes sure our army is fully provisioned so that it never has to be a burden on any farms nearby. More to the point,' he went on, earnestly, 'he'd never condone rape and pillage. I was shocked that anyone in a British uniform could behave like that.'

'Could you find out who those soldiers were?'

'I'll make it my business to do so,' he said. 'I've made some enquiries already but nobody knows of any patrol that might have been in that area. I won't stop looking,' he vowed. 'That farmer saved my life by putting his own in danger. However long it may take, what happened to him and his family needs to be avenged.'

'It must have been a gruesome sight.'

'It was, Amalia. I've been forced to see some hideous things in battle over the years and accepted them as the fortunes of war. This was very different – kind, innocent, defenceless people, left dead in the smoking ruins of their home. It's preyed on my mind ever since.'

'I'm not surprised,' she said, touching his arm in sympathy.

'However,' he went on, brightening, 'I didn't come here to dwell on the miseries of warfare. You've seen enough of those for yourself at first hand. I came because I missed you so much.'

'How long will you be in Amsterdam?'

'Only for a couple of days, I fear.'

Her face clouded. 'Is that all?'

'I have to sail for England.'

'Can't you stay here for a week at least?'

'My passage is already booked,' he explained, 'and His Grace is expecting me.'

'Tell him you had to spend more time with Father, advising him about his tapestry of the battle of Ramillies. After all, it was commissioned by the Duke himself and he ordered you to help.'

'I've spoken to your father at great length about the battle and he must already be well advanced on the tapestry.'

'Not at all,' she said. 'Her Grace, the Duchess of Marlborough, wrote to say that there was no immediate hurry. It may be years before it can be hung in Blenheim Palace. Building work is very slow, apparently. Father is engaged on other commissions at the moment. You'd have to jog his memory about Ramillies.'

Daniel sighed. 'I'll have to jog my own memory,' he

26

confessed. 'It seems such a long time ago now. When we routed the French that glorious day, I thought it would be a turning point in the war and that King Louis would agree to peace on our terms.'

'Father says that he'll never concede defeat.'

'Failing that, I hoped that we could build on the success of Ramillies in last year's campaigns and strike into France itself but, somehow, it just didn't happen. We had endless disappointments.'

She smiled sadly. 'I know all about disappointments.'

'Cheer up, Amalia,' he said, kissing her on the cheek. 'Make the most of me while I am here. I only have one other call to make and then I'm entirely at your disposal.'

'I think I can guess what that other call is.'

'I have to pay my respects to another very special woman.'

'You want to visit your mother's grave.'

'She was born and brought up in the city. Though she enjoyed living in England with my father, she felt that it was only right that she should be buried here.'

'An English father and a Dutch mother,' she observed.

'It's a case of divided loyalties.'

'Which has the stronger pull on you?'

'Each of them.'

'That doesn't make sense, Daniel.'

'It does to me,' he said. 'When I'm fighting in a British regiment, I feel English blood coursing through my veins and a sense of true patriotism. When I'm here in Amsterdam, however,' he continued, pulling her close and looking deep into her eyes, 'I feel as Dutch as a field of tulips and want to stay here for ever.'

'Why have you never remarried?' asked the Duke of Marlborough.

'Oh, I'm much too senile for such things, John.'

'Nonsense, man – you're only five years older than me.'

'I'll not see sixty again,' admitted Godolphin with a shrug. 'Besides, there's an insuperable barrier to my ever entering into holy matrimony again.'

'You can't mourn Margaret for ever.'

'It isn't just out of respect to my late wife. Margaret was a godsend and I could never find anyone else like her. No, there's a much simpler reason, John – I've never been wholly at ease in the company of women. The truth of it is that I feel far more comfortable with racehorses.'

Marlborough laughed. 'Does that mean you'd prefer to propose to a bay mare?'

'It means that I'm a contented widower and relieved that I won't ever have to go through the frightening process of selecting a wife.'

'Choosing Margaret was not frightening, was it?'

'That was different – she was an angel.'

The two men were enjoying a glass of brandy after an excellent dinner at Holywell House, the favourite home of John Churchill, Duke of Marlborough. He and Sidney, Earl of

Godolphin, were more than friends and political allies. After a marriage of barely a year, Margaret Godolphin had died in childbirth. Francis, the baby son who'd lived, had grown up to marry Marlborough's daughter, Henrietta, thus uniting the two families. Long commitments abroad meant that Marlborough didn't see as much as he would have liked of the man who, as Lord Treasurer, provided the substantial funds needed for the continuance of the war. In order to do that, Godolphin had to become an adroit manipulator of Parliament.

'What news of Blenheim?' asked Godolphin, stroking the dark periwig that reached down to his chest.

'Are you referring to the battle or the palace?'

'The one led to the other.'

'Indeed,' said Marlborough, 'and we are eternally grateful to Her Majesty for her kindness in bestowing the palace on us. Unhappily, it's proceeding at a snail's pace. There's been definite progress in the grounds but the building itself has yet to take on any real shape. Sarah is there at the moment, cracking the whip over them.'

Godolphin smiled fondly. 'I can imagine her doing that.'

'My dear wife likes to have things her way.'

'How is she getting on with the architect?'

'Not too well,' conceded Marlborough. 'It was never going to be a marriage of true minds, alas. Vanbrugh came up with some splendid drawings and was very enthusiastic at the start of the project. Then Sarah decided that she wanted some changes.'

'Oh, dear – have there been arguments?'

'Let's call them extremely warm discussions.'

'Well, I, for one, can't wait for Blenheim Palace to be finished,' said Godolphin, firmly. 'It's not just a fitting home for you. It will be a visible reminder to everyone – including Her Majesty – of just how much you did for us as captain general of the Allied armies. Blenheim was a remarkable triumph.'

'So it seemed at the time,' said Marlborough. 'Unfortunately, this damnable War of the Spanish Succession obliges me to produce a Blenheim year after year and that's just not possible.'

He reached for the decanter and poured more brandy into both the glasses. There was a tap on the door and a liveried servant came into the dining room. He spoke with profound respect.

'Captain Rawson presents his compliments, Your Grace, and asks if this is a convenient moment to see you.'

'By all means,' said Marlborough. 'Bring the fellow in.'

'Yes, Your Grace.'

The man bowed and withdrew silently.

'Captain Rawson,' said Godolphin. 'That's a name I know.'

'You met him once in this very house, Sidney. Daniel Rawson was the boy with the sword.'

'I remember now. It was after the battle of Sedgemoor. He was only ten but, when one of your soldiers tried to molest his mother, the lad killed the man with his own sword.'

'In recognition of his courage, I presented the weapon to him even though his father had fought against us in the rebel army. Daniel has put that sword to good use over the years. He's a fine soldier.'

'Coming from you, that's a real compliment.'

'I promoted him to my personal staff.'

'That's a signal honour.'

'It was well deserved.'

The servant escorted Daniel into the room then bowed and went out again. Marlborough gave the visitor a warm welcome. Daniel was pleased to find him in such a convivial mood. The last time he'd seen his commander, Marlborough had been weary and downhearted after a series of setbacks in the field.

'Do join us, Daniel,' said Marlborough, pointing to a chair. 'We've not drunk all of the brandy yet.'

Daniel sat down beside him. 'Thank you, Your Grace.'

'We've met before, Captain Rawson,' said Godolphin. 'I hear nothing but good things of you.'

'That's very gratifying, my lord,' said Daniel.

Marlborough rang a small bell and a servant appeared at once. He found a glass for the visitor and poured him some brandy before quitting the room. It was not the first time Marlborough had invited Daniel to join him at a table. Unlike some commanders, he didn't distance himself from his officers in order to preserve his authority. He willingly sought their company.

'Your good health!' said Daniel, raising his glass to them then taking a first sip. 'That's very welcome after a long ride.'

'Have you come from London?' asked Godolphin.

'Yes, my lord. My ship docked this morning.'

'What sort of crossing did you have?'

'A cold and cheerless one – we were caught in a squall.'

'It's not the ideal time of year to put to sea.'

'I managed to get here in one piece,' said Daniel before turning to Marlborough. 'I have several letters and dispatches for you in my saddlebag, Your Grace.'

'Then I must decline them,' said Marlborough, holding up a palm. 'They no longer hold any relevance for me.'

'But I've brought reports of troop movements by the French.'

'They've come to the wrong address.'

'Your orders were to deliver everything to you in person.'

'Things were different when I issued those orders.'

Daniel was bewildered. 'In what way, Your Grace?'

'During your absence, there have been some changes.'

'Yes,' confirmed Godolphin, 'some very radical changes at that. It's the reason you find us at leisure for once. We are no longer burdened by the affairs of state.'

'I'm not sure that I understand, my lord,' said Daniel.

'Let me explain,' volunteered Marlborough. 'The Lord Treasurer no longer holds the office and I have ceased to be the captain general. A situation arose that made it necessary for us both to offer our resignations. In short, Daniel, you are answerable to me no more.'

Daniel was astounded. 'This is dreadful news!'

'That was our view initially. Now, however, having had the time to savour retirement, Sidney and I are coming to see its attractions.'

'There's no attraction whatsoever in it for the Allied forces,' said Daniel, stoutly. 'If I may be candid, it smacks of disaster. You are the one person in Europe capable of leading a coalition army against the French. Without you, we'll be in a sorry state.'

'It's very kind of you to say so.'

'Who created this situation of which you speak? It must be someone well versed in the black art of politics.' Godolphin chuckled. 'I apologise, my lord. I meant no offence to politicians.'

'None was taken, Captain Rawson,' said Godolphin. 'Black art is an appropriate description. Parliament has rather more than its share of would-be sorcerers. They are always mixing potions designed to bring about one man's rise and another's downfall. His Grace and I have been victims of such sorcery. We are both ousted.'

'This is madness,' asserted Daniel, rising indignantly to his feet. 'You've kept our army and our navy in fighting trim between you. His Grace has supplied the leadership while you, my lord, have helped to raise the money to make that leadership effective. To dispense with your services is an act of sheer lunacy. Have they forgotten Blenheim? Don't they remember our victory at the Lines of Brabant? Does the name of Ramillies mean nothing to them?' He lowered his voice. 'I'm sorry to speak out so boldly, Your Grace, but I'm only saying what every British soldier will say. To lose you is an absolute catastrophe.'

'Kind words, Daniel,' said Marlborough, 'and inspired by your loyalty to me. Others, alas, have forsaken loyalty.'

'Then they must be brought to their senses. This is a decision that must be reversed at the earliest opportunity. I refuse to believe that Her Majesty approved of your resignations.'

Godolphin winced slightly. 'She did so with equanimity.'

'And there the matter ends,' said Marlborough, dismissively. 'You've performed some remarkable deeds in your time, Daniel, but even you couldn't make our beloved Queen change her mind on this issue.' He hunched his shoulders. 'Our time is over. We've learnt to accept that.' He waved an arm. 'Now why don't you sit down again and drink some more of this exceptional brandy?'

a battle had earned him a reputation unmatched in military circles. He was revered by his men who called him Corporal John because of his readiness to take notice of the lower ranks. At the same time, he was feared by French marshals and by other commanders who'd faced him in the field. He'd been such a dominating presence in European warfare for so long that he'd acquired almost legendary status. Yet that legend had now been discarded. Daniel could foresee the utter dismay in the Allied army when the word spread. By the same token, he could envisage the sheer delight among the enemy when they realised that their conqueror had relinquished his office. The whole balance of the war would shift in favour of the French. Daniel was troubled.

Reaching his destination, he dismounted and tethered his horse before he even realised where he was. The church tower cast a long, all-embracing shadow over him as if in reproach at his lack of due respect. He'd come to mourn a dead father not to bewail the loss of a living soldier. Daniel was sobered. With the image of Nathan Rawson before him, he went penitently into the churchyard and sought out his father's grave. Kneeling beside it, he offered up a prayer and apologised for being so distracted. Then he began to clear some of the weeds that encroached on the little headstone.

He was still on his knees when he heard the excited voices of children. Daniel looked up to see a small boy being chased by an even smaller girl. They were running through the churchyard with such joyful irreverence that he was mildly shocked for a moment. He rose to admonish them but their father saved him the trouble. Calling the children over to him, he told them to play on the village green instead. As they raced off happily again, Daniel crossed over to the newcomer.

'Is that you, Martin?' he asked, peering intently at him.

'Indeed, it is,' replied Martin Rye with a surprised grin. 'And unless my eyes fail me, I'm talking to Dan Rawson.'

'Yes, it's me.' They shook hands warmly. 'It's good to see you again after all this time. You're a married man now, I see.'

'I've two lovely children to show for it. I couldn't bring myself to punish them just now. After all, when we were their age, we used to play games here in the churchyard.'

Daniel smiled. 'The verger chased us away many a time.'

It was over twenty years since he'd seen his old friend. Martin Rye was a boy from the village who'd worked on the Rawson farm for a short while. He'd grown up to be tall and sturdy. Apart from memories of childhood fun together, they shared something else. When the Monmouth rebellion had been crushed at Sedgemoor, Nathan Rawson had been a captain in the defeated army. Rye had two brothers who'd also responded to the call to arms and fought on the losing side. All three of them had been condemned to death at the Bloody Assizes.

'I know what brought you here, Dan,' said Rye with envy. 'When your father was hanged, you cut down his

37

body so that it could lie here in the churchyard.'

'Yes, we did.'

'I wish we could have rescued my brothers but Will and Arthur had already been tossed into a common grave with all the other poor wretches who danced on the gallows that day.'

'We were lucky enough to reach my father in time. We brought him here in the dead of night and buried him under the bushes where nobody could find him. It was many years later,' recalled Daniel, 'that I was able to dig up the body and see that it had a proper Christian burial.' He touched Rye's arm. 'I'm sorry that your brothers don't lie in consecrated ground as well. They were brave lads.' He stood back to look his friend up and down. 'You've filled out since we last met. What are you doing with yourself now?'

'I've taken over the forge from my uncle. Being a blacksmith is hard work but I've never been one to shy away from that. What about you, Dan?' he went on. 'When I heard you'd fled to Holland with your mother, I thought you'd find a farm there.'

'I chose to follow the drum instead.'

'I can see that from your uniform. What regiment are you in?'

'The 24th Foot,' said Daniel, 'with the rank of captain.'

Rye was impressed. 'You've done well for yourself.'

'Soldiering is a dangerous occupation, Martin. I'd feel a lot safer if I was a blacksmith like you.'

'Don't be so sure about that,' said the other with a laugh.

'I've got burns all over my arms and horses can give you a nasty kick if they don't want to be shoed.'

'At least you don't have someone trying to kill you every time you go into battle.'

'That's true. I'd hate that. How do you put up with it?'

'You learn to survive.'

'Are you married?'

'Not yet.'

'I don't blame you.'

'Why do you say that?'

'Too many soldiers' wives end up as widows.'

'There's always that risk,' admitted Daniel, thinking wistfully of Amalia Janssen. 'Casualties are often very high. It's something you have to live with, Martin.'

'I could never do that.'

'It's surprising what you can do when you're put to the test.'

'I like my life as it is, Dan.'

There was an endearing simplicity about Martin Rye. He was a big, strong, healthy man in his thirties with limited needs and narrow horizons. The village provided him with everything he wanted and he'd never dream of moving away from it. Had he stayed on the family farm, Daniel mused, he'd probably have grown up to be like his friend and to enjoy a stable existence in the rural tranquillity of Somerset. He'd have employed Rye to shoe the farm horses and drunk with him from time to time in the village tavern. It was a tempting prospect but well beyond his reach now.

'Why do you serve in the British army?' asked Rye. 'I heard that you and your mother had fled to Amsterdam.'

'That's exactly what we did.'

'So why didn't you join the Dutch army?'

'I served in it for years when King William was on the throne,' said Daniel, 'before deciding to wear a redcoat instead. British and Dutch armies fight side by side now.'

'Have you fought in many battles?'

'My whole life has been marked out by battles and sieges.'

'What about Blenheim?'

'I was there, Martin.'

Rye whistled in admiration. 'Were you – what was it like?'

'If you want the truth, it was desperate.'

'Yet you don't have a scratch on you.'

'I was lucky,' said Daniel, modestly.

'We heard so many tales about Blenheim,' said Rye. 'The French were well and truly whipped that day. You're a hero, Dan Rawson. What a wonderful thing to be able to tell your grandchildren – that you fought at Blenheim.'

'In its own way, Ramillies was an even greater triumph. We beat the French into the ground and lost fewer of our men. I had a much better view of that battle,' Daniel continued, 'because I had the honour of serving on the Duke of Marlborough's personal staff.'

Rye's manner changed at once. 'Don't mention the name of that bastard!' he said, vehemently.

'But he was our captain general.'

'Yes, Dan, and he was also one of the leaders of the army that mowed down the rebels at Sedgemoor. Because of him, and other cruel devils like him, my brothers ended up with a rope around their necks and so did your father.'

'That's all in the past, Martin.'

'Is it?' demanded the other with passion. 'Then what are you doing *here*? Why are you still tending your father's grave after all these years?'

'It's a duty. I'm proud of what my father did.'

'You're no more proud of him than I am of Will and Arthur. Before he became a farmer, your father was a trained soldier. He had proper weapons and knew how to use them. My brothers were raw lads with fire in their veins and a pitchfork in their hands. They stood no chance against that monster, Marlborough, and his army.'

'He wasn't a duke at the time of Sedgemoor,' corrected Daniel. 'He was John, Lord Churchill with the rank of major general and he wasn't in overall command.'

'What difference does it make?' snarled Rye. 'He was one of *them*. That's all that matters. I detest him for what he did.'

'He wasn't directly responsible for the deaths of your brothers.'

'Why are you defending him?'

'Because I've had the advantage of getting to know His Grace,' said Daniel, proudly. 'In my opinion, he's the finest soldier alive.'

'Well, I think he's a barefaced traitor.'

'That's absurd.'

'I'm not stupid, Dan,' said Rye, tapping his chest. 'You may think we're cut off down here in this little village but we get to hear things and we remember them. When the Duke or Lord Churchill or whatever you want to call him beat the rebels on that bloodthirsty day, he did so in the name of King James. Am I right or wrong?'

'You're quite right, Martin.'

'Yet three years later, when he should have supported his king once again, he turns his back on him and joins up with a Dutchman, William of Orange. King James was forced into exile. That's treachery to me.'

'It's a little more complicated than that.'

'He stabbed King James in the back.'

'That's not what happened at all.'

'I see what I see,' affirmed Rye, thrusting out his jaw. 'You can lick the Duke of Marlborough's arse all you want but I'll never forgive him for what he did to my two brothers.' He nodded at the gravestone. 'Unlike you, I could never serve a butcher who helped to put my father in the ground.'

Turning on his heel, he stalked off and gathered up his children. Daniel was chastened. Caught up in his uncritical veneration of Marlborough, he'd forgotten that the Duke didn't enjoy universal praise even in his own country. It was not only scheming politicians who harboured a grudge against the great man. Humble people like Martin Rye had long memories and still nursed wounds inflicted at the battle of Sedgemoor. Daniel stared down at the grave with unease. He wondered what Nathan Rawson would say if he knew that his son had now served a man who'd once helped to quash the rebellion to which the farmer and retired soldier had dedicated himself.

When Daniel rode off, the words of Martin Rye rang in his ears.

The blacksmith would be one of many people who'd rejoice when he heard that Marlborough had effectively been stripped of his command.

On 19 February, 1708, the customary meeting of the Cabinet Council was held on a Sunday morning. The Queen's most trusted advisers shuffled into the room and took their places either side of the long oak table. The pervasive air of solemnity was offset by the suppressed glee of one man. Robert Harley, Secretary of State, was now at the head of an administration with a distinct Tory bias. Not for nothing did he bear the nickname of Robin the Trickster. In appearance, he was small and rather insignificant yet he wielded great power behind the scenes. It had taken guile and perseverance to supplant Godolphin and to bring an end to Marlborough's glittering military career. Harley was in the ascendant now. As he looked around the table, he was confident that a new and better political era was about to begin. It was time to flex his muscles.

When a door opened, everyone struggled to their feet. Queen Anne hobbled into the room and cut anything but a regal figure. Flat-faced, overweight and plagued by gout, she wore apparel that verged on the drab. When she took her seat at the head of the table, there was a loud scraping of chairs as the others lowered themselves down again. After looking around the faces that peeped out from their periwigs, she gave Harley a nod. He was a poor speaker with a dry voice but for once it had some sparkle in it.

'Thank you, Your Majesty,' he began. 'As Secretary of State, it is my duty to open this meeting and to set before you the business that we have to discuss.'

Though he carried on, he did so over audible murmurs of protest from some ministers. The noise slowly built until it was too concerted to be ignored. Harley came to a halt and glanced at the Queen in consternation. Feeling that his position was secure, he'd never anticipated that he might face opposition. He looked down at the notes in front of him but he was quite unable to read them out. While Harley dithered and while the Queen shifted uncomfortably in her seat, the Duke of Somerset rose with dignity. His eyes flicked meaningfully at the two empty chairs at the table.

'I do not see how we can deliberate,' he boomed, 'when the Commander-in-Chief and the Lord Treasurer are absent.'

The announcement was greeted with murmurs of agreement and someone patted the table by way of approval. Somerset had clearly voiced a general opinion. Robin the Trickster made no reply. Facing humiliation, he had no idea what to do. Queen Anne was unable to help him out of his predicament. She, too, was squirming with embarrassment. Somerset pressed home his advantage and repeated his earlier statement. After a long and extremely awkward silence, the Queen realised that a form of mutiny was taking place and that she had no means of quelling it. The unthinkable had occurred. She'd lost her control of the Council table.

'This meeting is formally ended,' she said.

Flushing angrily, and with lips pursed in exasperation, she got up and tottered out of the room. Muted laughter broke out and a few handshakes were exchanged as ministers congratulated each other on having made their point so forcefully. An important event had just occurred and it had constitutional significance. They'd openly defied the wishes of their sovereign and won a victory.

Harley was mortified. He could only sit there in hurt silence and reflect that, for once, his trickery had woefully miscarried.

Daniel Rawson's second visit to Holywell House was in marked contrast to the first one. He'd left on that occasion in a mood that bordered on despair but he now returned with alacrity. He was shown into the library and found Marlborough there, talking with his private secretary, Adam Cardonnel. They looked up as Daniel entered.

'Come in, come in,' said Marlborough, affably. 'Your

honour was but lately in our thoughts.'

'I rode here as soon as I received your letter, Your Grace,' said Daniel. 'Let me congratulate you on being restored to the command that you should never have relinquished.'

'It was very gratifying.'

'A gross injustice has been righted.'

'I agree with you, Daniel,' said Cardonnel. 'Her Majesty has been saved from making the most calamitous mistake of her reign.'

'And there have been a few of those,' said Marlborough under his breath. 'But don't just stand there, man. Take a seat.'

'Thank you, Your Grace.'

Daniel sat down opposite them. Delighted to find Marlborough in such high spirits, he was also pleased to see Cardonnel again. The secretary was a vital member of the captain general's staff. A neat, handsome, engaging man, Cardonnel was a model of efficiency. He was also tireless, tactful and intensely loyal. He and Daniel had something in common. Both were refugees. In 1685, when Daniel and his mother fled after the battle of Sedgemoor, Cardonnel and his Huguenot family hastily left France to avoid the slaughter that followed the Revocation of the Edict of Nantes.

'Order and common sense are restored,' observed Cardonnel.

'They should never have been abandoned in the first place,' said Daniel. 'What on earth persuaded Her Majesty to dispense with her acknowledged champion?'

'Someone whispered in her ear, Daniel.'

'Who was that?'

'It matters not. He's been summarily dismissed now.'

'It's no more than Robin the Trickster deserves,' opined Marlborough, 'but he wasn't the only villain here. A maggot had wriggled its way into the royal apple. It goes by the name of Abigail Masham, one of Her Majesty's bedchamber women. My dear wife will tell you all about that devious little baggage. Suffice it to say that we are – if not exactly in favour again – firmly in charge of operations.'

'Those are the best tidings I could wish to hear, Your Grace.'

'Thank you, Daniel.'

'What are my orders?'

'I'll come to those,' said Marlborough. 'First, I wish to tender my apologies for sending you away so brusquely when you last called. I've now read the correspondence you brought and it's been enlightening.'

'There was another matter I'd hoped to raise with you.'

'Speak on. This is your opportunity.'

'It concerns a harrowing incident, Your Grace.'

Daniel told them about the destruction of the farm and the murder of its occupants. Marlborough was aghast when he heard that it was the work of British soldiers.

'Are you *sure* about this, Daniel?' he asked, bristling.

'The farmer was very precise.'

'No soldiers under my command would dare do such a thing.'

'I can only report what I saw and heard.'

'This is outrageous,' said Marlborough, slapping his thigh. 'I'm grateful that you brought this to my attention. I'll institute a search for these devils at once. When you return to Flanders this week, you can bear a letter on the subject to General Cadogan.'

'I'll gladly do so, Your Grace,' said Daniel, 'and I'll pursue the matter on my own account as well. I have a strong personal interest in seeing these men caught and hanged. Wearing our uniforms, they behaved like savages.'

They came by night. While some of them rustled the cattle and seized the rest of the livestock, others set fire to the barn and to the stables. When the flames began to lick hungrily at the farmhouse itself, its occupants flung open the shutters to see what had caused the conflagration. They were instantly shot dead. As the fire roared on with deafening force, their bodies were soon burnt and blackened beyond recognition. The redcoats took on a deeper hue in the dazzling light. They had struck again. All that would be left behind him were sizzling embers. On a command from their leader, the men rode off with their booty, their harsh laughter echoing through the night.

Chapter Four

'Oh, you're still alive then,' said Welbeck with heavy sarcasm. 'I thought you were either dead or that you'd run off to join the enemy.'

'You know me better than that, Henry.'

'In the old days, I did, but I saw a lot more of you then.'

'Things have changed,' said Daniel. 'Since I joined His Grace's personal staff, I can't spend as much time with the regiment as I'd like. I have other duties.'

'Yes…chasing women around the bedroom.'

Daniel grinned. 'There's not much chance of doing that.'

'You can't fool me, Dan Rawson. I've got your true measure. You simply can't resist a pretty face and a nice pair of bubbies.'

'That's where you're wrong, Henry. My roving days are over. I've finally met the woman I want above all others.'

Welbeck was sardonic. 'That's what you tell each and every one of them,' he said. 'But when you've had a gallop on your latest filly, you probably can't even remember her name.'

'I have a name that I'll never forget,' said Daniel as an image of Amalia Janssen popped into his mind. 'And it's very precious to me. But,' he added, 'I didn't come here to discuss my private life. I'm here because I missed seeing your ugly old face.'

'Flattery will get you nowhere, you damnable liar.'

They shared a laugh and embraced.

Spring had brought the army out of winter quarters and Daniel had returned to his regiment. He'd watched Welbeck drilling his men with a stentorian voice that cowed them into obedience. Those who fell below the sergeant's high standards earned themselves some harsh criticism. They soon learnt to march in step and in line. Daniel had waited until his friend had dismissed the troops before he stepped forward to surprise him. Welbeck's mockery didn't offend him in the least because it was grounded in affection.

'So,' said the sergeant, 'where have you been?'

'Here, there and everywhere, Henry.'

'And where might that be?'

'Well, I spent some time in England at the start of the year.'

'I doubt if I'll ever do that again,' moaned Welbeck. 'This bleeding war will drag on for ever.'

'Don't be so pessimistic,' said Daniel.

'We take one step forward and two back. After we battered the Frenchies at Ramillies, I was rash enough to believe that the end might finally be in sight. But what happened?' he asked, jabbing a belligerent finger in the air. 'Last year we managed to lose almost everything we'd gained the year before. Marshal Villars stormed the Lines of Stollhofen before surging on into Germany and any hope we had of making headway in Spain vanished at the battle of Almanza. As for the naval attack on Toulon, it came to nothing – just like every other bloody thing we tried to do. I sometimes wonder if our so-called commanders have a clue how to win this war.'

'Now that's unfair, Henry.'

'Is it? I don't think so. We're supposed to be part of the Grand Alliance but, if you ask me, it's neither grand nor allied.'

Daniel grimaced. 'I'd have to agree with that.'

'Time and time again, we've been let down by the Dutch or by some other foreign frigging idiots who are meant to be on our side.'

'Be careful,' warned Daniel, indulgently. 'Bear in mind that my dear mother was Dutch. I'm one of those foreign frigging idiots you're talking about.'

'I knew there was something peculiar about you.' He

slapped his friend familiarly on the shoulder. 'Nevertheless, it's good to have you back in camp again, Dan.'

'Thank you.'

'And while you've been gallivanting here, there and everywhere, I've not been idle. I've been thinking about those British soldiers who burnt that farm down.'

'Yes, they're still very much on my mind as well.'

'According to Lieutenant Ainley, they've added some other victims to their list.'

'Oh?'

'Reports came in of another farm razed to the ground. The people who lived there were burnt to a cinder and all the livestock was driven off. Whoever these buggers are,' he went on, rancorously, 'they obviously eat well. While they have fresh pork and as much beef as they want, we're stuck on army rations.'

'How do you know it was the same men?'

'A witness saw them riding away from the blaze and claims they wore red uniforms. There can't be *two* raiding parties of British soldiers who like killing people and starting bonfires.'

'I agree,' said Daniel. 'It's too big a coincidence. They must be from one of our cavalry regiments. What puzzles me is why they're trying to spread terror throughout the countryside. That will only turn people against us.'

'Corporal John is always telling us to be kind to local farmers. After all, we're not fighting against *them*. We're supposed to treat them well, not burn them to death in their homes.'

'I mentioned the first incident to His Grace.'

'What did he say?'

'He was as shaken as we were, Henry. He's determined to find out who brought such disgrace on a British uniform.'

'And what else did he say?' wondered Welbeck. 'Did he have any idea at all how to achieve peace or are we going to keep floundering on for another year?'

'We won't flounder,' said Daniel. 'There's a definite plan.'

Welbeck raised a sceptical eyebrow. 'Really...what is it?'

'I'm not at liberty to tell you the full details but I've just come from The Hague where His Grace met with Grand Pensionary Heinsius and with Prince Eugene of Savoy.'

'What did the three of them do – play cards together?'

'Don't be so cynical, Henry.'

'I'd just like to know where the hell we're going.'

'Nowhere.'

'Oh, I see. We just stay here and twiddle our thumbs, do we?'

'Of course not,' said Daniel. 'We remain in Flanders. This is where the decisive action will take place. It's one of the things I found out while I was sniffing around in Paris.'

'Which general's wife did you seduce this time?'

'That opportunity didn't arise and, even if it had, I'd never have taken it.'

Welbeck rolled his eyes. 'You expect me to believe *that*?'

While gathering intelligence, Daniel had a reputation for resorting to any means necessary. On a previous stay in Paris, he'd befriended and wooed Berenice, neglected wife of General Salignac. It never occurred to her that some of the things she confided about her husband's commitments by way of pillow talk were duly passed on to the Duke of Marlborough. She'd been a useful, if unwitting, source of military information. In trying to combine espionage with pleasure, however, Daniel had taken an enormous risk, a fact later borne in upon him when the cuckolded general sent two men to kill him.

'What else did you find out between nights of madness in someone's boudoir?' asked Welbeck.

'I discovered that King Louis had personally chosen the ground on which this year's battles will be fought. It's right here in Flanders,' said Daniel with a sweeping gesture. 'We'll be up against a strong French army of 100,000 men under the command of the duc de Vendôme.'

'Vendôme!' The name was spat out in disgust. 'He's no match for us. The Duke has outwitted far better soldiers than Vendôme. We beat Marshal Tallard at Blenheim and Marshall Villeroi at Ramillies.'

'Both of them experienced commanders.'

'Poxy old Vendôme is useless.'

'Give him his due, Henry,' urged Daniel. 'He had a lot of success in Italy then kept us completely pinned down here last year. He's a worthy adversary and we should respect him.'

'I respect nobody in a French uniform.'

'Not even royalty?'

'What do you mean?'

'It's another little titbit that fell into my lap. Louis is sending his own grandson, the Duke of Burgundy, to put us to the sword. That shows you how seriously he's taking this year's campaign. Keep your men well drilled and ready for combat,' said Daniel. 'They may have the chance to spill some royal blood.'

Louis de France, duc de Burgundy, was a well-bred yet mettlesome young man in his mid twenties, deeply religious, inclined to arrogance and confident that he had the ability to lead a huge army to victory against the Confederate forces. Notwithstanding a lack of experience, he felt able to make critical military decisions in the field. With so many troops gathered at the French camp in Valenciennes, he didn't even contemplate defeat. Burgundy was a royal prince in every particular. Impeccably attired and courtly in manner, he was therefore highly offended when the scruffily dressed duc de Vendôme barged his way into the tent without warning. Burgundy turned away instinctively from the unpleasant smell that always accompanied the older man. Vendôme was over twice his age and had notoriously dirty habits. His shirt was badly soiled and hadn't been changed for several days. There was tobacco on his cravat, wine stains on his coat and his periwig was beginning to unravel. He was brusque, irreverent and angry. Vendôme made little effort to show any respect.

'I wondered if you'd come to your senses yet,' he said.

'I fancy that it's your senses that are deficient, my lord Duke,' said Burgundy with exaggerated courtesy. 'I hoped that you'd come to appreciate the wisdom of my argument.'

'Wisdom arises from experience.'

'That's why I'm careful to draw on the experience of older heads such as your own. I'll always seek the best advice before I make a decision.'

'Then why have you ignored it?'

'In this case, I found your counsel unhelpful.'

'Unhelpful!' spluttered Vendôme. 'That's an insult. We're in a position to take the initiative and I believe that we should do so.'

'On that point at least we're in agreement.'

'Then give the order to besiege Huy.'

'I've chosen another course of action.'

'Think of its situation, for heaven's sake! Huy sits on the Meuse. Those wide, open plains nearby will favour a cavalry engagement and we have a marked superiority there. Why not use it?'

'Because I've conceived another strategy,' said Burgundy, evenly. 'I prefer our initial advance to be towards Brussels. There's a clear dissatisfaction with Dutch rule among the Flemish population. We must exploit that. Brussels will welcome us.'

'All of Flanders will welcome us if you follow my plan.'

'The matter is settled, my lord Duke.'

Vendôme turned away and muttered some expletives under his breath. Forced to accept Burgundy as the titular commander-in-chief, he was seething with rage. The previous year he'd skilfully defended French positions in Flanders and kept the Allies at arm's length. As the new campaigning season began, he'd finally been allowed to risk a major battle, if it could be fought under advantageous conditions. To manoeuvre Marlborough and his army into the places where he wanted them, however, Vendôme needed a free hand but that was being denied him. Every decision had to be ratified by Burgundy.

'Could I simply ask you to think again?' said Vendôme, injecting a faint note of deference into his voice. 'On reflection, you may well come to see that the siege of Huy is the better option.'

Burgundy was peremptory. 'It's out of the question.'

'Will you spurn my advice in such a cavalier fashion?'

'We'll move towards Brussels.'

'May I remind you that I was in charge of operations in Flanders last year?' said Vendôme, cheeks reddening. 'I know the terrain well. I know how best to make use of its natural advantages. More to the point,' he went on as if playing a trump card, 'I understand the way that Marlborough thinks and acts. I can anticipate him.'

'Then it's a pity your anticipation wasn't more fruitful last year,' said Burgundy with a touch of condescension, 'or the campaign would not have ended in an impasse. That will not happen under my command, I assure you. I'm working to achieve a decisive result.'

Vendôme scowled. 'All that you're doing is to squander an opportunity to strike a telling blow.'

'You're entitled to your opinion, my lord Duke.'

'It's the advice of a veteran soldier.'

'Nobody questions your long record.'

'But that, by implication, is what you're doing,' said Vendôme with a hostile stare. 'In rejecting my plan, you're suggesting that it's worthless.' He pulled himself to his full height. 'I've fought and won battles. I think you should remember who I am.'

'It's rather difficult to forget,' said Burgundy, wearily. 'Perhaps it's you who should remember that I'm in command here. You are in the presence of a prince of the blood.'

Biting back a reply, Vendôme stood there fuming and looked as if he was about to explode. Burgundy remained composed and that drove his visitor to an even greater pitch of fury. Unable to put his feelings into polite words, Vendôme simply spun round and stormed out. As he strode through the camp with his eyes blazing, nobody dared to approach him. Instead, they stepped quickly out of his way. When he reached his own tent, Vendôme thrust the flap aside and burst in, reaching for a flagon of wine and pouring a full glass. He flopped down onto his chair and took a long sip of wine. Brooding on the way he'd been rebuffed, he was oblivious to everything else. He didn't even hear the tent flap open or see the head that popped tentatively in. Nor did he hear the deliberate cough made by the newcomer. It was only when the man stepped into the tent that Vendôme at last became aware of his presence.

'What do you want?' he growled, looking up.

'You sent for me, Your Grace.'

'The devil I did! Who, in God's name, are you?'

'Lieutenant Valeran.'

'Who?'

'Raoul Valeran.' With a slight bow, he moved backwards. 'I can see that I'm intruding. Pray, excuse me.'

'No, no,' said Vendôme, looking at him properly for the first time. 'Stay here. I do believe that I may have sent for you.'

'If this is an inconvenient moment…'

'Say no more, Lieutenant.'

Vendôme put a finger to his lips to reinforce the order then he gave a lazy smile. He studied Valeran from head to toe and was delighted with what he saw. The lieutenant was a tall, slender, handsome young man with an air of boyish innocence about him. He had a natural elegance that had caught Vendôme's attention and prompted him to find out the officer's name. Anger slowly gave way to desire. Vendôme needed something that would help him forget the

59

way his advice had been rejected by Burgundy. Here was the perfect distraction. Eyes never leaving his guest, he had a much longer drink then he reached for the flagon.

'Come on in, Raoul,' he invited, running a tongue over his lips. 'I'd like you to join me in a glass of wine.'

The last time that Daniel had disguised himself as Marcel Daron, he'd been hounded by a French patrol. He was more circumspect on this occasion, joining a group of other travellers who'd be passing through Valenciennes. They got him there without incident. Daniel sought out the best tavern within easy reach of the French camp and took a room there. Early that evening, some officers rolled in for a drinking bout. Daniel watched them carefully from a table in the corner. He picked up some of their names and heard snatches of conversation. There was a general air of optimism about the campaign ahead.

Daniel soon selected his target. Major Crevel interested him for two reasons. The man was sufficiently senior to have some knowledge of any tactical decisions that had been made, and he couldn't hold his wine. The more he drank, the more uninhibited Crevel became, laughing uproariously at the feeblest jokes and falling off his chair at one point. His companions hauled him upright again. Daniel chose his moment and crossed to their table.

'Good evening, my friends,' he said, 'I couldn't help overhearing what you've been talking about. I, too, wish to see the hateful Duke of Marlborough and his army ground into the dust. Allow me to buy you all a drink so that I may toast your success.'

Crevel giggled. 'I never refuse a glass of wine,' he said, peering at Daniel through bleary eyes, 'but I do like to know the name of the person who bought it for me.'

'My name is Marcel Daron and I'm a wine merchant by trade. That's why I insist on buying a better vintage than the one you've been drinking so far.' He snapped his fingers and the landlord bustled over. Daniel whispered into his ear and the man scuttled off. 'The sooner you win this war, the sooner I can export my wine again.'

'Oh, we'll win it, Monsieur Daron,' said Crevel, drunkenly. 'By God's grace, we'll beat the Grand Alliance this year.'

'You sound confident.'

'We are,' put in another man. 'We have a larger army and better commanders. Our enemies have been very lucky so far.'

'It's true,' said Crevel. 'They've escaped by the skin of their teeth time and again. We came close to routing them at Ramillies. I was there. We had victory within our grasp.'

It was not how Daniel remembered it but he didn't contradict the major. The battle had been a resounding triumph for the Allies. Major Crevel had been one of thousands of French officers who fled from the field in a panic. Pretending to be impressed, Daniel asked for details of Ramillies. The two flagons of wine that arrived at the table helped to lubricate the reminiscences of Crevel and his party. They gave the impression that the Allies had come close to extinction on the battlefield. In fact, as Daniel knew well, they'd suffered only limited casualties. It was the French army that had been cut to shreds.

'What manner of man is the duc de Vendôme?' asked Daniel.

Crevel cackled. 'A stranger one than you've ever met, my friend,' he said with a knowing wink at his friends.

'Is he as sanguine as you seem to be?'

'Why do you want to know that?' asked one of the men, eyeing Daniel with mistrust. 'Just because you bought us a drink, don't think you have the right to question us.'

'I apologise,' said Daniel, holding up both hands in a gesture of surrender. 'I was simply making conversation. I've only just arrived in the town and what I really want to know is where I can find a warm woman for the night.'

'We could all do with one of those,' declared Crevel, banging the table for emphasis. 'I like them warm and willing.'

'Then you're a man after my own heart.'

'And she must be French — I'll none of these Flemish doxies.'

'Nor me,' agreed Daniel, 'they're as plain as pikestaffs and as cold as a night in Siberia.'

'Stick a hot pizzle in them and it'll come out as an icicle.'

When the raucous laughter died down, they discussed local brothels they'd either visited or heard reports about. Feigning interest, Daniel said he'd call on one of them later. Crevel offered to do so with him but, when he tried to rise from the table, he collapsed back down onto his chair again. Ribald comments were made at his expense. Now that the talk had moved away from military matters, the men were more relaxed and unguarded. Daniel felt that he'd been accepted. He kept plying them with wine. When he mentioned a recent visit to Paris, all of them had boastful stories about their conquests in the French capital. Crevel nodded off to sleep at one point but woke up on cue when a fresh supply of wine arrived at the table.

'What kept you, landlord?' he complained. 'I'm dying of thirst.'

'Don't listen to him,' said one of the others. 'He's drunk more than the rest of us put together.'

'My throat is parched.'

'Then let's slake your thirst,' suggested Daniel, raising his cup.

'To victory in the field!'

'To victory in the field!' they chorused.

'And in the bedchamber,' added Crevel, wildly.

He took a long sip of wine then realised that he was in dire need of using the privy. Two of his friends helped him to his feet. Seeing his opportunity, Daniel got up.

'Let me take him,' he said, grabbing the major's arm. 'I

Chapter Five

Daniel was in great danger. It was evident from the tone in the man's voice that he wouldn't hesitate to kill his captive if he made a false move. He jabbed with the dagger. Daniel felt momentary pain then blood trickled slowly down his neck.

'I saw you watching us from the corner,' said the other, coldly. 'You were waiting for your chance to move in and ingratiate yourself. Well, not all of us were as drunk as you thought even though you kept buying us more wine. I can still see and think clearly. What's more,' he went on, sniffing noisily, 'I can still smell and what I've got in my nostrils is a nasty stink.'

'That's because we're too near the privy,' said Daniel.

'Don't jest with me,' warned the man. 'Who are you?'

'I've told you. My name is Marcel Daron.'

'What's your *real* name?'

'That's it, I swear it. I'm a wine merchant.'

'And why does a wine merchant suddenly turn up here at the very moment when the army happens to be in Valenciennes?'

Daniel shrugged. 'It's just a coincidence, my friend.'

'I'm no friend of yours,' said the other, 'and I'm certain that you're no friend of ours. You gave yourself away when you offered to help Major Crevel out here. You wanted to get him on your own so that you could wheedle information out of him. I *knew* there was something peculiar about you.' The dagger point drew more blood. 'Now for the last time, tell me who you are or I'll slit your throat.'

'I really am Marcel Daron,' said Daniel, earnestly.

'You're lying.'

'It's the gospel truth.'

'Then why are you here?'

'I'm breaking my journey on the way to see my sister in Lille.'

'You put your life in jeopardy by travelling alone?'

'I rode here with a score of others and will not venture on until I can enjoy the safety of numbers again. I know there's a war on,' said Daniel, 'and that perils may lie ahead. Believe me, I'd much rather have stayed at home to look after my business. But my sister is grievously sick. She begged me to visit her.'

The man put his face close. 'I don't think you *have* a sister.'

'I can prove it to you. I have a letter from her in my pocket. And you'll be able to see from my papers that I really am Marcel Daron. Step nearer to that lantern,' advised Daniel, 'and you'll be able to read more easily. Here,' he continued, taking out a sheet of paper. 'See for yourself what poor Hortense wrote.'

Glancing down to take it from him, the man gave Daniel the vital fraction of time that he needed. He moved like lightning. Seizing the wrist of the hand that held the weapon, he bunched the other fist and used it to deliver some fierce punches to the man's face, splitting his nose, closing both his eyes and knocking him senseless with a blow to the chin. As he slumped to the ground, the officer let go of the dagger. Daniel picked it up at once, easing it between the ribs and into the heart. He didn't bother to retrieve the letter from his phantom sister. It was really a tavern reckoning.

Daniel opened the privy door and found that Major Crevel was fast asleep. After hauling him out, he dragged the corpse into the privy and closed the door on it. Then he pulled up Crevel's breeches and more or less carried him across to the stables. Daniel's horse was already saddled in readiness for a quick departure. Reaching into a saddlebag for some lengths of rope, he bound Crevel hand and foot then used a handkerchief as a gag. The major was too drunk and fatigued to know what was going on. When he was lifted bodily and draped over one of the other horses, he made no complaint. Daniel used another rope to secure his cargo before leading both horses out of the courtyard.

Inside the tavern, the other officers continued to roister. It was a long time before they began to wonder where their friends were. One of them eventually went outside to investigate. When he discovered the corpse in the privy, he raised the alarm and a search began but there was no hope of their finding Major Crevel. He was lying in a ditch over a mile away, snoring up to heaven, blithely unaware of the fact that he was no longer in his uniform.

Even though it was far too big for him, it was being worn by Daniel along with Crevel's boots and hat. He knew that a major in a cavalry regiment would have far less trouble from any French patrol he met than a bogus wine merchant riding on his own. The disguise got him safely out of enemy territory. Night was a willing accomplice. Nobody noticed the baggy coat and the voluminous breeches in the darkness. When he was stopped by a patrol, Daniel had been treated with the utmost deference. It was an uplifting experience. He enjoyed his brief promotion to the rank of major even if it happened to be in the wrong army.

'Where have you been?' asked Emanuel Janssen.

'I went for a walk with Beatrix,' replied his daughter.

He smiled fondly. 'And I suppose that you just happened

to go past the shops in the course of your stroll. You've been looking at new dresses again, Amalia, haven't you?'

'It does no harm to look.'

'Of course not – I wasn't criticising you. It's only natural that a young woman like you should want to see the latest fashions.'

She sighed. 'There's no such thing in Amsterdam, Father.'

'Isn't there?'

'Clothing here is so drab and dull.'

'Oh, I don't think it's that bad.'

'You don't have to wear such dresses,' she argued. 'For the most part, they're so plain and uninteresting. It's the one thing I miss about our time in Paris. The ladies there dressed beautifully.'

'Your memories of Paris are much happier than mine.'

'Think of that day you took me to Versailles. It was amazing to see the King and his court in their finery. The ladies' dresses were magnificent and so intricate.'

'I felt that some of them were rather gaudy,' he said.

'There was so much bright *colour*,' recalled Amalia. 'Wherever I turned, my eyes were dazzled. It was a different world. There's nothing like that anywhere in our country. The only real colour in Amsterdam is right here in front of us.'

She pointed to the vivid tapestry on the loom. They were in the large workshop at the rear of the house, the place where Janssen created his masterpieces, sewing them from the back and viewing the front of the tapestry in a mirror to make sure that he was keeping exactly to the design. Though she loved watching her father at work, Amalia had no ambitions to emulate him. She restricted herself to needlework, seeing it as a female accomplishment rather than a source of income. Weaving tapestries was an art practised by men like her father, a self-effacing genius whose hand-sewn work hung in several European palaces. Whenever she thought about the future – and she did so most days – she never envisaged having to toil at a loom or sew battle scenes with meticulous skill. Her abiding fantasy was one of domestic bliss with a certain British officer.

Her father was well aware of her high expectations.

'When did you last hear from Captain Rawson?' he asked.

'It must be almost a month now, Father.'

'I suspect that you can tell me the correct day and the precise hour when his letter arrived.'

'I'm always so pleased to hear from him,' she said, cheerfully.

'Well, don't fret if there's a long wait for the next letter. The captain moves around so much that it's difficult for him to write to anyone, especially when he's on French territory. You simply have to be patient, Amalia.'

'I accept that.'

'And you must prepare yourself for the possibility of bad news.'

70

She frowned. 'Why should I do that?'

'Captain Rawson is a *soldier*.'

'He knows how to look after himself, Father.'

'When he goes into battle, anything can happen.'

'Daniel is always very careful.'

'Yet he sometimes puts courage before caution,' said Janssen. 'Look how he contrived to rescue me from the Bastille. He took the most terrible risks to do that. A careful man wouldn't even have tried to get me out of there.'

'Things are different now.'

There was such a hopeful note in her voice that her father couldn't bring himself to contradict her. He'd seen the way that she and Daniel Rawson had fallen in love and had given their romance his blessing. At the same time, however, he was realistic enough to know that a soldier's life could come to a sudden end at any moment. Daniel never hid from action. Instead, he deliberately went out in search of it. When he'd been commissioned to make a tapestry depicting the battle of Ramillies, Janssen had been delighted to have Daniel as his adviser but he'd quailed at some of the details he'd learnt. Glorious victories were based on blood and agony. Even during such a triumphant battle, there'd been hideous deaths among the Allies as well and many who survived were afflicted with horrendous injuries. Given the way he'd taken part in a cavalry charge – a fact that Janssen chose to keep from Amalia – Daniel could easily have been one of the casualties at Ramillies.

Next time, fortune might not favour the daring captain.

Loving his daughter dearly, Janssen didn't want to dash her hopes. He was an old man now, his hair and beard silvered by time, his shoulders rounded by long years at his loom. Most of his life was behind him. Amalia, however, had a whole future ahead of her and Janssen wanted it to be as happy and fulfilled as possible. On almost every test of suitability, Daniel Rawson would make an ideal husband for her. What cast a menacing shadow over any thoughts of marriage was the fact that he was engaged in a war that had already claimed thousands and thousands of victims. Janssen prayed that Amalia would not be one more stricken woman, doomed to pass her days by weeping over the grave of her dead lover.

'Yes,' he said, summoning up a grin. 'Things are different now.'

'Daniel leads a charmed life,' she said, confidently.

'That's why he met you, Amalia.'

With a light laugh at the compliment, she kissed him on the cheek in gratitude. Though her father embraced her warmly, his face was lined with apprehension.

Major General William Cadogan was a big, genial man in his early thirties with a reputation as an inveterate gambler. He was also a brilliant cavalry officer and a resourceful Quartermaster General of the Confederate army. But it was his work as head of intelligence that brought him into contact with Daniel Rawson. It fell to Cadogan to collate all the information gathered from prisoners and deserters, or from those who'd been captured by the French then exchanged. He also maintained his own cadre of spies. In this way, he built up a clear picture of the activities of the enemy.

'By what strange and mysterious witchcraft did you learn all this?' he asked in wonderment.

'I happened to be in the right place at the right time, sir.'

'That's arrant nonsense, Daniel, so don't try to fool me. It's almost as if you rode into the heart of the enemy camp.'

'I went to an inn nearby,' explained Daniel, 'and waited until some of the officers came there for a drinking bout. When I bought Major Crevel some wine, he was kind enough to reward me with details of the French plans.'

'There's more to it than that,' said Cadogan, 'and I want to hear the full story. No more of your modesty either. You've earned the right to boast a little.'

'I was lucky, sir.'

'You were both lucky and infernally clever, if I know you.'

Daniel gave him an abbreviated account of events at the inn near Valenciennes and Cadogan was soon laughing heartily. Even the details about the killing of the French officer didn't stop his guffaws. He loved the notion that a tavern bill had been passed off as a cry for help from a non-existent sister in distress. Cadogan saved his real mirth for the news that Crevel had been stripped of his uniform and left in a ditch. He positively rocked with laughter.

The two men were in Cadogan's tent, sharing a drink while they talked with easy familiarity. They had much in common. Both had fought in Ireland and taken part in the attacks on Cork and Kinsale under the command of the future Duke of Marlborough. Cadogan had been a cornet in the Enniskillen Dragoons while Daniel had been a humble corporal in a Dutch regiment. Both had shown conspicuous gallantry throughout their careers. When Cadogan married a Dutch heiress, he learnt her native language and was able to converse fluently in it with Daniel. It brought them closer together.

'It must have been a terrible shock for Major Crevel,' said Cadogan. 'To wake up half-naked in a ditch, I mean.'

'I think our picquets had an even greater shock,' noted Daniel. 'They thought they'd captured a French officer and they carried me off as if I was a wondrous prize. Imagine their disappointment when they discovered that I was a captain in a British regiment.'

'They should have applauded your audacity, Daniel.'

'They cursed me for not telling them the truth at the start.'

'Your mission was a success, that's the main thing.'

'Yes, I expected to be there for days before I gleaned anything that I could report back to you. It was pure happenstance that information fell into my hands on that first night.'

'There's that modesty creeping in again,' observed

Cadogan. 'Nothing in your life occurs by accident, Daniel. You're the most deliberate human being I've ever met. You went there in search of intelligence and, by Jove, you found it straight away. Your secret was to pick the right man.'

'It was a case of *in vino veritas*.'

'None of us is immune to the seductive power of the grape.'

'As a wine merchant,' said Daniel, taking a sip before holding up his glass, 'I'm inclined to agree.'

Cadogan laughed again. In spite of his weight and girth, he was really in his element when mounted and adored nothing more than leading his cavalry into battle. Daniel had seen and admired his fearlessness in action. But he also admired Cadogan's ability to carry a whole range of responsibilities so lightly. Here was the man who drew up the order of battle for the Confederate army, taking account of the differing priorities of the various nations and making sure that commanders between whom there was friction were kept well apart. Soldier, diplomat, spymaster, gambler and quartermaster, Cadogan radiated life. Daniel found it a pleasure to be in his company.

'What you've told me accords with my own instincts,' said Cadogan. 'I sensed that Burgundy was a complete novice. Why march towards Brussels when he could test our horse near Huy? That's the direction he should be taking.'

'It's exactly what the duc de Vendôme suggested,' said Daniel, 'but he was overruled. His plan was to lay siege to Huy.'

'That's because he's an experienced soldier. It must be galling for him to have to listen to a posturing ninny like Burgundy. I'll wager that the pair of them have some rare old arguments.'

'Vendôme is known for his blunt speech.'

Cadogan chuckled. 'That's not *all* he's known for! If rumours are correct, he has a taste for pretty young officers.'

'Then Major Crevel is safe from his attentions,' said Daniel with a grin. 'Even his own mother would never describe him as pretty. After a night in a ditch, he must have looked a sorry sight.'

The duc de Vendôme read the report with gathering fury. When he'd finished, he tossed it on the ground in disgust then rounded on Lieutenant Valeran who was alone with him in the tent.

'Can this be true?' he demanded.

'I fear that it is, Your Grace.'

'Were there witnesses to this disgrace?'

'Yes,' replied Valeran. 'Major Crevel was hauled out of a ditch by a patrol. At first, they refused to believe he was what he claimed to be. They took him for some kind of madman.'

'I can well understand that. Send for him, Lieutenant.'

'I took the liberty of doing so. The major will be here directly.'

'Crevel may arrive as a major but he certainly won't leave as one,' said Vendôme, vengefully. 'I don't reward

76

incompetence.' He looked meaningfully at his companion. 'Those who displease me get short shrift. Only those who impress me can look for promotion.'

'Thank you, Your Grace,' said Valeran, obsequiously.

Hearing the sound of footsteps outside, they turned towards the tent flap. A guard entered, ushered Major Crevel in, then withdrew. Vendôme glowered at the newcomer. Valeran made as if to leave but the general signalled that he was to remain. Crevel, meanwhile, was standing to attention as he braced himself for the onslaught. Now restored to a uniform, he was uneasy and shamefaced.

'Major Crevel,' began Vendôme.

'Yes, Your Grace?' answered the other.

'Is it your habit to sleep unclothed in a muddy ditch?'

'No, no, it's most uncharacteristic of me but I had no choice. I was set on by three villains. When they'd beaten me black and blue, they stole my uniform and left me unconscious.'

'I see no bruising on your face.'

'They punched and kicked my body,' claimed Crevel, 'then left me to die of my injuries. As you see,' he continued, straightening, 'I returned to duty at the earliest possible opportunity.'

'Yes,' said Vendôme, 'but only after the patrol had rescued you. According to the report, you behaved like a raving lunatic.'

'I deny that, Your Grace. I may have been a little

outspoken but I was entitled to be in the circumstances. The truth is that I was still distracted after my beating.'

'Is that the beating administered by those three rogues?'

'Yes, it was.'

'Then where did they suddenly spring from?'

'They were lying in wait in the privy,' said Crevel, trying to brazen it out. 'As I approached, they ambushed me. I had no chance against such odds.'

'Ah, I see…and what about your friend, Lieutenant Jauzion?'

'Sebastien?'

'At the time you say you were set on by three men, his dead body was in the privy.' Crevel gulped. It was news to him. 'Are you asking me to believe that it was big enough to conceal four human beings?'

'Sebastien is dead?' croaked Crevel. 'How could that be?'

'If you'd stayed awake long enough, you might have saved his life. He was stabbed to death with his own dagger. When they found his corpse in the privy, your friends were certain that the killer was a wine merchant whom you befriended in the course of the evening.' He snapped his fingers and Valeran retrieved the report from the ground before handing it to him. Vendôme glanced at it. 'The man's name was Marcel Daron. Do you have any memory of him?'

'Yes, I do. He was good company.'

'Lieutenant Jauzion might not agree with that judgement.'

'Poor Sebastien…I can't believe he's dead!'

'It's more than probable that he was murdered under your very nose. And not by three ruffians,' Vendôme went on, curling his lip. 'He was stabbed by this so-called wine merchant, the same man who stripped you of your uniform and tossed you into a ditch.' He took a step closer. 'Why did you lie to me?'

'I was telling the truth,' bleated Crevel.

'The only person you told the truth to was that crafty wine merchant, who will no doubt convey everything you divulged to his masters in the Confederate army. You were duped by a spy, Major Crevel. And you allowed a fine officer like Lieutenant Jauzion to be killed because you were too drunk and incapable to save him. What have you to say for yourself?'

Crevel's head drooped. 'It won't happen again, Your Grace.'

'Oh, there's no danger of that,' said Vendôme, vindictively. 'Nobody will be able to filch the uniform of a major in the French army again because you, sir, are no longer entitled to wear it. Take it off.'

'I must protest,' howled Crevel. 'I hold my rank with honour.'

'Take it off!' roared Vendôme. 'Or I'll tear it from your body with my bare hands.'

'The matter must be referred to the duc de Burgundy.'

It was an unwise moment to remind Vendôme that he was not the commander-in-chief. Losing his temper, he lashed out with a hand and slapped Crevel hard across the cheek. He then unleashed such a gushing stream of vituperation that the erstwhile major cowered before him and plucked hastily at the buttons of his coat. When it had been removed, Vendôme snatched it from him and hurled it into the corner of the tent.

'Get out of my sight!' he yelled, quivering with rage. 'You're confined to your quarters until I can decide on your punishment.'

'At least, give me leave to apologise,' pleaded Crevel.

But there was no chance of that. Vendôme raised his hand to strike again and Crevel gave up. Waddling ridiculously, he hurried out of the tent. It was some minutes before Vendôme's ire gradually subsided. Lieutenant Valeran, meanwhile, lurked silently in his corner, too frightened to venture an opinion lest the ducal anger be turned on him. He was relieved when the older man seemed to calm down. Vendôme lowered himself onto a chair and was deep in thought for a while. Making a decision, he suddenly got up again.

'I want him,' he said.

'Shall I fetch Major Crevell back?' asked Valeran.

'I don't want *him*, Raoul. I never want to see that buffoon again. No,' he went on, 'the man I'm after is that venomous wine merchant. I won't allow anyone to humiliate us like this. I want Marcel Daron – or whatever his real name is – standing before me in chains.'

'How can we arrange that?'

'Use your imagination, man. We have intelligencers in the enemy camp. Let them earn their money for once. Someone will have boasted of how they stole the uniform of a French officer. I want to know who he is.' He put a hand on Valeran's shoulder then lifted it to brush back a wisp of the lieutenant's hair. 'I need a name, Raoul,' he said, eyes glinting, 'then the hunt can begin.'

CHAPTER SIX

Lieutenant Jonathan Ainley was a tall, thin, pale-faced man with a long, beaky nose competing for facial dominance against an unusually large and dimpled chin that curved upwards. An efficient officer, he'd settled well into army life and learnt to accept its many shortcomings without complaint. Set against its defects, however, there were definite advantages. One of these was the warm camaraderie that existed and Ainley relished this aspect of his chosen lot. Drawing on their support, he was excessively friendly and obliging to all his fellow officers. In the case of Daniel Rawson, he hovered close to hero worship.

'Tell me the story in your own words,' he urged.

Daniel shook his head. 'There's nothing to tell, Jonathan.'

'Nothing to tell?' echoed Ainley. 'If I'd abducted a French officer then used his uniform as a disguise, I'd be crowing about it from the rooftops.'

'That's perhaps why you're not involved in espionage,' said Daniel. 'When you gather intelligence, discretion is everything. How did you come to hear about it?'

'A little bird told me, Daniel.'

'Then he's been singing too loud. You might warn him that if I find out who he is, I'll tie his beak shut.'

'You're among friends. Why not share your adventures?'

'Loose tongues can cause trouble,' said Daniel. 'I'm sure that the major who loaned me his uniform has found that out by now. My guess is that he's been severely punished.'

'Whereas you should be feted for what you achieved.'

'I did what I was told to do, Jonathan – no more, no less.'

'You ought to take some pride in your exploits.'

'Oh, I do,' admitted Daniel, 'but only in private.'

They were standing outside Ainley's tent in the British camp, surrounded by activity and forced to raise their voices above the routine clamour. Drums were beating nearby as soldiers were being drilled. Supply wagons were rolling noisily past. Distant orders were being barked out. Artillery was arriving. Nobody took any notice of the light drizzle that started to fall. After the heavy rain that greeted the arrival of spring, it was a relief.

'I'm surprised that His Grace could spare you,' said Ainley. 'You're such an important member of his personal staff that he must want you constantly by his side.'

'You overrate my importance, Jonathan,' said Daniel. 'I'm a very junior member of the staff. I'm far more useful if I gather intelligence than I would be if I sat in endless meetings with His Grace.'

'I thought you acted as his interpreter.'

'I do on occasion. My command of Dutch, French and German has been put to good use. But I'm not needed when Major General Cadogan is there, because he speaks all three languages.'

'Heaven knows how he mastered Dutch. It's so complicated.'

Daniel smiled. 'That's exactly what the Dutch say about English because they find it so fiendishly difficult to learn.'

'All I've ever managed are a few phrases in French,' said Ainley, scratching his chin. 'Not that it matters, I suppose. On the battlefield, we speak the universal language of brute force.'

'It is tempered with some subtler tones,' replied Daniel.

He was about to explain what he meant when he spotted the unmistakable frame of Henry Welbeck coming towards him and hailed his friend with a wave. Since Daniel was in the company of another officer, the sergeant spoke with more formality.

'Good morning, Captain,' he said. 'Good morning, Lieutenant.' The two men exchanged greetings with him. 'I was wondering if there was any news about those men who

85

raided two farms then burnt them to the ground?'

'I've heard nothing more,' said Daniel.

'Neither have I,' added Ainley. 'What I can tell you is that nobody has been arrested for those outrages. To all intents and purpose, the villains got away with it.'

'Yes,' said Welbeck, sourly, 'and they did so in British uniforms. That's what irks me. We rarely get permission to forage and, even if we do, we try to show respect to any civilians. Word must have spread by now. Every time people see redcoats coming towards them, they'll shrink back in fear.'

'The raiders will be caught sooner or later,' said Daniel.

Ainley was doubtful. 'I fear that they've gone to ground,' he said. 'They could take more chances during the winter when very few people were on the roads. They could strike then disappear very quickly. That's no longer the situation.'

'No,' agreed Daniel. 'There's a lot more traffic about now and the evenings are drawing out. It's not so easy to escape being seen.'

'Those devils have probably returned to camp now,' said Welbeck. 'Without knowing it, one of our cavalry regiments is harbouring ruthless killers.'

'Some people might say that all soldiers are ruthless killers,' remarked Ainley with a half-laugh. 'It's an occupational necessity at times. However,' he went on, 'I'm sure that you didn't come to talk to me, Sergeant. I'll leave you to Captain Rawson.'

'Thank you, Lieutenant.' Welbeck waited until Ainley was

out of earshot before turning to Daniel. 'How ever did that blinking idiot get to become a lieutenant?'

'He did what most officers do, Henry – he bought a commission.'

'You didn't do that.'

'No,' said Daniel, 'but, then, I could never have afforded it. If I hadn't been promoted on merit, I'd still be stuck in the ranks being bullied by some black-hearted sergeant like you. As for Jonathan Ainley, he's better than some I could name. He's a competent officer and respected by his men.'

'Well, he'll get no respect from me.'

Daniel laughed. 'None of us can expect plaudits from you, Henry,' he said. 'I sometimes think that you joined the army for the express purpose of despising its officers. According to you, we're all complete dolts.'

'There are a few exceptions.'

'Does that mean we're slowly winning you over?'

'There's not a chance of that, Dan,' asserted Welbeck. 'I've spent too many years taking stupid orders from well-bred fops who simply want to shoot game, drink wine and play cards all day.'

'That sounds like an attractive prospect to me. I only wish it were truly like that but we both know that it isn't. Since we've been involved in this war,' Daniel told him, 'every spring and summer has consisted of nothing but marches, sieges, skirmishes and occasional major battles. That's the pattern we've been following.'

'So when will we be on the move this time?'

'We have to await orders.'

'You must know what they're going to be.'

'I wish I did, Henry, but His Grace hasn't confided in me as yet. There are a number of elements to be considered before any final decisions can be made. However,' added Daniel, 'I can tell you this. The likelihood is that we'll have an opportunity to meet the French on the battlefield again. They're eager to avenge their defeat at Ramillies with a decisive victory. That's why they've mustered such a large army against us.'

'We've beaten large armies before. The Frenchies hold no fears for me, Dan. I've killed too many of them. What I'm worried about are some of the people fighting on my side.'

'What do you mean?'

'The heartless bastards who destroyed those farms,' said Welbeck, bitterly. 'They're hiding somewhere in our ranks and that makes my blood boil.'

'They won't stay here indefinitely,' decided Daniel. 'I fancy that the temptation will be too strong. It won't be long before we hear of a marauding band on the rampage again.'

The boy was ten, old enough to do his fair share of the chores on the little farm yet young enough to yearn for childish pleasures. When he'd finished work that afternoon, therefore, he ran off to the stream nearby to dangle his bare feet in the water while he carved a boat out of a piece of wood. Happily engaged with his knife, he didn't even look up when he heard the clatter of hooves on the road behind him. After shaving the prow of his vessel, he held it up to examine it from every angle. Deciding that it was still not ready, he carved the stern into a more rounded shape then ran a finger over it. Primitive as it was, the boat felt smooth and capable of staying afloat. At the exact moment when he launched it on the water, however, shots rang out from the farm and he jumped to his feet in alarm.

He was less than forty yards away but shielded by the bushes growing along the bank of the stream. As he peered around them, he saw the most horrific sight. Three bodies lay on the ground. They belonged to his father and two elder brothers. Blood-curdling screams from the house were recognisably those of his mother and sister. His first instinct was to run to their defence, but what could he do against armed soldiers in red uniforms? There was an additional shock for the boy. He heard the crackle of fire and saw smoke rising from the barn. The next moment, he was forced to watch the livestock being driven off by some of the men. When the horses had been taken, the stables were set alight. His whole world was suddenly aflame.

If he couldn't stop them, he thought, he could at least get close enough to see who they were. Keeping low, he crept furtively towards the farm. The raiders didn't even look in his direction. They were too busy seizing what they wanted. The fire had taken a firm hold now and the crackle had turned into a deafening roar. The boy moved steadily forward until he hit a wall of blistering heat that stopped him dead. When he glanced at the farmhouse, telltale wisps of smoke were now coming through the windows. His mother and his sister had stopped screaming but they were still inside. Desperate to help them, he was held back by the billowing flames.

The attackers were pleased with their work and started to mount their horses. The last man to join them seemed to be their leader because he bellowed orders as he emerged from the farmhouse, doing up his belt. Throwing a glance over his shoulder, he cackled happily before putting his foot in the stirrup and heaving himself up into the saddle. A sudden gust of wind then blew the flames away from the boy for a second. It was as if a curtain had been drawn back. What he saw, and what he would always remember, was the red beard and mad eyes of their leader, a big man with an evil laugh, who took one last look at the bonfire before giving the command to ride off with the day's spoils. The wall of flame returned to block his vision and the boy could see no more.

Somewhere downstream, his boat sailed bravely on.

The Duke of Marlborough sat tight-lipped in consternation as Daniel delivered the report. Adam Cardonnel was the only other person in the tent and he was equally appalled at what he'd heard. Daniel tried to translate a garbled version of events into something more articulate. When the recitation was over, Marlborough wanted answers.

'This happened this very afternoon, you say?'

'Yes, Your Grace,' replied Daniel.

'And where exactly was the farm?'

'It's about ten miles west of here. If I may look over your shoulder for a moment,' he said, standing behind Marlborough then pointing with his index finger at the map on the table, 'it would be close to here.'

'Then it's on territory held by us,' said Marlborough, worriedly. 'Every farm on it has a right to our protection. The last thing we need to do is to turn the civilian population against us.'

'Where did this information come from?' asked Cardonnel.

'The protest was made by another farmer,' said Daniel. 'I was there when he came into camp. He was too agitated to make much sense at first but I managed to tease the relevant details out of him. It seems that the boy ran four miles barefoot to the next farm to tell his tale. The lad was in a terrible state, and who can blame him? He lost his home, his parents and his siblings in one dreadful swoop. As soon as the farmer heard what had happened, he galloped here to demand that we punish the culprits.'

Cardonnel nodded. 'I'd say that was a very legitimate demand.'

'They'll be punished,' vowed Marlborough, frowning deeply. 'I'll supervise their execution myself. First, however, we have to identify them.' He turned to Cardonnel. 'Send word to every cavalry regiment, Adam. I want to know details of every patrol that rode out of here.'

'I'll draft letters immediately, Your Grace.'

'Ask for a description of where the patrols went and the names of those men involved. We may have to do this by a process of elimination but we'll catch them in the end. They're not British soldiers – they're vicious criminals.'

'And they wear our uniforms,' said Cardonnel, ruefully.

'I'm not certain about that,' Daniel put in.

'You just told us that redcoats committed this atrocity.'

'They did, but that doesn't mean they belong to us. I've been thinking how difficult it would be for one of our patrols to rustle livestock then burn down a farm. Where would they keep the animals? They could hardly bring them back here to camp. Nor could they rely on being sent out on patrol again at a time of their choosing. Do you see the problem here?' he went on. 'The boy talked of nine or ten soldiers who raided the farm. When patrols are sent out, they vary greatly in size. It's unlikely that the same group would be dispatched together each time.'

'That's true,' agreed Marlborough, grasping at the possibility that his men might not, after all, be responsible. 'We may have a smattering of god-forsaken rogues in our midst but we also have thousands of honest, decent, responsible men who'd draw back at such horrors. If they had the faintest whiff of it, they'd report it to their superiors.'

Daniel became pensive. Cardonnel watched him carefully.

'I know that look in your eye, Daniel,' he said at length. 'You've been meditating on this, haven't you? I suspect you have a theory.'

'As it happens,' Daniel answered, 'I have two.'

'If either exonerates our soldiers, let's hear it.'

'The first theory does that. I believe that these redcoats might actually be French soldiers, deliberately wearing our uniforms to give the impression that we'll slash and burn for the sheer love of it. It would be easy for them to get hold of uniforms,' Daniel continued. 'After any engagement, the battlefield is littered with them.'

'That sounds very plausible,' said Marlborough, thoughtfully. 'Burgundy and Vendôme know that we don't enjoy the unqualified support of the Flemish population. We've yet to win their loyalty, let alone their affection. What better way to stir up enmity against us than to portray us as callous murderers? Thank you, Daniel. Your theory has the ring of truth about it.'

'Yet it is only a theory, Your Grace,' Daniel reminded him.

'And it's partnered with another,' noted Cardonnel.

'This one is not so reassuring, I'm afraid,' cautioned Daniel, 'because it puts the onus back on us. It would be very comforting to think that French soldiers have carried out the three raids, thereby lifting suspicion off British soldiers. However...'

'Go on,' Marlborough encouraged.

'I incline towards my second theory.'

'Which is?'

'That these men are deserters from our own ranks,' said Daniel, 'hiding behind our uniforms and initiating another attack whenever they want a fresh supply of food or some more excitement.'

'Ha!' cried Marlborough, smacking the table. 'What excitement can there be in shooting unarmed men and raping their womenfolk? What kind of warped minds take delight in the wilful destruction of property? They behaved like wild animals. If they really are British renegades, there's all the more reason to track them down.' He turned to Cardonnel. 'When you send those letters, Adam, ask for a list of any deserters from our cavalry regiments.'

'I will, Your Grace,' replied Cardonnel, reaching for pen and paper, 'and I'll do it promptly.'

'They may not all be from the cavalry,' said Daniel. 'Some of them could equally well have fled from regiments of foot and stolen some horses. May I suggest that we examine the lists of *all* deserters?'

'That's a wise precaution,' agreed Marlborough, studying the map. 'Meanwhile, I'll send out patrols to search for them. So far, there have been three raids. The victims have all been roughly in this area to the west,' he went on, tapping the map with his finger. 'That's where the search must start. The attacks are obviously planned with care. They always choose small, isolated farms where they can expect little resistance.'

He sat back. 'Where will they strike next, I wonder?'

'We can only hazard a guess, Your Grace,' said Daniel. 'With your permission, I'll pursue another line of enquiry. The third attack is very similar to the others but there's a significant difference.'

'What's that, Daniel?'

'We have a witness.'

'He's only a frightened ten-year-old boy.'

'Nevertheless, he may have seen something that could help us. When the lad has had a little time to recover, I'd like to talk to him. He may, for instance, have heard those men speak.'

'That would be valuable evidence,' said Cardonnel. 'At least, we'd know what language they used. It's a good suggestion.'

'I concur,' added Marlborough. 'Take a patrol with you.'

'I'd prefer to go on my own, Your Grace,' said Daniel.

'Why is that?'

'The boy has had enough of a scare already. If he sees another troop of redcoats descending on him, he'll be terrified. I'll go on my own and I won't wear my uniform.'

'That's very sensible.'

'I have to win the boy's confidence somehow,' said Daniel, 'and that will be difficult. Might I suggest that any patrols sent out are kept well clear of this farm where the lad is now staying?'

'I'll ensure that they are, Daniel.'

'Thank you, Your Grace. I'd like to think that this is all part of some French plot to discredit us in the eyes of the local people. In my heart, however,' Daniel went on, sadly, 'I have a lurking suspicion that the men we're after served in the British army and ran from their colours. That, in itself, is a heinous crime. What they've done since, I'm afraid, is quite monstrous. They soiled our reputation and stirred up hatred against us.' Daniel's face hardened. 'That's unforgivable.'

The farmhouse stood beside a stream in the shadow of a hill that protected it from the worst of the weather. The summit commanded views in all directions. A lookout posted on it could see anyone approaching across the plain from miles away so they always had advance warning of company. It was a paradox. Men who made a living by burning down farmhouses had actually restored this one. When they first found the place, it was little more than a shell, its walls crumbling, its roof collapsed, its stone-flagged floors overgrown with weeds. After stealing tools, timber and tiles, they'd set about repairing their new home, building a snug refuge to see them through the winter. There'd been no shortage of wood for the fire.

The roof was now sound, the rooms swept clean, the shutters mended and new doors kept out the wind and rain. They'd even made some crude furniture. Anything else they'd needed, they'd simply looted. From the ruins of the barn, a new one had risen, stocked with hay and straw.

Animals penned behind the farmhouse were killed and roasted when the need arose. A pig was turning on the spit today, the tempting aroma of pork wafting through the air. The men were already licking their lips.

There was another paradox. Soldiers who'd deserted from an army that imposed too much discipline on them had readily accepted an even stricter regimen. They knew that it was essential to follow orders now or forfeit their lives. There was, however, a difference. In the army, they were at the mercy of loathsome superiors against whom they had no redress. They were now part of a band that had elected their leader. Matthew Searle was one of them, a soldier from the rank and file, a strong-minded man who'd refused a chance to become a corporal out of sheer bloody-mindedness. Yet now he was wearing the uniform of a captain, albeit one that was stained with blood and ventilated by bullet holes. Searle was bold, cunning and decisive. He held the ragged band together by force of character.

Edwin Lock was a short, skinny, rat-faced man with bulging eyes and a twitching moustache. Sucking on his pipe, he sidled across to Searle, who was seated at the kitchen table, counting money.

'I need to speak to you, Matt,' he said.

'Shut up,' ordered Searle.

'We've been talking, you see.'

'I don't care what you've been doing, Edwin. You can just hold your tongue until I finish. Open that big mouth of yours again and I'll halve your share. Is that what you want?'

Lock held his peace and waited impatiently as Searle put the money into a series of piles. It was the life savings of the family who'd occupied the last farm they'd raided. At the time, it had seemed like a reasonable haul. Divided between ten of them, however, it looked less substantial. Searle was a natural democrat. He expected no privileges because of his position as leader. Ten equal amounts stood on the table. His arithmetic lesson was over.

'Well?' he asked, glancing up at Lock. 'What have you got to say for yourself this time?'

'It's really what the others have got to say, Matt. They get bored out here without women.'

'The town is only two hours away. All they have to do is to ride over there and they can buy the juiciest slit they want. They have the time and the money.'

'Wouldn't it be easier to have the women here?' said Lock with a sly grin. 'The girl in that last farm, for instance. Why did we have to kill her? She'd have given us sport for days out here.'

'Yes,' conceded Searle, 'but you'd all have been fighting each other over whose turn it was next. I want none of that here, Edwin. If they want to dip their wick, the men can ride into town. The whores are cheap and succulent there.'

'Then why don't we pay for some of them to come here?'

'No, I tell you.'

'They could cook and sew for us as well.'

'They'd be too busy on their backs,' said Searle, stroking his red beard. 'I love my fucking as much as the next man but I know the dangers of having women under our feet. They're a terrible distraction and they'd expect to be pampered.' Rising to his feet, he towered over Lock. 'We're on the run, Edwin. Never forget that. There'll be patrols out looking for us and it may be necessary for us to find another place to hide. That's why I keep a man on top of that hill in daylight hours. We must always be on our guard.'

'Women would help to pass the time.'

'They'd encumber us and there's an end to it.'

'We *miss* them, Matt. It's one of the reasons we deserted.'

'You'll have your share of cunny before too long,' promised Searle with a grin. 'I've picked out the next farm already. I went over there last week to get the lie of the land. There's a buxom wife, two daughters and two servants. That's five lovely women between us. Pass the news around to the men. We'll take our pleasure with them before we send them up to heaven in dancing flames.'

Lock was thrilled. 'I like the sound of that,' he said, panting. 'British soldiers will have another victory to enjoy.'

'Not this time, Edwin.'

'No?'

'This farm is in enemy territory so we'll change sides. Look out those blue uniforms we collected,' ordered Searle. 'When we burn down the next farm and swive the women, we'll be troopers in the French cavalry.'

CHAPTER SEVEN

Conversations with Vendôme were usually unpleasant occasions but the duc de Burgundy found them almost unbearable when they took place early in the morning. While the devout Burgundy began each new day by offering up his prayers, Vendôme preferred to occupy his *chaise-percée*, his camp lavatory, writing letters, issuing orders and receiving visitors while seated with his breeches around his ankles. When Burgundy called on him that morning and saw him in his customary position, he took care to stand a few yards away. It was a revolting sight for such a fastidious man.

'I need to speak to you about Major Crevel,' he began.

'There's no such person,' replied Vendôme, brusquely. 'Crevel has been reduced to the ranks where he belongs.'

'You are too hasty, my lord Duke. Crevel is a fine officer with a good record. More to the point, he comes from a family with a long history of military excellence.'

'He besmirched that history and deserves his fate.'

'That's a matter of opinion,' said Burgundy, noting the copious tobacco stains on Vendôme's shirt. 'I would have acted rather differently in this matter.'

'Are you saying that you'd *promote* that imbecile?'

'Major Crevel is not an imbecile. He's an intelligent man.'

'Then why did he let himself get ensnared so easily by an enemy spy? Why did he get so drunk that he could be kidnapped, stripped of his uniform and left in a ditch? What glimmer of intelligence can you perceive in that? No,' Vendôme went on, 'I stand by my action. When a man shows himself unworthy of his position – and when he lets himself be humiliated like that – he merits instant dismissal.'

'That's for me to decide.'

'I disagree, my lord.'

'The matter should have been referred to me.'

'That was quite unnecessary. After all,' said Vendôme with ill-concealed sarcasm, 'you have a vast army to lead. You have to draw up a plan of campaign that will end in a famous French victory. Why should you bother about such trivialities as the demotion of a useless officer?'

'I don't regard it as trivial,' retorted Burgundy. 'In responding the way that you did, you set a bad example.'

'I think I set a very good example. The best way to

preserve discipline is to crack the whip from time to time. And I've always believed that officers should be punished severely if their conduct warrants it. You, of course,' he added with a patronising smile, 'have much less experience of dealing with this sort of problem so you are bound to flounder.'

Burgundy blenched. 'I am not floundering, my lord Duke!'

'The matter is closed. Why not leave it at that?'

'Because,' said the other, 'I do not choose to do so.'

'Forget Crevel. I have.'

'I can't do that, I'm afraid. The major has appealed directly to me and shown true remorse. He admits his folly and has vowed to be more circumspect in future. Heavens!' he exclaimed. 'If every officer who gets involved in a drinking bout is to be punished, then we'll have nobody left to lead the men.'

'I've nothing against drink,' said Vendôme, expansively. 'I love it myself. However, I despise men who can't hold their wine and make themselves vulnerable as a result. In his stupor, Crevel gave away valuable information about us.'

'He concedes that and is duly repentant.'

'So?'

'I believe you should reconsider your decision.'

Vendôme gesticulated theatrically. 'Why are we talking about the fate of one man,' he asked, 'when we have a hundred thousand to take into account? Why waste our breath on a miserable wretch like Crevel? I thought that he'd at least accept his punishment with some grace but it was too much to ask. Instead, he goes crawling on his hands and knees to you.'

'There's a reason for that,' said Burgundy.

'Yes…he's a snivelling toad.'

'No, my lord Duke, he happens to be a distant relative of mine.'

'Ah!' said Vendôme, sitting back. 'Now we come to it.'

'I want him restored to his rank.'

'Were he your own brother, I'd not do that.'

Burgundy recoiled slightly from this open challenge to his authority. Anger slowly built inside him, mingling with the revulsion he felt at having a discussion in such gross circumstances. There was a long, strained silence. It was eventually shattered by Vendôme who broke wind with such trumpeting violence that he forced Burgundy to take a few steps backwards.

'May I remind you,' said Vendôme, mustering what dignity he could from his undignified position, 'that Crevel is under my direct command.'

'And may I remind *you*,' countered Burgundy with a sharp edge in his voice, 'that I have overall command of the army. In short, my lord Duke, I am the final court of appeal here. My judgement is that Major Crevel should resume his rank.'

Vendôme was horrified. 'Is he to suffer no penalty at all?'

'Being admonished by you was a penalty in itself, I

suspect. When he left your quarters, he did so in the utmost disgrace and that, I believe, had a sobering effect on him. I fancy that he'll be a credit to his uniform from now on.'

'I insist that my decision is upheld.'

'Protest is pointless,' said Burgundy. 'You've been overruled.'

'I see,' said Vendôme, simmering. 'In that case, my lord, perhaps you'd be good enough to point out any other distant relatives you have in this army before I inadvertently rob them of *their* commissions as well. As for Crevel, what he did was tantamount to betrayal. He readily offered information to a British spy.'

'He was tricked into doing so. Instead of taking out your spite on the major, you should be chasing the man who hoodwinked him.'

'I am already doing so.'

Burgundy was startled. 'Really?'

'I take this lapse very seriously, my lord,' said Vendôme. 'I'll not rest until we have full retribution. At this very moment, someone in the enemy camp is trying to identify the man who exposed Crevel as the inept, unguarded, drunken fool that he is. But then,' he went on, acidly, 'since the man is a relative of yours, you'd be familiar with the many flaws in his character.'

In spite of his many other commitments, Daniel Rawson made sure that he never neglected sword practice. The weapon was much more to him than the difference between life and death. It had great symbolic value. It had marked his premature coming of age when, as a boy of ten, he'd used the sword to kill its owner, a cavalry sergeant trying to rape Daniel's mother. Presented to him by the man who was now captain general of the Confederate army, it had been kept at Daniel's home in Amsterdam for years until he earned the commission that allowed him to wear a sword. Long before that time, however, he'd learnt how to use the weapon, mastering the finer points of swordplay and developing the strength of his right arm. The blade was always kept clean and razor sharp.

Daniel had used the sword with lethal effect in many battles and skirmishes. It had been exceptionally deadly at Blenheim and had taken part in a cavalry charge at Ramillies. Now, however, it was put to less dangerous use as Daniel went through a practice routine with Jonathan Ainley. The lieutenant was a competent swordsman with a long reach that could trouble any adversary but he had neither the power nor the speed of Daniel. As the two of them fought on some open ground behind the officers' quarters, the flash of blades was accompanied by the echoing clang of steel.

No matter how hard Ainley tried, he couldn't put Daniel under any sustained pressure. Every thrust was deftly parried, every attack was repelled with comparative ease. After twenty minutes or so, the lieutenant was flagging visibly. Daniel's superior stamina told. With a sudden increase of power, he drove Ainley back so fast that his friend tripped and fell to the ground. After holding the point of his weapon playfully at Ainley's chest, Daniel offered him a hand to pull him up. The lieutenant was panting.

'I could never beat you in a duel,' he gasped. 'You seem to know exactly what I'm going to do before I do it.'

'You fought well,' said Daniel, hauling him to his feet.

'But I came off worst yet again.'

'It's different in battle. There's none of the formal swordplay that we've just enjoyed. It's all slash, thrust and parry. Strength and agility are what you need there.'

'Yes,' said Ainley, 'and you have too much of both for me.'

'I intend to stay alive, Jonathan. That's why I try to keep myself ready for action.' He held his sword aloft. 'This is my protector.'

'Yet you wore no sword when you went to Valenciennes.'

'It would have looked out of place on a wine merchant.'

'You were very brave to travel unarmed.'

'I carried a dagger with me,' said Daniel, 'in case of emergency. It was concealed under my coat. I'm a born soldier. I feel naked without some kind of weapon.'

Ainley laughed. 'It was that French officer who felt naked after you'd finished with him.'

'I thought I asked you not to talk about it.'

'Even you are entitled to brag now and again, Daniel.'

'I'd much rather that incident remained secret.'

'It's far too late for that.'

'What do you mean?'

'Everyone seems to have heard of it somehow. Major Earnshaw was talking about it only this morning and so were some of the others. I daresay it's filtered down to the ranks as well. It's no use trying to keep these things to yourself,' he said, clapping Daniel amiably on the shoulder. 'Everyone wants to hear about the latest exploits of Captain Rawson. You have a *name*.'

'His name is Daniel Rawson,' said Valeran.

'What rank does he hold?'

'He's a captain in the 24th Foot.'

'A British regiment,' said Vendôme with contempt. 'How, in the name of all that's holy, could one of our majors be taken in by an Englishman?'

'Rawson is something of a linguist, Your Grace. According to the report, he speaks French fluently enough to deceive anyone. Here,' he went on, offering the letter. 'Read it yourself. This is a copy, of course. I had the original decoded.'

Vendôme took the missive. 'Thank you, Raoul.'

Not daring to interrupt, Valeran waited while the other man studied the letter. It had been sent by one of their spies in the British camp. The two men were in Vendôme's tent, a place where the lieutenant spent more and more time. As a result, he'd had to endure the barbed comments and sly innuendoes of his friends but he ignored them in the interest of winning favour. Given an opportunity, he'd decided to seize it at whatever cost. Part of that cost involved being compliant but there were other duties as well. He'd been put in direct contact with French intelligencers and that gave him a definite status. In bringing Vendôme the letter, he hoped for praise. It was not forthcoming.

When he read the last sentence, Vendôme let out a cry of rage.

'Did you see this?' he demanded.

'Yes, Your Grace.'

'This spy of theirs is no mere captain in a regiment of foot. He's also a member of Marlborough's personal staff. He'll have been very popular after his little escapade. The Duke and his entourage are no doubt still slapping him on the back as they laugh at our expense.'

'The only person they're laughing at is Major Crevel.'

'Don't mention that abominable creature.'

'As you wish,' said Valeran, obediently.

'I never want to hear his accursed name again.'

'I see.'

'*This* is the only name I'm interested in at the moment,' stressed Vendôme, waving the letter in the air. 'Captain Daniel Rawson. I want him here in front of me, Raoul.'

'That may be difficult to arrange,' warned Valeran.

'Why?'

'We can't simply abduct a man from the British camp.'

'We don't have to do that.'

'Then how do we get him here?'

'We simply lure him to us.'

Valeran was puzzled. 'Lure him?'

'All it takes is a little imagination.'

'Then I must confess that I lack it, Your Grace. I fail to see what could possibly lure such a man out of the safety of his army.'

'Read this again,' suggested Vendôme, thrusting the letter at him. 'Rawson is clearly an adventurer. He's ready to take chances and court peril. What we need to find is something that would tempt him to come here.'

'And how do we do that?'

'We gather more information about this fellow and we do so with some urgency. It's clear that the bold captain has many strong points. But he'll also have weaknesses.'

'What sort of weaknesses?'

'Does he have a wife, a lover, a family – or what about a favourite child? There must be *someone* for whom he'd risk his neck, someone who isn't surrounded by an army and is therefore easier to get at. That's where we need to strike. Who is the most important person in his private life?'

'I have no idea,' admitted Valeran.

'Then find out. Send a coded message back to the British camp.'

'What must it say?'

'We need more detail about this Daniel Rawson. I don't

care how brave and resourceful he is. Everyone has an Achilles' heel. Discover what the captain's is,' said Vendôme, rubbing his hands together, 'and he's ours. That's the message to send, Raoul. Whom or what does he love most?'

Amalia Janssen gazed longingly through the window. Most of the shops they'd stopped at were filled with the neat but plain dresses that were the fashion among the women of Amsterdam. This shop was different. It displayed a colour and cut that reminded her of the months in Paris yet there was no hint of vulgarity. All the dresses she could see had such style and beauty. Amalia simply goggled.

'We always come here,' noted Beatrix.

'It's the best way home.'

The servant smiled. 'The best for you, maybe,' she said, 'because it lets you stare through that window for as long as you like. I've no call to be looking at dresses like that. I could never find one to fit me and, even if I could, I could never afford to buy it.' She pointed a finger. 'Can you imagine what your father would say if he saw me in something like that?'

'He'd be amazed, Beatrix.'

'He'd order me to take it off at once.'

'Well, you could hardly do any chores wearing that. And – I don't mean this at all unkindly – you don't really have the shape for any of the dresses on display here.'

'But you do, Miss Amalia.'

'Yes,' said Amalia with a sigh. 'I believe that I do.'

'Then ask Captain Rawson to buy one of them for you.'

Amalia giggled. 'Oh, I couldn't do that.'

'Why not?' asked Beatrix. 'I'm sure that he'd oblige.'

'That's not the point.'

'He's bought you gifts before.'

'Father might not approve.'

'That's not true at all, Miss Amalia. Your father dotes on him almost as much as you do – and with good cause. But for Captain Rawson, all three of us would be lying somewhere in a French grave. And the same goes for Kees.'

'I know all that,' said Amalia. 'What I meant was that Father wouldn't approve of my choice. He adores colour in his tapestries yet prefers sober hues in everything I wear. I still have dresses in my wardrobe that belonged to my mother.'

'Your mother was always very smart,' said Beatrix with a nostalgic smile. 'You are very much like her in that respect.'

Amalia was about to point out that she was developing rather different tastes but she broke off instead. Talking about her mother always brought back unhappy memories of her untimely death. If the conversation had continued, Amalia knew that she and Beatrix would eventually end up in tears. Turning away from the shop, she put aside any thoughts of a new dress and set off for home. Beatrix, a servant, friend and chaperone, fell in beside her.

'How much longer will this war drag on?' she asked, wearily.

'I wish I knew, Beatrix.'

'What does Captain Rawson say?'

'He has no more idea than the rest of us.'

'Yet he's very close to the Duke of Marlborough. He must know what's going on.'

'The fighting will continue until one side gives in,' said Amalia with a helpless shrug, 'and that's an unlikely prospect at the moment. There was talk of peace after the battle of Ramillies but, as usual, it came to nothing.'

Beatrix was morose. 'I think it could go on for ever.'

'Oh, don't say that, Beatrix. We must never give up hope.'

'It's the same thing every year – more killing, more misery. I'd hate to be the mother of sons in the army. You'd never know if they'd come back alive. To be *married* to a soldier would be even worse. You'd spend all your time worrying and...' Her voice tailed off as she realised what she was saying. She became apologetic. 'I'm sorry, Miss Amalia. I didn't mean to upset you. I wasn't talking about Captain Rawson.'

'Let's just change the subject, shall we?' said Amalia, firmly.

'He rides beside the Duke of Marlborough so he's in no danger at all. Captain Rawson is safe. That must be a comfort to you.'

But Amalia was no longer listening. She had drifted off into a private world where there was no comfort at all. As long as the war continued, no British soldier was completely safe, especially one who took on the hazardous assignments that fell to Daniel Rawson. At any moment, his luck might finally run out. Filled with apprehension, she kept asking herself the same question.

'Where are you *now*, Daniel?'

Because Daniel had changed out of his uniform, the farmer didn't recognise him at first. When it dawned on him who his visitor was, however, he became hostile and ordered Daniel to leave at once. After what had happened at the neighbouring farm, he wanted nothing to do with British soldiers. It took Daniel a long time to calm him down and an even longer one to persuade him to bring the boy down from his room. Only when the farmer was convinced of Daniel's sincerity did he agree that his visitor could talk to Jules, the young lad who'd witnessed the atrocities at his farm.

The boy came downstairs reluctantly. Since the outrage, he'd been weeping into his pillow, convulsed by a grief that was shot through with a burning desire for revenge. Daniel saw something of himself in Jules and was reminded of a time when his own world had been turned upside down by the arrival of soldiers. Daniel had at least been able to defend his mother. Jules had been utterly powerless and was plagued by guilt as a consequence. In the boy's face, Daniel saw the same anger, hatred and confusion that he'd felt in the wake of the battle of Sedgemoor. The one consolation was that Jules had not actually seen his family being murdered. Daniel, by contrast, had watched his father being hanged.

When the farmer explained that their visitor was a British soldier, Jules lost his temper and hurled himself at Daniel, managing to land a few punches. He had to be restrained for a while. Daniel took his time, letting the boy's rage die down a little.

'I come as a friend, Jules,' he said at length. 'I want to catch the soldiers who attacked your farm. They were not acting on orders. I'm as anxious as you to make sure that they'll pay for what they did to your family.'

'Go away!' said the boy.

'Listen to him, Jules,' coaxed the farmer. 'I believe what he says. He wants to stop these men from killing anyone else.'

'He's lying. I don't trust him.'

'Hear him out.'

'No…he's just as bad as the others.'

Daniel was grateful that the farmer was present. Though he had a good grasp of their Flemish dialect, Daniel found it easier to talk through the farmer than directly to Jules. It spared the boy from the feeling that he was being interrogated by an enemy. Daniel whispered the first question into the farmer's ear.

'Tell him what you saw, Jules,' urged the farmer.

'I don't want to speak to him,' retorted the boy.

'Do you want those soldiers to get away with what they did?'

'No...I want to kill them myself!'

'I can understand why you feel like that,' said Daniel. 'But you need us to hunt these fiends down.'

'Tell him everything,' said the farmer.

Jules scowled. 'He already knows what his soldiers did.'

'He doesn't. Captain Rawson says that they were not part of a British patrol. He thinks they were renegades.'

'They wore red uniforms,' asserted the boy, sullenly.

'That doesn't mean they were British,' said the farmer then he paused to take a prompt from Daniel. 'Did you hear them speak? Did you recognise their language?'

'I'm saying nothing.'

'You must help the captain.'

'He's like all the rest of them.'

'Just tell us, please. This is important, Jules. You want these men hunted down, don't you?'

'I want them burnt alive!' shrieked the boy.

'Captain Rawson tells me that, if they're British soldiers, they'll face execution. Now, what language did they use?'

Jules glowered at Daniel then spat out his reply.

'English,' he said. 'They spoke in English.'

Daniel's heart sank. He fed another question to the farmer.

'Did you get a good look at them?' said the man.

'No, there was smoke everywhere.'

'Yet you were able to see their uniforms.'

'Yes, I was.'

The farmer turned to hear another whisper in his ear.

'Did you hear any names being called out?' he asked.

'No.'

'Think carefully, Jules. This could be helpful. Someone must have been shouting orders to the others. Did he mention any names when he did so?'

'All he did was to laugh,' said Jules with a shudder.

'Who did?' pressed Daniel.

'Their leader.'

'How do you know he was their leader?'

'He shouted at the others to ride off.'

'Then you must have been able to see him properly.'

'Is that right, Jules?' added the farmer. 'You saw their leader?'

'What did he look like?' asked Daniel.

'Describe him for us.'

The boy recalled the mad eyes and the blood-curdling laugh.

'He was a big, ugly man with a red beard,' he said, gritting his teeth, 'and I'm going to tear out his heart one day.'

CHAPTER EIGHT

The Duke of Marlborough was finally starting to look his age. Now in his late fifties, he had always defied the passage of time and retained his boundless energy and resilience. Years of campaigning, when he sometimes spent twelve hours a day in the saddle, had not weakened him to any degree. His zest for battle remained intact. Now, however, it was different. Looking at Marlborough as he sat hunched over his desk, Adam Cardonnel was worried about him. Their commander was clearly unwell. He'd been afflicted by a series of pounding headaches that were difficult to shake off. He had a fever of some sort and was unable to sleep. Fatigue had painted deep lines on his face. What disturbed his secretary even more was the fact that Marlborough had become so uncharacteristically downhearted. It was almost as if desolation had eaten into his soul.

They were alone in the tent. While Cardonnel had been writing some letters, Marlborough was poring over a map of Flanders. He was so motionless that his secretary began to wonder if he'd dozed off from exhaustion. Cardonnel reached out to touch his shoulder.

'Are you still awake?' he asked, softly.

Marlborough stirred. 'Of course I am, Adam. I can't *but* be awake. At a time when I most need it, I seem to have forgotten how to sleep.' He used a palm to suppress a yawn. 'If my wife knew how ill I feel, she'd probably rush here with a brace of physicians and a bag full of potions. That's why I keep the full truth about my condition from her.'

'You can't hide it from *me*, Your Grace.'

'I know. What you see is what I see in the mirror every day and it's a dispiriting sight. But for this periwig,' he went on, toying with the elaborate curls, 'you'd notice how grey my hair has become. I'm sinking into senility.'

'Yet you still have more vigour than the rest of us.'

'I don't feel that I do, Adam. But enough of my ailments,' he said, sitting up and trying to marshal his thoughts. 'Beside the work we have to do, they are an irrelevance. And I'll wager a king's ransom that the French army won't suspend their activities simply because the enemy commander is feeling a trifle unwell.' He indicated the map. 'What's their next move? That's what I want to know. What are Burgundy and Vendôme up to?'

'They are probably asking the same question of you.'

'And so they should. We must keep them guessing.'

'They are probably still wondering how we managed to thwart their planned attack on Antwerp. That was a setback for them.'

'Thanks to good intelligence, we nipped that plot in the bud and it was vital that we did so, Adam. We can't let a citadel like Antwerp fall into their hands. It's so well fortified,' said Marlborough. 'It's the reason I want it to become the capital of the Spanish Netherlands. Brussels is too difficult to defend for any length of time. Antwerp would be a much more secure base.'

'I agree with you, Your Grace, but the idea did not exactly win favour with the Dutch.'

Marlborough groaned. 'None of my ideas ever excite them,' he complained. 'I know I've said it a hundred times before, Adam, but trying to lead a coalition army is like fighting with my hands tied behind my back. I can never do exactly what I want at a precise time of my choosing.'

'Granted — then it's all the more credit to you for achieving such remarkable victories in this war. You've overcome both the might of the French army and the shortcomings of our Allies.'

'We may have to do so again, Adam,' said Marlborough, placing a finger on the map. 'Latest reports place the French here at Soignies. I'd hoped to divert part of their army by a feint to the Moselle but Prince Eugene's force is not even fully assembled yet. Do you see what I mean about having my hands tied?' he went on. 'We need Eugene here this very minute. Instead, he's held up in Vienna on government business. Don't they realise that this war is government business as well?' he asked, slapping the table for effect. 'While our best ally is still in Vienna, we are left facing the entire French army.' He took a deep breath then smiled apologetically. 'Forgive me, Adam. I'm telling you nothing you don't already know. It just eases my mind a little if I vent my spleen in private.'

'You certainly never do so in public, Your Grace,' said the other with admiration. 'Your forbearance is an example to us all. In your dealings with our allies, you always contrive to appear gracious and accommodating.'

'And you know the reason why.'

'Yes…we'll never win this war without them.'

'Too true, alas,' said Marlborough. 'That's why we have to tolerate Dutch caution and Prince Eugene's delay. Allies are such a crucial component of any success in the field – and it's high time we *had* a real success.'

'Nobody will ever forget Blenheim,' said Cardonnel, stoutly, 'and Ramillies was, I reckon, even more significant. The French have achieved nothing comparable in this war.'

'Yet they still keep coming back at us, Adam, turning our gains into losses. Even though they've sustained enormous casualties, they've somehow mustered an army of 100,000 men. Think how much money and sheer effort went into recruitment. They must have scoured every corner of France. And while they were rebuilding so furiously, how did our Parliament react?'

'Disappointingly, Your Grace.'

'Disgracefully is a better description. When the Recruiting Bill came before the Commons, the provision for a compulsory levy of men was thrown out. It's heartbreaking. If we get no backing from our own country, how can we possibly equal French numbers?'

'New recruits are no match for seasoned soldiers.'

'Burgundy and Vendôme have both at their disposal. They know that they're stronger than we are. I fear they're about to venture.'

'They've shown little sign of it so far, Your Grace. French armies in the past have tended to watch and wait.'

'This time it could be different,' said Marlborough, gloomily. 'Vendôme outwitted us last year so he's full of confidence. Then we have the Duke of Burgundy, fresh to the field, keen to show his mettle, anxious to impress his grandfather, the King. Yes, I know he lacks experience,' he went on as Cardonnel was about to speak, 'but Vendôme can provide that. What Burgundy offers is youthful enthusiasm and the natural conceit of royalty – he believes that's it's his *right* to win.'

'You'll soon relieve him of that misapprehension, Your Grace.'

'I might do if I had a full complement of men at my disposal. As it is, we're at a clear disadvantage. We just have to hope that the French don't launch a major attack in the near future,' confided Marlborough. 'Otherwise, we could be in grave danger.'

'When we left England,' remembered Cardonnel, 'you *wanted* to provoke an attack. You hoped that our apparent weakness would tempt Burgundy and Vendôme to offer battle. You even talked about abandoning Brussels, if need be, and withdrawing to Antwerp.'

'That plan was conceived on the assumption that Prince Eugene would already be on the Moselle and thus able to march north in support of us. But he's not even here yet. Oh, I would love a battle, Adam,' said Marlborough rising to his feet with a touch of his old defiance. 'I'd love to lock horns with the French again. We need a victory that will echo around the whole of Europe. It's the only way to bring the Grand Alliance back to life again.'

Daniel Rawson had to wait over a week after his visit to the farm before he had the chance to call on Henry Welbeck. The sergeant was in a typical pose, legs apart and hands on his hips as he berated the men who were digging some new latrines. On a hot day, they were positively dripping with sweat. Daniel's arrival prompted Welbeck to move well away from them. The men heaved sighs of gratitude.

'Good afternoon, Henry,' said Daniel, cheerfully.

'I see nothing good about it.'

'We've got some sunshine at last. Doesn't that gladden your hard old heart?'

'No, Dan, it doesn't.'

'Oh?'

'Fine weather might tempt the Frenchies to offer battle,' said Welbeck, grimly, 'and we'd be outnumbered. That's why everyone in the camp is so nervous. They feel an attack is on the cards. From the moment we moved here, we've been on the alert.'

'You've not been too alert,' said Daniel, peering at his friend's unshaven face. 'Have you forgotten where you put your razor?'

'I've had far too much to do, Dan. I've been so busy that I've barely had time to wipe the shit off my arse, let alone shave the whiskers off my chin. Down here in the ranks, we have to toil. It's only officers like you who know what leisure is.'

'We know what it is, Henry, we just don't have any of it.'

'Your life is much softer than ours,' insisted Welbeck. 'There's no argument about that. Most of our officers wouldn't last a week in the ranks.'

'I did,' Daniel reminded him. 'I survived for years.'

'You're the exception to the rule, Dan.'

'I daren't ask what rule that might be. But it's odd that you should have grown a beard. That's exactly what I came to talk about.'

'What – me not shaving?'

'No, Henry. I've brought news about the men who burnt down those farms.'

'It's about time!' muttered Welbeck.

'There's been a lot of work to do,' explained Daniel. 'But I think we've made progress. When I suggested that they might be deserters, His Grace called for details of everyone who'd fled from their colours. There were far too many of them, I can tell you.'

'Desertion has always been our bane and always will be.'

'While those details were being gathered in and collated, I spoke to the one reliable witness we had.'

'Witness?'

'He's a lad of ten named Jules.'

Daniel described the visit he'd made to the farm and talked about the difficulty he'd encountered in persuading the boy to speak. Without the farmer's help, Daniel would have got nothing from him but truculence. Welbeck was sympathetic.

'You can't blame him,' he said, quietly. 'It was a terrible ordeal to go through. In his shoes, I'd feel much the same – that everybody in a British uniform has supped with the Devil.'

'He'll never forgive us, Henry. Nor will the farmer who took him in. The only way to appease them is to catch the villains responsible.'

'Catch them and skin them alive.'

'They'll get their deserts, don't worry.'

'So what's this about a beard?'

'It's a red beard, to be exact,' said Daniel, 'and there aren't too many of those. It belonged to the leader of this marauding band. We trawled through the lists of deserters from the cavalry regiments and we eventually found out his name.'

'What is it – Beelzebub?'

'No, Henry, it's Matthew Searle.'

Welbeck scratched his whiskers. 'Now where have I heard that name before?' he said, racking his brains.

'Searle fits the description given by the boy. I've spoken to one of the officers in his regiment and he remembered the man well. Searle was something of a menace, it seems. He was always trying to stir up trouble among the other troopers. He was punished a number of times for insubordination and being drunk on duty.'

'They should have let *me* cut him down to size.'

'In every sense, he was an unsavoury character,' continued Daniel, 'yet not without his virtues. He was strong and fearless. He fought well in battle and could ride a horse as if he'd been born astride one. Also, he had the instincts of a leader. Had he not been so perverse, he could easily have been promoted.'

'What was the name again?'

'Matthew Searle.'

'I remember now,' said Welbeck, snapping his fingers. 'It's

all coming back to me. I used to have a slimy little snake of a man who always wished he'd joined the cavalry instead of the infantry. That's what his cousin had done. He kept on and on about him. I'm sure that the cousin's name was Matthew Searle – though he never mentioned a red beard.'

'Who was this fellow?'

'A good-for-nothing named Edwin Lock.'

'Is he still with us?'

'Not any more, Dan – he deserted months ago.'

'Can you remember the precise time?'

'Why?'

'It may be that he joined up with his cousin.'

'That's very unlikely,' said Welbeck, sceptically. 'Edwin Lock was bone idle. He was only ever interested in whoring, drinking or doing both at the same time. Lock was a shoemaker by trade. I doubt if he'd know which end of the horse the manure came out of. Besides,' he went on, 'he was in a regiment of foot. Where could he get a horse from?'

'There's no mystery about that, Henry.'

'Isn't there?'

'It was one of the many ways that Searle endeared himself to the regiment he left behind him,' explained Daniel. 'He didn't merely take to his heels. He stole some of their finest horses as well.'

Inclement weather delayed the attack for day after day and the men became restive. They ate well and drank as much as they wished but they grew tired of being cooped up in the farmhouse. Edwin Lock once again acted as their spokesman. He found Searle in the kitchen.

'It can't go on like this, Matt,' he complained. 'We're fed up.'

'Do you think I like being holed up here?' snarled Searle.

'It's a fine day at last. Why don't we go right now?'

'I give the orders, Edwin.'

'Yes, that's another thing.'

'What is?'

'They've been muttering,' said Lock, glancing over his shoulder to make sure that nobody was within earshot. 'They feel that you throw your weight around too much.'

'Somebody has to be in charge.'

'But why does that someone have to be you?'

Lock let out a yelp as he was grabbed by the throat, lifted into the air and banged against a wall. When Searle released him, his cousin slumped to the floor, rubbing his neck disconsolately.

'Does that answer your question?' challenged Searle.

'It's not what *I* said,' bleated Lock. 'I spoke up for you. I always do – and not because we're kinfolk. You planned everything. If it wasn't for you, we'd still be in the army, having our ears chewed off and our arses kicked. It was you that got us out of there, Matt.'

'I'm glad that someone remembers that.'

'You can always count on me.'

'Who was it?'

'Eh?'

'Give me a name, Edwin. Who was it who thinks he ought to take over from me? Was it Hugh Davey or Gregory Pyle?'

'It was neither of them.'

'Who was it then?' demanded Searle, grabbing him by the neck to pull him upright. 'If we have a traitor in our midst, name him.'

'He's not really a traitor,' said Lock, wishing that he'd never broached the subject. 'Ianto just said that he'd have done things differently. There's nothing more to it than that.'

'Ianto Morgan, is it?' said Searle. 'I might have known it.'

'He's like the rest of us, Matt – itching for a woman.'

'Then maybe it's time I cured his itch.'

Searle marched out of the house and into the yard where the other men were sitting in a group, smoking pipes and drinking from tankards. When they saw Searle rolling up his sleeves, they tensed. Ianto Morgan was a short, thickset, bald-headed Welshman with a dark complexion. Searle confronted him.

'So you want to replace me, do you, Ianto?' said Searle.

'Not me, Matt,' replied Morgan with an ingratiating grin.

'What about the rest of you? Do any of you think he's a better man than I am?' They all shook their heads in denial. 'Then I'll show you what happens to anyone who questions my leadership.' He crooked a finger. 'Get up, Ianto.'

'Why?' said the Welshman. 'I'm comfortable here.'

'Get up and fight, you bastard!'

'Ianto didn't mean to upset you, Matt,' said Lock, trying to intercede and earning a clip around the ear from his cousin. 'We're all friends here, aren't we?'

Searle ignored him. 'Come on, Ianto,' he said. 'We've got to settle this once and for all.'

'There's nothing to settle, Matt,' argued Morgan.

'You're too much of a coward, are you?'

The Welshman's eyes flashed. 'Very well,' he said, starting to get up. 'If it's a fight you're after, then you can have one.'

But he had no intention of slugging it out with the other man. Searle was bigger, stronger and much younger than Morgan. His fists would pummel the Welshman into submission. Morgan's only chance lay in using a weapon. As he rose to his feet, therefore, he let one hand slip to the dagger in his belt. It was the last action of his life. Leaping forward, Searle knocked him unconscious with a vicious uppercut, caught the body as it fell, got a firm grip on Morgan's head then twisted it hard and broke his neck. The others recoiled in horror at the awesome crack. Edwin Lock began to gibber.

Searle tossed the dead man to the ground and surveyed the ring of frightened faces, content that none of them would dare to challenge his leadership now. He adopted a reasonable tone.

'I'm sorry it's taken so long,' he said, 'but we could hardly raid the farm when we were soaked to the skin. In any case, it's not the best way to whet our appetites for rutting with the farm wenches.' There was uneasy laughter. 'The long wait is over, lads. We attack at nightfall.'

'Why wait till then?' asked Lock.

Searle glared at him. 'Do you have a better plan, Edwin?'

'No, no, Matt. Forget that I spoke.'

'The reason we wait for dark is this,' Searle continued. 'I've been to the farm three times now and watched it carefully. There are eight men working there as well as the five women. I don't like those odds. However, four of the men don't live at the farm. They walk home at night to the village a couple of miles away.' He glanced at Lock. 'Are you beginning to understand now?'

'Yes,' said Lock. 'Four men won't put up so much of a fight.'

'I'm more interested in the five women,' said Gregory Pyle, a sharp-featured man with a lopsided smirk.

'There's something else you should know,' Searle told them. 'The last time I was there, they drove some of the stock off to market. That means they came back with a lot of money. It's ours for the taking, lads.' He kicked the corpse aside. 'Ianto won't need his share now, will he? That means each of us will get more. How does that sound?'

'I like it,' said Pyle.

'So do I,' added Lock. 'When do we leave, Matt?'

'There's a job to do first, Edwin,' replied Searle, 'and

you're just the man to do it. Find a spade and bury that stupid Welshman before he starts to stink. And if anyone else is thinking of pulling a dagger on me,' he warned, 'remember what happened to Ianto Morgan.'

The Confederate army was on the move again, responding to French deployment by heading south of Hal, thereby blocking the approach to Brussels. Glad that the earlier rain had eased off, Daniel rode at the head of his regiment, proud that the 24th Foot was near the front of the long cavalcade. Somewhere behind him, Henry Welbeck and the other sergeants made sure that their men marched at a brisk pace. Jonathan Ainley rode beside Daniel, eyeing the woods in the middle distance with some trepidation.

'That would be a good place for an ambush, Dan,' he said.

'Our scouts have reported nothing suspicious.'

'They could have sent out troops to harass us.'

'I doubt if they'd take the risk, said Daniel. 'They won't commit enough men to trouble an army this size. I think it would be suicidal. Vendôme never sacrifices manpower if he can help it.'

'Neither does His Grace.'

'Every soldier is important to him.'

'Why can't the French just come out and fight?'

'It's not in their nature.'

'Not even when they have a numerical advantage?'

'They'll wait until they can choose the right moment. In the meantime, they'll be manoeuvring for position. They want to test us out,' said Daniel, 'and play a few games with us.'

'I still think they could be hiding in those woods.'

'Then we'll need to keep our wits about us.'

When they got within a hundred yards of the trees, they slowed their speed, intending to proceed with caution. In fact, they never even reached the woods. There was a low, rocky outcrop to their left and it was from behind this that the French onslaught came. Scores of blue uniforms that had been lying flat on the ground suddenly appeared and muskets began to pop, sending up wisps of smoke. There was momentary bewilderment then Daniel ordered his men to spread out and return fire. While the 24th responded with its first volley, he tried to assess the size of the enemy, keeping his horse on the move so that he didn't present a stationary target. French and British soldiers kept exchanging fire with deafening effect. A number of Daniel's men had been wounded in the surprise attack and a few had been killed outright but the French were starting to suffer casualties as well. Indeed, when they saw the speed and accuracy of the British retaliation, they decided to beat a swift retreat. They'd done what they came for, using the woods as a decoy while lying in wait behind the rocks. They'd drawn blood. It was time to withdraw. After less than fifteen minutes, the skirmish came to an end and the French soldiers vanished from sight.

Daniel led his men up the incline in pursuit but the enemy had too big a start. Horses had been waiting to spirit them away and they were riding hell for leather. There was no point at all in chasing them towards their camp because they'd have massive reinforcements to call upon there. It was all over. The regiment was left to lick its wounds and count its losses. Returning to the main track, Daniel was alarmed to see Ainley, kneeling on the ground with blood on his face. He dismounted and rushed over to the lieutenant.

'Are you all right, Jonathan?' he asked with concern.

'Yes,' replied his friend, gamely. 'It's only a scratch.'

'You need to see the surgeon.'

'No, Dan, I'd feel I was wasting his time when there are far more serious wounds for him to look at.' He used a handkerchief to stem the blood. 'I was grazed by a musket ball, that's all.'

'Then you were very lucky.'

'It's not a question of luck. I survived by willpower.'

Daniel was amused. 'Is such a thing possible?'

'Yes, it is,' said Ainley, seriously. 'I have to stay alive for six months at least because I'm getting married at Christmas. Elizabeth would never forgive me if I let myself get killed. That's why I've resolved that it won't happen.'

'I wish it were as simple as that,' said Daniel. 'Unfortunately, we don't have our destinies in our own hands.'

'I do, Dan. I promised Elizabeth that I'd meet her at the altar.'

'Then I hope you're able to keep that promise. Will you tell her about the narrow escape you had today?'

'Oh, no – it would only upset her. When she reads my letters, she likes to hear good news.'

'There's been precious little of that recently.'

'You've got a short memory.'

'Have I?' Seeing the other's grin, Daniel understood what he meant. 'I hope you haven't been telling her tales about me.'

'I just mentioned that one of our officers went behind enemy lines to abduct a French major, steal his uniform and return to camp with details of enemy plans. If that isn't good news, then what is? You're a hero, Dan.'

'I don't feel too heroic today, Jonathan,' confessed Daniel. 'I let us walk into a trap. When I saw those rocks, I should have sent scouts on ahead to take a look behind them. They seemed too low to conceal anyone. I hadn't realised that the ground falls away sharply at the back of those boulders. Like you, I was too busy worrying about the potential danger in the woods.' He glanced back along the line of soldiers. 'As it is, we came off relatively lightly – and, whatever you may claim, it was not because of willpower.'

'It was in my case,' asserted Ainley. 'I'll tell Elizabeth that I came through the skirmish untouched. That's the sensible thing to do. A white lie will prevent any tears from her. But what about the letters *you* send?' he asked.

'How much of the truth do you tell Amalia?'

'Very little, I suppose.'

'Women are such delicate creatures. It's incumbent upon us to conceal the horrors of warfare from them. I'm just grateful that Elizabeth is hundreds of miles away from here. I need to feel that she's completely safe.'

'It's the same with me,' said Daniel, wistfully. 'Because of my commitments here, my letters to Amsterdam are few and far between. Whenever I write one, however, I console myself with the knowledge that Amalia is out of harm's way.'

Respected by his men as a brilliant soldier, Vendôme liked to review his troops at regular intervals. Simultaneously, it fed his sense of importance and kept the men on their toes. As he watched them march past in serried ranks, he was pleased with what he saw. Even though many new recruits were on display, the soldiers were well drilled and primed for action. When the parade was finally over, he turned round to find Valeran waiting patiently for him. The lieutenant offered him a letter.

'We have the answer you wanted, Your Grace,' he said.

'Excellent,' replied Vendôme, taking it from him.

'I had it decoded for you.'

'Well done, Raoul. Let's see what we've discovered about the gallant Captain Rawson, shall we?' As he read the letter, he smiled. 'So his weakness has a name, does she? All we need to do now is to put a face to that name.' His smile broadened into a grin. 'I look forward to meeting Amalia Janssen.'

Chapter Nine

It was a long ride and they didn't reach their destination until evening shadows were lengthening. Waiting under cover of some trees, they watched until the farmyard was completely deserted. Through the open shutters, they could see candles burning.

Edwin Lock was impatient. He grabbed his cousin's arm.

'Let's go, Matt,' he urged.

'It's too early,' decreed Searle.

'But they'll be eating their supper now. They'll be off guard. Those four men left ages ago. We'll soon deal with the ones still there. Then we can help ourselves to the women.'

'I want the fat one,' said Gregory Pyle, almost dribbling. 'I saw her coming out of the byre with a pail of milk. She's mine – I like plenty to hold on to.'

'You'll do as you're told,' cautioned Searle.

'But you *promised*, Matt.'

'All I promised was that you'd get your turn.'

'Then I want it with that fat milkmaid.'

'This is not a common whorehouse, Gregory. You can't pick and choose. We have to kill the men, grab what we want then get out of there as quickly as possible.'

'What about me?' asked Lock.

'You set fire to the barn.'

His cousin pulled a face. 'I did that last time.'

'Then we know we can rely on you,' said Searle. 'When you've got a good blaze going, you check to see what livestock is worth rustling. They've still got some pigs left. We'll have to slaughter them first. That's another job for you, Edwin. The next thing we need is one of their horses. Hugh can take care of that. Tie the dead pigs together and sling them across the horse's back.'

'And where will you be all this time, Matt?'

'Inside one of the women like me,' said Pyle, sniggering.

'You'll obey orders,' Searle told him, 'or you'll end up like Ianto Morgan. Each one of us must have a particular job and make sure we do it quickly. Edwin and Hugh know what they have to do – now for the rest of you.'

Searle had planned the attack in advance. He gave his men their orders and reminded them that the village was only two miles away. When the fire was at its height, it would be seen from a long distance and help would soon arrive. They had to be well clear before anyone came galloping out from the village. Searle was wearing the uniform of a lieutenant in the dragoons. Like the ones donned by his men, it had been stolen from a corpse left behind after a skirmish. He ran a finger around the inside of the collar.

'I don't know how anyone managed to wear this,' he complained. 'It's so tight, it's almost strangling me.'

'You've been demoted, Matt,' said Hugh Davey.

'What are you on about?'

'Last time you were a captain in the British army.'

Searle grinned. 'Yes…that uniform could have been made for me. I know what it feels like to be an officer now.'

'I hate officers,' said Davey. 'All they do is piss on the likes of us. I wasn't putting up with it any more.'

'That's why you joined me, Hugh,' said Searle. 'I may make the decisions about where we strike but we have equal shares after that. Whatever the haul tonight, we'll all get the same amount.'

Lock grinned. 'That goes for the women as well.'

There was general laughter. They carried on bantering until the shutters were eventually closed and the occupants of the house had all rolled off to bed. At a signal from Searle, they came out of hiding and trotted towards the farm. Dismounting well before they actually reached it, they led their horses forward then tethered them to some bushes. They had an array of weapons, mostly filched from dead

French soldiers. Some had pistols, others had muskets and a couple of them preferred daggers. When they reached the farmhouse, Searle waved them to their positions. Lock and Davey stayed outside while three of them went to the rear entrance of the building. Searle led two of the others to the front.

Using the element of surprise, they suddenly forced their way in and went charging upstairs, flinging open the doors of the bedrooms without ceremony. One of the farmer's sons was shot dead but another was only wounded and leapt naked from the bed to grapple with his attacker. A third son was stabbed to death but the farmer himself was unharmed. When Gregory Pyle fired a musket at him in the dark, he killed the man's wife instead and found himself wrestled to the floor. The other women screamed at the top of their voices.

Searle took it upon himself to finish off the two male victims still alive, cutting the throat of the one who'd been wounded so that his own man was released. Though he repeatedly stabbed the enraged farmer who was on top of Pyle, he was too late to save his friend from having the life strangled out of him. With their bloodlust sated, three of the other raiders chose a woman apiece and hurled them down onto their respective beds. Searle, meanwhile, hurried downstairs again, lighting a candle before searching for the place where the money was kept. Outside in the yard, Lock had set the barn ablaze and was trying to catch one of the squealing pigs in the sty. The creature kept slipping from his grasp and Lock had difficulty staying on his feet in the slimy, dung-covered sty. Davey harnessed one of the animals in the stables and brought it out to act as a packhorse.

Things were not going well. On their previous raids, there'd been little resistance. The men were killed instantly and the women ravished. This time they had casualties. Pyle was dead and Regan, the man who'd grappled with the wounded son of the farmer, was badly bruised. When he tried to overpower one of the women, she fought back so hard that he could not subdue her. Searle was having no success downstairs. Though he searched every nook and cranny, he could find neither money nor any other valuables. He dashed back upstairs to continue the search there, using the candle to illumine each room and going past beds on which frantic women were trying to push their attackers away. None was submitting without a fight, shrieking, biting and using their nails to scratch.

Through a gap in the shutters, Searle could see the flames from the barn as the fire really got a purchase. It would soon be spotted by someone in the village. Flying into a panic, his search became even more frenzied. He ran into the main bedchamber, stepped over the corpses of Gregory Pyle and the farmer then flung open the door of the little wardrobe. Nothing of value was in it or in the wooden chest under the window. Searle even dragged the dead body of the farmer's wife off the bed so that he could lift up the mattress. No

'That's rather more than a bloody nose,' said Marlborough. 'How many of the attackers fell?'

'Only three of them,' replied Daniel, 'because they had the cover of the rocks. However, several were wounded. We captured a handful of them. The rest got away.'

Marlborough was philosophical. 'It was ever thus,' he observed. 'The French are always inclined to turn tail and run. We seem to have spent most of this war looking at their retreating backs. This incident was highly regrettable,' he went on, shrugging it off, 'but of no real moment. There'll no doubt be others like it during the campaign.'

Daniel thought that their commander looked better than he had done for some time. He knew that Cardonnel was worried about him and had noticed the signs of weariness and pessimism. Customarily, Marlborough radiated a quiet confidence, something he imparted to the ranks as well as to his officers. Corporal John knew how to raise the morale of his troops, though he had yet to do so in the current campaign. The best judge of his condition was his secretary and, from Cardonnel's face and manner, Daniel could see that he was less concerned about Marlborough. It was reassuring.

While he had his commander's ear, Daniel returned to the topic that preoccupied him. The memory of Jules, the boy whose whole family had been butchered, was never far from his mind.

'Are patrols still searching for those renegades?' he asked.

'They are, Daniel,' answered Marlborough. 'In spite of everything else that needs to be done, I'm resolved to hunt them down.'

'I think we've identified their leader.'

'Who is he?' asked Cardonnel.

'Matthew Searle of the 5th Regiment of horse,' said Daniel. 'When he deserted, he took a few other malcontents with him as well as some spare horses. He must have gathered the rest of his band after he left camp. One of them was Private Edwin Lock of the 24th.'

'How can you be so certain of that?'

'It turns out that Lock was Searle's cousin. The two of them deserted on the same day – I checked up from that list you compiled. It has to be more than coincidence.'

'I agree,' said Cardonnel.

'It's a small mercy, I know,' Marlborough put in, 'but at least we've had no reports of further outrages.'

'None that have reached us,' said Daniel, 'but then, we've moved well away from that area. Searle and his men could still be on the rampage. Given what we know of these renegades, I fancy that they'll continue their raids until they're stopped.'

'They will be, Daniel, I promise you.'

'I'd like to be there when that happens.'

'We can't waste your talents on a routine patrol.'

'My talents would be put to good use, Your Grace,' said Daniel. 'I'd be helping to catch some very dangerous men.

Every time they strike, they sew even more hatred of us in the minds of the local people. That irks me.'

'It irks me as well,' said Marlborough. 'I want the French army to fear the sight of redcoats, but not the ordinary folk of Flanders. We need them to accept us.'

'They won't do that if these men are allowed to run amok.'

'This means a lot to you, Daniel, doesn't it?' said Cardonnel. 'You have a personal interest in this.'

'Yes, I do.'

'Why is that?'

'I heard what that lad had been through,' said Daniel, 'and it was harrowing. He may have survived but he'll have nightmares about the raid for the rest of his life. When he heard that I was a British soldier, he flung himself at me like a terrier.'

'Boys of that age act impulsively,' noted Marlborough with a half-smile. 'I once met a young lad named Daniel Rawson with the same kind of raw courage. Whatever happened to him, I wonder?'

'I heard a rumour that he'd joined the army,' said Cardonnel.

'He showed great pluck. We should harness that.'

'My situation was slightly different,' said Daniel. 'Though I lived on a farm, I'd always wanted to be a soldier like my father. I don't think that Jules will ever end up wearing a uniform he despises. He just wants to be a farmer and live in peace.'

'We're striving to achieve that peace,' Marlborough pointed out, 'though it obviously doesn't seem so to this unfortunate lad. Much as I sympathise with your motives, Daniel, I can't let you ride off with one of the patrols. You must stay with us. We're striking camp again.'

'Already, Your Grace?'

'In response to our move here, the French have shifted their base eastwards over the River Senne. Reports put them at Braine-l'Alleud.'

Daniel knew his geography. 'That would mean Louvain was under threat,' he said.

'Precisely – that's why we must block their approach. We'll march through Brussels and set up camp at Terbanck, immediately south of Louvain.'

'That's more or less what we did last year, Your Grace.'

'Yes,' said Marlborough, sadly, 'and we may very well find ourselves repeating the manoeuvre again next year. We're playing a form of chess, Daniel. When they move a piece on the board, we have to counter it at once – until, that is, we can seize the initiative.'

'And when will that be?'

'Your guess is as good as mine. What I do know is that King Louis didn't send such a huge army to the Spanish Netherlands in order for them to sit on their hands indefinitely. Sooner or later, they mean to strike. That's why you're of more use to us here than chasing a band of deserters. Who knows?' he added. 'They may not even be here any more. They could have returned to England.'

'Oh, no,' said Daniel with feeling. 'They're still here – I *know* it.'

Vendôme was in the middle of a meal when the report was handed to him. He read it while chewing a mouthful of chicken. Captain Valeran, celebrating his recent promotion, was dining alone with him in the privacy of the tent. Vendôme passed the report across to his favourite then turned to the messenger.

'When did this happen?' he asked.

'A few days ago, Your Grace,' replied the man.

'How can they be sure that French soldiers were involved?'

'One of them was killed and left behind. When the fire had died down, they found that his uniform had been burnt to a cinder but the buttons had survived and so had his musket. The buttons and the weapon were both ours. They confirmed that the raid was carried out by French soldiers.'

'That's dreadful!' exclaimed Valeran.

'It's more than that, Raoul,' said Vendôme, angrily. 'It's utterly barbaric. I want the culprits identified and brought to me. If they're so fond of flames, I'll have them cooked over a slow fire.'

'The raid was a long way away from here.'

'That makes no difference. It occurred on territory we hold and which we should therefore safeguard.'

He dismissed the messenger with a flick of the hand and the man left the tent. Taking another bite out of the chicken, Vendôme brooded, ignoring the gravy that dripped onto his lapel. Valeran passed the report back to him.

'What are you going to do, Your Grace?'

'I'll make every effort to find them as quickly as possible. And I'll need someone to return to that village.'

'Why?'

'They have to be pacified and recompensed,' said Vendôme. 'No soldiers under my command should ever behave this way. When foraging is required, it's sometimes necessary to use a little force but there's never any call for a massacre like this.'

'The whole farm was razed to the ground.'

'Speak to the four men who used to work there.'

Valeran was taken aback. 'You want *me* to go there?'

'It's a sign of how much trust I put in you,' said Vendôme, swilling down his food with some wine. 'Find out more details of what went on and assure those four men that we'll make some kind of restitution. We can't afford to rebuild the whole farm, of course, but a gesture on our part will show them how seriously we take this whole business. Leave with a patrol first thing tomorrow morning.'

'Yes, Your Grace,' said Valeran without enthusiasm.

'But be sure to hurry back – I'll miss you.'

The captain rallied immediately.

* * *

'What's his name, Henry?' asked Daniel.

'Ralph Higgins.'

'And who is he?'

'One of the sutlers,' said Welbeck. 'At least, that's what he claims to be. I think he's here for another reason altogether.'

'And what's that?'

'It concerns you, Dan.'

When he received the note from his friend, Daniel had hurried across to the area of the camp occupied by the 24th Foot. Knowing that he would not be summoned on a trivial matter, he met Welbeck outside the sergeant's tent. Daniel was curious.

'What's the fellow doing among the 24th?'

'Pretending to sell provisions to the men,' said Welbeck. 'He sought me out because someone told him that I was a close friend of a certain Captain Rawson.'

'Go on.'

'Higgins was very plausible. He gave me some free tobacco to make me well disposed towards him. He's an affable devil, I'll give him that, and I was happy to chat with him for a while. Then he started to ask questions about you, Dan, far too many questions. That's what aroused my suspicions. I think he's a French spy.'

'Where is he now?'

'He's being held inside.'

'Then I'll go in and introduce myself,' said Daniel.

Crossing to the tent, Daniel pulled back the flap and

stepped inside. Welbeck followed him. Ralph Higgins was seated on a stool with an armed soldier beside him. Higgins leapt to his feet at once. He was a tall, well-built man in his thirties with curly brown hair above a swarthy face that wore an expression of mingled surprise and pain. 'Could someone tell me what's going on?' he begged.

'That's exactly what we want to ask you,' said Welbeck.

Higgins spread his arms. 'I'm a sutler. I follow the army and sell to the soldiers. It's how I make my living.'

'Then why did you show such an interest in me?' asked Daniel. 'According to Sergeant Welbeck, you peppered him with questions about me. Are you intending to write a biography?'

'Are *you* the famous Captain Rawson?' asked Higgins, beaming. 'It's an honour to meet you, sir,' he went on, offering his hand and giving Daniel a warm handshake. 'You're something of a legend in the 24th, I hear.'

'And from whom did you hear that?'

'From just about everyone I've spoken to. The first person to mention your name was Lieutenant Ainley.' The sutler laughed. 'If ever you *do* want a biographer, sir, he's the man for you. It was the lieutenant who told me that Sergeant Welbeck was your good friend.'

'That's right,' said Welbeck, gruffly. 'I was put on this earth to make sure that no harm comes to Captain Rawson. If I sense any danger – and you reek of it – then I become very suspicious.'

'I don't blame you,' said Higgins, amiably. 'In fact, I was very much counting on it.'

Welbeck blinked. 'Were you?'

'How else could I get to meet Captain Rawson? Now that he's a member of the Duke's personal staff, he's out of reach of humble folk like me. The only way to approach him was through you.'

Welbeck was indignant. 'Are you saying that I was *used*?'

'I meant no harm by it, Sergeant.'

'And why should you want to meet me?' asked Daniel.

'First of all, I wanted to see if you were human.'

'Oh, I'm very human, Mr Higgins, and I'm full of human failings. For instance, I'm very short-tempered when I find that someone is trying to waste my time.'

'Forgive me,' said Higgins with a placatory gesture, 'I don't mean to take up your time. I wanted to put a proposition to you, Captain Rawson. The truth of it is that I'm not only a sutler,' he went on, slipping a hand into his pocket to take out a sheet of paper. 'I'm something of an artist, as you can see.'

Unfolding the paper, he showed them a portrait he'd drawn. It was only a pencil sketch but it had discernible talent. They were both able to recognise the face smiling up at them.

'That's Lieutenant Ainley,' said Welbeck.

'It's a good likeness,' admitted Daniel.

'This is only a preliminary drawing,' explained Higgins.

'I'll use it to do a portrait in colour. I'm not a real artist like van Dyck, mark you. A sketch like this only takes me five minutes and I have the painting finished in little more than an hour.'

'Why are you telling me this, Mr Higgins?'

'I'm coming to that.' He glanced at the soldier beside him. 'Is there any chance that you can get rid of my guard? He intimidates me. I'm not going to run away.' Welbeck gave a nod and the soldier left the tent. 'Thank you, Sergeant. Having him stand over me was rather unnerving.' He smiled hopefully at Daniel. 'I wondered if I could possibly have the honour of painting a portrait of you, Captain Rawson?'

'I can't think why you'd want to do that,' said Daniel.

'Then you haven't heard Lieutenant Ainley in full flow. He idolises you. He was telling me what you did at Blenheim and how you rescued someone from the Bastille in Paris.'

'I shouldn't believe everything he says.'

'Are you interested in my offer?'

'I'm sorry, Mr Higgins. I must decline. I'm not vain enough to want my portrait painted.'

'In the time we've been talking, I could have done the sketch.'

'Not without my permission,' said Daniel, 'and I'd never give that. It's a tempting notion but I suggest that you choose someone else. If you can produce these things so swiftly, you must have had a lot of customers.'

'Oh, I have,' said Higgins, ruefully. 'Some of the

ugliest men in the army have wanted a pretty painting of themselves. I have to show them what they want to see so I make hideous, old faces look young and handsome. Then, of course,' he added, dropping his voice and rolling his eyes. 'There are the other drawings.'

'What do you mean?' asked Welbeck.

'You know what soldiers are like, Sergeant. Most of them dream of nothing but drink and women. I sell them both. The beer is in the back of my wagon and the women are on sheets of paper like this.'

'You're talking about *naked* women, aren't you?'

'I have to meet a demand.' His eyes flicked to Daniel. 'Do you think that you could persuade the captain to sit for me? I won't charge him a penny for the portrait. It will be a pleasure to paint.'

'Captain Rawson makes his own decisions.'

'And you've already heard what I think,' said Daniel, pleasantly.

'Well, he hasn't heard what *I* think,' warned Welbeck, squaring up to Higgins. 'I think you have a nerve, coming here like this and using me as bait. It's unforgivable. If I catch you anywhere near the 24th again, I'll kick seven barrels of shit out of you and shove your bleeding sketches down your lying throat. Do you understand?'

'I apologise profusely, Sergeant,' said Higgins, composing his features into a mask of contrition. 'By way of recompense, I'll happily do a portrait of you as well.'

'No, you won't, you cheating, two-faced scoundrel!'

'Don't yell at him, Sergeant,' said Daniel, reproachfully. 'Mr Higgins came here in good faith and he had a reasonable proposal to put to me.'

'Only after he tricked me into getting you here,' said Welbeck.

'That's as may be. No real hurt was intended.'

'Yes, it was – my pride has been wounded.'

'I had no alternative,' argued Higgins.

'In that case,' returned Welbeck, holding up a fist, 'I'll have no alternative but to punch the living daylights out of you.'

'There's no need for that,' said Daniel, stepping between them to protect the sutler. 'I'm certain that Mr Higgins won't rely on a device like this again. I suggest that we let him get back to his wagon.'

Higgins was relieved. 'Thank you, Captain,' he said. 'Can't I make you reconsider my offer?'

'I'm afraid not.'

'Would you like to hear my offer again?' shouted Welbeck, waving a fist in his face. 'Now, get out before I throw you out.'

Still muttering apologies, Higgins retreated from the tent. Welbeck was livid. He was about to speak when Daniel silenced him with a wave. He peeped out through the gap between the tent flaps.

'He's gone,' noted Daniel. 'I thought he'd stay to eavesdrop.'

'You should have let me teach him a lesson.'

'That will come later, Henry.'

'I hate being deceived like that.'

'You should be grateful to Ralph Higgins.'

'Why…for wasting our time like that? Using me like that makes me seethe. Left to myself, I'd have tipped him headfirst into the deepest latrine.' He took a deep breath. 'I'm sorry I dragged you over here for no reason, Dan. I was wrong about the man.'

'But you weren't – he's a spy.'

'How do you know?'

'I have done a little spying myself, you know,' said Daniel, smiling, 'and I know that the first thing you need is a glib tongue. Higgins certainly had that. In offering to do a portrait of me, he gave himself away.'

'Did he?'

'Who do you imagine would have got that portrait?'

'I thought he'd do it for you, Dan?'

'I might have been given the painted version but the original sketch would have been sent off to the enemy. Somebody has designs on me, Henry, and they need to know what I look like.'

Welbeck was lost. 'If you think he's a spy, why let him go?'

'I wanted to test my theory,' said Daniel. 'Find six men and we'll guard the road out of here. When Higgins drives his wagon towards us, we'll stop him and take him into custody.'

'How do you know that that's what he'll do?'

'Because,' said Daniel with a soft chuckle, 'it's exactly what I'd do in his shoes.'

Seated in his wagon, Ralph Higgins worked swiftly. After drawing the sketch of Daniel Rawson from memory, he put it on top of the letter he'd just written and folded the two pages tightly until he could insert them into a pouch of tobacco. He then jumped down from the wagon. A soldier who'd been watching strolled casually over to him.

'Ah, good afternoon, Corporal,' greeted Higgins.

'I've come for my tobacco,' said the man.

'It's all ready for you.' Handing him the pouch, Higgins spoke in an undertone. 'Have this delivered at once. It's important.' He took some money from his customer. 'Thank you, Corporal. It's always a pleasure to do business with you.'

As soon as the soldier had gone, Higgins clambered up onto the seat of his wagon and picked up the reins. Feeling the flick of leather, the horse responded by pulling the vehicle away. It went past the other sutlers and the baggage wagons until it came to the road out of the camp. Nobody challenged him. Higgins was free. He allowed himself a congratulatory smirk. It soon froze on his face. Six armed soldiers suddenly emerged from the trees to block his way, muskets trained on him. Henry Welbeck was with them.

'Stop there or we'll shoot the horse dead,' he called out.

Higgins was perplexed. 'What's the meaning of this,

Sergeant?' he asked, innocently. 'Have I done something wrong?'

'Yes, you have,' said Daniel, coming into view from behind a large bush. 'You made a fatal mistake. There's something I require from you, Mr Higgins,' he added. 'Hand it over, please.'

'Hand what over, Captain?'

'The codebook you use to send reports to your masters in the French camp.'

'I really don't know what you're talking about.'

Higgins tried to bluff his way out of the situation but he soon realised that it was futile. He'd been found out. As a last resort, he reached inside the wagon for the pistol he kept hidden there. Welbeck gave him no time to use it. Jumping forward, he grabbed the sutler by the leg and yanked him off the seat. As Higgins hit the ground, he groaned in agony and the weapon was discharged harmlessly into the air. Daniel went and stood over him.

'Now, then,' he said, politely. 'Will you tell me where your codebook is or must I ask Sergeant Welbeck to jog your memory?'

Ralph Higgins quailed. He was trapped.

CHAPTER TEN

Amalia Janssen sat in the parlour and read through the letters in chronological order. It was the one sure antidote to her sadness. Whenever she pined for Daniel Rawson, she took out the correspondence he'd sent over the years and undid the pink ribbon around it. There were few letters and they contained very little about what he was doing and where he actually was at any given time. That didn't concern her. Amalia understood the need for caution. In case the letters fell into the wrong hands, Daniel ensured that he gave away no information whatsoever of military value. The missives were therefore essentially personal. Short and hastily written, they brought immense comfort to her because they were steeped in so much affection. Daniel's words made her feel that he was sitting there beside her.

When her father came into the room, he could see at a glance what she was doing. He placed a paternal kiss on her head.

'Are you reading those letters *again*, Amalia?' he said.

She put them in her lap. 'Yes, Father.'

'You must know every word by heart now.'

'I like to see Daniel's hand,' she said. 'His writing is so neat.'

'Then it's at variance with his character,' opined Emanuel Janssen. 'Captain Rawson is such a brave, adventurous man that you'd expect his calligraphy to be much larger and bolder.' He sat down opposite her. 'When did the last letter come?'

'A fortnight ago – but it seems like a year.'

'Time hangs heavy when a beloved is absent. Console yourself with the fact that it must be the same for him, Amalia.'

'I doubt it,' she said, resignedly. 'Daniel has so many responsibilities that there's not much time to think about me. I'm not complaining about that,' she added. 'I'd hate to be a distraction.'

'My guess is that Captain Rawson needs a distraction now and then. He's told us often enough that this war consists largely of watching and waiting until the French make up their minds what they're going to do. No,' he said, 'I fancy that you're in his thoughts very often.'

'I hope so.' She put the letters aside. 'Have you finished work for the day?'

'I had to, Amalia. I had that pain in my fingers again.'

She was alarmed. 'You ought to consult the doctor.'

'He'll only tell me what's becoming more and more obvious. I'm getting old. It's as simple as that.'

'How bad is the pain?'

'I had a sharp twinge now and again, that's all. I could have carried on but I felt that it was more sensible to hand over to Kees. His fingers are younger and more nimble than mine.'

'But he doesn't have your experience.'

'That will come.'

'How much work is left on the tapestry?'

'A fortnight, at most, I'd say.' He saw the concern etched in her face. 'It's nothing to worry about, Amalia. It just means that I won't be able to work for such long periods. Hand-sewing requires such care and stamina. Eyes get tired. Fingers are bound to hurt.'

'Yet you've never had pain in the past, Father.'

He smiled. 'You mean that I've never told you about it before.'

'Has this been happening for a long time?' she asked, anxiously.

'No, it hasn't. At the end of a long day, my hands have often been sore but that's to be expected. One must suffer for one's art.'

'I was thinking about the Duke of Marlborough's tapestry.'

'What about it?'

'Well,' she said, fretfully, 'it would be a tragedy if your hands got so bad that you weren't able to complete it. I mean, it will be such an honour for you to have your work hanging in Blenheim Palace.'

'Have no fears,' he assured her. 'My fingers have lost nothing of their skill. They're not about to drop off yet, Amalia. Work on the battle of Ramillies will start again as soon as we've finished this tapestry. It's a much bigger project, of course, so I'll have to take on more assistants. We'll all work side by side on different looms. It may be a long time before it can go to England to take its rightful place at Blenheim Palace but at least it will be ready.'

Amalia was relieved. 'I'm so pleased to hear that.'

'I'll be producing tapestries for years yet. One of them, I trust, will commemorate the Duke's next triumph.'

'Where will that be?'

'I was counting on you to tell me that,' he teased. 'I hoped that Captain Rawson might have given us forewarning in his last letter.'

'He never mentions things like that.'

'One thing is certain, anyhow.'

'What's that, Father?'

'Wherever the next battle does take place, we can be sure that the captain will be in the thick of it.'

* * *

'Well done, Daniel,' said Marlborough, cheerily. 'It's yet another feather in your cap.'

'Thank you, Your Grace,' replied Daniel, 'but the person who deserves the praise is Sergeant Welbeck of the 24th. It was he who first suspected the fellow.'

'I'll make a point of writing to thank him.'

It was no idle promise. Marlborough was always ready to give credit where it was due. Daniel was part of the entourage that was following him on his tour through the camp on a beautiful June day. Corporal John had fought under commanders who were aloof and detached. One or two of them had openly despised the ranks, viewing them as no more than cannon fodder. Marlborough, by contrast, respected the most humble members of his army and let them see him in person from time to time. The sight of their captain general, striding through the camp in his finery, was always uplifting.

'Where's this sutler now?' asked Marlborough.

'He's still in custody, Your Grace.'

'Has he been interrogated?'

'Oh, yes,' said Daniel with a grin. 'Ralph Higgins was thoroughly examined. I invited Sergeant Welbeck to take part in the exercise. He has a rare talent for loosening a man's tongue.'

'What did you learn?'

'For a start, we know the cipher that he's been using.'

'Excellent!'

'And we've also identified his accomplice – a corporal in the Royal Scots Fusiliers. Higgins refused to give us the man's name at first but Sergeant Welbeck eventually drew it out of him. What we don't yet know is the name of the go-between.'

'The go-between?' echoed Marlborough.

'There were three of them involved. Higgins gathered the intelligence and gave it to the corporal. He in turn passed it on to someone who delivered it to the enemy. Corporal Rennie proved to be a harder man to crack,' said Daniel. 'He admitted nothing.'

'Couldn't you get the name of this third man from Higgins?'

'He swears that he doesn't know it and I believe him.'

'Keep interrogating him.'

'We will, Your Grace.'

Marlborough broke off to exchange a few words with some officers he encountered. When he moved on, he waved to a group of privates who were unloading a wagon. Daniel noticed how pleased they were to be acknowledged. The tour continued.

'You and Sergeant Welbeck are to be congratulated, Daniel,' said Marlborough. 'You caught this man red-handed, so to speak.'

'It takes a spy to recognise a spy.'

'Why did you suspect him?'

'He tried to be too clever,' recalled Daniel. 'To convince us that he was genuine, he told us far more than he needed.

I've learnt to keep explanations to a minimum. Higgins talked too much. The only way to be certain, of course, was to give him the chance to escape. That would be an obvious confession of guilt. So we prepared a little welcome for him.'

'How long has he been with us?'

'Since the start of the campaign, Your Grace.'

Marlborough pondered. 'I suppose that a sutler would be in a position to hear all the gossip in the camp,' he said at length. 'Soldiers are off guard when they're buying things from the back of a wagon.'

'Don't forget his sketches,' said Daniel. 'They were a means of wheedling himself into the company of officers. He'd flatter them by offering to paint their portraits then draw what information he could from them. He was an artist of no mean talent.'

'He should have put it to better use.'

'Higgins felt that it *was* put to good use, Your Grace. When he questioned him, he confessed that his father was English and had died when his son was just a boy. He was brought up by his mother, who was French by birth. That's where his allegiances lay.'

'Not any more,' said Marlborough. 'He's finished.'

'And so is Corporal Rennie. He comes from a proud regiment. They were appalled to discover that they had a traitor in their midst. However,' Daniel said, 'Higgins was the real danger. He was a spy. Rennie simply handed on reports to a courier.'

'We must find out who that courier was.'

Marlborough paused again to pass a few remarks to a sergeant major. There was no sense of condescension. He talked to the man as if they were on an equal footing and the sergeant major appreciated that. After a few minutes, they were on the move again.

'I'm surprised that I was not on Higgins' list,' said Marlborough.

'What list is that?'

'Well, the obvious way to get the most reliable intelligence was to try to inveigle me into providing it. To manage that, he'd have had to do a sketch of me.'

'That would have been unnecessary,' said Daniel.

'Why?'

'Every soldier in Europe would recognise you, Your Grace. It was different in my case. He was desperate for a portrait of me.'

'You're a handsome fellow, Daniel. Any artist would enjoy painting a picture of you.'

'Higgins wouldn't have done it for his own benefit,' said Daniel. 'I think the portrait had been commissioned. Somebody is very keen to know exactly what I look like.'

'So *this* is the intrepid Captain Rawson, is it?' said Vendôme, studying the rough sketch. 'He's just as I imagined him to be.'

'This note came as well,' said the messenger, offering the paper. 'It's been deciphered.'

'Thank you.'

Snatching it from him, Vendôme read it. As he did so, his eyes bulged and his mouth fell open. He was patently startled. He looked at the sketch again with renewed interest. Before he could make any comment, however, the flap of the tent was held open by a guard so that the duc de Burgundy could sail in. Greeting the newcomer with a bow, the messenger scurried out. Burgundy took up a pose.

'I'm glad that I find you standing up for once,' he said.

'I think best when seated on my *chaise-percée*,' Vendôme told him. 'Contemplation helps the bowels to function.'

'I'll take your word for it, my lord Duke. As it happens, that's not something I came here to discuss.'

'Have you heard from Versailles?'

'Word has just arrived from His Majesty.'

'Go on,' pressed Vendôme. 'What does he say?'

'He concedes that there's some degree of merit in your plan,' said Burgundy, pursing his lips in distaste. 'Grandfather can see the value of laying siege to Huy.'

'I knew he would! He thinks like a soldier.'

'I, however, remain opposed to the notion.'

'That's immaterial. The King's word is final.'

'I haven't finished yet.'

'Even though you were against it, I gave orders for preparations to be made for a siege. I felt certain that common sense would prevail in the end. You've been overruled by your grandfather.'

'Not exactly,' rejoined Burgundy. 'I questioned the order and it's been placed in abeyance.'

Vendôme exploded. 'Placed in abeyance?'

'News has arrived of Prince Eugene. He's gathering his forces at Coblenz. Until his purposes are definitely revealed, you must suspend preparations against Huy.'

'But the plan has royal approval.'

'It's been withdrawn,' said Burgundy, enjoying Vendôme's discomfiture. 'In time, His Majesty will come to accept the wisdom of my strategy.'

'We should move against Huy *now*,' maintained Vendôme.

'Stand your men down.'

'Will you consign us to another month of inactivity?'

'We're not inactive,' replied Burgundy. 'We gather intelligence, we anticipate the enemy's movements, we respond accordingly. In the end, our superior tactics will be vindicated.'

'What tactics? We have none worthy of the name!'

'There's no need for insults, my lord Duke.'

'Huy is at our mercy,' said Vendôme with passion. 'Seize that and we have control of that stretch of the River Meuse.'

'And what if Eugene is coming north? We'd be squeezed between his army and that of Marlborough's like a piece of cheese between two slices of bread.' Burgundy was adamant. 'Forget all thought of Huy.'

'Marlborough may be a threat but what kind of army

can Eugene raise? Not a very large one, in my estimation. Besides, we've no indication that he's heading this way. All the signs are that he'll stay in the Moselle Valley. It's the kind of ruse Marlborough always employs in an attempt to divert us.'

Burgundy was unmoved. 'We obey orders and stay here.'

'The King has given us latitude to act.'

'You heard me, my lord Duke.'

'What I hear is a recipe for stagnation.'

'We are merely keeping our powder dry.'

'That amounts to the same thing,' said Vendôme, mordantly. 'We should move swiftly while we still outnumber the Confederate forces and while Prince Eugene is still trying to muster an army. It's the perfect way to catch them off guard.'

'Your advice is – as always – welcome,' said Burgundy, loftily. 'On this occasion, however, I choose to ignore it.'

'You *always* choose to ignore it!'

'There's no need to shout, my lord Duke.'

'I apologise,' said Vendôme, struggling to regain his composure. 'All I ask of you is that you give this matter serious thought and take my opinion into account.'

'You've heard the decision – I take my leave of you.'

After a polite nod, Burgundy swept out of the tent with an imperious stride. Vendôme stamped his foot hard on the ground and rid himself of a few imprecations. During the previous year, he'd been in supreme command and able to trust his own judgement. It was galling to be at the beck and call of someone he considered to be a novice in the field. He paced up and down like a caged lion in search of someone to maul. When the flap of his tent opened, he rounded on the man who put his head through.

'Get out of here!' he bellowed.

'Yes, Your Grace,' said Valeran, retreating immediately.

'Is that you, Raoul?' Vendôme opened the tent flap to call him back. 'Step inside. I didn't realise it was you.'

'I don't wish to interrupt you.'

'You're not doing so. After what I've just been through, the sight of a friendly face is a godsend.' When they were both inside, Vendôme wrapped him in a warm embrace. 'How are you?'

'I'm very glad to be back at last.'

'Have you brought good news with you?'

'No, Your Grace,' said the lieutenant. 'The search continues but the raiders have yet to be found.'

'Then the patrols must be doubled – trebled, if need be. These fiends must be caught. We came to liberate these people, not to murder them in cold blood.' He sat down heavily. 'Tell me what you discovered.'

Captain Valeran described the scene of devastation and told how he'd spoken to the four men who'd worked at the farm. Once the alarm had been raised on the night, they were among the first to get there. They were appalled by what they saw. One of the men had been due to marry the farmer's daughter in the autumn. He arrived to find that his bride-to-be had been burnt beyond recognition.

Vendôme listened to the recital with gathering fury.

'Is there no evidence as to whom these devils were?' he asked.

'We know for certain that they were French soldiers.'

'How?'

'They were seen earlier in the day,' said Valeran, 'riding past a village about five miles to the west. An old man was repairing the scarecrow in his field. He noticed them because they took the trouble to come right around the village instead of riding straight through it.'

'That sounds as if they didn't want to be seen.'

'They were spotted by the old man.'

'How many of them were there, Raoul?'

'Eight or nine, it seems.'

'Were there no other witnesses?'

'The patrols have not found any as yet, Your Grace.'

'An old man with a scarecrow,' said Vendôme, dubiously. 'I'd want more reliable testimony than he could provide. At his age, he's probably half-blind.'

'You do him an injustice,' said Valeran.

'Do I?'

'In one way, we couldn't have had a better witness. He may have lapsed into old age now but he wasn't always a farmer. In his younger days, he saw service in the French army. That's why it puzzled him.'

'What did?'

'Well,' continued Valeran, 'they passed so close to him that he was able to take a good look at them and he noticed something very strange. The uniforms they wore didn't all come from the same regiment. Indeed, he had a strong feeling that one of the uniforms didn't even belong in the cavalry.'

Matthew Searle tossed his coat onto the fire and used a sword to stir up the blaze. It was the last of the French uniforms to be consumed by the flames. The other men looked on. Hugh Davey had doubts.

'Are you sure it's a good idea to destroy them?' he asked.

Searle was curt. 'Yes, it is.'

'But they might have come in useful, Matt.'

'They brought us bad luck. Also, as long as we keep them, we put ourselves in danger. If a French patrol finds them here, we'll have some awkward questions to face.'

'This part of Flanders is held by the Allies,' said Edwin Lock. 'I should know. We helped to capture it.'

'It's ours at the moment, perhaps – that could soon change.'

'What a pity!' said Davey, staring into the flames. 'I preferred that uniform. It was the only one that fitted me.'

There were six of them in all. Searle had allowed the other two members of the band to ride off to the town in search of carnal pleasure. When the first pair returned, it would be the turn of Lock and Davey. They were throbbing with anticipation. Searle saw the look of desperation in their eyes.

'Remember what I said to the others,' he warned. 'You take your pleasure and come straight back here. If I have to come looking for you, I'll cut your balls off and make you swallow them.'

'We'll come back, Matt,' said Lock, slipping a protective hand to his groin. 'I promise.'

'But only when we've had our money's worth,' added Davey.

'Tell them nothing,' ordered Searle. 'They don't need to know your name or where you came from. A careless word from either of you and we're done for. There'll be patrols out looking for us by now.'

'We won't be there for conversation, Matt,' said Davey with a sly grin. 'We'll have plenty of that on the way back when me and Edwin talk about what we got.'

Lock cackled. 'I'm getting *everything*, Hugh!' he boasted.

'So am I.'

'When is it your turn, Matt?' asked Lock. 'You didn't even touch any of those women at the farmhouse. You must be feeling as ripe for fucking as any of us.'

'I'll wait till last,' said Searle, 'when I've made sure that you've all obeyed orders and come back. Don't you dare try to run away on your own. Neither of you would last five minutes without me.' He threw a meaningful glance at the mound of earth around the grave of Ianto Morgan. 'If you do as you're told, everything will be fine. Cross me and you'll end up beside Ianto.'

'At least Ianto had a proper burial,' said Lock, morosely. 'I know that because I dug the grave. That's more than we can say for poor Gregory. He went up in flames.'

Searle was derisive. 'Gregory Pyle was an idiot,' he said. 'If he couldn't tell the difference between a man and a woman, he deserved to go up in smoke. Everything would have been so much easier if he'd killed the farmer instead of his wife.'

'There's only eight of us left now, Matt,' said Davey. 'We'll have to choose smaller farms from now on with less people to kill.'

'Leave all the decisions to me, Hugh.'

'I always do.'

'And so do I,' said Lock, sycophantically.

'Riders are coming!' yelled the lookout on the hill.

The three men immediately grabbed their weapons and a fourth rushed out of the house with a musket. Hand over his eyes to shield them from the evening sun, the lookout peered into the distance.

'How many are there, Will?' asked Searle.

'Two of them, I think,' replied the lookout. 'Yes, just the two of them – they're clear of those trees now.'

'Are they wearing uniforms?'

'Yes, they both have redcoats. You can put your weapons away,' he said with a laugh of relief. 'It's Luke and Peter, back from the town.'

'Thank heavens for that!' said Searle to himself.

'That means it's our turn!' declared Lock.

'Come on, Edwin,' said Davey, slapping his thigh in delight. 'Saddle up. We're off to town.'

They watched her for days before deciding on their plan of action. Seizing her from the house would be difficult because it would involve subduing her father, his assistant and the various servants. Amalia Janssen would be a far easier target in the open. She was methodical. Every day she ventured out, either to visit the market or simply to stretch her legs. The same servant always accompanied her, a plump woman who waddled along the streets with a basket over her arm. At some point in their walk, they invariably stopped to look in the windows of some dress shops. They then made their way home down a series of lanes. An almost identical route was taken each day and – if the weather was fine – they ventured out at roughly the same time.

Following that same pattern would be Amalia's downfall.

The day began with great excitement when a letter arrived from Daniel Rawson. It had come via The Hague. Marlborough was in regular contact with Heinsius so that the Grand Pensionary was kept well informed about the army's movements and strategy and thus able to discuss them with the States-General. Daniel's letter had been included with dispatches sent by Marlborough and forwarded to Amsterdam. Amalia was overjoyed. Though the letter was as brief as its predecessors, it made her glow for hours. It showed that Daniel was still thinking about her.

When she was ready to go out, Amalia didn't want to be parted from her latest letter. Instead of joining the others inside the pink ribbon, therefore, it was tucked up her sleeve so that she could feel it against her skin. It was like a good luck charm. Beatrix was waiting for her with a large basket on her arm. They left the house together, unaware that someone was watching them from the opposite side of the street. As the two women went on their familiar route, the man followed them.

'What do we need today?' asked Amalia.

'Cook has given me a list,' replied Beatrix.

'She usually forgets something.'

'Then she can go out and buy it herself when we get back because I'm not making two trips to market in one day.'

'I thought you liked to be out in the fresh air.'

'Once a day is all the exercise I need, Miss Amalia,' said Beatrix. 'I have far too many jobs to be done in the house. I don't want your father complaining.'

'Father *never* complains,' said Amalia.

'That's only because I never give him cause.' They turned a corner and headed for the market. Beatrix had a knowing smile. 'I think that someone had a letter this morning.'

'How do you know that?'

'I can always tell. You never stop grinning.'

Amalia laughed. 'Oh dear!' she exclaimed. 'Do I give myself away so easily? I shall have to be more careful in the future.'

'It's wonderful to see you so happy, Miss Amalia.'

'Thank you, Beatrix.'

'And is Captain Rawson well?'

'He's very well indeed.'

The market was as busy and noisy as ever. When they plunged in among the stalls, the basket soon began to fill. Amalia paid for the items but left all the haggling to Beatrix, who examined all the food carefully before she agreed to buy it. Their last purchase was the bread, still warm from the oven and giving off a bewitching aroma. Once everything on the list was safely in the basket, they wended their way slowly home. Amalia made her obligatory stop outside the shop that displayed the dresses she coveted. She was transfixed for a long time and her companion was restless.

'We must get back,' said Beatrix.

'Give me a few more minutes.'

'This basket is heavy, Miss Amalia.'

'Then put it down for a moment.'

Beatrix obeyed, folding her arms and hoping she'd not be kept waiting too long. In fact, Amalia's vigil was promptly interrupted. A young man came round the corner from the lane and approached them at speed.

'There you are,' he said, breathlessly. 'I was told I might

find you here. Your father's been taken ill, I'm afraid. I was sent to fetch you.'

Amalia was disconcerted. 'What's wrong with him?'

'Come and see for yourself. The doctor's been sent for.'

'Wait a moment,' said Beatrix, her instincts aroused. 'Who exactly are you, sir?'

'I'm a friend of Emanuel Janssen,' said the man. 'I was in the house when he had the seizure. Please hurry – I'll explain everything on the way.'

Amalia was too worried to have any suspicions. She allowed herself to be guided around the corner. A coach was waiting in the lane. As soon as they drew level with it, the man opened the door and bundled her into the vehicle, jumping in beside her. Beatrix tried to protest but she was grabbed from behind by the man who'd been following them since they'd left the house. Spinning her round, he threw her violently to the ground then clambered into the coach. Beatrix was left face down on the pavement, hurt, dazed and surrounded by the contents of the upturned basket. The driver cracked his whip and the coach rolled swiftly down the lane. Amalia was inside it, being overpowered by two men so that she could be bound and gagged. She was terrified.

Daniel's letter had not brought her luck, after all.

CHAPTER ELEVEN

'Can this be true?' asked Jonathan Ainley, incredulously.

'As true as I stand here, Lieutenant,' said Welbeck.

'But he seemed such an engaging fellow.'

'That's what made me suspect him.'

'He promised to paint my portrait.'

'You'll never receive it now,' said Daniel. 'Ralph Higgins' career as an artist is at an end – and so is his work for the French.'

'Upon my soul!' exclaimed Ainley. 'This is most extraordinary.'

The three of them were standing beside the stream that looped around the edge of their camp. Cooks were filling buckets of water to use in the preparation of the day's meals. A little way upstream, horses were being allowed to slake their thirst. Camp followers were washing clothes so that they could be hung out to dry in the warm sunshine. A boy was trying to fish with a rudimentary rod.

The lieutenant had just been told that the sutler with whom he'd talked so freely was, in reality, an enemy spy. It was sobering news. Guilt made Ainley wince.

'I should have been more alert,' he admitted.

'I think you should, Lieutenant,' said Welbeck, muffling his contempt under a token respect. 'I would have thought a man in your position would not be taken in so easily.'

'How right you are, Sergeant!'

'Before you confided in him, Higgins should have been sifted.'

'I can see that now.'

'Better men than you have been deceived,' said Daniel, trying to soften the blow for his fellow officer. 'The fact is that Higgins has been gathering intelligence under our noses since this campaign started and nobody had the slightest idea of his true purpose. We must be thankful to Sergeant Welbeck that he was finally unmasked.'

'I endorse that wholeheartedly – congratulations, Sergeant.'

'Thank you, sir,' said Welbeck.

'You deserve commendation for this.'

'His Grace was kind enough to write to me, sir. Yet I look for no praise.' Welbeck straightened his shoulders. 'I was only doing my duty.'

'You were doing it very well.'

'It was Captain Rawson who got the proof that Higgins was a spy. We caught him as he tried to flee.'

'And we caught his accomplice as well,' added Daniel. 'One of them, anyway – there's a third man who acted as courier but we've been unable to identify him. The chances are that he's already left with whatever intelligence Higgins had managed to collect.'

Ainley swallowed hard. 'I see.'

'That brings us to you, of course. What exactly did you tell him?'

'We had a pleasant conversation, that's all.'

'Can you recall what it was about?'

'I divulged no secrets,' said Ainley, defensively.

'You must have divulged something, sir,' said Welbeck, 'or the fellow wouldn't have come to me.'

'I simply said that you were Daniel's – Captain Rawson's – friend and that you probably knew him better than any of us.'

'What else did you say?' wondered Daniel.

'I talked about you, mainly.'

'Sutlers are only here to sell their provender. Didn't it strike you as odd that this particular one wanted to talk to you about a fellow officer?'

'That's the curious thing,' said Ainley, 'We didn't *begin* by discussing you. Higgins was too cunning for that. He worked around to it as he did that sketch of me. I suppose,' he went on with obvious discomfort, 'that I was drawn in.'

Welbeck was forthright. 'You were too gullible, sir.'

'I suppose that I was.'

'It's not for you to criticise an officer, Sergeant,' said Daniel, coming to the lieutenant's aid. 'We both know how credible Higgins was. Anyone could have been fooled.'

'I wasn't, sir,' said Welbeck. 'But I was too late.'

'Why do you say that?'

'The damage was done by the time he came to me.'

'What damage?' said Ainley, hurt by the accusation. 'On my word of honour, I said nothing about Captain Rawson that wasn't common knowledge. I talked about him leading a forlorn hope at the Schellenberg and of his gallantry at Blenheim. There's no secret about any of that.'

'What else did he want to know?' asked Daniel.

'How you'd risen from the ranks.'

'That was done purely on merit,' said Welbeck, pointedly.

'You were more aware of the details, Sergeant, so I took the liberty of mentioning your name. Had I had the slightest inkling of his true motives, of course, I'd never have dreamt of doing that.'

'No, Lieutenant, I'm sure that you wouldn't.'

'I told Higgins nothing he couldn't have got from elsewhere,' said Ainley. 'He'd already heard rumours of what you did in Paris. In fact – now that I remember – it was your adventures in the Bastille that really interested him. He couldn't believe that you could rescue a prisoner then bring him and three other people all the way back to

Holland. He was laughing in wonder.'

'He was laughing at you,' said Welbeck to himself but he didn't translate the thought into words. Stone-faced and bordering on disrespect, he put a question to Ainley.

'How long would you say that you and Higgins talked, sir?'

Ainley considered. 'I can't really put a time on it, Sergeant.'

'He boasted to us that he could draw a sketch in five minutes. It sounds to me as if the pair of you went on a lot longer than that so you must have told him a great deal about Captain Rawson.'

'I suppose that I did.'

'I trust that you didn't mention Major Crevel,' said Daniel.

'No, no, I swear it,' replied Ainley. 'On that subject, my lips were sealed. I obeyed your orders on that score, Captain.'

'I'm glad to hear it.'

'Honestly, I feel so deuced embarrassed by all this.'

'You've nothing to reproach yourself with, Lieutenant,' said Daniel with a forgiving smile. 'I just wanted to hear what had happened between you and Higgins. You've put my mind at rest and I'm grateful to you.'

Ainley brightened. 'Oh, I'm not under fire, then.'

'Not at all – I'm sorry that I kept you so long.'

Daniel put a hand in the middle of his back to ease him gently away then he strolled along the bank in the opposite direction with Welbeck. The sergeant was able to lapse into familiarity.

'You let that silly bugger off lightly, Dan,' he said.

'Lieutenant Ainley means well.'

'No wonder Higgins picked on that simpleton. He could see how naive the lieutenant was. He probably got the entire life story of Daniel Rawson out of that fool.'

'We caught Higgins,' said Daniel, 'so no harm was done.'

'The lieutenant should learn to keep his big gob shut.'

'And you should learn to be less censorious of an officer, Henry. I concede that Ainley has his shortcomings but he's assiduous in his duties and has distinguished himself in battle.'

Welbeck snorted. 'I'll believe that when I see it, Dan.'

'He may surprise you yet.'

Before he could speak up for the lieutenant, Daniel saw someone walking briskly towards him. The man was carrying a letter in his hand. When he reached them, he gave it to Daniel.

'His Grace wanted you to have this as a matter of urgency, Captain,' said the messenger. 'It was sent from the French camp.'

'Thank you.'

Daniel waited until the man had gone before he opened the letter. When he realised what he was holding, he recoiled as if from a heavy blow. His mind clouded for an instant. There was no need to read the letter because, having written it to Amalia Janssen, he already knew its contents. Daniel was shocked that something so private had been made public. If it had been sent by the enemy, the message was clear.

Amalia was in dire trouble.

Flanked by two guards, Amalia Janssen stood in trepidation while Vendôme ran a searching eye over her. His scrutiny made her blood run cold. Being abducted and smuggled out of Holland had been a frightening experience but her captors had treated her with a measure of respect. She got little of that from Vendôme. His gaze was so direct and penetrating that it was almost as if he were slowly undressing her until she was stark naked before him. Bound and defenceless, Amalia felt abused. She turned her face away in embarrassment.

Vendôme nodded so one of the men removed the gag from her mouth and the rope that pinioned her hands behind her back. Amalia rubbed her wrists. During her stay in Paris, she'd learnt a fair amount of French but was far from fluent. When Vendôme spoke rapidly to the two guards, she could only pick out certain words. The two men withdrew and she was left alone in the tent with Vendôme. After circling her to appraise her from every angle, he came back to face her, lifting her chin with a finger so that she was forced to look into a pair of dark, burning, uncompromising eyes.

'Captain Rawson is a fortunate man,' he began, slowly. 'I'm sure that he realises that. He wrote you a very touching letter.'

'That was private,' she said.

'You no longer have any privacy, mademoiselle. You left it behind you in Amsterdam.' He saw her glancing around. 'And before you think of trying to run away, let me warn you that guards are posted outside. There's no escape.' He beamed at her. 'You're *mine*.'

'What do you want from me?'

'I want you to tell me about Captain Rawson.'

'There's nothing to tell.'

'Then you have a very short memory,' he chided. 'Have you so soon forgotten your rescue from Paris? Don't you remember how the captain managed to release your father from the Bastille? That was a remarkable achievement. I look forward to hearing how it was done.'

'I don't know.'

'Your father must have told you. Emanuel Janssen is one of the very few people who escaped from the Bastille. I'm certain that he must have boasted to you about it.' Amalia remained silent. 'Well? What did he tell you?' Biting her lip, she let her head fall to her chest. 'You're not in a very talkative mood yet, I see,' he continued. 'That's understandable. You're still shocked at being kidnapped. You need time to grow accustomed to the idea.'

'Where am I?' she asked, raising her head.

'You're in our camp at Braine l'Alleud and I,' he said, proudly, 'am the duc de Vendôme, commander of the French army.'

Amalia trembled. Because of his aristocratic bearing, she knew that he must hold a high rank but it never occurred to her that she was talking to a duke. Vendôme was so slovenly. He looked nothing like the magnificent grandees she'd once seen on parade at Versailles. She couldn't imagine why she'd been plucked from the streets of Amsterdam to stand before one of the most celebrated commanders in the French army. He noted her confusion.

'You'll have plenty of time to think about it, mademoiselle.'

'I don't understand.'

'You have no idea why you're here, do you?' She shook her head. 'It's because I want to witness a reunion.'

'What do you mean?'

'I wish to be there when you and Captain Rawson meet again.'

She was still bewildered. 'How can you do that?'

'He's probably read that letter he wrote to you by now. I had it sent to him. By all accounts, he's an astute man. He'll know that you'd never have returned something that was so precious to you. The captain will reach the obvious conclusion – his beloved is in danger.'

Vendôme spoke too quickly for her to translate every word but Amalia caught the gist of what he was telling her. She was being used as bait. In order to lure Daniel to the French camp, Amalia was to be held hostage. Her brain was swimming and her heart fluttering. She was consumed by feelings of guilt. Because of her, Daniel would now be imperilled. Because she'd been so unguarded as to let herself be captured, his life might be at risk. It was a devastating thought. Stifling a sob, Amalia brought both hands up to her face.

'I see that you've finally comprehended,' said Vendôme, gloating. 'Since you won't tell me how your father escaped from the Bastille, I shall have to wait until I can put the question to Captain Rawson.'

Daniel had hoped in vain that there was another explanation. It was conceivable that his letter to Amalia had been stolen from her or even intercepted before it ever reached Amsterdam. Deep down, however, he knew that he was grasping at straws and, when news came from her stricken father, the truth was unavoidable. Emanuel Janssen's letter told of his daughter's abduction and of the inabilities of the Dutch authorities to find any trace of her. That confirmed it. Amalia was in enemy hands. She was being held in the French camp.

'We can't be absolutely certain of that,' said Marlborough.

'I think we can, Your Grace,' insisted Daniel.

'Amalia could be held anywhere in French territory. She may even have been taken back to Paris.'

'I think that highly improbable. The only use that Amalia has for them is to act as an enticement for me. They'd hardly want to draw me all the way to the French capital.'

'That's a fair point, Daniel,' said Cardonnel. 'They went to great trouble to arrange the kidnap. It must have taken a lot of planning. Why go to such lengths?'

'They want me very much,' replied Daniel.

'I can't think why.'

'I can,' said Marlborough. 'It might well have something to do with Daniel's kidnap of Major Crevel. That must have rankled with the French high command. They may even be aware of his part in the liberation of Emanuel Janssen from the Bastille.'

'How could they know that, Your Grace?'

'Ralph Higgins will have told them,' decided Daniel. 'Before we caught him, he'd set himself the task of finding out as much as he could about me. I know for a fact that he was aware of my work in the Bastille. The information was volunteered to Higgins.'

'What happens now?' asked Cardonnel.

'I go to Amalia's rescue.'

'But you'd never succeed – they'd be expecting you.'

'Besides,' said Marlborough, 'I'm not willing to let one of my most able officers fall into their hands. This requires thought.'

The three of them were in the captain general's tent. Now that he was convinced of Amalia's whereabouts, Daniel wanted to get to her as soon as possible. The others were more circumspect.

'There may be another way out of this,' suggested Cardonnel. 'We could request that Miss Janssen is exchanged for one of our French prisoners.'

'They'd never agree to that,' said Daniel.

'They might do if the request came directly from me,' argued Marlborough. 'And we do have some high-ranking officers in custody.'

'It would be pointless even to make the offer, Your Grace. The only person for whom they'd exchange Amalia is me. It's only a matter of time before they propose it.'

'We can't just surrender you, Daniel.'

'You won't have to – I'll devise a plan.'

Cardonnel was sceptical. 'How can you rescue someone when she's surrounded by a massive French army?'

'There has to be a way.'

'If anyone can find it,' Marlborough commented, 'then Daniel is the man to do it. On the other hand, this may pose rather more of a challenge than the Bastille. How many men will you need?'

'I won't need any, Your Grace.'

Marlborough gaped. 'You'll go *alone?*'

'I went alone to Paris.'

'That was different. You could hide among the civilian populace there. It won't be so easy to get inside the French camp.'

'I think it will,' said Daniel, confidently. 'Though he didn't realise it, someone has given me a good idea how to go about it.'

'Really?' said Cardonnel. 'Who was that?'

'Ralph Higgins.'

* * *

Amalia was in despair. She wasn't only afraid of what might happen to her. It was Daniel's situation that troubled her even more. The love that had brought them together might well turn out to be fatal. She sensed that he couldn't resist a rescue attempt and that a trap would be laid for him. One or both of them could be put to death. Amalia believed that she'd been safe in Amsterdam but war had suddenly taken on a frightening immediacy for her. She also feared for Beatrix and for her father. When she was hurled into the coach, Amalia had heard the scream of pain from her servant. Had Beatrix been badly hurt or even killed? Either way, Emanuel Janssen would be deeply upset but he'd reserve even more anxiety for his daughter. Amalia was his only child and, since his wife had passed away, he'd grown very close to her, cherishing her, nurturing her and planning for her future. She knew how mortified he'd be by the turn of events.

Thinking about others helped to distract her from contemplating her own predicament. Her confrontation with Vendôme had been truly harrowing. Amalia had never been looked at in such an unashamedly lecherous way. The memory of it was enough to give her a hot flush. She was at the mercy of a man who might have dark designs on her and she was completely vulnerable. Though she was no longer bound and gagged, she was being held in a tent with guards outside. Escape seemed impossible. Against two armed men, she stood no chance. Against the lustful Vendôme – should he take advantage of her – she'd have no

Yet here we are with the whole matter settled.'

'Then we need to deal with the correspondence, Your Grace.'

Marlborough grimaced. 'Must we?'

'I know we're both tired but it has to be done.'

'You're right, Adam. Grand Pensionary Heinsius will expect an account of the latest developments – not that there's much to report. Then there are dispatches to be sent to England.'

'I think that we need to respond to General Vendôme first.'

'Why?'

'You were too engrossed in the council of war to see the letter that was passed to me. It bears Vendôme's seal.'

'Then let me see it,' said Marlborough, taking it from him.

'I think we both know what it will contain.'

'You're right,' said the other, opening the letter and reading it. 'An exchange is being offered.'

'We can have Amalia Janssen in return for Captain Rawson.'

'Yes, Adam – Daniel warned us that the offer would be made.'

'What do we do, Your Grace?'

'Well, we certainly won't comply with the request.'

'It's impossible to do so,' said Marlborough. 'Daniel has already left camp.' After thinking it through, he handed the letter to his secretary. 'That must be our response,' he went on. 'Tell Vendôme that we can't consider his offer because Captain Rawson is unavailable. That will at least buy us some time.'

'At least we know for certain where Miss Janssen is.'

Marlborough sighed. 'I just hope that no harm has come to her.'

'I was tricked,' said Sophie Prunier, mournfully. 'One of the officers befriended me and invited me to look at the camp. He was charming until we actually got here. Then I realised my mistake.'

'What happened?' asked Amalia.

'I was taken to see the duc de Vendôme.'

'Yes, I met him as well.'

'Then you'll know what a beast the man is,' Sophie told her. 'It was he who tore my dress. The handsome young lieutenant who brought me here was acting on his commander's orders. He had to provide a woman – and it turned out to be me.'

'That's disgusting!'

'I come from a good family. They'd be horrified if they knew that I'd ended up here.'

'Didn't you tell them that you were visiting the camp?'

Sophie looked sheepish. 'No,' she admitted. 'My parents are away. They would have objected and I was so pleased to be asked. I'd always wanted to see inside an army camp.

How was I to know that it was all a ruse?'

'The way you were deceived was cruel,' said Amalia.

Sympathy welled up inside her. The sudden and unheralded arrival of Sophie Prunier had done something remarkable. It had taken Amalia's mind off her own troubles. Instead, she was caught up in the plight of the Frenchwoman. Though she could not understand every word that Sophie said, there was no mistaking the look of fear on her face or the horror in her voice. Amalia had been abducted as a means of ensnaring Daniel Rawson. Sophie, on the other hand, was being held captive until Vendôme chose to send for her. Having been alone with him, Amalia sensed that he'd be ruthless and malevolent.

'My uncle was once the Mayor of Mons,' resumed Sophie. 'When the army passed through, he invited some of the officers to dinner. That's how I came to meet Lieutenant Bouteron. He was so kind and attentive to me. It's only now that I realise why.' Taking out a handkerchief, she used it to wipe away her tears. 'But I'm so selfish, Amalia,' she said. 'All that I can think about are my own troubles. You're a prisoner as well. Who enticed you here?'

'I was kidnapped.'

Sophie was startled. 'That must have been terrifying for you.'

'It was, Sophie.'

'What exactly happened?'

'To be honest, I'm not entirely sure.'

Amalia told her about the incident and about how she'd been smuggled out of the country by her abductors. Since she'd been bound, gagged and blindfolded most of the time, she was never quite sure where they were or how they'd eluded border patrols. The only violence she encountered was during the kidnap. From that point on, Amalia had not been maltreated in any way. It was a concession that helped to make her ordeal bearable.

'Oh, you poor thing!' said Sophie, putting a tender arm around her. 'You've suffered far more than I have. I'm only here because of my own stupidity. Against your will, you were dragged here all the way from Amsterdam.'

'My father will be sick with worry.'

'I still don't see *why* they picked on you, Amalia.'

'It's not me they want. They're trying to capture a friend of mine in the British army. I'm simply a worm on the hook. When he knows where I am, you see, he'll try to rescue me.'

'How on earth could your friend do that?' said Sophie, mystified. 'Lieutenant Bouteron told me that they have 100,000 soldiers here. No man has a chance against those odds.'

'No ordinary man, perhaps,' agreed Amalia, warmed by the thought. 'But then, Captain Rawson is far from ordinary.'

Shedding his uniform once more, Daniel had put on the coarser attire of a sutler, wearing a wide-brimmed hat that concealed some of his face. He borrowed the wagon that had once belonged to Ralph Higgins. Instead of travelling in a direct line to the French camp, thereby signalling his starting point, he went in a wide arc so that he could reach Braine l'Alleud from the south-west. His route took him past the ruins of the farm where he'd once hidden from a French patrol in a pigsty. The sight of the blackened remains served to stir up his anger at those responsible and to reinforce his determination to hunt them down.

For the moment, however, he had other concerns. Travelling alone through a country ravaged by war was always hazardous. Daniel had a dagger hidden beneath his coat and his sword was within easy reach under the seat. He hoped that he'd have to use neither of the weapons. The first part of the journey was uneventful. He even sold a few items in a village he passed through. It was when he was back out in open country that he encountered trouble. As the road dipped down an incline, a small forest appeared on his left. Out of the trees, moving at a leisurely pace, came two riders. When they got close, they waved their hands in a friendly greeting. Daniel replied with a smile and brought the wagon to a halt.

The bigger and older of the two men did the talking.

'Good day to you, friend,' he said, speaking in French.

'And good day to both of you,' replied Daniel.

'How far do you mean to travel?'

'I'll be on this road for the rest of the day.'

'Then you need to be warned,' said the man. 'You could be in danger if you don't turn off.'

'That's right,' added his companion. 'There's a band of redcoats somewhere ahead of you. We've seen them twice now. There's a rumour that they burnt down a farm. They'd certainly have no hesitation in stealing your wagon.'

'Thank you for the warning,' said Daniel, keen to know more. 'Someone has already mentioned these men to me. What exactly did you see? How many of them were there?'

The big man inhaled deeply. 'Eight or nine, I suppose.'

'And they were British soldiers?'

'Yes. They were only a few miles away from here.'

'How close did you get?'

'We kept well away from them,' said the second man. 'As soon as they came into sight, we galloped away both times. They're preying on travellers. You'd best avoid them.'

'How can I do that?'

'We know a track through the forest that will get you safely past them. Follow us and we'll show you where it is.'

'That's very kind of you,' said Daniel. 'Lead on.'

'This way, my friend,' invited the big man.

Swinging his horse round, he headed towards the forest with his companion at his side. Daniel was not deceived by their offer of help. Though their manner was pleasant and unthreatening, he sensed that they were highwaymen. What they'd told him about the marauding redcoats was probably true and he was grateful for an indication of the whereabouts of the band. At the same time, he didn't believe for a moment that the two men were going to show him a path through the forest. They'd use their sighting of the redcoats as a convenient excuse to lure Daniel off the road. Their intention was clear. Once inside the trees, they planned to kill him.

CHAPTER TWELVE

As the two men rode ahead of him, they were deep in conversation. The rattle of the cart prevented Daniel from overhearing what they were saying but he knew they were discussing his fate. When they reached the forest, his fears were amply justified. Once they were covered by the leafy canopy and shielded by the tall tree trunks, the younger of the two guides broke away from his friend and dropped back behind the wagon. Certain that it would be needed, Daniel used one hand to ease his dagger out of its sheath. It was only a question of waiting now.

The wagon rumbled on along a rutted track until it came to a clearing. When the big man raised a hand, Daniel pulled on the reins and his horse stopped. The next moment, a pistol was being held on him. There was no friendliness in the voice now.

'Get down,' he ordered.

Daniel mimed confusion. 'Why?'

'Just do as you're told.'

'I thought you were helping me.'

'Get down or I'll shoot you where you are.'

'There's no need to kill me,' said Daniel, hand tightening on the blade of the dagger. 'If you want the wagon, take it.'

'We can't leave you alive to tell your tale.' He levelled the gun. 'I won't tell you again – get down *now*.'

Daniel pretended to obey and the man lowered his weapon. He never lived to regret his mistake. In a move he'd practised many times, Daniel hurled the dagger with speed and accuracy. It buried itself deep in the man's chest, knocking him from the saddle and making him drop the pistol. With a yell of rage, the other man dismounted at once and clambered on the back of the wagon to take revenge. Daniel was ready for him, whisking his sword out from its hiding place under the seat. Armed only with a dagger, the man was at a disadvantage but he was resourceful. Grabbing a wooden bucket from among the provisions, he used it to flail away at Daniel, dislodging some of the hoops over which the sheet of canvas was spread to protect the wagon from bad weather.

The confined space made it difficult for Daniel to evade him and the sword was no match for a bucket being wielded frantically by a wild young man. When he tried a thrust at him, the weapon was buffeted out of Daniel's hand and landed on the ground. He jumped down to retrieve it but his adversary was too quick for him, throwing the bucket at him and dazing him slightly with a glancing blow to the head. In the seconds it took for Daniel to recover, the other man had leapt to the ground and seized the weapon for himself. Dagger in one hand and sword in the other, he let out a roar of anger.

'You killed my brother!' he shouted.

'He deserved to be killed,' replied Daniel, edging his way towards the dead body. 'Both of you are thieves and murderers.'

'I'll cut you to threads!'

'Stay back,' said Daniel, stooping down swiftly to pick up the discarded gun and aiming it at him. The man laughed derisively. 'What's so amusing?'

'It's not loaded. We have no ammunition.'

'Then you'd better have it back,' said Daniel, throwing it at him and hitting him full in the face.

Nose streaming with blood, the man staggered back a few paces. In the brief time he was given, Daniel pulled his dagger from the chest of the corpse and picked up the bucket as well. He was now able to defend himself and circled his attacker warily. The bucket was a crude but effective weapon. Every time his adversary tried to thrust or hack at him, Daniel used the bucket to ward him off. Time and again it was a life-saving shield even though splinters were hacked off it by the sharp blade. The longer the fight went on, the more frustrated the man became and the less careful. Hoping to overpower Daniel by the sheer force of his attack, he suddenly lunged at him with the sword flashing through the air.

Daniel was far too agile for him. Leaping nimbly sideways, he swung the bucket hard against the side of the man's head, knocking him to the ground. Howling in pain, the highwayman sat up and flung his dagger with murderous force, only to see it embedded in the bottom of the bucket that Daniel held up in front of him. Daniel tossed away his improvised shield and dived on top of him. At close quarters, the sword was useless. It was the blood-stained dagger that made the difference. Though the man grabbed Daniel's wrist and tried to twist the weapon from his grasp, he lacked the strength to hold out for long. His breathing was heavy, his grip weakening. The stink of his breath was foul. After punching him repeatedly with his free hand, Daniel pulled his other wrist free and stabbed the man through the heart, holding the dagger up to the hilt inside the body as the life drained slowly out of him and the frenzied resistance finally stopped.

'How long have you known Captain Rawson?' asked Sophie.

'It must be well over two years now,' said Amalia, fondly.

'Do you see much of him?'

'Not as much as I'd like, Sophie.'

'My sister married a soldier. He's away for months on end. She's worried to death in case he's injured or even killed in battle. The danger is always there. I suppose,' Sophie went on, 'you must have the same fears.'

'I try not to think about such things.'

'That's very sensible.'

'Daniel – Captain Rawson, that is – always claims that he has the luck of the devil. But there's more to it than that. I think he's just a very fine soldier.'

'I thought that of Lieutenant Bouteron. He looked so wonderful in his uniform – so wonderful and so trustworthy.' Sophie's head sagged. 'I didn't realise that he was misleading me. When he handed me over to the duc de Vendôme, I was shocked. I've never been looked at like that before. It was horrible.'

'He looked that way at me as well.'

'The man is so revolting.'

Since they supported opposing sides in the war, they were unlikely friends but adversity made light of their differences. They were both victims and their fate would be determined by a man they'd both detested on sight. Amalia was glad to have company. In talking about her situation, she'd gained a small measure of relief. Listening to Sophie, she realised that they lived in very different worlds. The other woman seemed so much more sophisticated and her beautiful dress made Amalia feel dowdy. Sophie's father was a wealthy merchant who was away from home a great deal. His daughter was bored and restless. When invited to dine at her uncle's house in Mons, she'd accepted with alacrity and revelled in the company of soldiers. It was there that she met the man who'd brought her to the camp under false pretences.

'Isn't it strange?' said Sophie, musing.

'I don't follow.'

'Well, by rights, we ought to be trying to tear each other's hair out. You support one army and I'm loyal to another. In my heart, I want the whole British and Dutch armies to be defeated.'

'I want the French to be beaten,' confessed Amalia.

'Yet none of it matters now, does it?'

'No, it would be silly for us to argue. In some ways, we're on the same side now. We're both at the mercy of that dreadful man.'

'Mercy?' echoed Sophie, resignedly. 'I don't think he knows the meaning of the word.' She wrung her hands. 'I should have stayed at home where I belong.'

'Does anyone else know that you're here?'

'No, that's the trouble. Nobody can come to my aid.'

Amalia felt another upsurge of sympathy. Before she could put a consoling arm around her, however, the tent flap opened and two guards stepped in. One of them pointed at Sophie.

'You're wanted – now.'

'Where are you taking me?' asked Sophie, tremulously.

'You'll soon find out.'

He grabbed her by the arm and took her out of the tent. When Amalia tried to follow, the other guard raised his musket at her and she drew back instantly. He, too, then went out of the tent, leaving her to worry about what might happen to her new friend and whether or not she herself might also be the victim of the commander's lust.

Though they'd tried to kill him, Daniel nevertheless believed that the two men were entitled to a decent burial. After digging two shallow graves, therefore, he lowered each of them into the ground and covered them with earth. He mouthed a silent prayer then turned to see what they'd bequeathed him. The two horses were a valuable acquisition and might come in useful if he was unable to sneak Amalia out of the French camp in his wagon. The saddlebags yielded up some welcome surprises. Apart from food and wine, they contained a telescope, a tattered map of Flanders and lots of stolen money. Evidently, other travellers had not been as cautious as Daniel. After pocketing the money, he kept the telescope and the map. He also put his sword back in the wagon and, after wiping it clean in the grass, he slipped his dagger into its sheath. The weapons belonging to the two men were concealed beneath the upturned bucket. Daniel repaired the wooden hoops then pulled the canvas back over them so that the contents of the wagon were hidden from view.

With the horses tied to the vehicle, he climbed up to the seat again and set off, driving back along the track he'd taken to reach the clearing. When he emerged from the shadows of the forest, he blinked in the bright sunshine until his eyes became accustomed to the glare. While they'd lied about most things, Daniel believed that the men had told him the truth about the band of redcoats. If they roamed the area in search of prey, they may well have heard rumours about burnt farmhouses and butchered people. It was more than possible that they'd actually caught sight of the marauders.

As a result, Daniel kept his eyes peeled as he moved along, using the telescope to scan the landscape ahead. He saw other travellers a mile or more before he actually passed them but it was when he crested a hill that he spotted something of real interest. Far off to his right was a copse. At first glance, he noticed nothing and the telescope swept on. When it returned to the copse, however, Daniel saw something glinting in the sun. Concentrating his gaze on the trees, he watched for a couple of minutes until he realised what he was looking at. The object that glinted was a sabre and the man wearing it was in the uniform of the British army.

Matt Searle was enjoying a wrestling contest with one of the men when he heard the call from the lookout on the hill. The combatants immediately broke off and used the back of their hands to wipe away the sweat on their brows. The lookout descended the hill.

'It's Edwin,' he told them, 'and he's in a hurry.'

Searle tensed. 'Is anyone after him?'

'No, Matt.'

'He'd better not be leading anyone here, that's all I can say.'

The thunder of hooves got closer then Lock came galloping into the yard before reining in his horse. He remained in the saddle.

'I've just seen a wagon, Matt,' he announced.

'Where was it?' asked Searle.

'It was only a couple of miles from here.'

'How many people were on it?'

'There was just the one,' said Lock, pleased that he was able to pass on good news. 'The wagon was pulling two horses along.'

'Which way was it heading, Edwin?'

'It was going south, towards French territory.'

'Then we'd better catch it before it gets there,' decided Searle. 'Mount up, everyone! It's time for some highway robbery.'

When all seven of them had climbed into the saddle, Lock led them back in the direction from which they'd come. Burning a farmhouse after ravishing the women inside it was a more exciting venture for them but a lone wagon was too good a windfall to resist. Spare horses could always be sold at market for a high price and the wagon was bound to have something of value aboard. Searle rode beside his cousin who, after so many months with the band, had become such a competent horseman that he could be sent out on foraging expeditions. This particular one had delivered a prize.

'Who was driving the wagon?' asked Searle.

'It was too far away for me to see that,' said Lock. 'All I know is that there was only one person.'

'Well done, Edwin.'

'He won't try to run away from us. When he sees us coming, he'll think we're going to offer him our protection. We'll have a sitting target, Matt.'

'We will – and you can have the pleasure of killing him.'

They rode on until they reached the copse in which Lock had been hiding then veered off to join the road far beyond. Once on that, it was only a case of maintaining a steady speed and they'd overhaul the wagon. Searle yelled a command and the riders who'd been spread out behind him moved in to ride in twos. Seen by the driver of the wagon, they'd look like a British patrol. Mile after mile went by until they finally caught a glimpse of their quarry. Yet even as he came into view, they realised that their journey had been futile. A line of wagons was rolling along and the man they were after was about to join the convoy. The prize had slipped through their fingers.

'Shit!' exclaimed Searle before spitting on the ground. 'Let's go back, lads. There are far too many of them now. He was lucky.'

* * *

Sophie Prunier was away for almost half an hour and Amalia feared that she might not come back. If she'd been taken to Vendôme, she reasoned, the woman might be forced to spend the night there. What would happen to her in those circumstances was unimaginable. While she clearly had some spirit, she could not hold a strong man at bay. Amalia was just about to give up all hope of seeing her again when the tent flap opened and Sophie stumbled back into the tent. She was even more dishevelled than before and was close to tears. Amalia helped her to one of the stools.

'What happened?' she asked.

Sophie was panting. 'It was awful,' she said.

'Did they take you to the commander?'

'No, Amalia.'

'Then where did you go?'

'I went to Lieutenant Bouteron's quarters. He apologised for bringing me here and said it was a big mistake. He begged me to forgive him.'

'You should have asked for his help,' said Amalia. 'You should have appealed to his sense of honour.'

'That's exactly what I did.'

'How did he react?'

'He gave me his word that he'd get me out of the camp.'

'That's marvellous – when do you leave?'

'I'm not going anywhere, Amalia.'

'But you just said that you were.'

'There's something I haven't told you,' said Sophie. 'My

freedom came at a price. Lieutenant Bouteron promised that he'd secure my release but on one condition.'

'And what was that?'

'I had to give myself to him.'

She buried her face in her hands. Amalia was too shocked to speak. The other woman had been cruelly betrayed. Brought into the camp in order, as she thought, to be shown around, she was unable to leave without sacrificing her virginity. Amalia felt desperately sorry for her and alarmed about her own position.

'There was something else he told me,' said Sophie, uncovering her face. 'The lieutenant swore that he'd be considerate to me but that I wasn't to look for the same consideration from the duc de Vendôme. He has a terrible reputation where women are concerned, it seems. There's no way out, Amalia,' she went on, helplessly. 'If I stay here in the camp, then sooner or later, I'll be summoned to his tent to let that monster have his way with me.'

The council of war held in the French camp was relatively brisk. Since they were approving royal commands sent from Versailles, none of the generals present raised any objection. Hoping to bask in the sun of supreme command, the Duke of Burgundy was irritated when he wasn't allowed to do so. Instead, people kept deferring to Vendôme and putting the questions to him. When the meeting had ended and everyone had dispersed, Burgundy was left alone with his second in command. He was in a bad mood.

'There was no need for you to speak so much, my lord Duke,' he said, tetchily. 'We could have done without your lectures.'

Vendôme smiled. 'When answers are requested from me, it would be impolite not to provide them. I said nothing with which you disagree, my lord, did I?'

'That's beside the point. They all kept looking at you.'

'I'll be the first to acknowledge that you are a more handsome spectacle. Why they stared at me, I simply can't imagine.'

Burgundy was piqued by the complacency in his voice. Trying to hide his displeasure, he tackled Vendôme on another matter.

'I hear disturbing rumours about you,' he began.

'Ignore them,' advised Vendôme. 'They're bound to be lies.'

'They concern the business with Major Crevel. It's come to my attention that you won't consign the matter to the past and have taken steps to identify the man who actually humiliated Crevel.'

'His name is Captain Rawson of the 24th Foot.'

'So?'

'He must be punished for what he did.'

'Our aim is to punish the armies of the Grand Alliance not to single out an individual member of them. This fellow can surely not deserve the time and attention lavished upon him.'

'Your grandfather might think otherwise, my lord.'

'Why ever should he do that?' asked Burgundy.

'Because this same Captain Rawson was the instrument of great annoyance to His Majesty,' said Vendôme. 'Emanuel Janssen, a tapestry maker of renown, was commissioned to work at Versailles. Instead of devoting himself to the weaving of the tapestry, he acted as a spy and sent intelligence to the enemy. Janssen was imprisoned in the Bastille for his crime. Captain Rawson rescued him.'

'Nobody ever escapes from the Bastille.'

'Janssen is living proof to the contrary. I fancy that His Majesty would be extremely interested to meet the man who achieved that astonishing feat.'

'I do believe he would,' conceded Burgundy. 'I'd be curious to see the fellow myself but he's hardly likely to oblige us by coming here of his own volition.'

'That's where you're quite mistaken.'

'Oh?'

'A stratagem has been set in motion,' said Vendôme with a self-important smirk. 'My guess is that Captain Rawson is on his way here at this very moment.'

Travelling as part of the cavalcade gave Daniel the safety of numbers. The other wagons were taking supplies and munitions to the camp at Braine l'Alleud and were protected by a detachment of soldiers in the blue uniforms of the French army. Daniel hadn't been accepted without close questioning. He'd had to show his forged papers and explain why he was on his own. Only after he'd given satisfactory answers was he told to fall in at the rear of the column. While progress was slow, he at least had the reassurance that he'd be admitted to the camp without undue interrogation. Certain that Amalia Janssen was there, he prayed that she was unharmed.

After a long journey, he finally saw the canvas tents spreading endlessly across the fields and got ocular proof of the sheer size of the enemy army. What particularly interested him were the positions of the picquets and the proximity of trees. Leaving the camp with Amalia, he knew, would be far more difficult than entering it in his wagon. His hopes of success rested on careful preparation. The telescope enabled him to inspect all of the outposts on the western approach and he resolved to study the map he'd inherited from the highwaymen in order to have a clearer sense of the local geography.

When he got to the area where the other camp followers were drawn up, he made sure that his wagon stayed on the outer edge so that it could slip away easily in the night. He then fed and watered the three horses. His arrival had been noted by some of the other sutlers and they were not pleased to have competition. Daniel was confronted by three of them. Their spokesman was a wizened old man with a goatee beard and a single, inflamed eye.

'Who are you?' he demanded, pointing a skeletal finger.

'My wagon should tell you that,' replied Daniel.

'We don't need another sutler.'

'Why do you say that? In an army this size, there's surely enough trade for us all.'

'We were here first.'

'Then you'll already have regular customers who rely on you. I'm not here to take them away.'

'We don't want you here at all,' said a short, wiry individual who, from his close resemblance to the old man, was obviously his son. 'We think you should leave camp.'

Daniel smiled defiantly. 'Thank you for your advice,' he said, 'but that's a decision I'd like to make for myself.'

'We're making it for you.'

'Leave now,' ordered the old man, folding his arms, 'or we'll have to persuade you.'

Daniel looked at each of them in turn. The old man posed no problem in a fight but his son was a very different matter. The real challenge, however, would come from their companion, a big, broad-shouldered man in his thirties with a drooping black moustache. If he was to survive a brawl, Daniel would have to tackle the bigger man first. Pretending to accept their warning, he offered his hand.

'I bid you farewell, gentlemen,' he said, meekly.

The big man reached out to shake the hand and found himself yanked forward, tripped up by Daniel and kicked so hard in the groin that he lay writhing in agony on the ground. Shocked by what he'd seen, the young man came at Daniel with both fists swinging but none of the punches landed where they were intended. Daniel dodged or parried them with his arms, using clever footwork to put his attacker off balance. At one point, when his back was to the old man, Daniel felt a blow to the nape of his neck. He responded by digging a sharp elbow into the old man's stomach, taking all the wind out of him and making him stagger back.

The son was already puffing and panting, his energy depleted and his confidence waning when he realised that he was now fighting alone. As a last resort, he aimed a violent kick at his opponent's groin, only to be upended as Daniel grabbed the foot and pulled hard. A relay of punches to the son's head quickly subdued him. But the brawl was not over. The big man was sufficiently recovered to be able to get to his feet. One hand on his tender genitals, he circled Daniel and threatened to tear him apart. When he finally launched himself, however, he was far too slow and ponderous. Daniel ducked and dodged every wild punch. Growling with rage, the big man flailed away with his massive fists and had to take a number of well-directed counter punches to the face and stomach. Fatigue eventually got the better of him and Daniel was able to jump in and fell him with an uppercut to the chin.

Seeing his other attacker rise to his feet, Daniel seized him by his collar and was about to dash him against the side of the wagon when the old man cried out.

'That's enough!' he said. 'Don't touch Alphonse. The fight is over. You can stay.'

Daniel released the son then turned to his other adversary. Dazed and sobered, the man held up a hand to indicate that he'd had enough. Daniel helped him to his feet and apologised for hitting him so hard. The three men laughed ruefully. Having come to evict him, they now gave him a warm welcome. Daniel was one of them. After introducing himself as Gustave Carraud, he brought out a flagon of wine and they were soon chatting together as friends.

'I haven't come to take away your business,' said Daniel. 'In fact, I've got provisions that I can sell to you at very low prices.'

'I like the sound of that,' said Alphonse.

'Do you have any ointment for sore balls?' asked the big man, still rubbing his testicles.

'Find a pretty woman to kiss them better, Victor.'

Victor guffawed. 'She can do more than that while she's down there, Alphonse.'

The wine flowed, the laughter increased and the friendship slowly deepened. Daniel was quick to enlist them as allies. They told him how the camp was laid out and where best to sell his goods.

'You obviously know your way around,' he said.

'It's part of our job,' Alphonse told him. 'We stay close to regiments who've bought from us in the past. We have a reputation.'

'A *good* reputation,' added the old man. 'If you want to take a look at the camp for yourself, Alphonse will show you the way.'

'I'd appreciate that,' said Daniel.

'Wait till this evening,' advised Alphonse, 'when the light fades. There won't be so many soldiers about then so we're less likely to be stopped.'

'That suits me.'

'Watch him, Alphonse,' warned Victor, chuckling. 'If he offers to shake you by the hand, refuse or you'll have a boot in your bollocks.'

'I'm sorry I had to do that,' said Daniel. 'I was up against unfair odds so I had to disable one of you.'

'The brawl is over now, Gustave,' said the old man. 'We're all friends.'

'Let's drink to that.'

Daniel found another flagon of wine in his wagon and passed it round. The mood became even friendlier and the sutlers began to reminisce about the years they'd spent trailing after French armies. It was interesting to hear their descriptions of battles in which Daniel had fought. When they cursed the Duke of Marlborough in colourful language, Daniel didn't object. It was a perverted form of flattery. What was evident was that all three of them felt that a French victory was now inevitable.

'Why do you believe that?' asked Daniel.

'We've talked to the soldiers,' said Alphonse. 'They've told us they can't fail this time.'

'That will depend on their commanders.'

'Vendôme is a good general,' said the old man,

knowledgeably. 'He made a fool of Marlborough last year. We know – we were there.'

'What about the duc de Burgundy?'

'He's young but he has royal blood. That counts for a lot. His Majesty wouldn't have put him in charge if he didn't have faith in his grandson. The duc is a fine-looking man.'

'You've seen him, then?'

'We've seen them all,' boasted Alphonse. 'I'll show you where his quarters are, if you wish.'

'Thank you,' said Daniel. 'I'd like that. And I'd very much like to see where Vendôme has his quarters as well.'

'Then you will, Gustave. You can count on me.'

Daniel was grateful. If Amalia was in the camp, he surmised that she'd be kept somewhere close to Vendôme. Thanks to his friendship with the three men, he wouldn't have to grope around in the dark, trying to locate the right area of the camp. Alphonse would lead him right to it. Unaware that they might be aiding and abetting an enemy soldier, the sutlers talked and joked for hours. They told Daniel everything he needed to know. It was a good omen.

CHAPTER THIRTEEN

With every hour that passed, Emanuel Janssen became more anxious. Unable to sleep, he was so concerned about his daughter's safety that he was also unable to work. All that he did during the day was to pace the house restlessly then dash to the front door whenever someone rang the bell. However, the good news for which he yearned never came. Beatrix was equally despondent and kept blaming herself for the abduction. She'd been Amalia's chaperone at the time and felt that she'd let her down badly. Janssen had to reassure her constantly.

'It was my fault,' she wailed yet again.

'Don't think that for a moment,' he said. 'You were up against strong and determined men. You had no chance.'

'I should have fought back.'

'How could you when you'd been shoved to the ground?'

'I failed.'

'That's nonsense!'

'Wherever Miss Amalia is,' said Beatrix, stricken by remorse, 'she's probably blaming me for letting her get kidnapped.'

'Amalia would never do that. She's more likely to be wondering how you are. According to your story, you let out such a scream when you were thrown to the ground that she must have heard it.' He peered solicitously at her. 'How *are* you now, Beatrix?'

'The bruises still hurt.'

'You were lucky that no bones were broken.'

'Forget me,' she said, bravely. 'The only person we should both be thinking about now is Miss Amalia. *Why* did someone do that to her? I just can't fathom it out.'

'No more can I,' admitted Janssen, running a nervous hand across his furrowed brow. 'I keep returning to the notion that it must somehow be connected with me.'

'Oh, I don't believe that.'

'The French must have been very angry when I slipped from their grasp in the Bastille. This could be a means of revenge.'

'Then why wait so long to take it?'

'Who knows?'

'Besides,' she went on, face puckered in concentration as

she thought it through, 'if they wanted revenge, why didn't they kidnap *you* instead? I think there's another reason, sir.'

'I've been racking my brains trying to think what it is.'

'So have I.'

They were in the *voorhuis*, the entrance hall to the Janssen house. While he was continually on the move, rubbing his hands and chewing his lip, she was standing in a corner, her face still bruised from the fall. Beatrix kept searching through her memory of the fateful day for a forgotten detail that might shed some light on the motives of the kidnappers. Because she could find no explanation, her fears became more and more extreme.

'We're not even sure that Miss Amalia is still alive,' she said.

Janssen was firm. 'Don't say that, Beatrix. We *have* to believe that she's alive. If they intended to kill her, then they'd have done so when they attacked the pair of you. No,' he decided, fighting off a rising despair, 'I won't entertain the idea that my daughter is dead. Amalia is alive.'

'But where is she?'

'I wish I knew.'

'My fear is that she may have been smuggled on board a ship and taken off to be sold into slavery. You hear tales of beautiful young women being handed over to Turks or Arabs so that they can...'

Her voice tailed off but her expressive face completed the sentence. Janssen refused to consider the possibility. Once he let such terrible thoughts into his mind, he'd be in torment. He was an intelligent and rational man. Having to calm his servant's nerves helped him to keep his own demons at bay. Unlike the fretful Beatrix, he was no martyr to a vivid imagination.

She suddenly remembered the letter he'd sent.

'Have you heard from the Duke of Marlborough?' she asked.

'Not yet, I'm afraid.'

'Will he pass on your message to Captain Rawson?'

'I'm sure of it, Beatrix.'

'The captain will be as anxious as we are. He adores Miss Amalia.' She gave an involuntary shiver. 'He'll probably think it was my fault that this happened.'

'He's far too sensible to do that.'

'Then why do I feel so *guilty*?'

'For the same reason that I feel guilty,' he replied. 'We both feel a duty of care to Amalia. Yet at the very time she needed us most, we weren't able to save her. You're not the only one to feel responsible. I lie awake at night, squirming with guilt. I keep telling myself that, as her father, I should have been there.'

'Amsterdam is such a safe city as a rule,' said Beatrix, dolefully. 'When we walked the streets, we never sensed any danger.'

'That's why you and Amalia were caught off guard.'

'Where on earth can she *be*?'

As if in answer to her plea, the bell rang and they both turned to the front door. Beatrix rushed to open it wide, only to meet with grave disappointment. Instead of word from Amalia, it was a delivery of wool and silk. Janssen asked the servant to take it into the workshop. Left alone, he clasped his hands in prayer and looked upward.

'Dear God,' he said, '*please* keep Amalia free from harm.'

'Father will be driven insane by worry,' said Amalia, 'and so will Beatrix. She's been like a second mother to me. But then,' she went on, looking at Sophie, 'your parents will be suffering as well.'

'They won't,' said Sophie, 'because they have no idea that I've gone astray. Father had business in Paris so he took Mother with him. I thank heaven that they know nothing at all about this.'

'If they did, they could come to your rescue.'

'They'd be shocked that I let myself get into this position.'

'You were deceived. They can't blame you for that.'

'Yes, they can, Amalia. They think that I've always been too headstrong. Mother will be horrified but Father will chastise me. He brought me up to be wary of invitations from men. To be honest, I hope that my parents never learn the truth.'

'But they're *bound* to, Sophie.'

'Only if I tell them and I'm too ashamed to do that.'

It was evening and the two women were talking in

their tent over the remains of the meal they'd been served. Candles cast flickering shadows on the canvas. Seated on a stool apiece, they sipped cups of wine. The food had been good and the wine was more than tolerable so they were at least being cared for properly. Amalia still clung to the hope that Daniel would somehow come for her but Sophie had lapsed into a dull resignation. Accepting what she feared was inevitable, she stared at the ground. Amalia was upset at the way her companion's spirit seemed to have drained out of her.

'All may yet be well,' she predicted.

Sophie was inconsolable. 'How can it be?'

'You must never give up hope.'

'What possible hope *is* there for me, Amalia?'

'I can't say for certain. What I can tell you is that, when my father disappeared in Paris, I never gave in to horrid thoughts. Difficult as it was, I simply kept faith that it would somehow all come right in the end.' Amalia smiled at the memory. 'And it did.'

'That was only because you had someone to ride to your rescue. I have nobody in my life like that. Captain Rawson treated you with respect,' said Sophie, enviously, 'but I've had little of that. Lieutenant Bouteron is more interested in capturing me than helping me escape.'

'He may yet relent.'

'You don't know him, Amalia.'

'He can't keep you here against your will.'

'Yes, he can,' said Sophie. 'I'm not the first woman to be tricked like this and I don't suppose I'll be the last. The lieutenant told me that the last one was glad to offer herself to him in return for her freedom — though I'm not sure that I believe that. Quite frankly, after what's happened so far, I can't trust anything he says.'

Sophie fell silent. Wanting to comfort her new friend, Amalia couldn't think of anything to do or say. Her fear was that both of them might be victims of the duc de Vendôme's lechery. Whenever she thought of the way that he'd looked her up and down, she felt nauseous. It was a new and unsettling experience for her. Though Amalia had been brought to the camp to act as a hostage, it might not be her only function. She, too, could be forcibly deflowered. The very notion made her feel faint. Amalia was highly sympathetic to Sophie's plight but she was now even more in dread of what might befall her as well. Her hopes began to wane. Even if Daniel did eventually come for her, he might well be too late to save her from molestation. As the evening wore on, Amalia felt increasingly defenceless.

When the summons finally came, it was not for her. The tent flap was pulled abruptly back and two men stepped into the tent. One was an officer and the other a guard. Amalia and Sophie rose to their feet and retreated a few paces. The officer stood with both hands on his hips.

'Well,' he said to Sophie, 'have you made your decision yet?'

'Leave me alone,' she pleaded.

'Since you reject me, I'll hand you over to someone else.'

'Is this how you treat guests to the camp, Lieutenant Bouteron?'

He grinned. 'That depends how pretty they are.' His eyes flicked to Amalia. 'And it's a long time since we've had two visitors as pretty as both of you.' He extended a hand to Sophie. 'Are you coming?'

'No,' she retorted with a show of defiance.

'Then you'll need some assistance.'

Bouteron nodded to the guard. Moving quickly, the man took Sophie firmly by the arm. When Amalia tried to stop her from being dragged off, she was brushed aside by the lieutenant who then followed the others out. Fired by a mixture of fear and anger, Amalia tried to go after them, only to find that she was staring down the barrel of the musket that the outside guard aimed at her. All that she could do was to withdraw into the tent. Sophie had gone. It might be Amalia's turn next. Dropping onto a stool, she burst into tears.

The tour was very thorough. As they walked through the camp, Alphonse was able to make clandestine deliveries of tobacco and wine to some of his customers. He'd been following French armies all his life yet had somehow managed to avoid being recruited. He told Daniel that he came from a family of sutlers who'd spent the best part of a century meeting the needs of soldiers on the march. Daniel was less interested in this personal history than he was in the way that the camp was laid out. Everywhere they went, he made a mental note of what he saw. When campfires pierced the gloom from time to time, they kept to the shadows to evade attention. Eventually, they came to the quarters occupied by Vendôme. From inside the tent came sounds of revelry.

'He likes to enjoy himself,' said Alphonse.

'I see.'

'There's no trade for us here, Gustave. Commanders have their own source of supplies. We do our business with the lower ranks. Victor, of course, is always in demand.'

'Why is that?' asked Daniel.

'He's a blacksmith. The cavalry always have need of him.'

'Then he had no call to attack me.'

'You're lucky that it was Victor and not his wife,' said Alphonse with a chortle. 'She's even bigger and stronger than he is. While Victor is shoeing horses, Josette sells from the back of their wagon. He didn't want you to take away any of her trade.'

Daniel let him babble on, only half-listening to Alphonse's mixture of advice, reminiscence and crude humour. Eyes now accustomed to the darkness, Daniel kept looking for the most likely place where Amalia might be detained. There were guards outside Vendôme's quarters but few other people were about. What he was looking for was another tent protected by armed guards but none presented itself. He and Alphonse were about to move on when two figures emerged like ghosts out of the murky heart of the camp. A woman was being hustled along by a soldier with a musket. Daniel's stomach lurched. Suspecting that it was Amalia, he instinctively took a few steps forward before checking himself. To attack her escort now would be foolish. He'd be giving himself away. He and Amalia were certain to be caught. Alarmed as he was at the way she was being manhandled, Daniel had to bide his time.

As the couple approached a tent in the shadows, another guard came out of it. He and the first man pushed the woman inside then remained where they were on sentry duty. Daniel was at once angry and grateful, incensed by the rough treatment he'd witnessed yet indebted to the soldiers for the guidance they'd given. The trip around the camp with Alphonse had yielded a bonus.

He knew where Amalia was being held.

In fact, the woman he'd seen only in outline had been Sophie Prunier. Thrust into the tent, she had difficulty staying upright at first and Amalia had to steady her. Something had clearly happened. Sophie had a hunted look to her. Sinking down on to a stool, she put her face in her hands and sobbed quietly. Amalia didn't disturb her. The other woman patently wanted to be alone with her thoughts. To ask her to describe her ordeal would be unkind and improper. When she was ready to talk, she would. Amalia therefore kept a silent vigil beside her, noting the way that she hunched her shoulders and kept her face hidden. Sophie had been away from the tent for some time so her fellow prisoner was bound to speculate on where she'd been. Having met Lieutenant Bouteron – albeit fleetingly – Amalia was in a position to make a judgement. Compared to Vendôme, he was definitely the lesser of two evils.

It was well over twenty minutes before Sophie lowered her hands and sat up. She was too embarrassed to meet Amalia's gaze. All she did was to mumble a few words.

'Please don't ask me.'

'No,' said Amalia. 'I promise.'

'I'm so tired, so very tired.'

'Then you must rest.'

It was difficult to tell if Sophie was genuinely fatigued or simply unable to bear the weight of humiliation. At all events, she stretched herself out on one of the camp beds and turned her face away. Amalia placed a blanket gently over her. Nothing more was said. Sophie either fell asleep or went off into a reverie. Amalia decided to get what rest she could while she still had the opportunity. There was always the possibility that she, too, might be hauled out during the night to satisfy someone's lust. As she lay on the other camp bed, she pulled the blanket up over her head in the vain hope that it might shield her from her worst fears. They continued to gnaw at her brain.

Amalia had lost all track of time. She would never know if it was an hour or two before she finally dozed off. What was certain was that sleep did nothing to soothe her troubled mind. It confronted her with new and more hideous terrors. Twisting and turning on the camp bed, she was lucky not to fall off. At one point in her nightmare, she felt as if someone was trying to cut open her skull with a sharp knife. Amalia could hear the bone being sawn through by the blade. A hand then closed over her mouth and she came awake with a start to discover a figure bending over her in the darkness. Thinking that someone had come to kill her, she fought back with her puny strength.

'It's *me*, Amalia,' whispered Daniel. 'Don't struggle.'

She almost cried with relief. 'How did you get here?'

'I cut through the canvas.'

'So that was the noise I heard. I thought my head was being split open by someone.' She sat up and embraced him. 'Oh, I'm so glad to see you, Daniel.'

'Keep your voice down,' he said. 'I've come to rescue you.'

'What about Sophie?'

'Who is she?'

'She's my friend,' said Amalia, indicating the other bed. 'We can't leave without her.'

Speaking softly into his ear, she gave him a terse account of what Sophie Prunier was doing there. Daniel was forced to make a hasty decision. Crossing to the other bed, he put one hand over Sophie's mouth and used the other to rouse her.

When the woman's eyes blinked open, Amalia reassured her that she was in no danger. Introduced to Daniel and offered the chance of escape, Sophie took time to come fully awake and make up her mind. She kept glancing nervously in the direction of the two guards outside the tent.

'Would you rather stay here?' asked Amalia.

'No,' said Sophie, getting up. 'I'll come.'

'Hold on for a moment,' said Daniel.

The women watched while he put a stool on each of the camp beds and covered it with the blanket to make it look as if someone was still there. Then he blew out all but one of the candles. In the dark, all that could be seen were the lumps in the two beds. Daniel believed they'd be enough to deceive anyone who happened to glance in.

He led the way through the slit in the rear of the tent then folded it back in position. Signalling for them to stay low and keep silent, Daniel set off and took them on a meandering path through the camp, skirting any signs of activity. Amalia and Sophie obeyed every order. When he dived full length on the grass and told them to follow suit, they did so without hesitation. Nor did they object to crawling through a hedge then wading up to their knees through a stream. It seemed to take an age to reach the perimeter of the camp. In order to elude the picquets, they had to go down on their stomachs again and inch their way along the ground as soundlessly as possible. By the time they reached the safety of a stand of trees, Amalia and Sophie were soaked, filthy and trembling with fright.

Daniel tried to instil confidence in them by stressing that the worst was over. Under the cover of the trees, he was able to lead them to the place where he'd earlier concealed the two horses he'd brought into the camp. They were sufficiently far away from danger to be able to speak to each other at last.

'I know that Amalia can ride,' he said. 'What about you, Sophie?'

'Yes,' she replied, 'I learnt to ride as a girl.'

'Mount up and follow this road until you come to an old mill. It's quite dilapidated but a useful place to hide. I noticed it on the way here. Wait for me at the mill.'

'Where will you be?' asked Amalia, worried.

'I have to retrieve my wagon,' he explained. 'If I can get that out of the camp, you'll be able to travel in a little more comfort.'

'What if we get lost?'

'Stay on this road and there's no chance of that, Amalia.'

'How long will you be?'

'That will depend on how lucky I am. I should be no more than an hour. If I'm not there by dawn, ride off without me.'

Amalia was aghast. 'We can't do that, Daniel.'

'Do you want to be recaptured?'

'No, no…it's frightening in there.'

'Then do as I say,' he went on, handing her his map. 'There's a road that runs north from the mill. When you have enough light, you'll see from the map that it will take you to Terbanck where our army is camped. I'll follow you somehow.'

'I still can't believe that you got here, Captain Rawson,' said Sophie, unable to understand his conversation with Amalia in Dutch. 'How did you get inside the camp?'

'I'll tell you that in due course,' he replied, speaking in French. 'Ride off to the old mill with Amalia. There's food and wine in the saddlebags to sustain you.'

'Thank you. I can't tell you what this means to me.'

'There's no time to talk,' he told them. 'I need to sneak back into the camp for the wagon. I'll be as quick as I can.'

After helping Amalia up into the saddle, he did the same for Sophie, repeating his orders once more. Scared that he'd no longer be with them, they left with misgivings. Daniel watched them go until they were swallowed up by the darkness. He then went back to the camp along the same route used to leave it, eluding the picquets and going in a wide circle towards the area where his wagon was waiting. The horse was harnessed and the vehicle was ready to leave even though he wasn't entirely sure how or if he'd get it out of the camp. Alphonse had unwittingly shown him one possibility. It would involve taking the wagon across the stream higher up where the noise he'd create was less likely to be overheard.

The main object of the exercise had been achieved. Amalia had been rescued and she was now relatively safe. The presence of Sophie Prunier was an unforeseen complication but one that had to be accommodated. Daniel had seen the bond that had grown up between the two women during their imprisonment. Sophie had obviously helped Amalia endure the horrors of being in French hands and, for that reason alone, Daniel was willing to involve her in the escape. First, however, he had to retrieve his wagon.

Creeping between the tents, he reached the area where the camp followers were stationed and moved between their carts and wagons like a phantom. Nobody stirred. When he was almost there, Daniel allowed himself a moment of self-congratulation. So far his plan had worked to perfection. There was only one problem.

His wagon had disappeared.

'They should have caught them by now,' complained Welbeck.

'I agree, Sergeant,' said Jonathan Ainley. 'But, as far as I know, they haven't had so much of a glimpse of the band.'

'They must be hiding somewhere.'

'That's the problem. In this terrain, there are far too many excellent hiding places. Whenever they see one of our patrols, the villains simply go to ground. At least,' he added, 'there have been no more incidents.'

'That proves nothing, sir.'

'No, I suppose that it doesn't.'

They were standing outside Lieutenant Ainley's quarters and Welbeck was showing impatience. Having seen the way that the marauding redcoats had destroyed a farm, he was desperate to hear of their arrest and annoyed that he could take no part in it. He found it frustrating that the patrols sent out after the men had made no apparent progress.

'In a sense,' said Ainley, 'it's really not our problem. Most of them deserted from the same cavalry regiment.'

'You're forgetting Private Lock, sir. He's from the 24th.'

'We can't be absolutely certain that he's involved.'

'I can,' said Welbeck. 'I feel it in my bones. It's just the kind of thing that would attract a man like Edwin Lock. He has no respect for authority or for other people's property. When I caught him stealing from the other men, I beat him to a pulp.'

'You should have had him flogged, Sergeant Welbeck.'

'I didn't want to let him off so lightly.'

Welbeck gave a grim chuckle. Though he was no admirer of Ainley, he found him the most approachable of the officers and, as such, a useful source of information.

'Is there any news of Captain Rawson?' he asked.

'I fancy that I should be asking that question of you,' said Ainley with a smile. 'You always seem to know far more about his movements than I do. All that I can tell you is that he left camp on his own.'

'That much I already know. What he didn't tell me is why.'

'I can't help you on that score, Sergeant. If he's been given another assignment, then he could be anywhere.

As you know, His Grace places the greatest trust in the captain.'

'He sometimes asks too much of him.'

'I'm not sure that that's possible,' said the other, admiringly. 'Captain Rawson has nine lives. He's gathered intelligence in the most dangerous places and always returned unharmed. And I don't need to tell you how utterly fearless he is in battle.'

'No, sir, I've served under him for a long time.'

'He relies heavily on people like you.'

'He does, sir,' said Welbeck, meaningfully. 'He knows that I can always tell if a man is lying or telling the truth. At first glance, I had my suspicions of Ralph Higgins.'

Ainley was contrite. 'I'm still embarrassed about that little lapse on my behalf,' he said. 'I'll be more careful in the future.'

'I'm sure that you will, Lieutenant.'

Behind the deferential comment, Welbeck kept his scorn for the officer well concealed. He was on the point of taking his leave when he heard shouts and laughter. They were prompted by the arrival of two horses. One was ridden by an attractive young woman while the other carried a man and a woman. Ainley couldn't understand why they were given such a noisy welcome but Welbeck recognised Daniel immediately, even though he was still in disguise.

Seeing his two friends, Daniel came across to them and whisked off his hat. Ainley was amazed to see who it was.

Dismounting swiftly, Daniel helped Amalia down from the same horse then lifted Sophie down from the other animal. He introduced the two women to Ainley.

'Lieutenant,' he said, 'would you be so kind as to escort the two ladies to His Grace? They have useful intelligence to impart. I'll join them in His Grace's quarters directly.'

'Yes, Captain,' said Ainley, pleased to be given the task. 'I'll pass on that message.' He smiled at the women. 'Follow me, ladies.'

'I might have known there'd be a woman in the case,' said Welbeck as he watched the others walk away. 'You had two of them this time, Dan.'

'That was unintentional,' said Daniel. 'Mademoiselle Prunier was being held captive with Amalia in the French camp. I had to rescue both of them.'

'I see that you only brought *two* horses so that you had an excuse to put your arms around Amalia.'

'That's not true at all, Henry. I'd hoped to bring all three of us back in Ralph Higgins' wagon but it went astray. I had to leave the French camp without it.'

'Is that how you got there – in Higgins' wagon?'

'Yes…but I'll have to find another way next time.'

'You're surely not going back.'

'When I've given my report to His Grace, I have to return.'

Welbeck grinned. 'How many more women need to be rescued?'

'I'm not trying to release a hostage this time. I'm going back for my sword. It was hidden in the wagon that was stolen.'

'Spare yourself the trouble and buy yourself another sword.'

'I can't do that. This one is very special to me. I've told you the story of how I came to acquire it.'

'Yes,' recalled Welbeck. 'You were given it after the battle of Sedgemoor by His Grace – except that he was Lord Churchill in those days, and your father had fought against him.'

'It's because of what happened then that I'm certain His Grace will give me permission to go back, especially when I tell him that I have an inkling of where those renegades might be hiding.'

'You do – where are they, Dan?'

'You'll be able to see for yourself,' Daniel told him. 'There's something I forgot to mention – you'll be coming with me.'

Chapter Fourteen

The raid was a disappointment. After their setback at the preceding farm, they'd chosen a smallholding on this occasion so that they ran no risk of losing any of their number. In fact, there were only three people inside the little cottage and – to their disgust – they were all male. Deprived of their ritual assault on any available women, they killed the men with particular savagery, stole what little money there was and took some of the livestock. As they rode away, the night sky was lit by flames from the bonfire and the loud crackle pursued them for half a mile. It was almost dawn by the time they reached their refuge. Lurching into their farmhouse, the first thing they did was to assuage their fury with beer or wine.

'That was a waste of time, Matt,' said Edwin Lock, bitterly. 'We rode all that way just to warm our hands at a fire.'

'I'm sorry about that,' said Searle. 'I expected more.'

'We all did. At the very least, we hoped for a tumble with a farmer's wife or with a milkmaid.'

'I definitely saw women there when I rode past a few days ago, Edwin. They must have been visitors.'

'This life is starting to get me down,' moaned Hugh Davey, undoing the buttons on his jacket. 'I've had enough.'

'Nobody walks out on me,' warned Searle. 'When you agreed to join us, Hugh, you swore to accept my leadership.'

'Things have changed, Matt.'

'We've had a little upset, that's all.'

'It's not all,' corrected Lock before taking another swig from the flagon of wine. 'We've been let down twice in a row now. Last time, we had to leave Gregory behind.'

'That was his own bleeding fault,' snapped Searle.

'This time, we got little money and no women.'

'Edwin is right,' said Davey. 'It was a complete waste of time.'

'What would you rather do?' demanded Searle, rounding on him but addressing the other six of them as well. 'Would you prefer to be in the army and have someone else running your lives, telling you when you can eat, drink, shave and shit? Is that what you want?'

'No, Matt, you know it isn't.'

'But for me, the rest of you would still be stuck in

uniform. Yes,' he went on over the mocking laughter, 'I know that you're wearing army uniform now but you're doing it of your own free will. You can take it off whenever you like. Let's be frank about this,' he continued, 'there's not a man among you who could have organised everything the way I did. I got all of you out of the clutches of the army and I've kept you alive ever since.'

'You didn't keep Gregory Pyle alive,' said Lock, sullenly.

'Nor Ianto Morgan, for that matter,' said Searle, using the name to counter any stray thoughts they might have of mutiny. 'You all know the penalty for desertion. Without me, most of you would've paid it by now.'

'That's not the point, Matt,' said Davey.

'Then what is, Hugh?'

'Well, we can't go on like this for ever, can we?'

'No,' said Lock, smirking. 'We'll run out of farms to burn down.'

'I'm serious, Edwin. When does it all end?'

'It ends when I say so,' declared Searle.

Davey was blunt. 'I think the time has come now.'

'If that's how you feel, off you go.' Davey hesitated and looked around the others. 'The same goes for the rest of you,' said Searle. 'If any of you are stupid enough to imagine that Hugh can get you safely back to England, then you can leave now. I'm not keeping you here.'

He sat back and took a long swig of wine. There was general unease among the others and sheepish glances were exchanged. Worried by the lack of support, Davey began to lose his nerve.

'Perhaps we're better off with you, Matt,' he conceded.

Searle was sarcastic. 'Oh, you've finally realised that, have you?' he said. 'You've shown a glimmer of intelligence at long last.'

'I just want to know when we leave.'

'Then I'll tell you. We leave at the right moment and that's not when there are so many patrols out looking for us. We bide our time, Hugh. We stay here and enjoy good food and good beer or wine. It won't be long before there's another battle,' he predicted. 'Patrols will be recalled then because every man will be needed. *That's* when we make our move. That's when we find our way to the coast and take ship to England. Does anyone disagree with that?'

He met each pair of eyes with an assertive stare. None of the men dared to speak. Matthew Searle had rescued them from an army routine they'd all hated. In spite of its drawbacks, their new life was much more enjoyable. They'd been able to savour a freedom they'd not known for years. Lock was the first to speak up.

'I'm staying with you, Matt,' he said.

'So am I,' said Davey.

'What about the rest of you?' There was a murmur of agreement from the others. Lock turned to his cousin. 'There you are, Matt. We all want to stay if you can find us some willing women.'

'There's more to life than a hole between a woman's legs,' said Searle, philosophically. 'Money is the key to everything. We need all we can get in order to sail to England and start a new life. When we have money, we can buy whatever we want.' He raised his voice for emphasis. 'Bear in mind that the hunt for us won't end when we get back home. Our names will be listed among other deserters in the *London Gazette* and elsewhere. There'll be a description of each one of us. We'll be fugitives.'

'I'll change my name,' decided Davey.

'So will I,' said Lock.

'Take care to change your appearance as well,' advised Searle, 'and stay away from people who know you. If they realise you're a deserter, they could inform on you.'

'I never thought about that.'

'You've got me to think of it for you, Edwin.'

'Thank you, Matt. I can't wait to get home to England.'

'Nor can I,' said Searle, tapping his flagon, 'though I'll miss this lovely wine. I never thought I'd learn to enjoy it more than beer.'

'What I'll miss,' said Davey with a lascivious grin, 'are these gorgeous Flemish women. Apart from them, I leave Flanders with no regrets.'

Lock was wistful. 'Oh, I have one regret,' he confided, 'and I think about it every day. My regret is that I never had the chance to kill that swine of a sergeant, Henry Welbeck.

He made my life a misery – God rot his soul!' He held his flagon aloft. 'Here's to the long and agonising death of Sergeant Welbeck!'

Henry Welbeck rode beside Daniel Rawson at the head of a patrol. While the two friends wore civilian garb, the soldiers trotting in pairs behind them were in uniform. The patrol wasn't simply protecting them, it was scouring the countryside for the deserters who'd caused so much havoc. Reports of the burning of a smallholding and the murder of its occupants had come in to the camp. It was another charge to add to the gruesome record.

'This is a long way to go for a sword, Dan,' said Welbeck.

'I'm hoping we might catch some renegades along the way.'

'Where did you see them?'

'I'm not sure that I did, Henry,' admitted Daniel. 'I just thought I saw a glimpse of a redcoat where it wasn't supposed to be.'

'Then we could be hunting moonbeams.'

'Someone else spotted them in the same part of the country and they had a clearer view. If the deserters have a hiding place, then it's there or thereabouts.'

'That sounds like a hopeful guess to me.'

'Hopeful guesses sometimes hit the mark.'

'More often than not,' said Welbeck, 'they're miles wide of it. Still,' he went on, sardonically, 'I suppose that hunting for a handful of men in a country as big as this is no worse than searching for a sword in the middle of a vast French army. Both are fairly simple undertakings.'

Daniel chuckled. 'You were ever the eternal optimist.'

'I don't like a wild goose chase, Dan.'

'Yet you'd enjoy eating the goose if we actually caught it.'

'Of course,' said Welbeck. 'And while we're at it, couldn't we catch a flying pig or two? I'm very partial to pork.'

Daniel was glad of his friend's company and happy to put up with his rumbling cynicism. Since one of his own men was involved, Welbeck had a personal stake in the arrest of the deserters. Daniel was driven by the desire to exact revenge on behalf of the farmer who'd helped to save his life. The problem, he knew, was visibility. A patrol as large and conspicuous as the one at his back could be seen from miles away, giving the renegades plenty of time to go into hiding. When they got nearer to the copse where he'd seen the stray redcoat, therefore, Daniel intended to proceed with only Welbeck for company. Two men in rustic attire would blend more easily into the countryside.

'Who was the other woman?' asked Welbeck.

'Mademoiselle Sophie Prunier – she'd been lured into the camp to provide sport for one of the officers.'

'That's nothing new. We have officers who've done that.'

'Not while His Grace is around,' said Daniel. 'He takes a dim view of anyone who entices women into the camp.'

'I agree with him. One disease-ridden whore can infect

dozens of men with the pox. They're useless as soldiers then. Nobody can shoot straight while he's scratching his balls with the other hand.'

'Sophie is not in that class, Henry. As you saw for yourself, she's very wholesome. Her only fault was to be too trusting when a handsome lieutenant invited her into the camp.'

'What will happen to her?'

'Eventually, I daresay, she'll be escorted back to Mons.'

'And what about Amalia – will she return to Amsterdam?'

'No,' said Daniel, 'she'll remain in camp for a while. His Grace has promised to write to her father with the news that she's been rescued. Their ordeal has had one benefit.'

'Has it?'

'Yes, since Amalia and Sophie have been inside the French camp, they were able to describe what they saw and heard. That sort of intelligence is always valuable. What they both need now is time to recover. They went through a very harassing experience and our journey back was not without its adventures. We had some narrow escapes from French patrols along the way. I was relieved when we finally got back to camp.'

'So was I, Dan,' said Welbeck. 'It meant that I could have a decent conversation with an officer instead of listening to a brainless dolt like Lieutenant Ainley.'

The patrol continued for hour after hour, pausing at a small village to take refreshment before pressing on. Though they kept their eyes peeled, the soldiers saw nothing that could lead them to the deserters. Daniel took them on past the forest where he'd had to fight off the two highwaymen and down the road that he'd followed in his wagon. Bringing the column to a halt with a raised arm, he used the telescope to pick out the copse where he'd seen what he believed was a British soldier. Nobody appeared to be there now. He set off again and the patrol followed him until it reached the copse. When all the horses were concealed by the trees, he brought them to a halt and spoke to the lieutenant in charge of the patrol.

'Sergeant Welbeck and I will go on alone,' he said.

'What if you need help, Captain?' asked the man.

'We'll find a way of summoning you. While you're here, you won't catch the attention of any lookouts. And after the long ride, I think your men deserve a rest.'

'What about me?' protested Welbeck. 'I'm exhausted.'

'Do you want to miss the chance of catching Private Lock?'

'I'd ride another thousand miles to do that, Dan.'

'Then stop moaning about being saddle-sore.'

Welbeck accepted the reproach. 'Lead on, Dan,' he said.

The copse was on a rise that commanded a view across the plain they'd just crossed. When they went down the other side of the rise, they found themselves in open countryside that was dappled with trees and bushes. Bathed in the light of a summer evening, it was an idyllic scene. After a while, they encountered a brook that trickled its way across their path. Leaving Welbeck to water the horses, Daniel dismounted and continued on foot, walking up a gentle gradient until he finally came to a ridge. Realising that he'd be silhouetted against the sky if he remained standing, he lay on his stomach and crawled forward until he reached the crest. The telescope now came into play, searching the horizon in a wide sweep before making a second, more detailed inspection. Daniel stared intently through the lens until it settled on what at first looked like a clump of trees. Rising out of them was a hill on which a figure was sitting as he gazed in every direction. There was no redcoat this time because the man was in his shirt. It was his breeches and boots that identified him. Daniel recognised them as belonging to a cavalryman in a British regiment.

He was thrilled. The wild goose might yet be caught.

By the end of the evening, most of the men had drunk themselves close to a stupor. Two of them played cards while one of them threw horseshoes at a stake he'd set up outside. Searle was studying a map when Hugh Davey came into the house and reached immediately for some beer.

'I'm finished, Matt,' he announced.

'Who's supposed to relieve you?'

'It's Edwin's turn now.'

'Wake up,' said Searle, kicking his cousin. 'You're on duty.'

'I'm too tired,' groaned Lock, opening an eye.

'Then I'll duck your head in a bucket of water.'

'No, no, Matt – don't do that!' Lock was sufficiently scared to haul himself up. He staggered to the door and used it to steady himself. 'What's the point of going up there now? It will be dark soon.'

'That's when you come down and not before.'

'Go on, Edwin,' urged Davey. 'Take your turn. I was up there while the rest of you were roistering down here.'

'I'm weary,' said Lock, yawning by way of illustration.

'Are you still here?' said Searle, rising to his feet and pulling out a dagger. 'Do as you're told or you'll get this up your arse.'

'All right, all right,' said Lock, holding up both palms. 'There's no need to be violent. I'll act as lookout. Just give me time to wake up properly first.'

To encourage him on his way, Searle jabbed playfully at him with the dagger. Lock jumped quickly out of the way and fled from the house. As he crossed to the hill, he had to dodge a wayward horseshoe that missed the stake by several yards. Climbing upwards was an effort for a man with tired limbs and blurred vision. When he reached the top of the hill, he picked up the loaded musket that had been left there by Davey and used it for support. His head slowly cleared. He surveyed the landscape in every direction, seeing how the shadows were lengthening across the grass.

Lock knew that his cousin was right. A lookout was

essential to their survival and it was only fair that each of them took it in turns. Searle himself was not excluded from the duty. He'd been up on the hill earlier in the day until he was relieved by the next man. Lock hated the chore. It reminded him too much of the army from which he'd fled. He'd always found sentry duty to be boring and dispiriting. When he'd deserted, he hoped that he'd put it behind him. Yet here he was again with a musket in his hands, staring at an empty landscape for a danger that never appeared. It was demoralising.

After a while, he lowered the weapon to the ground and sat cross-legged beside it. That offered him some relief. The grass was long and the ground soft. Birdsong acted as a gentle lullaby. Lock's eyes soon began to flutter. Minutes later, he was asleep.

After waiting until dark, Daniel deployed his men around the old farmhouse. He and Welbeck then approached on foot to take a closer look. There was nobody on the hill now. The deserters were all fast asleep inside the building. The first place that Daniel checked was the stables. Six horses were inside and two others were tethered to a fence nearby. That told them how many men they were up against. Welbeck led one of the horses away and Daniel followed with two more in tow. Leaving the animals with members of the patrol, they went back for three more and took them a safe distance away. Daniel brought out the last two horses on his own.

'I didn't know we came here to act as horse thieves,' said Welbeck in an undertone. 'Are we just making sure that they can't gallop out of there?'

'That's one reason,' said Daniel, 'but there's another as well.'

'And what's that?'

'I didn't want the horses waking them up.'

'Why should they do that, Dan? They were as good as gold when we led them out of there. I didn't hear a peep from them.'

'It would have been different when the blaze started.'

Welbeck was stunned. 'Are you talking about a fire?'

'Yes,' said Daniel, remembering the gutted farmhouse, 'I think it's high time that they had a taste of their own medicine.'

Going back to the stables, he took armfuls of dry hay from the manger and Welbeck did the same. They made a pile in front of the door and beneath the windows. Daniel even tossed some up onto the roof. When he was ready, he lit the piles of hay and waited for the fire to take hold. It was the signal for the patrol to move forward with their weapons at the ready. Searle and his men were deeply asleep and it was several minutes before any of them heard the noise of the fire or inhaled the clouds of smoke that began to fill the house. The door itself was alight before anyone finally stirred and the front of the building was a sheet of flame.

Screaming, yelling and cursing, the deserters were roused

from their beds and came hurtling out half-naked. The first man through the door was Matthew Searle, howling in pain as the fire licked him. Seeing his red hair and beard in the bright glare, Daniel realised who he must be. He showed Searle no mercy. He pounded away at him with a succession of punches then threw him to the ground and stood over him. Searle was cunning. Pretending to be dazed, he suddenly reached out for Daniel's foot and pulled him to the ground before leaping up and running towards the stables. Expecting to find horses, he was horrified to see that they'd all vanished.

'There's no escape, Matthew Searle,' said Daniel, back on his feet and closing in on him.

'Who the hell are you?' roared Searle.

'My name is Captain Daniel Rawson of the 24th Foot.'

'Well, Captain Rawson, here's a 25th fucking foot for you.'

Rushing at Daniel, he aimed a kick at him but Daniel caught his foot and pushed hard. Searle fell backwards and struck his head on the hard timber of the stables. This time he really was dazed. Daniel stepped in to administer some more punishment with his fists before throwing him to two men from the patrol. Covered in blood, Searle was almost out on his feet. He was dragged swiftly away.

The other deserters, meanwhile, had all been captured and were struggling in the arms of the soldiers. Welbeck had waited for Edwin Lock, the last of them to emerge, grabbing him by the scruff of the neck and rushing him across the yard to plunge him head first into the water trough. After holding him down for a minute, he brought him up for air, only to thrust him underwater once again. On his second appearance from the trough, Lock was gurgling madly and pleading for release. Welbeck ducked him for a third time before lifting him out of the trough altogether. The sergeant put his whiskery face close.

'Remember me, Edwin?' he asked, sweetly. 'I'm Henry Welbeck. We've come to take you back to the army.'

Burgundy made the most of his rare chance to embarrass Vendôme. When they met in the commander-in-chief's quarters, he was smiling for once and looked down his nose at his visitor.

'Your plan seems to have unravelled, my lord Duke,' he said with well-mannered glee. 'You invest immense time and effort in the capture of a single British soldier and you not only fail to catch him, you lose the hostage who was supposed to tempt him here.'

'That was unfortunate,' grunted Vendôme.

'It might be all for the best.'

'I fail to see how, my lord.'

'You can now attend properly to your duties as a commander.'

'I've always done so,' said Vendôme, stung by the criticism. 'My duties include the arrest of dangerous enemies, and Captain Rawson, I submit, answers that description.

He's been a thorn in our flesh for years now and needed to be plucked out.'

'Then where is he?'

'I have no answer to that.'

'In other words, your plan was ill-conceived from the start.'

'I dispute that, my lord. To some degree, it worked perfectly in that the hostage I took did bring him to the camp. I'd hoped that Captain Rawson would be exchanged for the young lady and made overtures to that effect. The Duke of Marlborough sent word that the captain was no longer in his camp.'

'No,' said Burgundy, seizing the opportunity to twist the dagger a little, 'he was already on his way here. Did it never occur to you that the fellow would attempt to rescue the lady?'

'Of course,' riposted Vendôme. 'She was closely guarded.'

'Not closely enough, it seems.'

'Captain Rawson is very resourceful.'

'You should have taken account of that fact.'

'I didn't expect him to get here so soon.'

'Do you have any idea how he managed to penetrate the camp?'

'Not yet,' confessed Vendôme, 'but I have men searching for that information. We'll soon know what device he employed.'

'You should have anticipated it,' said Burgundy. 'What use

is wisdom *after* the event? All that you can do now is to shut the stable door after the horse has bolted. The resourceful captain is unlikely to use the same stratagem again.'

Vendôme was livid. The rescue of Amalia Janssen had annoyed him intensely but he'd hoped to keep it secret. That was clearly impossible. Burgundy had been watching him, noting his every move and waiting for him to make a slight mistake so that he could enjoy reprimanding him. It was a means of enforcing his authority and it wounded Vendôme to the quick. As a commander, he had infinitely more flair, experience and tactical skill than the younger man yet he had to withstand a rebuke. It was time to hit back.

'May I ask how you come to know of the escape, my lord?' he asked, politely. 'It seems such a trivial matter to come to your attention.'

'When I taxed you earlier with its triviality, you swore to me that the capture of Captain Rawson would have some significance. You intended,' said Burgundy, 'to send him back to Versailles.'

'That's true, my lord.'

'Persuaded by your argument, I made it my business to keep abreast of any developments relating to your hostage.'

'And what exactly did you learn?'

'That the young lady was held under armed guard and yet she miraculously disappeared.'

'Is that all you learnt?'

'What else is there?'

'Evidently, your spies missed something.'

'They were not spies, my lord Duke,' said Burgundy, hotly. 'They were members of the army that both you and I serve.'

'Then they should be more vigilant,' argued Vendôme, 'because they gave you an incomplete report. Our hostage was not alone in that tent. She was accompanied by a young lady named Mademoiselle Prunier. Both of them were rescued by Captain Rawson.'

'That's a double blow to your reputation, then. You contrive to lose two prisoners at the same time. I scent carelessness here.'

'Your nostrils deceive you, my lord.'

'Pray, tell me how.'

'My plan was never as simple as you believed it to be,' said Vendôme with a touch of pride. 'While offering to exchange the hostage for Captain Rawson, I never expected Marlborough to give him up so easily. That left a rescue attempt as the most likely outcome and I felt that we were prepared for that.'

'That was a bad mistake on your part, my lord Duke.'

'I allowed for that eventuality.'

Burgundy gaped. 'You *expected* the rescue to succeed?'

'I accepted it as a possibility.'

'Then your plan was doomed from the start.'

'Not so,' said Vendôme, savouring his moment. 'You forget Mademoiselle Prunier. When she was thrown into the tent with our hostage, she was posing as the victim of a cruel trick. The two ladies were drawn closely together – I know that for certain.'

Burgundy was perplexed. 'What are you telling me?'

'That the tables have been turned on Captain Rawson. He was far too gallant to leave Sophie Prunier behind. Instead of rescuing a young lady in distress,' said Vendôme with a triumphant smile, 'he was escorting one of my spies into the very heart of the British camp.' He raised an eyebrow. 'Does that not merit congratulation, my lord?'

Sophie Prunier was delighted to meet the Duke of Marlborough and be received with the courtesy for which he was renowned. While she freely volunteered information about her stay in the French camp, she took care to pass on nothing of real value to the Allied commander. Since he was fluent in French, it was Adam Cardonnel who actually questioned her while Marlborough looked on.

'What else can you tell us, mademoiselle?' he probed.

'Only that I never wish to return to that camp again,' she said, fearfully. 'You are the enemy yet you've treated me with more respect than my own countrymen. I thank you for that.'

'You'll come to no harm here.'

'That's what Lieutenant Bouteron promised me. I'd never have dared to accept his invitation otherwise. I'd hate you to think that I'm the sort of woman who would encourage what the lieutenant had in mind. When he revealed his true colours,' she went on, 'I was shocked beyond belief.'

'It's obviously been a great trial for you.'

'I can't bear even to think about it.'

'The sooner we can reunite you with your family, the better.'

'My parents are away at the moment, monsieur,' she told him. 'Would it be possible for me to stay here for a few days?'

'Naturally,' said Marlborough. 'Stay as long as you wish.'

'We'll provide accommodation for you,' added Cardonnel.

'What about dear Amalia?' she asked. 'Will she be going home to Amsterdam now?'

'No, Mademoiselle Janssen will also remain here.'

'Then I hope to see her because I owe her so much. Amalia was such a wonderful support to me. And without her, I'd still be held in custody at that dreadful camp.'

'You were fortunate to be there when Captain Rawson arrived.'

Sophie beamed. 'He's the person I must really thank,' she said with apparent conviction. 'When may I see him?'

'Not for a while, I'm afraid,' said Cardonnel. 'He has urgent business elsewhere.'

'Yes,' explained Marlborough in his halting French. 'He's gone back to the place from which he rescued you.'

'Whatever for?' she gasped.

'It's a matter of honour, mademoiselle.'

'Oh?'

'Captain Rawson has to retrieve his sword.'

'I don't understand,' she said, interest aroused. 'Why did he leave this sword there in the first place? And how will he get it back?'

Daniel spent the night sleeping under the stars with Henry Welbeck. The patrol set off at dawn, taking the deserters back to the Allied camp. Matthew Searle and his men were a sorry sight, blackened by the fire, wearing almost nothing, seated astride their horses with their hands tied behind their backs. When the column moved off, Welbeck couldn't resist waving farewell to Edwin Lock.

'They'll never wear redcoats again,' said the sergeant with gruff satisfaction. 'Their uniforms were destroyed by fire. I just hope that we get back in time to see them executed.'

'Their fate is irrelevant now, Henry,' said Daniel. 'We need to think only of what lies ahead.'

'Yes…a pointless search for something you'll never find.'

'You told me I'd never find those deserters.'

'That was different, Dan. You had clues to help you.'

'I have even more clues as to the whereabouts of my sword,' said Daniel. 'It's hidden beneath the seat in the wagon I borrowed from Ralph Higgins. All I have to do is to track it down.'

'And will the whole French army put their hands over their eyes while you're doing that?'

'They won't even know that I'm there.'

Welbeck shook his head. 'It's far too risky – even for you.'

'I've been in and out of that camp before.'

'You're tempting Providence by trying to do it again, Dan.'

'I want that sword.'

'Does it *really* mean that much to you?'

'Yes,' replied Daniel. 'The day I picked up that weapon, I came of age. It was the moment I knew I'd be a soldier.'

'I had a moment like that,' said Welbeck, sorrowfully, 'and I've regretted it for the rest of my life.'

Daniel laughed. 'That's arrant nonsense and you know it. We're two of a kind, Henry – born soldiers with the urge to fight.'

'The only urge I have is to stay alive and I'm not likely to do that if I go barging into the French camp with you.'

'That's exactly why you'll stay outside and wait for me.'

'And how long am I to wait?' asked Welbeck.

'Until you're certain that I'm not coming out again.'

'Then what do I do?'

'Come in search of me, of course.'

Welbeck shuddered. 'And how am I supposed to do that?'

'Oh, you'll think of something,' said Daniel, happily. 'That's why I brought you with me.'

CHAPTER FIFTEEN

Amalia Janssen had been so exhausted by the events of recent days that she slept without interruption for almost fourteen hours. She awoke with the delicious feeling that she was free, unharmed and completely safe. A letter from Marlborough had been dispatched to Amsterdam to assure her father that she was alive and it had been accompanied by a scribbled note from Amalia. Knowing how guilt-stricken Beatrix would be, she'd made a point of absolving her from any blame for the abduction. In making sure that her father and her servant would no longer fret over her disappearance, she'd removed a crushing weight from her mind. Unfortunately, it had been replaced by a lighter but not inconsiderable one.

'When did Captain Rawson leave?' asked Sophie Prunier.

'I don't know,' replied Amalia.

'Didn't he bid you farewell?'

'No, Sophie, he left Lieutenant Ainley to do that on his behalf. Daniel – Captain Rawson, I mean – knew that I'd try to persuade him to stay here.'

'Would he have listened to you?'

'I'm afraid not.'

'Yet he was not under orders to go, was he?'

'No, it was his decision.'

'The Duke of Marlborough called it a matter of honour.'

'We might not think so,' said Amalia, 'but that's how Captain Rawson would see it.'

The two women were pleased to be reunited and were sharing a late breakfast in the tent assigned to Amalia. Both of them had been able to wash off the filth collected during their escape and clean clothing had been found for them, albeit of a utilitarian kind. As they ate their meal, Amalia explained why Daniel's sword had such a symbolic importance in his life. Sophie began to understand why he was driven to retrieve it.

'Do you feel afraid for him?' she asked.

'Yes, I do – very afraid.'

'It's a reckless thing to do. I'm surprised that the Duke of Marlborough let him take the risk.'

'His Grace knows what that sword means. After all, it was he who presented it to him. Captain Rawson was only ten when he used that sword to prevent his mother from being—'

'Yes, yes,' said Sophie, interrupting. 'There's no need to talk about that. It seems that British soldiers can be just as brutish as the French. It's disgusting.'

Amalia was tentative. 'Did you tell His Grace what happened?'

'How could I? It was too embarrassing.'

'Lieutenant Bouteron should be called to account.'

'I'd sooner forget his foul name.'

'He should be punished.'

'It would be a case of his word against mine,' said Sophie. 'If I made a complaint, it would be heard by the duc de Vendôme and he'll always support his officers. That's the tragedy of it all, Amalia. I have no recourse to justice. I have to bear my disgrace.'

'It's not a disgrace – it was forced upon you.'

'I'd much rather pretend it never happened.'

'*Somebody* should pay,' insisted Amalia.

Sophie looked dejected. 'I wish that they would.'

They ate on in silence for a while then Sophie brightened a little.

'I never thought I'd get to meet the Duke of Marlborough,' she said. 'He's so charming. I expected a much older man.'

'His Grace is always very considerate.'

'He and his secretary, Monsieur Cardonnel, were kind to me and I was surprised. When all is said and done,' she said with a shrug, 'I'm French. I'm one of the enemy.'

'I only think of you as a good friend,' said Amalia.

'Thank you.' Sophie reached across the table to give her hand an affectionate squeeze. 'One day, perhaps, when this war is over, we shall be able to meet again – in Paris, perhaps.'

'I'd prefer it to be in Amsterdam.'

'Then that's where it will be.' They traded a warm smile. 'You're blessed to have a man like Captain Rawson in your life.'

'You don't need to tell me that, Sophie. I say it to myself every day. He's been my saviour. This time, he was yours as well.'

'In your place, I'd be very concerned about him.'

'Oh, I am, Sophie.'

'We both saw how many soldiers there are in that camp.'

'He managed to reach us, nevertheless.'

'But can he get in there all over again?'

'I hope so,' said Amalia, sounding far more confident than she actually felt. 'This time, he only has himself to worry about. That should make it a lot easier.'

'Yes, it should,' agreed Sophie. 'I'd just love to know how he'll go about it. You're as close to Captain Rawson as anybody. What sort of a plan do you think he'd have?'

'It won't work,' said Henry Welbeck with categorical certainty.

'I believe that it's worth a try,' said Daniel.

'It could be suicide.'

'That's the talk of a defeatist and I'd never call you that, Henry. You've always believed that we could succeed in the past.'

'Granted,' said Welbeck, 'but that was when we were surrounded by a British army and its allies. When we have sufficient numbers, we're a match for anyone. This time, there are only two of us.'

'I see that as an advantage.'

'Well, I don't, Dan.'

'It's so much easier for one person to remain hidden. You must see that, surely.'

'All I see is that I may end up as the fox with a pack of slavering hounds on my trail – and I can't run fast enough.'

'You won't have to run at all, Henry.'

'I won't?'

'No,' said Daniel. 'You'll be hiding up a tree.'

Welbeck quaked. 'Hell and damnation!' he yelled. 'This gets worse and worse!'

They were about three miles from the French camp at a point where the road ran through the woods. Any traffic going to the camp would have to pass that way and Daniel was counting on deliveries of food or other supplies. What troubled Welbeck was that the plan had been made on the spur of the moment, as was Daniel's habit when he needed to improvise. The sergeant lacked his friend's ability to make things up as he went along. He liked order, control and the sense of being part of a huge military unit. Cut off from his regiment, he felt isolated. Welbeck was uncomfortable enough being so close to the French camp. The idea of implementing Daniel's plan only brought him out in a cold sweat.

'I have a better idea,' he said.

'And what's that, Henry?'

'I'll buy you a *new* sword – two or three of the bloody things, if necessary. Now, please let's be sensible and leave.'

'Don't you want the excitement of deceiving the enemy?'

'We'll talk about it when we get back to our camp.'

'We're staying here,' said Daniel, 'until the right chance comes. All that you have to do is to fire the pistol.'

'Then what happens? Every one of the soldiers guarding the wagons will race to see who can hack me to pieces first.'

'They won't even notice you high up in a tree.'

'And how am I supposed to get up there? I hate climbing.'

'Then I'll help you. We brought rope with us. I'll climb up there first then haul you up after me.' He touched Welbeck's shoulder. 'I can't do this without you, Henry.'

'In my view, you can't do it at all.'

'Why do you think that?'

'To begin with,' said Welbeck, 'you've forgotten our horses. As soon as they hear a pistol being discharged above their heads, they'll probably bolt off through the trees.'

'They won't be anywhere near you,' Daniel told him. 'They won't even be on this side of the road. If they were, they could easily be discovered. We'll tether them deep in the woods on the other side so that you can collect them after we've gone.'

'And what am I supposed to do then?'

'Watch and pray, Henry. Think inspiring thoughts.'

'The only thing that's inspired me about this venture is that we finally caught those deserters. That's the kind of work I like, Dan. Rounding up dirty renegades is what I do well.'

'You can do anything well if you put your mind to it.'

'Not if it involves climbing,' protested Welbeck. 'I like to fight with my feet on the ground, not perched up in a tree.'

'You won't have to fight at all,' said Daniel. 'You're my decoy.'

After a lengthy argument, Welbeck was finally cajoled into taking part in the plan. They first took their horses into the woods on the opposite side of the road and tethered them in a clearing. Returning to the place from which they'd started, they searched for a hiding place. The trees were in full leaf and many had high branches strong enough to support a man's weight. Daniel chose with care, shinning up a trunk with ease then throwing the rope over the sturdy bough on which he wanted his friend to sit. When the rope was tied in position, he used it to haul Welbeck up through the fretwork of branches. The sergeant was spluttering as he was pulled upward through the air and he didn't dare to look down. He eventually reached safety and he put a hand to his chest. Sitting side by side astride the bough, they were like two birds of prey discussing what they'd managed to catch that day.

'Don't ever ask me to do that again, Dan,' said Welbeck.

'Why not?'

'My heart won't stand it.'

'You'll survive,' said Daniel.

'I don't like it up here.'

'It may not be for long.'

'How do I get down?'

'It's easy,' said Daniel, dropping the rope and sliding effortlessly down to the ground. 'Pull it up out of sight.' The rope vanished behind the leaves. 'Well done, Henry,' he called to the now invisible sergeant. 'Make sure that you have the pistol ready.'

Welbeck took the weapon from the holster attached to his belt.

'I may use this to kill myself,' he warned.

'Stand by – no more words.'

Daniel slipped quietly away and concealed himself behind some thickets on the other side of the road. It was a long wait and he began to fear that Welbeck would be unable to stay aloft indefinitely. The sergeant's fear of heights could only worsen as time went by. Daniel was still wondering if anybody would come when he finally heard the distant rumble of wagons. A convoy was on its way and it was soon making so much noise that the sergeant was sure to hear it. There were twenty vehicles in all, packed with provisions and flanked by soldiers. As the first set of wheels rolled past him, Daniel was only a few feet away. A second cart passed, then a third, then a fourth. When over half of the convoy had gone, there was still no sound from Welbeck. Daniel felt certain that his friend must have sustained an injury, dropped the pistol or simply decided to abandon the plan.

Then, when it was almost too late, there was the sudden report of a gun, reverberating through the woods to the left. It caused immediate consternation, sending dozens of birds squawking into the sky. Horses neighed shrilly between the shafts and some tried to rear up on their back heels. There was great confusion. An order was barked and the convoy juddered to a halt. Soldiers drew their swords and spread out so that they could search the wood opposite. The sound had been deceptive. Some thought it came from the right, others from the left and others again from a point straight ahead. They kicked their horses forward. While the soldiers combed the woods, the drivers stayed on their carts, staring in dismay at the trees opposite and wondering if an ambush was imminent. Everyone had his back to the woods behind them.

The search was swift but methodical. They looked everywhere, using their swords to hack at bushes and shrubs. The one thing they never thought to do, however, was to look upwards so they never saw the chunky figure of Henry Welbeck, clinging on to the bough for dear life. At length, when they were convinced there was no danger, the soldiers trotted back to the convoy. One of them waved an arm to signal that there was no need for alarm.

'It must have been a hunter!' he shouted. 'There's nobody there now. Move on!'

Whips cracked and the vehicles creaked slowly into action again, rolling noisily towards the French camp. The interruption was over and all was well again. With their eyes fixed on the road ahead, nobody noticed that they now had a passenger. Daniel had crept under one of the wagons and was suspended between the axles.

Welbeck, meanwhile, had to solve the problem of how to descend from the tree without hurting himself. Daniel had made it look easy but his friend was much heavier and far less agile. After waiting until the noise of the convoy had faded away, Welbeck dropped the rope so that it dangled to the ground. Then he took a firm grip on it and rolled slowly off the bough, bringing both legs together around the rope. He was now hanging in mid-air and assaulted by fears that the bough might break, the rope might slip from his grasp or that he'd somehow lose consciousness and plunge to his death.

Lowering himself with painful slowness, he waited until he had gone down a few yards before swinging on the rope so that he could get within reach of the trunk of the tree. That promised solidity. It needed several attempts before his legs closed gratefully around the trunk and he was able to discard the rope altogether. Confidence restored, Welbeck climbed down through the lower branches until he could jump to the ground. Hurrying to the road, he saw that it was utterly deserted. He let out a cry of amazement.

'Bugger me!' he exclaimed. 'The plan *worked*.'

Known for his considerate treatment of his men, Marlborough could be ruthless when time served. As soon as he heard that the deserters had been apprehended, he ordered a court martial and presided over it in person. Matthew Searle and his followers were arraigned on charges of desertion, arson, rape, theft and wilful murder. Because the evidence against them was overwhelming, the trial was short. It was time to pass judgement. Cowed and pathetic, they pleaded for mercy. Marlborough was outraged.

'How dare you ask for mercy,' he said with vehemence, 'when you showed none to your unfortunate victims. How dare you have the audacity to imagine that you deserve anything but the death sentence for your appalling crimes. Had you repented of your desertion and returned immediately to this camp, I should have been inclined to be more lenient. But that was not the case here. Oh, no,' he went on with controlled anger. 'Wearing the uniform of the British army, you started a reign of terror that consisted of rape, theft, murder and the wanton destruction of property by fire. You brought untold shame upon us and that is unforgivable.'

He consulted briefly with the officers seated either side of him. They agreed wholeheartedly with what he proposed. Marlborough rose to his feet and looked hard at each man in turn before speaking.

'You have been found guilty of heinous crimes,' he declared, 'and you've brought disgrace to the uniforms you once wore. The sentence of this court is that each and every one of you will be hanged by the neck until you are dead.'

'No, no,' cried Edwin Lock. 'We'd rather be shot, Your Grace.'

'It's more honourable,' said Searle.

'For that reason alone, it's denied you,' said Marlborough. 'You have no right to talk of honour. What you did was so dishonourable that it defies belief. How could British soldiers behave with such unconscionable barbarity? How could you sink so swiftly to the level of savages?' He snapped his fingers. 'Take them away and hold them in custody until a gallows has been built.'

Now in chains, the prisoners were dragged away, two armed guards to each of them. Marlborough thanked the other members of the court martial and they began to disperse. Adam Cardonnel had been watching the whole event. He walked across to Marlborough.

'You showed too much compassion, Your Grace,' he said.

'I certainly felt none, Adam.'

'Hanging is too good for them. Those men were *evil*. They should have been burnt alive at the stake.'

'That sentence is not permitted, alas,' said Marlborough, sadly, 'though I can see that it would be a form of poetic justice.'

'What will happen now?'

'Word must be sent out to other farms to assure them that the culprits have now been caught and will answer with their lives. We must try everything we can to win back their goodwill.'

'It may already be too late for that, Your Grace.'

'Then there's the boy who survived the raid on his farm. When you write to the people who are looking after him, send them my personal apology. I hope they'll take some consolation from the fact that the deserters will be put to death.'

'When will the sentence be carried out?'

'Not until Captain Rawson and Sergeant Welbeck have returned. According to the report, it was they who led the attack on the place where those vile men were hiding. We must wait,' said Marlborough. 'Rawson and Welbeck would hate to miss the occasion.'

'You're assuming that they will come back,' said Cardonnel.

'Do you harbour any doubts about that?'

'One is bound to feel some qualms, Your Grace.'

'I don't,' said Marlborough. 'If I did I'd never have sanctioned the enterprise. To be candid, Daniel Rawson is one of the few people in the Confederate army who *doesn't* give me qualms. Somehow – and some day – he'll come safely back to us.'

* * *

It was not the most comfortable way to enter the camp. Hanging under the wagon, Daniel had had to put up with persistent noise, choking dust and an intense ache in every muscle. To add to his problems, one of the horses ahead of him rid itself of several pounds of manure and Daniel's back grazed it as he passed over the stinking pile. It would have been easier for him to have sneaked into the rear of the wagon and hide among the provisions but he would certainly have been discovered that way. As it was, he was carried into the camp and was able to loosen his hold, drop to the ground and roll over swiftly before the horse pulling the next wagon trampled on him.

Getting to his feet, he stepped behind one of the tents so that he could gather his strength, dust himself off and take his bearings. He also spared a thought for Henry Welbeck, wondering if he'd managed to descend the tree without hurting himself. In Daniel's view, the sergeant was the ideal person to take on such a hazardous errand. He'd always choose his friend before anyone. Welbeck was tough, reliable and a veritable tiger in combat. He'd also been desperately keen to help in the capture of the deserters and had acquitted himself well when they'd been arrested.

The sword took precedence now. Daniel knew that it was in the camp somewhere and that fact sent a thrill through his entire body. Making light of his aches and pains, he began his search. The first person he needed to speak to was Alphonse, the helpful young sutler who'd shown him around the camp. Daniel headed for the area where he was likely to find him. Alphonse was at work, seated on the ground while he repaired a shoe. When Daniel approached, the sutler didn't recognise him at first because he was wearing different apparel. Then he looked at the newcomer more carefully.

'It's Gustave!' he said, getting up to welcome him. 'Where have you been? We thought something must have happened to you.'

'I had to leave the camp for a while, Alphonse.'

'Where did you go – and where are those horses of yours?'

'I'll tell you later.' He glanced at the shoe. 'I didn't know that you were a cobbler.'

'You have to learn all trades to make a living these days.'

'I'm sure. Now, what I'm looking for is my wagon.'

Alphonse sighed. 'I thought you might be.'

'Where is it?'

'I don't know, Gustave.'

'It seemed to vanish in the night.'

'So did you, if it comes to that.'

'Well, I'm back now and I want my wagon.'

'Then you'll have to speak to Victor's wife,' said Alphonse, 'because she's the one who took it.'

'What possessed her to do that?' asked Daniel.

'Josette wanted revenge. You kicked her husband so hard that his balls swelled up and turned black. He couldn't bear to let anyone touch them. Josette is a woman who likes her pleasures,' he went on, 'and you deprived her of them. She's had long, cold nights with Victor. That made her angry.'

'Where is she, Alphonse?'

'Be nice to her. If you try to bully Josette, she'll turn nasty.'

'I just wish to get what's mine,' said Daniel.

Alphonse tossed the shoe, the hammer and the nails into the back of his wagon before zigzagging between the other vehicles. The woman they were after was not far away. Daniel had been warned that Josette was big but he'd not expected the gargantuan proportions that greeted him. She was a positive mountain of flesh with bulging arms, flabby legs, a massive belly and a bosom so large, heavy and volatile that it threatened to burst through her bodice. Being married to a blacksmith was appropriate inasmuch as her face had the gleaming hardness of something hammered out on an anvil. When the two men arrived, she was sitting on the ground and smoking a pipe.

'Who's this?' she asked, giving Daniel a hostile glance.

'This is Gustave, the man I told you about,' said Alphonse.

She got to her feet at once. 'So you're the villain who kicked my husband, are you?'

'It was only in self-defence,' said Daniel.

'Then I'll knock your frigging teeth out in self-defence.'

'Gustave is a friend,' said Alphonse.

'He's no friend of mine.'

'Victor forgave him for what happened.'

'Well, I haven't. Take him away before I hit him.'

'I simply want to know where my wagon is,' said Daniel, politely. 'After what I did to Victor, you were right to take it. I deserved that. But I think that we're even now.'

'Oh, do you?' she said, hands on her hips.

'I did apologise to your husband.'

'That means nothing to me.'

'Listen,' said Daniel, trying to mollify her, 'I'll be happy to let you have some of the goods in my wagon by way of compensation.'

'We don't need your charity!' she snarled. 'What I want is a proper husband not someone with a purple prick that hangs between his legs all night like a dead snake.' Raising a fist, Josette advanced a few steps. 'That was your doing!'

Daniel moved back and bumped into Victor, who came up behind him. The blacksmith was in an affable mood.

'Are you brawling again, woman?' he said to his wife with a laugh. 'Who are you battering this time?' He took a closer look at Daniel. 'Why, it's Gustave!' he exclaimed, embracing him. 'It's good to see you again, my friend. We'd given you up for dead. Where have you been?'

'I had to go away on business,' explained Daniel. 'When I tried to take my wagon with me, it had disappeared.'

'That's right. Josette took it – but only in jest.'

'Jest!' she howled. 'I'll tell you what my idea of a jest is. I'd like to bury this bastard up to his neck in horse dung and throw stones at his ugly face.'

Victor chuckled. 'My wife has a bit of a temper, Gustave,' he said. 'You mustn't take offence – it's only her way. I'll show you where the wagon is, if you wish.'

'Yes, please,' said Daniel. 'I'd be very grateful.'

'There might not be much left in it, mark you. This camp is full of scavengers. If it had stayed where it was, Alphonse could have kept an eye on it.'

'That's what I was doing,' said Alphonse, 'until Josette came.'

'I should have torn that wagon to pieces,' she growled.

'I'm very glad that you didn't,' said Daniel. 'Please take me to it, Victor.'

'Get him out of here,' roared Josette, 'before I sit on his head and fart in his mouth.' As the blacksmith led Daniel away, she fired a Parthian shot. 'And I hope his rotten wagon has been stolen and used as firewood.'

Glad to get out of her reach, Daniel was disturbed by the news that the wagon might have been pillaged. His sword had been hidden under the seat and held in place with some nails. Most people who searched the wagon would not even see the weapon but there was always the possibility that someone might chance upon it.

'Where did your wife drive it?' asked Daniel.

'Down by the stream,' replied Victor. 'It was all I could do to stop Josette from tipping it into the water. You upset her, Gustave.'

Daniel looked over his shoulder. 'Yes, I gathered that.'

'She likes to get her own back.'

They picked a way between the wagons until they came to a grassy incline. At the bottom of it, perched on the very edge of the stream, was the wagon taken from Ralph Higgins. There was no sign of the horse. When he saw what had happened, Daniel grimaced. Most of the canvas had been torn away from the hoops and the back of the wagon was almost empty. Whoever had stolen the provisions had been very thorough.

Daniel ran quickly down the hill and climbed onto the back of the wagon. Reaching under the seat, he felt for the sword but all that he found was a sharp nail that drew blood from his finger. Daniel was impervious to the pain. He was too numbed by a horrible realisation. His precious sword had gone. He might never find it again.

Still courting his commander's favour, Captain Raoul Valeran delivered his report with the quiet smile of someone expecting praise for his efforts. Seated at a table in his tent, Vendôme was leafing through some papers as he listened.

'I believe that I've found how he got into the camp,' said Valeran. 'Posing as a sutler, he joined some wagons that came here a few days ago. I've spoken to some of the soldiers who guarded them.'

'Do we know what name he used?' asked Vendôme.

'It was Gustave Carraud.'

'How can you be sure of that?'

'I made enquiries among the other sutlers, Your Grace. A man of that name came and went, leaving his wagon behind him.'

'Why should he do that?'

'I can only imagine that he had no need of it.'

'Then how did he escape?' pressed Vendôme, looking up at him. 'He could hardly have walked all the way back to the British camp, especially as he had two women with him.'

'I have the answer to that,' said Valeran, eager to impress. 'It seems that he arrived here with two horses. They vanished at the same time as Captain Rawson and the women.'

'I see. You've done well, Raoul. I congratulate you.'

Valeran beamed. 'Thank you, Your Grace.'

'It's a pity that your investigation into the burning down of that farm was not so fruitful. That crime remains unsolved. However,' he continued as Valeran's face crumpled, 'you've made amends here. At least we now know how Captain Rawson entered the camp. What is not clear is how he left it during the night.'

'That takes us into the realm of guesswork.'

'Quite so,' said Vendôme, standing up. 'I assume that you searched this wagon of his?'

'I did, Your Grace,' said Valeran, 'though, by the time I got to it, most of its contents had been stolen. What was left behind, however, confirms my belief that Gustave Carraud was indeed Captain Rawson.' Lifting up the sword that he was carrying, he showed it to Vendôme. 'This was concealed beneath the seat of the wagon.'

'How interesting,' said Vendôme, taking the weapon and examining it. 'This has seen good service, by the look of it. I think your supposition is correct – it must belong to Rawson. What use would a sutler have of an army sabre?'

'That was exactly the question that I asked.'

'Did you get a description of this Gustave Carraut?'

'He's a well-built man in his thirties who can fight like a demon.'

'How did you find that out?'

'He had a brawl with some of the other sutlers. I spoke to witnesses who saw him overpower them with relative ease. Evidently, he's very fit and strong.'

'That accords with what we already know of Captain Rawson.' Vendôme studied the sword again. 'He's fit, strong, daring and imaginative. He can pass himself off as a wine merchant or a sutler with equal facility. For all that, the captain is not infallible.' He tapped the sword. 'This proves it, Raoul.'

'Does it, Your Grace?'

'Most assuredly,' said Vendôme. 'I don't need to tell you how soldiers cherish their weapons. They grow to have a superstitious reliance on them.'

'I'd certainly never part with my sword, Your Grace.'

'I dare swear that Captain Rawson has the same attitude. He'd never have abandoned this unless he was forced to do so. That's what I mean about his fallibility,' said Vendôme. 'He made a mistake. I suspect that he's the sort of man who'll take steps to rectify it.'

Valeran was dubious. 'Surely, he'd never try to retrieve it.'

'I think that's precisely what he might do, Raoul. Perhaps we don't need Mademoiselle Janssen, after all.' He brandished the sword in the air. 'I could be holding a far better hostage in my hand.'

CHAPTER SIXTEEN

There was a pervasive gloom in the house in Amsterdam. It was almost as if the occupants were in mourning. The longer they waited for news about Amalia Janssen, the more depressed they became. Her father did his best to keep up the spirits of the others but even he was starting to lose hope. Unable to work, he instead watched Kees Dopff, his chief assistant, a short, skinny man in his late twenties who'd once been Emanuel Janssen's most gifted apprentice. Dopff was a tireless worker, quick to learn, meticulous in all he did and devoted to his master. Conversations between them were largely one-sided because the little weaver had been mute from birth. Since he could use no words, Dopff had to communicate by means of his mobile features and gesticulating hands.

During a break from the loom, he turned to Janssen and offered him a quizzical smile. The old man shook his head.

'There's no news as yet, Kees,' he said, regretfully. 'I've been left in such a daze that I've lost count of the number of days that Amalia has been missing now.' Dopff held up fingers on both hands. 'Has it really been that short a time? It seems like months. I haven't had a decent night's sleep since Amalia was taken. I'm so grateful to have you to continue work on the tapestry because I'm far too tired and preoccupied to concentrate. However,' he went on, straightening his shoulders, 'we mustn't despair. That's what the Duke of Marlborough said. In his letter, he advised us to bear up and not succumb to fearful thoughts. He also promised to take every step possible to find out where Amalia is and seek to rescue her.' Dopff nodded eagerly. 'The trouble is that she could be hundreds of miles from here. Then again,' he added, 'she might still be here in Amsterdam. It's conceivable that someone might be playing a cruel joke on us.'

Dopff stood up and used both hands to convey what he was thinking, tracing elaborate patterns in the air and reinforcing them with a range of facial expressions. Janssen was able to translate.

'I agree with you, Kees,' he said. 'This whole distressing business is probably linked to the fact that we escaped from Paris. Well, you were there. You saw how desperate they were to recapture us.' Dopff's head bobbed again. 'You had the better of it, I fancy,' he went on, trying to lighten his misery with a touch of humour. 'You and Amalia got away by boat. I had to be smuggled out of the city, dressed as a woman. I don't think that Beatrix has ever forgiven me for wearing some of her clothes.'

The two men laughed at the memory. Janssen then left the workshop and went into the house, walking through to the *voorhuis* so that he could be close to the front door in case any mail was delivered. Beatrix was already there, pretending to dust the furniture while she hovered. She gave Janssen a dutiful smile.

'Kees and I were just recalling our escape from Paris,' he said.

'I'd hate to go through that again.'

'We all would, Beatrix. It was frightening.'

'I think it took years off my life,' she said. 'I don't think I'll ever feel the same again. Yet in some ways, this is even worse. When we had problems in France, we could do something about them. That's not the case now.'

'No, it isn't. We simply don't know where Amalia is or how we might go to her aid. Being kept in the dark like this is maddening.'

'We should have heard something by now.'

'I agree.'

'The house is not the same without Miss Amalia.'

'It feels so empty.'

'Are they still searching the city?'

'They've given up, alas,' said Janssen, failing to keep a forlorn note out of his voice. 'They found nothing.'

In the wake of his daughter's abduction, he'd raised the alarm and a search had been set in motion by the authorities. A handful of witnesses had come forward but none of them had seen the actual kidnap. All that they remembered was a coach hurtling away from the place where Amalia had been seized. Janssen was a man of influence in Amsterdam so no effort was spared and the search was extended well beyond the bounds of the city. After days of disappointment, it was finally abandoned. The conclusion was that she was not there.

Beatrix had spent all her time brooding on the kidnap.

'I don't think Miss Amalia is still in Amsterdam,' she said. 'I'd *know* it if she was still close. Someone has taken her far away.'

'Whoever he is, I do hope that he's been treating her well.'

'She's very brave, Master Janssen. I saw that when we lived in Paris and you disappeared. Miss Amalia was a tower of strength for Kees and for me. She doesn't deserve this to happen to her.'

'I know, Beatrix,' he said. 'I keep repeating it to myself.'

'I *swear* I'll take more care of her next time,' she said with passion. 'If – God willing – there *is* a next time.'

'I'm certain that there will be.'

His voice was firm but his mind troubled. He was trying to reassure himself as much as his servant. The disappearance of his beloved daughter had induced a kind of paralysis in him. He couldn't work, relax, think, act or enjoy his food. He drifted aimlessly through each day in a kind of all-enveloping mist. It was unsettling.

'This is no way for us to behave,' he said, attempting to shake himself out of his lethargy. 'We both have better things to do than to lurk out here, Beatrix. I suggest that we get on with them.'

'Very well,' she said, reluctantly.

After a glance through the window at the empty street, she retreated into the parlour. Summoning up his willpower, Janssen returned to the workshop and clapped his hands.

'It's time I did some work in here,' he announced. 'I've been resting far too long. I need something to engross me, Kees.'

His assistant gave him an understanding nod but that was all that he had time to do. Shortly after Janssen came in, the doorbell rang and he immediately turned tail and headed back to the *voorhuis*. Beatrix won the race to the door, flinging it open and snatching the letter from the hand of the messenger. She thrust it breathlessly at Janssen and watched him tear it open. As he read it, his face was ignited by joy.

'Amalia is safe!' he cried. 'She's with the British army. And look,' he added, waving the enclosed note, 'here's a message in her own hand. She's unharmed and in good health. Captain Rawson rescued her.'

Janssen was not simply talking to Beatrix and to the

messenger who stood at the open door. His loud cry had brought Dopff and the other servants running. They gathered around him with mounting excitement as he read out what Amalia had actually written. It was wonderful news. They were so overcome by a collective relief and elation that they hugged each other for several minutes. The long and agonising wait was finally over.

Lieutenant Ainley was delighted to be given the privilege of escorting the two ladies around the camp. Neither Amalia Janssen nor Sophie Prunier wanted to be cooped up in a tent all day and so they readily accepted the invitation to combine a tour of inspection with a walk in the fresh air. The only thing that dampened Amalia's enjoyment was the fact that Daniel was not escorting her. To stroll through the camp on his arm in such fine weather would have been a treat for her.

She'd met Jonathan Ainley more than once and liked his courteous manner and the way that he cheerfully venerated Daniel Rawson. What she didn't know was that he had a good command of French and so was able to converse freely with Sophie. As the three of them walked between the avenues of tents, the women gathered many approving stares and admiring comments. Sophie didn't need an interpreter. The looks on the men's faces were self-explanatory. Civil and attentive, the lieutenant pointed out various aspects of the camp and talked about battles in which the army had been involved. Out of deference to Sophie's presence, he chose not to dwell on the casualties suffered by the French and their allies.

Amalia sensed that he was developing more than a passing interest in their companion. Even in borrowed attire, Sophie was a striking young woman. Most of what Ainley said was directed at her and she, in turn, asked most of the questions. It almost reached a point where Amalia began to feel that she was in the way.

'When will you return to Mons?' asked Ainley.

'I have to wait until my parents come home from Paris,' said Sophie, 'so I may be here for a few days yet.'

'I won't complain about that, mademoiselle.'

'Thank you, Lieutenant.'

Amalia watched as she acknowledged the compliment with an engaging smile. She'd never seen Sophie's smile before and realised how it released the full beauty of her face. Ainley was captivated. For the first time since their escape, Sophie was relaxed and able to enjoy something. Amalia was glad that the horrid memories of the woman's ordeal had been put briefly behind her and that she could be in an army camp without feeling endangered.

'And what do *you* do, Lieutenant?' wondered Sophie.

'I simply obey orders,' he replied.

'You have to give them as well, don't you?'

'It's more a question of passing them on. The structure of command in an army is crucial. I occupy a particular place in it with very particular duties.'

'How long have you served under His Grace?' asked Amalia, determined not to be left out altogether.

'Ever since this war started,' he said. 'Captain Rawson and I have served side by side – though he hadn't attained a captaincy when we first met.'

'Yes, I've heard the story of his career.'

'It bears retelling time and again, Miss Janssen.' He switched from English back to French. 'You must be an admirer of Captain Rawson as well, I daresay.'

'He rescued me,' said Sophie. 'I can never thank him enough. I was beginning to fear that I'd never get away from that camp.'

He was amused. 'When you did so, however,' he noted, 'you ended up in another army camp. It was a case of jumping out of the frying pan and into the fire.'

'Oh, no, I think that I am very safe here.'

'And why do you feel that?'

'To begin with, it has gentleman like you in it, Lieutenant.'

Ainley was not sure how to cope with the flattering remark so he turned away. Amalia wasn't watching him. Her eyes were on the smile that Sophie had given him. It was almost coquettish and it worried her. The Frenchwoman was behaving oddly and Amalia didn't know why. Once again, she felt that she was intruding.

'Well,' said Ainley, facing them again, 'you've seen almost everything there is to see.'

'We haven't seen the big guns yet,' said Sophie.

'I didn't think that cannon would hold any appeal for you. Artillery is not something that usually interests ladies.'

'I'm very interested,' said Sophie. 'What about you, Amalia?'

'Yes, I'm happy to view the cannon,' replied Amalia.

'In that case,' said Ainley, obligingly, 'follow me.'

It took hours. Distraught at the loss of his sword, Daniel began the search by going from wagon to wagon and asking if anyone had the weapon. From the shifty looks he collected from certain people, he could see that they'd been involved in looting his supplies but none of them had even seen the missing sword. When he offered to pay handsomely for its return, he still had no response and had to accept that he'd not find the weapon among the camp followers. The one person he didn't question was the blacksmith's wife, Josette. Had she possessed the sword, he was certain that she'd have used it on him now that she realised that Daniel was responsible for her husband's inability to enliven the marital couch at night.

The search took him on a meandering route that ended at the wagon owned by Alphonse and his father. The old man was there this time and he recognised Daniel instantly.

'Why, it's Gustave,' he said, pointing. 'My son told me that you'd come back. Where have you been?'

'I had to leave camp for a while,' said Daniel.

'That was a mistake. You left your wagon unguarded.'

'I know that. Almost everything in it has been looted.'

'Well, don't look at me,' said the old man, truculently. 'We never steal from friends. Josette drove your wagon away. Speak to her.'

'I already have,' said Daniel, 'and she wasn't pleased to see me.'

The old man cackled. 'Did she try to hit you?'

'I didn't stay long enough.'

'Josette has fire in her belly – and with a belly that size, that means a real inferno.'

Daniel waited until the old man stopped shaking with mirth.

'I'm trying to find something that was in my wagon,' he said.

'Then you may as well give up now.'

'This is too important to give up.'

'Listen,' said the old man, screwing up his one eye. 'Most of what was stolen has already been sold or eaten. You'll never find it.'

'I'm not after the provisions.'

'Your horse has vanished into thin air as well.'

'That doesn't worry me either.'

'Really – then what *are* you after, Gustave?'

'The only item that I want back is a sword. It was hidden under the seat and now it's gone.'

'Oh?' The old man was curious. 'And why would you be carrying a thing like that?'

'It's a family heirloom,' lied Daniel. 'It belonged to my father and I promised to keep it for his sake.'

'Did he serve in the army?'

'Yes, he did.'

'Which army was that?'

'It was the French army, of course. He was a true patriot.'

'What about you, Gustave?' asked the old man, regarding him shrewdly. 'Would you call yourself a true patriot?'

'Yes, I would,' affirmed Daniel.

'You'd be willing to die for France?'

'If it was necessary, I would.'

'Then you'd better volunteer for the army,' said the old man, 'because that's the only way you might get your sword back.'

Daniel's eye lit up. 'You know where it is?'

'I might do.'

'Then please tell me – I must know.'

'Earlier today, I went for a walk along the stream.'

'That's where my wagon was left,' said Daniel.

'I know. I saw it. I also saw the soldiers who were climbing all over it. I took care not to get too close,' continued the old man, 'because some of them are too free with their bayonets. I watched them search all over and underneath the wagon.'

'Did they find anything?'

'Yes, they did. I didn't get a proper look at what it was because they were all clustered together but I think it must have come from under the seat.'

'It was my sword!'

'If it was, the army has it now, Gustave. I daresay it's been handed over to a senior officer. You may have lost it for ever.'

When they put their minds to it, Burgundy and Vendôme could work effectively together. Their meeting that afternoon bordered on friendliness. They dealt with correspondence together, reviewed the latest intelligence and – should battle arise – discussed the deployment of their men. It was only when Vendôme was about to leave that the commander-in-chief introduced a note of discord.

'I'm pleased to see that you've come to your senses at last,' he observed. 'It's very gratifying.'

Vendôme tensed. 'I'm not sure that I follow.'

'Your mind is now centred on the task in hand, my lord Duke. It's no longer befuddled by your obsession with a captain in the British army.'

'It was not an obsession.'

'Let's not be pedantic. We'll call it an undue interest, shall we?'

'You can call it what you like, my lord,' said Vendôme, sharply. 'I see it as a legitimate subject of concern.'

'Then let's leave it at that,' said Burgundy with a patronising smirk. 'Suffice it to say that you've learnt your lesson.'

'And what lesson was that, may I ask?'

'That it's wrong to give priority to a single individual

when we have a whole army to fight.'

'Yet that's exactly what you do,' rejoined Vendôme. 'I've just spent a couple of hours listening to you repeating Marlborough's name over and over again. You, too, it seems, have your gaze fixed on a single individual.'

'Marlborough is their captain general.'

'Captain Rawson is a valued member of his personal staff and is entrusted with missions that nobody else could accomplish. That alone makes him a person of exceptional interest.'

'The fellow made you look like a fool.'

'I see no fool when I peer into a mirror, my lord.'

'Why do you keep arguing over my choice of words?' said Burgundy, irritably. 'Let me rephrase what I'm trying to say. You set a trap for Captain Rawson and he cleverly eluded it. I would have thought you'd be glad to forget about him altogether.'

'I can't do that,' said Vendôme.

'Why go on scratching the itch of your complete failure?'

'The failure was by no means complete. It was tempered with success. Even you were impressed at the way I contrived to get one of our ablest spies – Sophie Prunier – inside the British camp.'

'That was a pleasing stratagem, I admit.'

'Then you'll also admit that the capture of Captain Rawson is a pleasing stratagem when I bring him before you.'

Burgundy sniffed. 'It will never happen.'

'Would you care to place a wager on that?'

'I wouldn't demean myself by doing so. Mademoiselle Prunier, I am sure, is a lady of immense ability but even she is not going to walk into our camp with the captain over her shoulder.'

'I fancy that he'll walk into the camp on his own, my lord.'

'That's a preposterous notion!' said Burgundy, laughing.

'It's not too late to accept that wager.'

'I don't have the slightest interest in Captain Rawson.'

'Well, you should do – your grandfather certainly will.'

Burgundy flicked a hand. 'Be off with you!'

'Very well, my lord,' said Vendôme, frothing at being dismissed in such a peremptory manner. 'But I may be back before long and I'll be ready to accept your apology.'

Turning on his heel, he swept angrily out of the tent.

When he joined his father at their wagon, Alphonse found the old man in a reflective mood. Nudged out of his reverie, he told his son about the conversation with Gustave Carraud.

'I met him earlier,' said Alphonse, 'and told him what happened to his wagon. He was keen to speak to Josette.'

'What did you make of him?'

'He seemed very upset that his wagon had gone.'

'That's the funny thing,' said the old man, stroking his chin. 'It wasn't the wagon that he was worried about. He didn't even mind that his horse had been stolen. How can he stay in business with no animal to pull the wagon? It doesn't make sense. All that he was after was his sword.'

'I didn't know he had a sword,' said Alphonse.

'Gustave told me it was hidden under the seat. I knew he didn't find it there because I saw soldiers searching the wagon this morning. I think they took the sword away.'

'What does he want with it?'

'He claimed that it belonged to his father.'

'Did you believe him?'

'No,' said the old man, 'and I don't believe that he's a sutler. None of us would dare to leave our wagon unguarded for a few days. That's what Gustave did. Where did he sneak off to in the night?'

'I wondered about that.'

'I've been thinking, Alphonse.'

'Well?'

'There may be money in this for us,' said his father. 'There's something else I remembered about him, you see. Gustave wanted to be shown around the camp.'

'That's right – I took him. We went everywhere.'

'Put all those things together, Alphonse. He arrives here out of nowhere. He beats you and Victor in a fight. He gives us wine to buy our friendship. You walk around the camp with him. The next minute, he's nowhere to be seen. And when he comes back, the only thing that he's really after is a sword.' The old man narrowed the lids on his remaining eye. 'Do you see what I mean?'

Alphonse needed time to absorb all that he'd been told and to weigh its significance. His brain was slow but it eventually reached the same conclusion as his father.

'We need to speak to someone,' he decided.

'Leave that to me,' said the old man. 'I know how to haggle. We have useful information. That costs money.'

Daniel was agitated. The chances of getting his sword back seemed remote. If it was in the hands of the army, it meant that they'd had a specific reason for searching the wagon. They must have known who its putative owner was. That being the case, it was almost certain that a link had been established between the arrival of a sutler by the name of Gustave Carraud and the disappearance of two women from custody. Daniel was in a quandary. Common sense told him to get out of the camp as soon as possible but nostalgia urged him to continue the search for his sword. It was a question of head versus heart. As he sat beside the stream, a fierce battle was raging within him.

Another factor had to be considered. Henry Welbeck was hiding in the woods not far away, waiting to ride back to Terbanck with his friend. He would already be fretting. Daniel had assured him that he would soon return with his sword, possibly even with his wagon. That plan had been shattered. He was now cut adrift in the enemy camp with no means of warning Welbeck that his mission might take a great deal longer than anticipated. Daniel scolded himself for being too confident. Having made false assumptions, he was now suffering the consequences.

Should he go or should he stay? Daniel agonised over the decision until it was suddenly taken out of his hands. As he gazed at the stream, he noticed human figures dancing on the water and turned round quickly to discover that he was facing a dozen bayonets.

'Where the hell *are* you, Dan Rawson?' said Welbeck to himself. 'I want to get out of this bleeding place.'

Though he had the cover of the woods, he could never feel safe being so close to the French camp. His one source of comfort was the ample supply of food and drink they'd brought with them. Crouched beside the horses in the clearing, he munched some bread and cheese. He'd reloaded the pistol that Daniel had given him and carried a dagger as well but the weapons didn't reassure him. The wood was full of wild animals. Welbeck never actually saw any of them but the horses were aware of any potential danger. Every so often, they'd neigh, become restive and pull at their reins. When he heard a noise in the undergrowth yet again, Welbeck jumped to his feet and drew the pistol in readiness, hoping that he wouldn't have to fire a shot in case it was heard by any French soldiers on the road nearby. The sound of something scuttling rapidly away allowed him to relax a little and put the weapon back in its holster.

Finishing his meal, he brushed the crumbs from his

clothing then made his way furtively back towards the road. Welbeck hid in the thickets where Daniel had earlier concealed himself, remaining out of sight yet able to see the road in both directions. Once he'd worked out how to use it, the telescope proved a useful aid. Settling down, he found that he'd just put one knee into some animal dung. As he was trying to wipe off the mess with a handful of grass, an insect stung him on the back of the neck. Welbeck killed it with a slap but it had bequeathed a sharp pain. He swore at Daniel under his breath.

'Why on earth did I let you talk me into this, you bastard?'

Vendôme studied the papers with interest then held them up.

'These appear to be in order,' he said, blandly.

'Does that mean I can be released?' asked Daniel.

'Oh, no – these papers are the property of Gustave Carraud.'

'That's my name, Your Grace.'

'It's one of them, I grant you. I'm told that you also answer to the name of Marcel Daron when you pose as a wine merchant. I've no doubt that you have other names at your disposal as well and that, in each case, your papers will be expertly forged.'

Daniel had been hauled off to Vendôme's quarters and was being held by two guards. Raoul Valeran, who had been in charge of the arrest, was also there, anticipating extravagant praise if not a tangible reward for his work. When he was searched, Daniel had his pockets emptied and was deprived of the dagger he was carrying. His situation seemed hopeless but he wrested a tiny moment of joy out of it. On the table in front of Vendôme was what looked very much like Daniel's missing sword. He had difficulty in keeping his eyes off it.

'Let's dispose of Monsieur Carraud, shall we?' said Vendôme, holding the papers over a candle until they caught alight. He tossed them to the ground where they were consumed by flame. 'That takes care of that, I think. Perhaps you'd be so kind as to tell us your real name.'

'I'm Gustave Carraud,' said Daniel, doggedly.

'And what is your occupation?'

'I'm a sutler.'

'Then where is your wagon?'

'It's down by the stream.'

'Yes, so I believe. It's more or less empty and your horse has gone. How can you conduct business without something to sell?'

'The wagon was pillaged.'

'Why didn't you take more care of it?'

'I was…distracted for a while,' answered Daniel.

'That's not surprising,' said Vendôme with an oily smile. 'A woman like Mademoiselle Janssen would distract any man and so would Mademoiselle Prunier. You obviously have an eye for beautiful women.'

'I think you're confusing me with someone else.'

'I don't think so.' He turned to Valeran. 'Show him.'

Valeran stepped forward and lifted the sword from the table.

'Have you ever seen this weapon before?' he asked.

'No,' said Daniel, averting his gaze.

'Look at it more carefully.'

'I don't need to – it's an army sabre.'

'A *British* army sabre,' corrected Valeran, 'and it belongs to Captain Daniel Rawson of the 24th Foot.'

'I've never heard that name before.'

'It was Captain Rawson who rescued the two ladies to whom His Grace has just referred. The captain is very close to Amalia Janssen which is why she was taken hostage. Sophie Prunier was also held in custody and, unable to resist helping someone in distress, the captain agreed to take her with him as well.' He glanced at Vendôme to see if his questioning met with the other's approval. 'Does any of this sound familiar to you?'

'I'm afraid that it doesn't,' said Daniel.

'Are you speaking as Gustave Carraud or as Marcel Daron?'

Daniel remained silent. Unable to resist looking at his sword, he weighed up the possibilities of escape if he suddenly seized it. The weapon was only two feet away, balanced on Valeran's outstretched hands. There were four people in the tent with Daniel and all of them were armed. Outside, he'd seen two guards. Even if he managed to hack his way out of Vendôme's quarters, he wouldn't get far.

Valeran seemed to read his mind. He held the sword closer.

'Go on, Captain Rawson,' he urged. 'Take it. I know it's yours.'

'I'm a sutler. I have no need of a sword.'

'You're a soldier. You have no need of a wagon, especially as you've no idea how to protect it.'

'My name is Gustave Carraud,' said Daniel, stoutly.

'Are you still clinging to that ridiculous lie?'

'My papers were in order.'

'What papers?' asked Vendôme, taking over. 'I see no papers. Monsieur Carraud has been burnt out of existence so you must be someone else. We've spoken to one of the sutlers you befriended,' he went on. 'He told us how you disappeared from the camp for days and came back with some flimsy excuse. I had a feeling that we'd be seeing you again, Captain Rawson. You were so desperate to reclaim your sword, weren't you? That's the mark of a true soldier.'

Daniel was caught. They knew far too much about him. He wondered which of the sutlers had betrayed him. Alphonse had been too ready to accept him and Josette too eager to assault him. It had to be the old man. Daniel had been wrong to admit that he cared far more about a sword than he did about his horse and wagon. In doing so, he'd lowered his guard. Alphonse's father had been astute enough to realise that Gustave Carraud had something very important to hide. The arrest had been set in motion by the old man.

'Do you still deny that you are Captain Daniel Rawson?' said Vendôme, walking across to confront him.

'I do,' replied Daniel.

'Then perhaps it's time for you to meet an old friend.'

Vendôme gave a nod and Valeran went briskly out of the tent. Though he showed no sign of it, Daniel was profoundly alarmed. He feared that Henry Welbeck had been apprehended as well. A spasm of guilt shot through him. In bringing his friend, he'd imperilled him. Daniel could speak French fluently but Welbeck had only a limited grasp of the language. He could never pass for a Frenchman. If caught, his disguise would be useless. Daniel's face was impassive. Yet inwardly, he was berating himself.

As the tent flap was drawn back, he braced himself for the sight of his friend but it was not the sergeant who was led in by Valeran. It was a big man in the blue uniform of a major. Strutting across to him, the newcomer snatched off Daniel's hat so that he could take a good look at him. He required only a couple of seconds. Satisfied, he drew back his hand and delivered a resounding slap across Daniel's face.

'That's him,' he said with leering certainty. 'Marcel Daron.'

'Thank you, Major Crevel,' said Vendôme. 'You've proved his identity beyond doubt. Henceforth, however, you must call him by his real name – Captain Daniel Rawson.'

Chapter Seventeen

Amalia Janssen spent most of her time wondering where Daniel was and worrying that he might be in danger. But she also found herself recalling the inspection of the camp that she and Sophie Prunier had made in the company of Lieutenant Ainley. Something about the other woman had troubled her deeply yet she was not quite sure what it was. Sophie had never been less than friendly and confiding towards her. During their imprisonment, they'd been able to offer each other mutual support. Even in so short a time together, a trust had built up between them. It was the reason that Amalia had felt able to talk so freely to Sophie about her relationship with Daniel.

Something had changed and it disturbed Amalia so much

that she lay awake that night, trying to solve the puzzle. Why had Sophie been so anxious to see the entire camp? What had made such a difference? Why had a woman who'd sworn that she'd never trust a soldier again been so ready to talk with Lieutenant Ainley? Why did she now seem at ease? What exactly was behind Sophie's ambiguous smile? As the questions multiplied in Amalia's mind, they combined eventually into one – who *was* she?

Amalia was confused. Part of her felt guilty that she should even question the character of a woman who'd endured such maltreatment in the French camp. At the same time, another part of her began to entertain nagging doubts. Jonathan Ainley had trusted Sophie implicitly and, in the course of their tour of the camp, had shown polite interest in her. Amalia was tempted to accept the lieutenant's judgement and to dismiss her feelings of unease about the woman. Yet they still persisted. Indeed, by morning they were beginning to plague her. She resolved to speak to someone.

Since Daniel was not there, Amalia had to find someone else who'd offer a sympathetic ear. Ainley was an interested party so she ruled him out at once and she didn't want to bother Marlborough with what might well turn out to be a mistaken assessment on her part. The person to whom she turned, therefore, was Cardonnel, a man of surpassing discretion and one on whom she could rely to be wholly dispassionate. After she'd eaten breakfast in her tent, she went in search of the secretary.

Amalia intercepted him on his way to Marlborough's quarters. When they'd exchanged greetings, she asked him for a few moments of his time. Cardonnel could not have been more agreeable.

'Take as much time as you wish,' he invited, 'though if you're hoping for news of Captain Rawson, you'll be disappointed. We've heard nothing from him.'

'I just wanted to mention something to you,' she said. 'I could be speaking out of turn here and, if that's the case, I apologise in advance. But I felt I must raise the matter with somebody.'

'And what matter might that be, Miss Janssen?'

'It concerns Sophie Prunier.'

'I understand that she's remaining with us for a few days.'

'That's one of the things that worries me,' admitted Amalia. 'She says that she'd rather stay here until her parents return from Paris. Yet, when we were held in the French camp, she was adamant that she'd never tell her parents a word of what had happened to her because it was too shameful. If that's the case, surely Sophie would be eager to return home *before* her mother and father do. She'd want to give the impression that she'd been there all the time.'

'That's a reasonable point,' said Cardonnel.

'It only popped into my mind yesterday.'

Amalia told him about the way that Lieutenant Ainley had conducted them around the camp and how Sophie – who'd expressed a hatred of the army when in custody – had suddenly developed a curiosity. Cardonnel was a good listener, giving her full rein then gently pressing for more detail.

'I mean no criticism of the lieutenant,' said Amalia. 'It was very kind of him to act as our guide. He found nothing untoward in Sophie's manner, but then, he didn't know her before she came here. This could all be nothing but silliness on my part,' she added with a diffident smile, 'and I'd be grateful if you'd tell me so. Then I could stop it from buzzing around in my head.'

'I'm very glad that it *did* buzz around, Miss Janssen.'

'Do you really mean that?'

'I do,' said Cardonnel. 'This is something that should be taken seriously and I'm grateful to you.'

'What would you advise?'

'Are you expecting to see Mademoiselle Prunier today?'

'Yes, I am.'

'Then I'd urge you to carry on as if nothing had happened. You must give her no indication at all that you've been harbouring any suspicions. Meanwhile,' said Cardonnel, 'I'll make His Grace aware of what you've told me. He might well want us to contrive a casual meeting with the lady so that we can sound her out a little.'

'It's strange,' said Amalia, gripped by remorse. 'I feel as if I'm betraying a friend.'

Before he could reassure her, Cardonnel saw someone walking rapidly towards him. After giving him a salute, the soldier handed him a message. Cardonnel read it then dismissed the man with a nod.

'Your fears were far from groundless, Miss Janssen,' he told her. 'It seems that Sophie Prunier is no longer in the camp. Somehow, she left during the night.'

Bound hand and foot, Daniel had found it impossible to sleep. All that he could do was to lie on the bare ground while two armed guards occupied the tent with him. It had been a time for recrimination. He rebuked himself for letting his search for the sword blind him to the hazards of such a quest. In thinking that the weapon would still be in the wagon, he'd been misled. In imagining that Alphonse and his father were friends of his, he'd not even considered that one of them might report him. In bringing Henry Welbeck – then getting himself caught – he'd stranded his friend in enemy territory. The momentary relief of actually seeing his sword had been completely erased by the confrontation with Major Crevel. He was in dire straits. Daniel had been captured, identified and exposed for what he was. He could look for no quarter from the enemy.

'So this is the infamous Captain Rawson, is it?' said Burgundy, regarding him with distaste. 'His audacity has finally got the better of him, it seems.'

'Too true, my lord,' said Vendôme, delighted to be able to show off his captive. 'He felt that he could walk in and out of the French camp with impunity. His calculations went awry this time.'

'I'm pleased to hear it.'

'I daresay that you're also pleased that you spurned my wager.'

'That's immaterial, my lord Duke.'

'Your purse would have been seriously lightened.'

With his hands tied behind his back, Daniel stood in Vendôme's quarters while the two commanders looked at him as if he was an animal in a cage. He was taunted, laughed at and humiliated. What made his suffering more intense was the fact that his sword was on a table over a yard away. The weapon with which he'd killed so many Frenchmen in battle was now in the possession of the enemy.

'What do you intend to do with him?' asked Burgundy.

Vendôme grinned. 'I know what I'd like to do,' he said, 'and that's to flay him alive for all the trouble he's given us.'

'That would be ignoble and improper.'

'It would also be wasteful. The captain is a worthy prize. I'm sending him to Versailles where he can be sternly interrogated and where His Majesty can appraise him.'

'My grandfather will be intrigued to meet him.'

'I'm sure that he'll devise a suitable punishment. It may even be,' he went on with a vindictive laugh, 'that he sends Captain Rawson to the Bastille.' He turned to Daniel. 'You'll not find it so easy to escape from there when you're kept in chains.'

Retaining his composure, Daniel was determined to show no fear. While the two commanders were gloating over him, he was taking their measure, noting the sharp contrast in their age and appearance, and the occasional moments of friction between them. Burgundy was nominally in command, but since the prisoner was in Vendôme's hands it was he who'd assumed control and was effectively boasting about it. As he looked into Vendôme's unforgiving eyes, Daniel could see why Amalia had been so frightened of him.

After goading the prisoner for a few minutes, Vendôme signalled to the guards to take him out. Burgundy blocked their exit.

'Wait there,' he said, a regal hand bringing the guards to a halt. 'Aren't you forgetting something, my lord Duke?'

'I don't think so,' replied Vendôme.

'What about his sword?'

'I thought to keep that as a souvenir.'

'There are much finer trophies with which to remember this war. I feel that the sword should travel to Versailles with its owner. After all, it was his pursuit of the weapon that brought about his downfall. My grandfather may be amused to hear the tale.'

'I'd rather it stay here,' said Vendôme.

'Then I must overrule you,' insisted Burgundy, taking the sword and examining it before handing it to one of the guards. 'See that this goes with Captain Rawson,' he said, curtly. 'It may well be that His Majesty uses it to cut off his head.'

Henry Welbeck had spent the night in a tree before. Accustomed to sleeping rough, he'd always done so in the company of other soldiers. Now that he was alone, he was more aware of danger. Darkness brought the wood alive and he heard all sorts of threatening noises in the undergrowth. Perched on one of the lower branches of a tree, he eventually managed to doze off. He was roused from his slumber at dawn by melodic birdsong and was immediately aware of the cramp in his limbs. Descending to the ground, he stretched himself to ease the pain then searched for breakfast in a saddlebag.

There was a rivulet nearby and he allowed the horses a drink before using the water to wash his face and to bring himself fully awake. Tethering the horses once more, he returned to the thickets adjoining the road and maintained his vigil. On the previous day, he'd been irritated by Daniel's failure to return swiftly. Any irritation was now swamped beneath his concern for his friend's safety. Welbeck used the telescope to scan the road in both directions then pointed it in the direction of the French camp.

It was hours before his patience was rewarded. A patrol came round the bend towards him, a dozen soldiers riding in pairs at a brisk trot. It was not their disciplined riding that interested the sergeant. His attention was fixed solely on the cart that rattled along with them. Trussed up, and seated in the rear of it, was Daniel.

'A pox on it!' muttered Welbeck, removing his eye from the telescope. 'What the devil am I supposed to do now?'

* * *

Jonathan Ainley was writhing with embarrassment. Summoned to Marlborough's quarters, he'd hoped for an assignment that showed how much he was valued by the captain general. Instead, he was being admonished for his lack of perception.

'When did this happen, Your Grace?' he asked.

'Some time during the night,' replied Marlborough. 'Clearly, Mademoiselle Prunier could not escape without assistance. It remains to be seen who actually provided it.'

'Are you certain that the lady was a spy?'

'Why else would she depart so abruptly?' said Cardonnel. 'It seems that we were all duped by her.'

'Not all of us,' observed Marlborough. 'Miss Janssen was deceived by her at first but it was she who actually sensed that our French guest was not the harmless victim she claimed to be. Her suspicions were communicated to my secretary but, by that time, it was too late. The bird had flown.'

Ainley winced. 'I feel such a fool, Your Grace.'

'You were not to know her true intentions. We, too, accepted her at face value and so did Captain Rawson. The lady was devious.'

'I should have been more alert when Mademoiselle Prunier asked to see our artillery. What woman likes cannon?'

'One who's offered the chance to count their number for the benefit of the enemy. In future,' said Marlborough, 'make it a rule never to conduct any stranger around the camp.

I'm sure that you did it out of courtesy and – because the stranger in this particular case was a beautiful woman – no whisper of doubt was heard in your ear.'

'No,' confessed Ainley. 'I was gulled.'

'Learn from the experience, Lieutenant.'

'I will, Your Grace. What can I do to make amends?'

'I can tell you that,' said Cardonnel. 'You can help to find the person or persons who aided her escape. Since Mademoiselle Prunier had quarters near your regiment, the likelihood is that someone from the 24th Foot was also in the pay of the French. Find out who is missing and report back to us.'

'I'd sooner lead a patrol in pursuit of the lady,' said Ainley.

'One has already left camp,' Marlborough told him, 'but I suspect that she will have too good a start to be overhauled.' Seeing his extreme discomfort, he felt a pang of sympathy. 'Comfort yourself with this thought, Lieutenant,' he went on. 'Sophie Prunier learnt nothing that Ralph Higgins had not already discovered. She will merely confirm intelligence already supplied.'

'That's no consolation to me, Your Grace. I failed.'

'You were misled by a pretty face,' said Cardonnel. 'That is all.'

Marlborough gave a wry smile. 'It's happened to every one of us at some time or other, Lieutenant,' he remarked. 'You suffered the fate of all mankind.'

* * *

Because he had so few advantages, Henry Welbeck made the most of them. The map that Daniel had given him was accurate enough to spark an idea. He should be able to get well ahead of the patrol. It was keeping to the road and moving at a moderate pace. By riding across open country at a gallop, Welbeck believed that he could rejoin the road at a point where it looped south, and arrange some kind of ambush. His pistol could only account for one soldier and there were a dozen guarding Daniel, not to mention a driver who would have some sort of weapon. An indifferent horseman, he didn't even notice the pounding of the saddle in his crotch and the lurching sensation in his stomach. The hectic journey gave him thinking time and that proved critical.

How could he stop and disable a French patrol? How could he rescue his friend? How could he ensure that Daniel was unharmed? How could he retrieve the sword? How could they get back to the safety of the British camp? These were the questions he kept firing at himself but the answers were elusive. As he sped along, his eyes were raking the terrain ahead for a suitable place, somewhere where he could make use of natural features. Occupying his mind like a dead weight was the image of Daniel, tied up, defenceless and bouncing in the rear of the cart. He knew that the one thing sustaining the prisoner in his hour of need was the conviction that Welbeck would come to his aid. The sergeant couldn't let him down.

Unable to answer any of the questions that continued to besiege him, Welbeck asked himself another one. If their roles were reversed, what would Daniel Rawson do in the same circumstances?

It was tantalising. Seated in the cart with his hands securely bound behind his back, Daniel was only feet away from his sword. It was travelling with him and had been placed nearby as a visible taunt. He endured plenty of other taunts from the two soldiers riding behind the cart but he ignored their jeers. They would soon tire of mocking him. All that concerned Daniel were the whereabouts of his friend. He knew that Welbeck would have spent the night in the wood but wasn't at all sure that the sergeant had witnessed the patrol as it passed by. His friend might still be in the clearing with the horses, wondering what had happened. Daniel couldn't rely on him.

The sword was his only means of escape. Indirectly responsible for his capture, it might also be his salvation. If he could get close enough, its sharp blade would soon cut through his bonds. Somehow he had to distract the soldiers riding behind him. As long as they were there, he had no hope of reaching the weapon. The road was pockmarked with ruts and holes, making the journey a painful one. As the wheels of the cart explored each ridge or depression, Daniel was tossed helplessly to and fro. Whenever he fell sideways onto his shoulder, he had to haul himself upright again. His antics provided endless amusement for the two soldiers.

Emerging from the wood, the patrol kept up a steady pace for the next few miles. Daniel saw nothing of what lay ahead. The only road that he could see was the one that he was facing. When he heard sounds of commotion behind him, therefore, he didn't at first know what had caused them. Horses neighed, men shouted and the cart came to such an abrupt halt that Daniel was thrown sideways. He could smell smoke and hear the rumbling sound of a small avalanche that descended on the patrol. One of the horses behind him reared and unseated its rider. The other horsed neighed frantically and danced out of the way of the cascading stones.

Daniel responded swiftly. Rolling over, he reached his sword and angled the blade so that it sawed through the rope that held his wrists. Once his hands were free, he seized the weapon and was just in time to ward off an attack from the soldier who'd been unsaddled. Parrying the slash of the man's sword, he flicked his wrist and took the soldier's eye out, making him scream in agony. One glance told Daniel what had happened. As they came round a bend, the patrol had been confronted by a fire then pounded by rocks that came hurtling down the rocky incline to their right. Horses were frenzied, their riders unable to control them. Stones kept coming. When one of the soldiers dismounted and tried to scramble up the gradient, he was shot dead by Welbeck.

The driver of the cart was the next victim, hacked from

behind by Daniel then thrown bodily off the vehicle. Seizing the reins, Daniel snapped them hard and set the two horses off into a mad gallop, buffeting a soldier who'd been unsaddled and knocking him senseless. In the general mayhem, most of the patrol had been disabled because their mounts had been lamed by the vicious flurry of stones. Two of them, however, had the presence of mind to go in pursuit of the prisoner, riding through the flames and galloping along the road after the cart. When it veered off the track and went careering across a field, they went after it, sabres drawn and blood pumping.

Daniel could not outrun them. The most he could do was to put distance between himself and the rest of the patrol so that he was only up against two men. He had an advantage. Their orders were to take him to Versailles and hand him over alive. If they killed their prisoner, they'd have to answer to Vendôme and they'd have no wish to do that. Their instinct would be to maim him in order to disarm him. Daniel was still well ahead of them but they were gaining on him. It was time for a change of tack.

When he spotted a copse off to the right, he guided the cart towards it and vanished into the trees, swerving past their gnarled trunks, ducking low branches and seeing bushes thrash at the sides of the vehicle. For a few minutes, the canopy blocked out the light. As he emerged once more into the sunshine, he saw that he was in a field that rose gently towards a ridge. Going halfway up it, Daniel brought his horses in a complete circle and headed back towards the copse. When the soldiers came galloping out of the trees, therefore, they saw the cart aimed directly at them. One of the horses flew into a panic, rearing up on its hind legs then bolting so uncontrollably that its rider struggled to stay in the saddle.

Daniel tugged on the reins and brought the cart skidding to a halt, sending clods of earth spinning into the air. Then he picked up his sword, jumped into the rear of the cart and beat off the attack from the other soldier. Hacking away at him, the man was trying to dislodge his weapon so that he could overpower him and take him prisoner. Daniel had no time for the niceties of swordplay. Snatching up the rope that had earlier held him, he lashed out at the horse's head and made the animal neigh in terror. As it tossed its head sideways and came round in a half circle, Daniel ducked under the swishing sabre that was aimed at his shoulder then thrust upwards with his own sword. Its point went deep into the stomach of the soldier and caused him to drop his weapon.

Swearing loudly, he fell into Daniel's arms and used the last of his strength to beat feebly at his chest. Daniel lowered him to the ground, withdrew his sword and thrust it through his heart to spare him a lingering death. Then he mounted the horse and rode off at a gallop with blood still dripping from his sword.

* * *

Vendôme was pleased to welcome Sophie Prunier back into the French camp and to hear a full account of her adventures. He was grateful for the detail she was able to provide of the enemy and was amused at the way she'd deceived even the Duke of Marlborough.

'I'd be the first to admit that I never expected you to be rescued by Captain Rawson,' he said, 'but I feel that it worked out to our benefit in the end. You are to be congratulated.'

'Thank you, Your Grace,' she said.

'I think you've earned a reunion with your husband now. You'll find Lieutenant Bouteron waiting for you in his quarters.'

'Before I go, I must give you a warning. Captain Rawson set out for this camp for the second time. According to what I was told, he's anxious to retrieve his sword.'

Vendôme gave a throaty chuckle. 'I assisted him,' he said. 'The captain was arrested and brought before me. Since he was so keen to have his sword, I sent it with him to Versailles. I've left it to His Majesty to determine the fate of Daniel Rawson. My guess is that we shall never hear of the fellow again.'

Henry Welbeck ate the last of the cheese then washed it down with a swig of wine. The loaded pistol lay beside him. He was sitting in the darkness on top of the hill near the farmhouse used by the deserters as their refuge. His thighs were smarting and his crotch felt as if it were on fire. He'd never ridden so hard or so recklessly as he had when he fled from the scene of the ambush, and he vowed that he'd never do so again. One of the horses had had to be left behind. The other was now munching what was left of the hay stored at the farmhouse.

He heard the jingle of a harness first. The slow clip-clop of hooves followed. Pistol in hand, Welbeck was ready to shoot. Then he saw a familiar profile coming out of the gloom and laughed happily.

'Here he is at long last,' he teased. 'What kept you, Dan?'

The first thing that Daniel did when they returned to camp was to seek out Amalia Janssen in her tent and assure her that he was safe. He gave her only an attenuated version of what had happened and – when he showed it to her – his sword had been wiped clean of blood. Daniel was shocked to learn that Sophie Prunier had fled and shaken to realise that he'd been taken in so completely.

'I should have been more careful,' he said.

'It was my fault,' said Amalia. 'I was the one who urged you to bring her with us when we escaped from the French camp. The person who has really been left with a red face is Lieutenant Ainley.'

Daniel smiled tolerantly. 'That's not unexpected,' he said. 'The sight of a gorgeous woman usually makes Jonathan blush and so his judgement is impaired. Like the rest of us, he was cleverly exploited by Mademoiselle Prunier. It took another woman to unmask her in the end. Your instincts were sound, Amalia.'

'Where will she be now?'

'Someone will have helped her to get back to Braine l'Alleud and she'll be laughing at our expense. However,' he went on, kissing her, 'I can't stay. His Grace will be expecting a report.'

Amalia smiled. 'In the space of a couple of days,' she observed, 'he lost Sophie Prunier but gained Daniel Rawson. He'll consider that a profitable exchange.'

Marlborough received a much more detailed account of what had happened in the French camp. While playing down his own role in the escape, Daniel emphasised how heroic and imaginative Henry Welbeck had been. Without the sergeant's ambush, he stressed, he would have been taken all the way to Versailles for an unpleasant confrontation with the French king.

'That's an honour I'm happy to forego,' said Daniel.

'I'm sure that he'd have been very interested to meet you,' said Marlborough. 'Your escapades at the Bastille have made you a marked man, Daniel. Make no more visits to the enemy camp – that's an order rather than a suggestion.'

'It's one that I'm happy to obey.'

'We heard about your part in the arrest of the deserters,' said Cardonnel. 'Sergeant Welbeck featured there as well, I believe.'

'He did indeed,' confirmed Daniel. 'Where are they now?'

'Awaiting execution – they faced a court martial.'

'Yes,' added Marlborough. 'Had you been here, they'd have been hanged already. We felt that both you and the sergeant would like to be present when those rogues dance on the scaffold. It will serve as a warning to anyone else contemplating desertion.'

'What's happened here in my absence?' asked Daniel.

'Nothing,' said Cardonnel, pursing his lips, 'absolutely nothing. It's been a case of hesitation and inactivity. I fancy that the French are trying to *bore* us into submission. The impasse has been going on for weeks now.'

'I had the dubious pleasure of meeting their commander-in-chief in company with the duc de Vendôme. My impression was that there was some discord between them,' said Daniel. 'If they are bickering about what strategy to employ, that could explain their indecision.'

'It's a mixture of indecision and natural caution, Daniel,' said Marlborough. 'We saw how Vendôme played his hand last year. He'd rather hold on to what they already have than risk a major battle. When I saw the size of his army, I hoped that he'd at last come out of his shell but he seems far too snug inside it.'

Daniel gave a hollow laugh. 'Snug is not a word I'd apply to him, Your Grace,' said Daniel. 'He struck me as a man who'd prefer action. All that he requires is approval from Versailles.'

'There's the rub. The French have to get word from King

Louis before they can move and we must have our strategy ratified by our allies. Neither of us can act independently. It's the besetting sin of war by coalition.'

'We could never win on our own, Your Grace.'

'I know,' said Marlborough with a melancholy sigh. 'Allies are a necessary evil. I'd find them less of a hindrance if they managed to arrive on time. After all these weeks, Prince Eugene has still not made an appearance. Latest reports put his troops somewhere between here and the Moselle.'

'Their movements will at least distract the French.'

'We need them here, Daniel.'

'I agree, Your Grace.'

'If we are to save Brussels, we require all our troops.'

'Only if the French launch an attack, and there seems to be very little indication of that happening.'

'There's none at all,' said Marlborough. 'There was a time when their armies were the finest in Europe, sweeping aside all before them. Now they seem to have lost their stomach for a fight.'

'We sapped their strength at Ramillies,' observed Cardonnel.

'We did, Adam. Their appetite for war has never fully been regained. What possible hope do we have of ever bringing this conflict to a satisfactory conclusion when the enemy simply cools its heels and watches us? It's soul-destroying,' said Marlborough, shaking his head. 'The French refuse to budge.'

* * *

328

On 5 July, 1708 the French moved with speed and precision. After the long lull, they burst into life in the most unexpected way. While advance guards hurried on ahead of them, they left Braine l'Alleud with dramatic suddenness and marched westwards. Their first prize was the beautiful town of Bruges. Knowing of the general discontent felt towards the Confederate army, French sympathisers had worked hard to win over the citizens. They'd been forewarned of the dash to the west and, as soon as the army appeared before Bruges, its gates were flung open and the French were hailed as deliverers. A major prize had fallen into enemy hands without a shot being fired.

Ghent was a slightly more problematical target in that it had a garrison of three hundred British soldiers under the command of Major General Murray. They were not there merely to protect the city but to suppress any dissident elements within it. In the event of attack, they'd offer stout resistance. Careful planning was the secret of French success. General de Chemerault and his men infiltrated the city, disguised as peasants, with the aid of the former Grand Bailiff, M de Fouille. Its gates were firmly shut against the British. They were isolated in their castle and besieged by a French army whose numbers swelled by the hour. After holding out bravely for a couple of days, Murray and his men were forced to surrender.

Two places of great strategic importance had changed hands at a stroke. What the British had thought were foraging expeditions were, in fact, armies with specific targets in mind. Marlborough had been completely outfoxed. The French had made themselves masters of the middle reaches of the River Scheldt and of the canals leading to the coast. Marlborough was decisively cut off from his North Sea base at Ostend, the port with the shortest route from England. Any supplies coming from there would henceforth be involved in a longer and more onerous voyage.

Burgundy and Vendôme had earlier had their differences over which tactics to employ. What this operation showed was that they could combine their men into a highly effective fighting force. The capture of Bruges and Ghent delivered more than a profound shock to the Allies. They had to stand by and watch nearly all the gains made at the battle of Ramillies taken ruthlessly from them. Marlborough was rocked. The disastrous news stunned him. The French had achieved the kind of swift, unheralded, brilliant victory that was more usually associated with the captain general of the Allies.

The Duke of Marlborough had been beaten at his own game.

CHAPTER EIGHTEEN

Reeling from the shock of the French victories, the Allied armies took time to recover. Their morale was visibly lowered. They'd been led for so many years by the outstanding military mind of his day and, as a consequence, enjoyed a magnificent record of success. The sudden reversal of fortunes called that success into question. Marlborough had failed them. There could be no equivocation about that. His prestige – so vital a factor in controlling an army of British, Dutch, Austrian, Hanoverian, Prussian and Danish soldiers – had been severely weakened.

Henry Welbeck was never a man to mince his words.

'What's got into the bloody man?' he demanded. 'We work our balls off to hold onto Bruges and Ghent then he hands them over to the French on a silver plate.'

'That's not what happened,' said Daniel.

'Well, that's what it looks like to me, Dan. While we're stuck here, waiting for signs of life from the enemy, they race off and capture two major towns. Why didn't His Grace see it coming? Is he blind as well as fucking stupid?'

'Moderate your language, Henry.'

'I'm only saying what everyone else is thinking.'

'Nobody can accuse His Grace of stupidity,' said Daniel, roused to defend Marlborough. 'He's a man of exceptional gifts who's waged this war with exemplary skill.'

'Until now, that is.'

'Even the best horse stumbles. I concede that mistakes were made but let me say this in extenuation. His Grace has been ill since the start of this campaign. I've never seen him in such poor health. To his credit,' Daniel went on, 'he's never simply taken to his bed and abandoned his responsibilities. He's forced himself to press on and give us the leadership that we need.'

'We don't need a leader who gives territory away.'

'You're being far too harsh.'

'I'm being honest, Dan,' said Welbeck, fiercely. 'Our captain general has lost his way and I've lost my faith in him.'

Daniel was upset to hear such biting criticism of Marlborough from someone as experienced as the sergeant. It was symptomatic of a deep malaise that had spread throughout the ranks. The Allied armies had met with setbacks before but they'd never been blamed on its commander-in-chief. This was different. Such was the scale of their loss that Marlborough was being singled out as the scapegoat. Daniel felt that it was unjust.

They were trying to hold their conversation above the turmoil all round them. The army was striking camp. Along with all the other regiments, the 24th Foot would soon be on the march but they'd do so with a diminished confidence in their leader.

'What are we going to give to the French next?' asked Welbeck, cynically. 'Are we going to sacrifice Brussels to them as well?'

'We're going to do what we always do – fight back hard.'

'We have to find the enemy first.'

'Our scouts are already at work, Henry.'

'Where were they when the Frenchies made their dash for Bruges and Ghent? Why didn't they raise the alarm?'

'There's no point in dwelling on the mistakes of the past.'

'There's every point, Dan. It's the only way to stop the mistakes being repeated. Everyone in this army knows that forewarned is forearmed. Yet we had no bloody warning at all.'

'The French deceived us,' conceded Daniel. 'They disguised their initial movements as large-scale foraging and we were thrown off the scent. They achieved a remarkable coup.'

'In other words, they have better generals than we do.'

'No, Henry, it simply means that they caught us napping this time. It won't happen again.'

Welbeck was unconvinced. 'I wish I could believe that.'

'There's something you're forgetting,' said Daniel. 'I was inside the French camp only days ago. I know when an army is about to go on the march and I saw no sign of that whatsoever.'

'That's easy to explain,' said Welbeck, bluntly. 'You were too busy looking for your damn sword to notice anything else.'

The sergeant went off to yell at some soldiers who were too slow in taking down their tent. Wounded by the tart comment, Daniel had to admit that there was some truth in it. His single-minded pursuit of the sword had blinkered him. On his second visit to the camp, he should have taken more notice of what was going on there. He was still reflecting on his failure when Jonathan Ainley came up to him.

'We're on the move at long last,' said the lieutenant.

'It's going to be a forced march. We can't let the French outmanoeuvre us again. I hear that their main army has already crossed the River Dender and their pioneers will no doubt be breaking down the bridges at places like Alost and Ninove.'

'What sort of a mood is His Grace in?'

'I'm more concerned about his health,' said Daniel. 'His

mood is as defiant as ever but he's suffering from a fever as well as a migraine. His Grace is hardly in the best condition to wage a war.'

Marlborough put on his hat, straightened his back and adjusted his coat. He looked pale, drawn and in obvious pain. Alone with him in the tent, Cardonnel was anxious.

'You shouldn't push yourself like this, Your Grace,' he said.

'An army needs its captain general.'

'Not if he's indisposed. Your doctor advised complete rest.'

'At a time like this,' said Marlborough, 'I can't afford to rest.'

'Your migraine has been worse than ever today.'

'That's why I'm so determined to strike back at those who gave it to me. Burgundy and Vendôme are the authors of my headache.'

'Too much activity will only make it worse, Your Grace.'

'Then I'll have to endure it.'

'I think it's time that you put your health first for once.'

'Stop fussing over me,' said Marlborough, good-humouredly. 'You're sounding like my dear wife. If I so much as cough, she thinks that I'm about to expire. Take heart, Adam,' he went on, 'I'm not nearly as bad as I must look.'

Though he recognised it as a patent lie, Cardonnel said nothing. Nobody had been in such constant contact with Marlborough as his secretary and he'd been able to gauge the steady deterioration of the other's health. More worryingly, he'd also seen him sink lower and lower into melancholy. Physical exhaustion was matched by a mental fatigue that had taken its toll on Marlborough's brimming confidence. There'd been moments when he'd lapsed into unqualified despair.

For his part, Marlborough steeled himself to withstand the drumming inside his head and the creeping heat that turned his body into a furnace. In the face of a daring French strategy, he'd been found wanting and that had inflicted a deep wound on his pride. Accustomed to receiving unstinting praise, he was now being roundly condemned in some quarters. Ordinarily, when he walked around his camp, he floated on a wave of respect and affection. Both, he feared, had been forfeited. Silent reproach from his officers could be borne far more easily than his loss of esteem among the common soldiers. Corporal John had to earn back their regard immediately.

As Marlborough was about to leave, Cardonnel had a request.

'At the very least, travel in your coach,' he said.

'No, Adam,' replied Marlborough, stoically. 'I need to ride at the head of the army. I have to be *seen*.'

The hasty departure meant that Daniel had little time to take his leave of Amalia Janssen. While he was going in one direction, she was about to be taken back to Amsterdam with an armed guard.

'When will I see you again?' she asked.

'It may not be for some time, Amalia,' he warned.

'Please write to me, if you can.'

'I'll endeavour to do so.'

She took his hands. 'I'm sorry that I caused so much trouble.'

'You caused none at all,' he said.

'I let myself be taken as a hostage, Daniel. That put your life in danger and I still shudder when I think about it.'

'You didn't get kidnapped deliberately.'

'Nevertheless, I put you to a lot of trouble.'

Daniel smiled. 'Coming to your rescue was no trouble at all, Amalia,' he said. 'My only regret is that I brought Mademoiselle Prunier with us. I should have left her with her paymasters.' He looked over his shoulder as another regiment marched past. 'I'll have to go now. Think of me.'

'Nothing could stop me doing that.'

'Have a safe journey!'

'Thank you,' she said, 'but I'm far more concerned about your safety than mine. You could be involved in a battle.'

'I'm ready for it,' he said, patting the sword that hung by his side. 'Now that I have this back, I can't wait for action in the field.'

Amalia trembled. 'It worries me when you talk like that.'

'Then don't listen to what I say.'

'You seem to welcome danger.'

'The only thing I welcome is an end to this interminable war,' he told her, 'and I'm prepared to do anything I can to bring it about. Only then can I think about spending more time with you, Amalia.'

She squeezed his hands. 'Good luck, Daniel!'

'I was hoping for a farewell kiss.'

'You don't need to hope,' she said with a laugh.

'Thank you – this is the best way to part.'

Enfolding her in his arms, he gave her a long, lingering kiss, relishing every luscious second of it and ignoring the envious jeers of the soldiers who went swiftly past them.

One thing for which Marlborough's soldiers were justly famed was their ability to put on a superb display of forced marching. They kept their shape, negotiated any undulations in their path with ease and maintained a considerable speed. Indeed, they moved so fast that they almost caught the French army in two separate columns halfway between Tubize and Ninove. In the event, all that the French rearguard lost was its baggage. The duc de Vendôme saw it a reason for congratulation.

'We fooled them again,' he said, chortling. 'We flourished our colours in the scrub and gave the impression that our entire army was about to give battle. That made them back off at once.'

'Marlborough has been tricked once more,' said Burgundy, sipping a celebratory glass of wine. 'That won't improve his temper.'

'Or his health, for that matter – he's a sick man.'

'Is that what your intelligencer told you?'

'Sophie Prunier – Madame Bouteron, I should say – met him in person. She said how old and ill he appeared.'

'We're not here to act as his physicians, my lord Duke. A sick commander is a serious handicap. We must exploit his weakness to the limit. The best way to do that, I feel, is to lay siege to Menin.'

'That would take us farther west,' argued Vendôme, 'and our real destination should be Oudenarde. Seize that and we'd have complete control of the central part of the Scheldt before the Allies have time to bring in reinforcements.'

'I still favour Menin as our target.'

'Then I beg you to reconsider, my lord. Our first task should be to occupy the river crossings at Lessines. That would prevent the enemy from getting over the river and severing our communications with Lille and Tournai.'

'I've taken that into account.'

'Then respond accordingly.'

'You advice is welcome,' said Burgundy with a lordly smile, 'but I choose to disregard it in this instance.'

Vendôme bristled. 'Oudenarde has to take priority over Menin.'

'That's for me to decide.'

'It's the crucial fortress town on the Scheldt. Until we capture it, the Allies will always be masters of that stretch of the river.'

'I know that, my lord,' said Burgundy, irritably, 'and I promise you that we'll attack it in due course. Before that, however, I wish to invest Menin.'

'That operation would divert too many of our men.'

'Yet I find myself minded to attempt it.'

'*After* we occupy the crossings at Lessines,' insisted Vendôme, 'and after Oudenarde has fallen. Everything must be done in order. Even you must accept that.'

Burgundy was brusque. 'I wish that you wouldn't keep questioning my decisions, my lord Duke,' he said.

'If you made the right ones, there'd be no need to question them.'

'I take that as an insult.'

'It was not meant to be,' said Vendôme, trying to smother his rising fury under a pillow of politeness. 'I defer to you at all times and, as we've shown, we can devise a strategy that's both guileful and effective. On this point, however, there's a diversity of opinion. May I suggest that you consult the other generals? I think you'll find that they'll agree to a man with me.'

'I refuse to wage war by means of a show of hands,' snapped Burgundy, putting his glass down on the table. 'That has echoes of democracy about it and there's nothing I abhor more than that. I don't deny that most of the generals would side with you. It's only natural that old friends will support you against someone less seasoned.'

'They will see exactly what I see, my lord.'

'Then they are looking in the wrong direction. What they should bear in mind is that I was appointed by His Majesty to lead this army and my orders are above reproach.'

'I accept that,' said Vendôme in a voice that contained no hint whatsoever of acceptance. 'I just ask you to depend for once on my experience in the field.'

'Menin must come before Oudenarde.'

'Is that a command or an opinion?'

Vendôme met his gaze and there was a crackle of animosity in the air. Burgundy could not back down, yet, at the same time, he could not disregard the advice of a man who'd tussled so successfully with Marlborough in the past. Moving his glass aside, he looked down at the map that was laid out on the table. Oudenarde was less than twenty miles to the south-west of Ghent. Once taken, it would form a triangle with Bruges. Menin, by contrast, was farther to the west and north of Lille, a citadel so well fortified that it was the jewel of French fortresses. To take Menin would be to nullify any possibility of an attack on Lille from that direction. Burgundy made up his mind.

'This decision needs to be referred,' he said, settling for a compromise.

'That would waste valuable time,' protested Vendôme.

'We need royal approval here, my lord Duke. His Majesty will decide which we besiege first – Menin or Oudenarde.'

'If we wait for His Majesty's decision, it may be too late.'

'Without it, we can do nothing.'

Vendôme wanted to storm out of the tent in a rage but managed to maintain a measure of control. All that he could do was to wait and hope that his plan gained royal assent. He gave a rueful nod.

'So be it, my lord,' he said, darkly. 'So be it.'

Now that the campaign had at last been set alight, Marlborough acted with speed and authority. Brigadier Chandos was sent post-haste to Oudenarde, travelling at night with sizeable reinforcements. The main army was still at Assche and it was there that Daniel Rawson attended a council of war as an interpreter. Aware of how feverish Marlborough was, he was amazed at the coherence of the plan that was outlined.

'We must reach the river crossings at Lessines as soon as is humanly possible,' declared Marlborough, brooking no dissension. 'I've already ordered eight days of bread to be baked so that we're not hindered by shortage of food. In the interests of speed, our baggage and transport must be reduced to an absolute minimum.'

'What exactly does that mean, Your Grace?' asked a voice.

'If you want chapter and verse,' said Marlborough, picking up a list, 'I'll give it. Generals of foot are permitted to retain three wagons and a coach.' There was an audible gasp from around the table. 'Other generals are allowed only two wagons and a coach. Brigadiers must manage with one of each and colonels with only a pair of wagons. Yes,' he went on over the heavy murmur, 'I know that it will lead to inconvenience but it can't be avoided. If we lose the race to Lessines, then we'll be trapped on this side of the river.'

Daniel was impressed by his masterly performance. It was just like old times. From where he was sitting, however, he couldn't see the perspiration dribbling down Marlborough's face or assess how weak he now was. When the meeting broke up, a number of generals clustered around their commander-in-chief to clarify certain points in his orders. Daniel had the opportunity to take Cardonnel aside.

'What is the state of His Grace's health?' he asked, quietly.

'It's a cause for concern, Daniel.'

'Concern is not alarm.'

'We've not reached that stage yet, thank God,' said Cardonnel. 'His doctor bled him today and advised him to sweat out the fever. He's suffering badly but will, as you saw, rise above any discomfort he may feel.'

'His bravery is a lodestar for us all.'

Cardonnel grinned. 'I've heard that said about you.'

'Oh, I could never emulate His Grace,' said Daniel with humility. 'He can inspire a whole army. All that I can offer is the kind of blind courage that enables me to risk my life for the sake of a sword. I'm already beginning to feel ashamed of that episode.'

'Why is that?'

'I put my selfish needs before my duty to the army.'

'You'll discharge your duty much better if you have the right sword in your hand, Daniel.'

'That's true.'

'And if you have any twinges of conscience, there's a simple way to get rid of them. Distinguish yourself in battle and you'll feel that you made amends.'

'That depends if there *is* a battle,' said Daniel. 'We know that the French like to skirmish but will they meet us in a frontal attack? I must say, I have my doubts about that.'

'I don't,' returned Cardonnel, 'and, as you heard, His Grace is convinced that they are ready for battle this time. There's far too much at stake for them to pull back now. They want to erase the memory of Ramillies. Our task is to renew it.'

When the Allies marched south to camp at Herfelingen, their spirits were raised by the appearance at last of Prince Eugene. Unfortunately, he only arrived with an advance guard, having pressed on four days ahead of his cavalry. The bulk of his men were still approaching Brussels. They were being shadowed by Marshal Berwick, the hero of Almanza, where he'd crushed the Allied forces with a combined French and Spanish army. Berwick's orders were to watch Eugene's forces until their intentions became clear.

At the sight of his tardy ally, Marlborough rallied at once and gave Eugene a cordial welcome. Prince Eugene's bold leadership had earned him immense respect during the preceding years. He heard and readily agreed with Marlborough's plan of action. When Cadogan set off for Lessines with an elite body of men, hand-picked for their valour and for their experience, Eugene wished them well. He followed with the main army which broke camp at two in the morning.

Night marches were familiar to Marlborough's soldiers. They would never be popular but they usually achieved the desired result. So it was in this case. The French were heading for Lessines from the opposite side of the River Dender, bent on seizing the crossings and keeping the Allies at bay. They were mortified to learn that Cadogan and his men had been in the town since dawn and that the main army reached the river hours ahead of them. In all, Marlborough's forces had covered an astonishing thirty miles in less than thirty-six hours. Their speed completely disrupted French plans.

Seeing what had happened, Vendôme was puce with anger. He turned on Burgundy, riding beside him, and spat out the words.

'They got here before us,' he said with disgust.

'We moved as fast as we could, my lord Duke.'

'Had you listened to me, we'd have been here yesterday and in a position to keep them on the opposite bank. By seeking the authority of His Majesty before we acted, we squandered our opportunity.'

'May I remind you,' said Burgundy, piqued by his tone, 'that His Majesty approved of my suggestion to invest Menin?'

'He won't approve of this catastrophe, my lord.'

'I don't view it as such.'

'My advice was to secure the crossings here with all due haste and besiege Oudenarde. Neither objective is now possible.'

'The siege of Oudenarde was not sanctioned by His Majesty,' said Burgundy, taking refuge behind the authority of his grandfather. 'You read his dispatch, my lord Duke. The most that he recommended was that we should blockade the town.'

'It's too late for that now as well. Their men are already pouring over the Dender in large numbers.'

'In that case, we must withdraw.'

'But we have a chance to force a battle,' urged Vendôme. 'Their main army has not arrived in full yet and Prince Eugene's cavalry are still days behind. This is a moment for us to strike.'

'I think not,' said Burgundy after using a telescope to

review the strength and disposition of the Allied forces. 'We'll move north of Oudenarde and camp on the bank of the Scheldt.'

'I beg of you to think again, my lord.'

'I will only reach the same decision a second time.'

'What is the point of bringing our army here if we are not prepared to fight?' asked Vendôme with exasperation. 'Marlborough will not withdraw. He'll not yield one inch. If we attack, he's bound to close with us. Circumstances may not favour us again,' he went on. 'We must take advantage of them while we can.'

Burgundy paid him the courtesy of considering his advice. He surveyed the enemy through his telescope again then pulled out his saddle map. Opening it up, he indicated a point on the river.

'We'll withdraw,' he said at length, 'and head northwards towards Gavre, camping here.' His finger tapped the map. 'That will put the Scheldt between us and our enemy. There'll be other opportunities for battle, my lord. For the moment, we need to pitch camp so that we can gather our strength and decide on our next move. There's no hurry,' he went on, complacently. 'Their army and its reinforcements will not reach the Scheldt for some time yet.'

Nightfall found both armies sited beside a river. While the French were on the east bank of the Scheldt, the Allies had lit their campfires on the west bank of the Dender.

The town of Oudenarde lay between them. Burgundy and Vendôme were stationed a mere six miles north of it. Marlborough and Eugene were some fifteen miles to the south-east. Unlike the French commanders, they were in agreement with each other. Anticipating the possibility of a siege train being sent to Oudenarde, they decided to advance rapidly towards the town. In the dead of night, the ever reliable Cadogan was once again sent ahead with a force composed of eight squadrons, sixteen battalions, thirty-two regimental guns – lighter pieces attached to each battalion – and a bridging train.

Cadogan's orders were explicit. He was to improve the road, allowing faster movement over it for those following, establish five pontoon bridges to the north of Oudenarde and build a protective bridgehead on the Scheldt. This, it was hoped, would allow the Allies to cross the river to the west bank before the French did so. Now attached to Marlborough's staff, Daniel was with him when a first report came back from Cadogan.

'He's in sight of the river,' said Marlborough with satisfaction.

'At what time was the message sent, Your Grace?' asked Daniel.

'Nine o'clock this morning.'

'They've moved fast.'

'William Cadogan is not a man to dawdle. According to this,' said Marlborough, holding up the missive, 'the French camp is at Gavre. They'll be crossing the Scheldt before long. We mustn't keep them waiting.'

Daniel was soon in the saddle, riding with Marlborough at the head of forty squadrons, eager to join Cadogan's advance guard before the French realised what their intentions were. By one o'clock in the afternoon, they were thundering across the wooden timbers of the pontoon bridges. Behind them, the infantry were already on the march from Lessines. Daniel was exhilarated. He was not only heartened to see Marlborough shaking off his physical debility and behaving with characteristic authority, he sensed that battle was finally at hand. The Allies would have an opportunity to avenge the loss of Bruges and Ghent, and the sword that Daniel had taken such pains to retrieve would be put to good use.

Vendôme's temper had not improved overnight. If anything, it was at an even higher pitch. When news of the enemy's movements reached him, wrath crimsoned his cheeks and put murder in his eyes. He rounded on his commander-in-chief.

'You assured me that the Allies wouldn't reach the Scheldt for days,' he said, accusingly. 'While our men are still crossing the river as if they have all the time in the world, Marlborough's soldiers are already here on the west bank.'

'His speed took me by surprise,' confessed Burgundy.

'When you match yourself against Marlborough, you must always expect surprises. Otherwise, you're doomed to fail.'

Burgundy was adamant. 'There's no chance of our failing when we have a much larger army,' he asserted. 'Evidently, a battle is imminent. We've been left with no alternative but to fight.'

'We should have been in a position to dictate the terms of the encounter,' complained Vendôme, 'and not have it forced upon us. If you'd listened to my advice at the start, the Allies would still be fretting outside the walls of Lessines.'

'That's all in the past,' said Burgundy, dismissively. 'We have to meet this new situation and do so with vigour.'

'On that, at least, we can agree. We should attack at once.'

'I think not, my lord Duke.'

'All that we're facing at the moment is the advance guard. If we fall upon them without delay, we can put them to flight then march on Oudenarde.'

'I have a better strategy.'

'Dear God!' exclaimed Vendôme. 'Have you learnt *nothing*? Every second we delay gives the enemy time to bring more men across the river. We should strike now before reinforcements arrive. With deference to your position,' he went on, trying to show a semblance of respect, 'I submit that there *is* no better strategy.'

'Then we must agree to differ,' said Burgundy with muted anger. 'I suggest that you calm down before you make a judgement. A cool head is required, my lord Duke.'

'What use is a cool head without a detailed knowledge of warfare?' said Vendôme under his breath. Controlling himself with a conscious effort, he became apologetic. 'Forgive my hasty words, my lord. The prospect of battle excites me somewhat. I implore you to follow my advice this time and act decisively.'

'That's exactly what I intend to do. Having inspected the terrain with care, I want the army to form into line of battle along the ridge to the north of the River Norken. From there, we'll be able to see the spires of Oudenarde.'

'The time to look at spires is when we've defeated the enemy,' said Vendôme, earnestly. 'Strike now and we can rout them.'

'You've heard my decision,' declared Burgundy, 'and it will stand. Like everyone else under my command, you must obey orders.'

Vendôme scowled. There was nothing more to be said.

By the time that Marlborough and Eugene caught up with him, Cadogan had already had a brush with the cavalry of the French advance guard. Undaunted by larger enemy numbers, he hailed the arrival of the others and was eager to attack. His unassailable buoyancy raised the spirits of his men. After conversing with Cadogan about what had already occurred, Marlborough watched the enemy deploying along a low, partly wooded ridge that was punctuated by three small villages.

'They've chosen well,' he said with grudging admiration. 'It's a strong position.'

'Do we still attack, Your Grace?' asked Cadogan.

'We came here to fight and that's what we'll do.'

'There are many risks involved.'

Marlborough grinned. 'That's never stopped you before, William.'

'And it won't do this time,' said Cadogan, heartily.

'Now that we have them in our sights, we'll offer them battle. We must do – nothing else will suffice. We need a victory to appease our critics. If it miscarries, I'm ready to shoulder the blame.'

Overhearing the exchange between the two men, Daniel was impressed. Both men were confident and clear-headed. Since most of the Allied army were still scrambling over the pontoons, their leaders would be courting danger with an attack. Simultaneously, however, they'd be signalling to the enemy that they felt capable of inflicting serious damage on them even with a depleted force. The boldness of the plan appealed to Daniel.

Cadogan's appetite for action had been whetted. He was keen to be in the field again. Ahead of him were seven enemy battalions, made up of Swiss mercenaries. Sent forward by Vendôme, they had, by an oversight, never been recalled.

Cadogan acted decisively. With the consent of Marlborough, he unleashed his attack on them with British redcoats to the front supported by Hanoverian cavalry to their flank and rear. When the two sides met, there was an ear-splitting cacophony of clashing blades and musket fire, supplemented by cries of agony from men and horses as they were shot, hacked or bayoneted to the ground. The popping of musketry became a roar and clouds of smoke marked the successive volleys. The Swiss had erected some rudimentary barricades but they failed to hold back the onslaught. Cadogan's men were well trained, quick to respond to orders and merciless in combat. As soon as some of them fell, others stepped over their bodies to continue the fight with an iron determination.

The result was never in doubt. The Swiss brigades had been taken unawares. Their leaders had never imagined that Allied forces in such strength could be so close. Shocked and unprepared, they were no match for Cadogan's infantry and were soon put under intolerable pressure by the surging waves of redcoats. Cadogan deployed his men with such skill and purpose that they overcame all opposition within an hour. As the Swiss retreated, the Hanoverian cavalry harried them ruthlessly. Daniel was thrilled at the early success. Cadogan had not merely vanquished the Swiss and taken masses of prisoners, he'd bought priceless time for reinforcements to catch up with them. It augured well for the battle ahead.

* * *

Burgundy was dismayed by what he saw. From his position on the ridge, he witnessed the complete destruction of his Swiss battalions. It made him think again about how to fight the battle. Vendôme, who'd been an ardent advocate for striking hard at the enemy, now felt that it was too late to attack. Once again, he was overruled. On the orders of Burgundy, the French right wing began to pick its way down the slopes and over the River Norken, one of the many streams that crisscrossed the area. It was close countryside with ditches, marshes, bushes, hedgerows, copses, brambles and thick undergrowth hindering progress.

At approximately five o'clock, the right wing attacked Cadogan's forces with ferocity, overlapping it to the west and threatening to engulf it. Some relief came from a battery posted by Marlborough to fire away incessantly at the advancing French hordes. To counter the threat of being enveloped, Cadogan changed his front to the left but his line remained thin and potentially fragile. Fortunately, the nature of the terrain left little scope for cavalry. At Blenheim and at Ramillies, they'd been offered a wide, open, uncluttered plain on which troops could be aligned in strict formation and cavalry charges used to effect. The battle of Oudenarde, it was now clear, would be decided by fierce, unrelenting, hand-to-hand fighting by the infantry.

Vendôme led from the front with a verve that inspired his men. While Burgundy remained on the ridge with the left flank, his second-in-command was in the thick of the action, wielding a half-pike with unflagging power and driving his army on. He was quick to notice that the only open ground was to Cadogan's left and that it was occupied by Prussian and Hanoverian horse with no supporting infantry. It was a weak point that needed to be exploited. Conscious of this, Vendôme sent an urgent message to Burgundy, telling him to overwhelm the cavalry by launching the left wing. In doing so, the French would be able to attack Cadogan from both flanks and crack his army like a walnut.

Like much of Vendôme's sound advice, it was disregarded. Burgundy's staff reported incorrectly to him that his troops would be hopelessly caught in a morass if they descended from the left. To the eternal chagrin of Vendôme, therefore, thirty thousand soldiers remained as passive spectators on the high ground. Instead of being crushed by greater numbers, the Allied forces were being steadily replenished. Tragically for the French, the messenger sent to inform Vendôme that the left wing would not come to his aid was killed before he even reached the general. The message was thus never received. Vendôme fought on courageously, waiting in vain for the requested left wing to join in, betrayed by Burgundy's inexperience and by the false information on which the commander-in-chief based his decision.

* * *

Daniel was encouraged by what he saw. The cultivated fields and the widespread thickets deterred a French cavalry that would have held a distinct advantage. Instead, it was the superior infantry of the Allies on which the result would rest. Marlborough ensured that the battle didn't drift into utter confusion. He gave it shape and direction. Daniel was employed as a galloper, carrying messages to and fro between the various generals. Seeing that Vendôme's forces were putting Cadogan under severe pressure, Marlborough brought up twenty battalions under the Duke of Argyll and extended the Allied flank westwards. In spite of repeated French attacks, the line held out. The very real danger of being swamped by enemy numbers had passed.

No sooner had Daniel returned to Marlborough's side than he was dispatched to bring some other reinforcements into action, riding across the battleground with sabres flashing murderously all round him and musket balls whistling past his ear. Eugene, meanwhile, was given command of the right flank, leaving Marlborough to operate on the left. Over to the west, the captain general observed a rim of higher ground swinging round the perimeter of the battle, largely free of vegetation and suitable for cavalry. It was time to use General Overkirk's troops, a combined force of Dutch infantry and cavalry. They were sent wide and deep to the enemy rear. Though he, too, was a sick man, leading his troops from the comfort of his coach, Overkirk responded to the call, following orders to send some of his men in a tighter turn against the flank of the French infantry line.

Daniel was galloping all over the battlefield, carrying orders and using his sword to hack a way past any opposition. He brought news to Marlborough that Eugene was hard-pressed on the right flank and twenty battalions of infantry and seventeen squadrons of British cavalry were immediately dispatched to his aid. When he looked down from higher ground at the field of battle, Daniel marvelled at the way Marlborough had marshalled his men, rushing reinforcements to vulnerable points and searching out points of potential weakness. It was in sharp contradistinction to the role of the French commander-in-chief. Still on higher ground, well behind the front, Burgundy was a helpless bystander who made no meaningful contribution. Far below him, the indefatigable Vendôme was flailing away with his half-pike, too engrossed in the battle to be able to impose any control over it. Marlborough looked up at the sky. Evening was closing in.

'How much more light do we have, Daniel?' he asked.

'No more than an hour, Your Grace,' replied Daniel.

'Then there's no time for delay.' After scribbling some orders, he handed them to Daniel. 'Take this to General Overkirk with all speed possible. He is to attack.'

Burgundy could not believe what he saw. Masses of Dutch infantry and cavalry seemed to appear from nowhere and surge down the slopes like a waterfall. French cavalry, aching with fatigue and thinned out by heavy losses, turned to face the newcomers but they were swept aside by Overkirk's men who rode deeper and deeper into the French rear, spreading panic wherever they went. Keeping a much tighter line, another part of the Dutch forces descended on the French to effect a double encirclement of them. The noose was slowly but inexorably tightened. One of the largest French armies ever to take the field was being strangled into submission. Indeed, so tight was the encirclement that the Dutch were, at one point, inadvertently firing at each other.

In the arrogance of youth, Burgundy had been composing in his mind the report he'd expected to send to Versailles of a magnificent victory. Instead, he would have to describe a humiliating defeat and try to explain why his left flank – comprising fifty battalions and a hundred and thirty squadrons – was marooned on a ridge throughout the whole six hours of battle.

Daniel claimed his share of the action. As the French were driven from ditch to ditch, splashing madly through stream after stream in their headlong retreat, Daniel hacked and thrust away with his sword, killing four men outright and wounding several others. When his horse was brought down by a stray shot, he jumped clear and fought shoulder to shoulder with the advancing line of redcoats. The noise was deafening, the smoke blinding, the battlefield littered with dead and dying. It was a complete rout. French cavalry, infantry and dragoons were mixed higgledy-piggledy. Battalions and squadrons became so hopelessly entangled with each other that there was no sense of order or definition. They fled in desperation.

Somewhere in the vast melee, Henry Welbeck was still fighting as well, using a discarded half-pike like the sail of a windmill and exhorting his men to pepper the backsides of the retreating French with volleys of musket fire. Lieutenant Ainley was also in his element, leading fearlessly and fighting with a ferocity that belied his mild temperament. After killing and wounding indiscriminately, his men rounded up prisoners by the score. Along with all the other British regiments of foot, the 24th had distinguished itself yet again.

As the rings of terror tightened even more around the enemy, the light gradually faded and the battle had perforce to be adjourned. Marlborough's delight was edged with disappointment.

'If we'd been so happy as to have two more hours of daylight,' he said, 'I believe we should have made an end of this war.'

As it was, unbeknown to him, the outcome had already been decided. His exhausted soldiers spent the night on the battlefield amid the butchered corpses of men and horses, sprinkled by gentle rain. Their captain general slept in the saddle, waking early in order to renew hostilities at dawn.

But there was no foe in sight.

The ridge above the River Norken was deserted. Burgundy and Vendôme had limped ignominiously away to Ghent with the remnants of their shattered army. It was all over. When Marlborough and Prince Eugene entered Oudenarde itself and rode into the square, they were cheered to the echo by their soldiers. Thousands of French prisoners were being held in the town, including some six hundred officers. When the full numbers of dead, wounded, prisoners and deserters were known, it amounted to twenty thousand men. Forty French battalions had been smashed out of existence and others had suffered savage losses. Marlborough was exhausted but exultant. He dashed off a note for the Earl of Stair to deliver to Sidney Godolphin in London.

I must acknowledge the goodness of God in the success he was pleased to give us; for I believe Lord Stair will tell you they were in as strong a post as it is possible to be found; but you know when I left England I was positively resolved to endeavour by all means a battle, thinking nothing else would make the Queen's business go well. This reason only made me venture a battle yesterday, otherwise I did give them too much advantage; but the good of the queen and my country shall always be preferred by me before any personal concern; for I am very sensible if I had miscarried, I should be blamed. I hope I have given such a blow to their foot, that they will not be able to fight any more this year. My head aches so terribly I must say no more.

* * *

Daniel stayed long enough in camp to see Matthew Searle, Edwin Lock, Hugh Davey and the other renegades hanged for their crimes. While the rest of the army were celebrating a glorious victory, eight men who could have taken part in it were dangling from the gallows. It was not a sight that Daniel enjoyed because it reminded him too much of the occasion when he watched his father being hanged with other rebels after the battle of Sedgemoor. He turned away from the scene. Welbeck was beside him.

'The bastards got what they deserved,' said the sergeant with grim satisfaction. 'It's as well that they're so fond of fires because there'll be plenty of them where they're going.'

'I didn't think you believed in heaven and hell,' said Daniel.

'I don't believe in heaven, Dan, but I know all about hell.'

'Do you?'

'It's called army life.'

Daniel laughed. 'Only you can be grumbling at a time like this,' he said. 'You helped to give the French another hiding and you've had the pleasure of seeing Searle and his men strung up. Yet you still can't find a good word to say. I suppose you'll even criticise His Grace for the way he led us into battle.'

'No,' said Welbeck, 'I salute him, Dan, and I take back what I said about him earlier. He's neither blind nor stupid. The way that he routed the enemy showed that he's still at the height of his powers. And while we're on the subject,' he continued, 'I'll admit that I was wrong about Lieutenant Ainley as well. He's not the complete idiot I took him for. Once the smell of battle got into his nostrils, he fought like a demon. I saw him scything his way through the French.'

'I must make a note of the date and time of day,' teased Daniel. 'I've never heard you praise two of your superiors at the same time. Such a rare event needs to be commemorated.'

Welbeck grinned. 'It won't happen again, I can tell you.'

'And you were wrong about heaven – it does exist, Henry.'

'I've never seen it.'

'Then you must have kept your eyes closed at Oudenarde. That's my idea of heaven – a wondrous victory that reminds me why I joined the army in the first place.'

'You only joined in order to use that bleeding sword of yours.'

After sharing a laugh, they exchanged farewells. News of their triumph had already been sent to The Hague. Daniel had been given the task of delivering a full account of the event to Grand Pensionary Heinsius. It was an honour he readily accepted because it would take him back to Holland and he didn't intend its capital to be the only place that he visited.

Glancing out of the window, Beatrix was the first to see him and her cry of delight roused the whole house. When

Daniel was admitted to the *voorhuis*, the welcoming committee comprised Amalia, Beatrix, Emanuel Janssen, Kees Dopff, the other weavers taken on by Janssen and the rest of the servants. Daniel only had eyes for Amalia. He greeted everyone individually but was pleased when all but one of them melted away into the house or the workshop. Left alone with Amalia, he was able to embrace her and kiss away the time they'd been apart.

'What are you doing in Amsterdam?' she asked.

'I was hoping that you'd be thrilled to see me, Amalia.'

'I'm overjoyed.'

'His Grace instructed me to deliver dispatches to The Hague,' he explained. 'I think he knew that I'd relish the opportunity of paying a brief visit to you.'

'We were so happy to hear what happened at Oudenarde,' she said, stepping back to look him up and down. 'What makes me even happier is that you seem to have come through the battle unscathed.'

'Good fortune attended me yet again.'

'Did you have no injuries at all?'

'None that prevented me from coming here,' he said. 'My horse was shot from under me and I collected a few painful bruises as I fell. Otherwise – thank God – I escaped unharmed.'

'Tell me all about it, Daniel.'

'I can't do that.'

'But I want to hear the details.'

'Then you'll have to find someone else who was there.'

She frowned. 'Why are you being so unhelpful?'

'Because I don't want to waste the little time we have together, talking about a battle. It was fierce, hectic and very bloody, Amalia. My sword gave me good service. That's all I'm prepared to say.' He picked her up in his arms and twirled her around a couple of times. 'Let me forget about the army for once in my life.'

'But you've just helped to conquer the French.'

'The only conquest I'm prepared to discuss is *you*.'

Face glowing, Amalia laughed with sheer joy.

If you enjoyed *Fire and Sword*, read on to find out about
more books by Edward Marston . . .

∽

To discover more historical fiction and to
place an order visit our website at
www.allisonandbusby.com
or call us on
020 7580 1080

THE CAPTAIN RAWSON SERIES

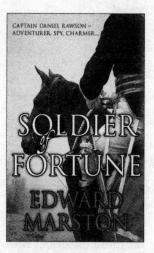

Soldier of Fortune
Drums of War
Fire and Sword
Under Siege

⊃⊂◊⊃⊂

'An enthralling and accomplished historical adventure'
Good Book Guide

'Abrim with heroism, tenderness, chicanery and suspense, while
crisply evoking a vivid picture of the era'
Kirkus Reviews

'Serious tone, a sense of historical presence and well-sketched
characters comprise a sterling performance'
Library Journal

THE RAILWAY DETECTIVE SERIES

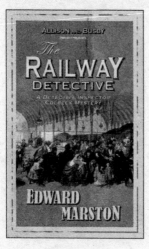

The Railway Detective
The Excursion Train
The Railway Viaduct
The Iron Horse
Murder on the Brighton Express
The Silver Locomotive Mystery
Railway to the Grave
Blood on the Line
The Stationmaster's Farewell

The Railway Detective Omnibus:
The Railway Detective - The Excursion Train - The Railway Viaduct

⇢◇⇠

'Told with great colour and panache . . . a wonderful sense of
inhabiting the period. This is how history mysteries should be'
Sherlock Magazine

PRINCE CASPIAN

Full of gloom, the Pevensie children are waiting at the railway station for the train to take them back to school. Lucy feels a sudden tug, then Edmund does, and a minute later Peter and Susan do too. In a trice the station has vanished, and they find themselves in an overgrown wood near the sea, close by the ruins of their former castle, Cair Paravel. They are back in the magical land of Narnia where they had such wonderful times when they ruled as Kings and Queens (in *The Lion, the Witch and the Wardrobe*).

But something is very wrong. Their glorious castle lies in ruins and everywhere is strangely silent and empty. With the startling arrival of the Dwarf, they learn of the sad fate that has befallen Narnia. Civil war is now destroying the land as brave Prince Caspian, realising his uncle King Miraz's evil ways, is trying to regain the kingdom that is rightfully his. But Caspian needs help and, with the guidance of Aslan, the children take up the challenge to save Narnia and restore the long lost days of freedom and happiness.

THE CHRONICLES OF NARNIA
are all available from Collins

C. S. LEWIS

Prince Caspian

The return to Narnia

illustrated by
Pauline Baynes

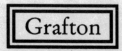

Grafton

First published in Great Britain by Geoffrey Bles in 1951
First published by Collins in paperback in 1980

This edition published by Grafton 2002
Grafton is an imprint of
HarperCollins*Publishers*
77-85 Fulham Palace Road, Hammersmith
London W6 8JB

9 10

ISBN 0 00 765011 6 (DMG Ltd.)
ISBN 0 26 167049 2 (Remainders Ltd.)

Printed and bound in Great Britain by
Bookmarque Ltd, Croydon, Surrey

To Mary Clare Havard

CONTENTS

WIL?

Miraz his Castle

Beaversdam

LANTERN

WASTE

A
MAP of
NARNIA
and adjoining
LANDS

NARN?

GREAT

RIVER

Aslan's Ho?

Dancing Lawn

Trufflehunter's
Cave

Bulgy Bears Home

ARCHENLAND

LANDS of the NORTH

BERUNA

ER RUSH

Cair Paravel

GLASSWATER

CHAPTER ONE

THE ISLAND

ONCE there were four children whose names were Peter, Susan, Edmund, and Lucy, and it has been told in another book called *The Lion, the Witch and the Wardrobe* how they had a remarkable adventure. They had opened the door of a magic wardrobe and found themselves in a quite different world from ours, and in that different world they had become Kings and Queens in a country called Narnia. While they were in Narnia they seemed to reign for years and years; but when they came back through the door and found themselves in England again, it all seemed to have taken no time at all. At any rate, no one noticed that they had ever been away, and they never told anyone except one very wise grown-up.

That had all happened a year ago, and now all four of them were sitting on a seat at a railway station with trunks and playboxes piled up round them. They were, in fact, on their way back to school. They had travelled together as far as this station, which was a junction; and here, in a few minutes, one train would arrive and take the girls away to one school, and in about half an hour another train would arrive and the boys would go off to another school. The first part of the journey, when they were all together, always seemed to be part of the holidays; but now when they would be saying good-bye and going different ways so soon, everyone felt that the holidays were really over and everyone felt their term-time feelings beginning again, and they were all rather gloomy and no one could think of anything to say. Lucy was going to boarding school for the first time.

It was an empty, sleepy, country station and there was hardly anyone on the platform except themselves. Suddenly Lucy gave a sharp little cry, like someone who has been stung by a wasp.

"What's up, Lu?" said Edmund — and then suddenly broke off and made a noise like "Ow!"

"What on earth —" began Peter, and then he too suddenly changed what he had been going to say. Instead, he said, "Susan, let go! What are you doing? Where are you dragging me to?"

"I'm not touching you," said Susan. "Someone is pulling *me*. Oh — oh — oh — stop it!"

Everyone noticed that all the others' faces had gone very white.

"I felt just the same," said Edmund in a breathless voice. "As if I were being dragged along. A most frightful pulling — ugh! it's beginning again."

"Me too," said Lucy. "Oh, I can't bear it."

"Look sharp!" shouted Edmund. "All catch hands and keep together. This is magic — I can tell by the feeling. Quick!"

"Yes," said Susan. "Hold hands. Oh, I do wish it would stop — oh!"

Next moment the luggage, the seat, the platform, and the station had completely vanished. The four children, holding hands and panting, found themselves standing in a woody place — such a woody place that branches were sticking into them and there was hardly room to move. They all rubbed their eyes and took a deep breath.

"Oh, Peter!" exclaimed Lucy. "Do you think we can possibly have got back to Narnia?"

"It might be anywhere," said Peter. "I can't see a yard in

all these trees. Let's try to get into the open – if there is any open."

With some difficulty, and with some stings from nettles and pricks from thorns, they struggled out of the thicket. Then they had another surprise. Everything became much brighter, and after a few steps they found themselves at the edge of the wood, looking down on a sandy beach. A few yards away a very calm sea was falling on the sand with such tiny ripples that it made hardly any sound. There was no land in sight and no clouds in the sky. The sun was about where it ought to be at ten o'clock in the morning, and the sea was a dazzling blue. They stood sniffing in the sea-smell.

"By Jove!" said Peter. "This is good enough."

Five minutes later everyone was barefooted and wading in the cool clear water.

"This is better than being in a stuffy train on the way back to Latin and French and Algebra!" said Edmund. And then for quite a long time there was no more talking, only splashing and looking for shrimps and crabs.

"All the same," said Susan presently, "I suppose we'll have to make some plans. We shall want something to eat before long."

"We've got the sandwiches Mother gave us for the journey," said Edmund. "At least I've got mine."

"Not me," said Lucy. "Mine were in my little bag."

"So were mine," said Susan.

"Mine are in my coat-pocket, there on the beach," said Peter. "That'll be two lunches among four. This isn't going to be such fun."

"At present," said Lucy, "I want something to drink more than something to eat."

Everyone else now felt thirsty, as one usually is after wading in salt water under a hot sun.

"It's like being shipwrecked," remarked Edmund. "In the books they always find springs of clear, fresh water on the island. We'd better go and look for them."

"Does that mean we have to go back into all that thick wood?" said Susan.

"Not a bit of it," said Peter. "If there are streams they're bound to come down to the sea, and if we walk along the beach we're bound to come to them."

They all now waded back and went first across the smooth, wet sand and then up to the dry, crumbly sand that sticks to one's toes, and began putting on their shoes and socks. Edmund and Lucy wanted to leave them behind and do their exploring with bare feet, but Susan said this would be a mad thing to do. "We might never find them again," she pointed out, "and we shall want them if we're still here when night comes and it begins to be cold."

When they were dressed again they set out along the shore with the sea on their left hand and the wood on their right. Except for an occasional seagull it was a very quiet place. The wood was so thick and tangled that they could hardly see into it at all; and nothing in it moved — not a bird, not even an insect.

Shells and seaweed and anemones, or tiny crabs in rock-pools, are all very well, but you soon get tired of them if you are thirsty. The children's feet, after the change from the cool water, felt hot and heavy. Susan and Lucy had raincoats to carry. Edmund had put down his coat on the station seat just before the magic overtook them, and he and Peter took it in turns to carry Peter's great-coat.

Presently the shore began to curve round to the right.

About quarter of an hour later, after they had crossed a rocky ridge which ran out into a point, it made quite a sharp turn. Their backs were now to the part of the sea which had met them when they first came out of the wood, and now, looking ahead, they could see across the water another shore, thickly wooded like the one they were exploring.

"I wonder, is that an island or do we join on to it presently?" said Lucy.

"Don't know," said Peter and they all plodded on in silence.

The shore that they were walking on drew nearer and nearer to the opposite shore, and as they came round each promontory the children expected to find the place where the two joined. But in this they were disappointed. They came to some rocks which they had to climb and from the top they could see a fair way ahead and – "Oh bother!" said Edmund, "it's no good. We shan't be able to get to those other woods at all. We're on an island!"

It was true. At this point the channel between them and the opposite coast was only about thirty or forty yards wide; but they could now see that this was its narrowest place. After that, their own coast bent round to the right again and they could see open sea between it and the mainland. It was obvious that they had already come much more than half-way round the island.

"Look!" said Lucy suddenly. "What's that?" She pointed to a long, silvery, snake-like thing that lay across the beach.

"A stream! A stream!" shouted the others, and, tired as they were, they lost no time in clattering down the rocks and racing to the fresh water. They knew that the stream would be better to drink farther up, away from the beach, so they went at once to the spot where it came out of the wood. The trees were as thick as ever, but the stream had made itself a deep course between high mossy banks so that by stooping you could follow it up in a sort of tunnel of leaves. They dropped on their knees by the first brown, dimply pool and drank and drank, and dipped their faces in the water, and then dipped their arms in up to the elbow.

"Now," said Edmund, "what about those sandwiches?"

"Oh, hadn't we better save them?" said Susan. "We may need them far worse later on."

"I do wish," said Lucy, "now that we're not thirsty, we could go on feeling as not-hungry as we did when we *were* thirsty."

"But what about those sandwiches?" repeated Edmund. "There's no good saving them till they go bad. You've got to remember it's a good deal hotter here than in England and we've been carrying them about in pockets for hours." So they got out the two packets and divided them into four portions, and nobody had quite enough, but it was a great deal better than nothing. Then they talked about their plans for the next meal. Lucy wanted to go back to the sea and catch shrimps, until someone pointed out that they had no nets. Edmund said they must gather gulls' eggs from the rocks, but when they came to think of it they couldn't remember having seen any gulls' eggs and wouldn't be able to cook them if they found any. Peter thought to himself that unless they had some stroke of luck they would soon be glad to eat eggs raw, but he didn't see any point in saying this out loud. Susan said it was a pity they had eaten the sandwiches so soon. One or two tempers very nearly got lost at this stage. Finally Edmund said:

"Look here. There's only one thing to be done. We must explore the wood. Hermits and knights-errant and people like that always manage to live somehow if they're in a forest. They find roots and berries and things."

"What sort of roots?" asked Susan.

"I always thought it meant roots of trees," said Lucy.

"Come on," said Peter, "Ed is right. And we must try to do something. And it'll be better than going out into the glare and the sun again."

So they all got up and began to follow the stream. It was very hard work. They had to stoop under branches and climb over branches, and they blundered through great masses of stuff like rhododendrons and tore their clothes and got their feet wet in the stream; and still there was no noise at all except the noise of the stream and the noises they were making themselves. They were beginning to get very tired of it when they noticed a delicious smell, and then a flash of bright colour high above them at the top of the right bank.

"I say!" exclaimed Lucy. "I do believe that's an apple tree."

It was. They panted up the steep bank, forced their way through some brambles, and found themselves standing round an old tree that was heavy with large yellowish-golden apples as firm and juicy as you could wish to see.

"And this is not the only tree," said Edmund with his mouth full of apple. "Look there – and there."

"Why, there are dozens of them," said Susan, throwing away the core of her first apple and picking her second. "This must have been an orchard – long, long ago, before the place went wild and the wood grew up."

"Then this was once an inhabited island," said Peter.

"And what's that?" said Lucy, pointing ahead.

"By Jove, it's a wall," said Peter. "An old stone wall."

Pressing their way between the laden branches they reached the wall. It was very old, and broken down in places, with moss and wallflowers growing on it, but it was higher than all but the tallest trees. And when they came quite close to it they found a great arch which must once have had a gate in it but was now almost filled up with the largest of all the apple trees. They had to break some of the branches to get past, and when they had done so they all blinked because the daylight became suddenly much brighter. They found themselves in a wide open place with walls all round it. In here there were no trees, only level grass and daisies, and ivy, and grey walls. It was a bright, secret, quiet place, and rather sad; and all four stepped out into the middle of it, glad to be able to straighten their backs and move their limbs freely.

CHAPTER TWO

THE ANCIENT TREASURE HOUSE

"THIS wasn't a garden," said Susan presently. "It was a castle and this must have been the courtyard."

"I see what you mean," said Peter. "Yes. That is the remains of a tower. And there is what used to be a flight of steps going up to the top of the walls. And look at those other steps – the broad, shallow ones – going up to that doorway. It must have been the door into the great hall."

"Ages ago, by the look of it," said Edmund.

"Yes, ages ago," said Peter. "I wish we could find out who the people were that lived in this castle; and how long ago."

"It gives me a queer feeling," said Lucy.

"Does it, Lu?" said Peter, turning and looking hard at her. "Because it does the same to me. It is the queerest thing that has happened this queer day. I wonder where we are and what it all means?"

While they were talking they had crossed the courtyard and gone through the other doorway into what had once been the hall. This was now very like the courtyard, for the roof had long since disappeared and it was merely another space of grass and daisies, except that it was shorter and narrower and the walls were higher. Across the far end there was a kind of terrace about three feet higher than the rest.

"I wonder, was it really the hall?" said Susan. "What is that terrace kind of thing?"

"Why, you silly," said Peter (who had become strangely

excited), "don't you see? That was the dais where the High Table was, where the King and the great lords sat. Anyone would think you had forgotten that we ourselves were once Kings and Queens and sat on a dais just like that, in our great hall."

"In our castle of Cair Paravel," continued Susan in a dreamy and rather sing-song voice, "at the mouth of the great river of Narnia. How could I forget?"

"How it all comes back!" said Lucy. "We could pretend we were in Cair Paravel now. This hall must have been very like the great hall we feasted in."

"But unfortunately without the feast," said Edmund. "It's getting late, you know. Look how long the shadows are. And have you noticed that it isn't so hot?"

"We shall need a camp-fire if we've got to spend the night here," said Peter. "I've got matches. Let's go and see if we can collect some dry wood."

Everyone saw the sense of this, and for the next half-hour they were busy. The orchard through which they had first come into the ruins turned out not to be a good place for firewood. They tried the other side of the castle, passing out of the hall by a little side door into a maze of stony humps and hollows which must once have been passages and smaller rooms but was now all nettles and wild roses. Beyond this they found a wide gap in the castle wall and stepped through it into a wood of darker and bigger trees where they found dead branches and rotten wood and sticks and dry leaves and fir-cones in plenty. They went to and fro with bundles until they had a good pile on the dais. At the fifth journey they found the well, just outside the hall, hidden in weeds, but clean and fresh and deep when they had cleared these away.

The remains of a stone pavement ran half-way round it. Then the girls went out to pick some more apples and the boys built the fire, on the dais and fairly close to the corner between two walls, which they thought would be the snuggest and warmest place. They had great difficulty in lighting it and used a lot of matches, but they succeeded in the end. Finally, all four sat down with their backs to the wall and their faces to the fire. They tried roasting some of the apples on the ends of sticks. But roast apples are not much good without sugar, and they are too hot to eat with your fingers till they are too cold to be worth eating. So they had to content themselves with raw apples, which, as Edmund said, made one realize that school suppers weren't so bad after all – "I shouldn't mind a good thick slice of bread and margarine this minute," he added. But the spirit of adventure was rising in them all, and no one really wanted to be back at school.

Shortly after the last apple had been eaten, Susan went

out to the well to get another drink. When she came back she was carrying something in her hand.

"Look," she said in a rather choking kind of voice. "I found it by the well." She handed it to Peter and sat down. The others thought she looked and sounded as if she might be going to cry. Edmund and Lucy eagerly bent forward to see what was in Peter's hand – a little, bright thing that gleamed in the firelight.

"Well, I'm – I'm jiggered," said Peter, and his voice also sounded queer. Then he handed it to the others.

All now saw what it was – a little chess-knight, ordinary in size but extraordinarily heavy because it was made of pure gold; and the eyes in the horse's head were two tiny little rubies – or rather one was, for the other had been knocked out.

"Why!" said Lucy, "it's exactly like one of the golden chessmen we used to play with when we were Kings and Queens at Cair Paravel."

"Cheer up, Su," said Peter to his other sister.

"I can't help it," said Susan. "It brought back – oh, such lovely times. And I remembered playing chess with fauns and good giants, and the mer-people singing in the sea, and my beautiful horse – and – and –"

"Now," said Peter in a quite different voice, "it's about time we four started using our brains."

"What about?" asked Edmund.

"Have none of you guessed where we are?" said Peter.

"Go on, go on," said Lucy. "I've felt for hours that there was some wonderful mystery hanging over this place."

"Fire ahead, Peter," said Edmund. "We're all listening."

"We are in the ruins of Cair Paravel itself," said Peter.

"But, I say," replied Edmund. "I mean, how do you make that out? This place has been ruined for ages. Look at all those big trees growing right up to the gates. Look at the very stones. Anyone can see that nobody has lived here for hundreds of years."

"I know," said Peter. "That is the difficulty. But let's leave that out for the moment. I want to take the points one by one. First point: this hall is exactly the same shape and size as the hall at Cair Paravel. Just picture a roof on this, and a coloured pavement instead of grass, and tapestries on the walls, and you get our royal banqueting hall."

No one said anything.

"Second point," continued Peter. "The castle well is exactly where our well was, a little to the south of the great hall; and it is exactly the same size and shape."

Again there was no reply.

"Third point: Susan has just found one of our old chessmen — or something as like one of them as two peas."

Still nobody answered.

"Fourth point. Don't you remember — it was the very day before the ambassadors came from the King of Calormen — don't you remember planting the orchard outside the north gate of Cair Paravel? The greatest of all the wood-people, Pomona herself, came to put good spells on it. It was those very decent little chaps the moles who did the actual digging. Can you have forgotten that funny old Lilygloves, the chief mole, leaning on his spade and saying, 'Believe me, your Majesty, you'll be glad of these fruit trees one day.' And by Jove he was right."

"I do! I do!" said Lucy, and clapped her hands.

"But look here, Peter," said Edmund. "This must be all rot. To begin with, we didn't plant the orchard slap up against the gate. We wouldn't have been such fools."

"No, of course not," said Peter. "But it has grown up to the gate since."

"And for another thing," said Edmund, "Cair Paravel wasn't on an island."

"Yes, I've been wondering about that. But it was a what-do-you-call-it, a peninsula. Jolly nearly an island. Couldn't it have been made an island since our time? Somebody has dug a channel."

"But half a moment!" said Edmund. "You keep on saying *since our time*. But it's only a year ago since we came back from Narnia. And you want to make out that in one year castles have fallen down, and great forests have grown up, and little trees we saw planted ourselves have turned into a big old orchard, and goodness knows what else. It's all impossible."

"There's one thing," said Lucy. "If this is Cair Paravel there ought to be a door at this end of the dais. In fact we ought to be sitting with our backs against it at this moment. You know — the door that led down to the treasure chamber."

"I suppose there *isn't* a door," said Peter, getting up.

The wall behind them was a mass of ivy.

"We can soon find out," said Edmund, taking up one of the sticks that they had laid ready for putting on the fire. He began beating the ivied wall. Tap-tap went the stick against the stone; and again, tap-tap; and then, all at once, boom-boom, with a quite different sound, a hollow, wooden sound.

"Great Scott!" said Edmund.

"We must clear this ivy away," said Peter.

"Oh, do let's leave it alone," said Susan. "We can try it in the morning. If we've got to spend the night here I don't want an open door at my back and a great big black hole that anything might come out of, besides the draught and the damp. And it'll soon be dark."

"Susan! How can you?" said Lucy with a reproachful glance. But both the boys were too much excited to take any notice of Susan's advice. They worked at the ivy with their hands and with Peter's pocket-knife till the knife broke. After that they used Edmund's. Soon the whole place where they had been sitting was covered with ivy; and at last they had the door cleared.

"Locked, of course," said Peter.

"But the wood's all rotten," said Edmund. "We can pull it to bits in no time, and it will make extra firewood. Come on."

It took them longer than they expected and, before they had done, the great hall had grown dusky and the first star or two had come out overhead. Susan was not the only one who felt a slight shudder as the boys stood above the pile of splintered wood, rubbing the dirt off their hands and staring into the cold, dark opening they had made.

"Now for a torch," said Peter.

"Oh, what *is* the good?" said Susan. "And as Edmund said —"

"I'm not saying it now," Edmund interrupted. "I still don't understand, but we can settle that later. I suppose you're coming down, Peter?"

"We must," said Peter. "Cheer up, Susan. It's no good behaving like kids now that we are back in Narnia.

You're a Queen here. And anyway no one could go to sleep with a mystery like this on their minds."

They tried to use long sticks as torches but this was not a success. If you held them with the lighted end up they went out, and if you held them the other way they scorched your hand and the smoke got in your eyes. In the end they had to use Edmund's electric torch; luckily it had been a birthday present less than a week ago and the battery was almost new. He went first, with the light. Then came Lucy, then Susan, and Peter brought up the rear.

"I've come to the top of the steps," said Edmund.

"Count them," said Peter.

"One – two – three," said Edmund, as he went cautiously down, and so up to sixteen. "And this is the bottom," he shouted back.

"Then it really must be Cair Paravel," said Lucy. "There were sixteen." Nothing more was said till all four were standing in a knot together at the foot of the stairway. Then Edmund flashed his torch slowly round.

"O – o – o – oh!!" said all the children at once.

For now all knew that it was indeed the ancient treasure chamber of Cair Paravel where they had once reigned as Kings and Queens of Narnia. There was a kind of path up the middle (as it might be in a greenhouse), and along each side at intervals stood rich suits of armour, like knights guarding the treasures. In between the suits of armour, and on each side of the path, were shelves covered with precious things – necklaces and arm rings and finger rings and golden bowls and dishes and long tusks of ivory, brooches and coronets and chains of gold, and heaps of unset stones lying piled anyhow as if they were marbles or potatoes – diamonds, rubies, carbuncles, emeralds, topazes, and amethysts. Under the shelves stood great chests of oak strengthened with iron bars and heavily padlocked. And it was bitterly cold, and so still that they could hear themselves breathing, and the treasures were so covered with dust that unless they had realized where they were and remembered most of the things, they would hardly have known they were treasures. There was something sad and a little frightening about the place, because it all seemed so forsaken and long ago. That was why nobody said anything for at least a minute.

Then, of course, they began walking about and picking things up to look at. It was like meeting very old friends. If you had been there you would have heard them saying things like, "Oh look! Our coronation rings – do you remember first wearing this? – Why, this is the little brooch we all thought was lost – I say, isn't that the armour you wore in the great tournament in the Lone Islands? – do you remember the dwarf making that for me? – do you remember drinking out of that horn? – do you remember, do you remember?"

But suddenly Edmund said, "Look here. We mustn't waste the battery: goodness knows how often we shall need it. Hadn't we better take what we want and get out again?"

"We must take the gifts," said Peter. For long ago at a Christmas in Narnia he and Susan and Lucy had been given certain presents which they valued more than their whole kingdom. Edmund had had no gift, because he was not with them at the time. (This was his own fault, and you can read about it in the other book.)

They all agreed with Peter and walked up the path to the wall at the far end of the treasure chamber, and there, sure enough, the gifts were still hanging. Lucy's was the smallest for it was only a little bottle. But the bottle was made of diamond instead of glass, and it was still more than half full of the magical cordial which would heal almost every wound and every illness. Lucy said nothing and looked very solemn as she took her gift down from its place and slung the belt over her shoulder and once more felt the bottle at her side where it used to hang in the old days. Susan's gift had been a bow and arrows and a horn. The bow was still there, and the ivory quiver, full of well-feathered arrows, but – "Oh, Susan," said Lucy. "Where's the horn?"

"Oh bother, bother, bother," said Susan after she had thought for a moment. "I remember now. I took it with me the last day of all, the day we went hunting the White Stag. It must have got lost when we blundered back into that other place – England, I mean."

Edmund whistled. It was indeed a shattering loss; for this was an enchanted horn and, whenever you blew it, help was certain to come to you, wherever you were.

"Just the sort of thing that might come in handy in a place like this," said Edmund.

"Never mind," said Susan, "I've still got the bow." And she took it.

"Won't the string be perished, Su?" said Peter.

But whether by some magic in the air of the treasure chamber or not, the bow was still in working order. Archery and swimming were the things Susan was good at. In a moment she had bent the bow and then she gave one little pluck to the string. It twanged: a chirruping twang that vibrated through the whole room. And that one small noise brought back the old days to the children's minds more than anything that had happened yet. All the battles and hunts and feasts came rushing into their heads together.

Then she unstrung the bow again and slung the quiver at her side.

Next, Peter took down his gift – the shield with the great red lion on it, and the royal sword. He blew, and rapped them on the floor, to get off the dust. He fitted the shield on his arm and slung the sword by his side. He was afraid at first that it might be rusty and stick to the sheath. But it was not so. With one swift motion he drew it and held it up, shining in the torchlight.

"It is my sword Rhindon," he said; "with it I killed the Wolf." There was a new tone in his voice, and the others

all felt that he was really Peter the High King again. Then, after a little pause, everyone remembered that they must save the battery.

They climbed the stair again and made up a good fire and lay down close together for warmth. The ground was very hard and uncomfortable, but they fell asleep in the end.

CHAPTER THREE

THE DWARF

THE worst of sleeping out of doors is that you wake up so dreadfully early. And when you wake you have to get up because the ground is so hard that you are uncomfortable. And it makes matters worse if there is nothing but apples for breakfast and you have had nothing but apples for supper the night before. When Lucy had said – truly enough – that it was a glorious morning, there did not seem to be anything else nice to be said. Edmund said what everyone was feeling, "We've simply got to get off this island."

When they had drunk from the well and splashed their faces they all went down the stream again to the shore and stared at the channel which divided them from the mainland.

"We'll have to swim," said Edmund.

"It would be all right for Su," said Peter (Susan had won prizes for swimming at school). "But I don't know about the rest of us." By "the rest of us" he really meant Edmund who couldn't yet do two lengths at the school baths, and Lucy, who could hardly swim at all.

"Anyway," said Susan, "there may be currents. Father says it's never wise to bathe in a place you don't know."

"But, Peter," said Lucy, "look here. I know I can't swim for nuts at home – in England, I mean. But couldn't we all swim long ago – if it was long ago – when we were Kings and Queens in Narnia? We could ride then too, and do all sorts of things. Don't you think –?"

"Ah, but we were sort of grown-up then," said Peter.

"We reigned for years and years and learned to do things. Aren't we just back at our proper ages again now?"

"Oh!" said Edmund in a voice which made everyone stop talking and listen to him.

"I've just seen it all," he said.

"Seen what?" asked Peter.

"Why, the whole thing," said Edmund. "You know what we were puzzling about last night, that it was only a year ago since we left Narnia but everything looks as if no one had lived in Cair Paravel for hundreds of years? Well, don't you see? You know that, however long we seemed to have lived in Narnia, when we got back through the wardrobe it seemed to have taken no time at all?"

"Go on," said Susan. "I think I'm beginning to understand."

"And that means," continued Edmund, "that, once you're out of Narnia, you have no idea how Narnian time is going. Why shouldn't hundreds of years have gone past in Narnia while only one year has passed for us in England?"

"By Jove, Ed," said Peter. "I believe you've got it. In that sense it really was hundreds of years ago that we lived in Cair Paravel. And now we're coming back to Narnia just as if we were Crusaders or Anglo-Saxons or Ancient Britons or someone coming back to modern England?"

"How excited they'll be to see us –" began Lucy, but at the same moment everyone else said, "Hush!" or "Look!" For now something was happening.

There was a wooded point on the mainland a little to their right, and they all felt sure that just beyond that point must be the mouth of the river. And now, round that point there came into sight a boat. When it had cleared the point, it turned and began coming along the channel towards them. There were two people on board, one rowing, the other sitting in the stern and holding a bundle that twitched and moved as if it were alive. Both these people seemed to be soldiers. They had steel caps on their heads and light shirts of chain-mail. Their faces were bearded and hard. The children drew back from the beach into the wood and watched without moving a finger.

"This'll do," said the soldier in the stern when the boat had come about opposite to them.

"What about tying a stone to his feet, Corporal?" said the other, resting on his oars.

"Garn!" growled the other. "We don't need that, and we haven't brought one. He'll drown sure enough without a stone, as long as we've tied the cords right." With these words he rose and lifted his bundle. Peter now saw that it was really alive and was in fact a Dwarf, bound hand and foot but struggling as hard as he could. Next moment he heard a twang just beside his ear, and all at once the soldier threw up his arms, dropping the Dwarf into the bottom of the boat, and fell over into the water. He floundered away to the far bank and Peter knew that Susan's arrow had struck on his helmet. He turned and saw that she was very pale but was already fitting a second arrow to the string. But it was never used. As soon as he saw his companion fall, the other soldier, with a loud cry, jumped out of the boat on the far side, and he also floundered through the water (which was apparently just in his depth) and disappeared into the woods of the mainland.

"Quick! Before she drifts!" shouted Peter. He and Susan, fully dressed as they were, plunged in, and before the water was up to their shoulders their hands were on the side of the boat. In a few seconds they had hauled her to the bank and lifted the Dwarf out, and Edmund was busily engaged in cutting his bonds with the pocket knife. (Peter's sword would have been sharper, but a sword is very inconvenient for this sort of work because you can't hold it anywhere lower than the hilt.) When at last the Dwarf was free, he sat up, rubbed his arms and legs, and exclaimed:

"Well, whatever they say, you don't *feel* like ghosts."

Like most Dwarfs he was very stocky and deep-chested. He would have been about three feet high if he had been standing up, and an immense beard and whiskers of coarse red hair left little of his face to be seen except a beak-like nose and twinkling black eyes.

"Anyway," he continued, "ghosts or not, you've saved my life and I'm extremely obliged to you."

"But why should we be ghosts?" asked Lucy.

"I've been told all my life," said the Dwarf, "that these woods along the shore were as full of ghosts as they were of trees. That's what the story is. And that's why, when they want to get rid of anyone, they usually bring him down here (like they were doing with me) and say they'll leave him to the ghosts. But I always wondered if they didn't really drown 'em or cut their throats. I never quite believed in the ghosts. But those two cowards you've just shot believed all right. They were more frightened of taking me to my death than I was of going!"

"Oh," said Susan. "So that's why they both ran away."

"Eh? What's that?" said the Dwarf.

"They got away," said Edmund. "To the mainland."

"I wasn't shooting to kill, you know," said Susan. She would not have liked anyone to think she could miss at such a short range.

"Hm," said the Dwarf. "That's not so good. That may mean trouble later on. Unless they hold their tongues for their own sake."

"What were they going to drown you for?" asked Peter.

"Oh, I'm a dangerous criminal, I am," said the Dwarf cheerfully. "But that's a long story. Meantime, I was wondering if perhaps you were going to ask me to breakfast? You've no idea what an appetite it gives one, being executed."

"There's only apples," said Lucy dolefully.

"Better than nothing, but not so good as fresh fish," said the Dwarf. "It looks as if I'll have to ask you to breakfast instead. I saw some fishing tackle in that boat. And anyway, we must take her round to the other side of the

island. We don't want anyone from the mainland coming down and seeing her."

"I ought to have thought of that myself," said Peter.

The four children and the Dwarf went down to the water's edge, pushed off the boat with some difficulty, and scrambled aboard. The Dwarf at once took charge. The oars were of course too big for him to use, so Peter rowed and the Dwarf steered them north along the channel and presently eastward round the tip of the island. From here the children could see right up the river, and all the bays and headlands of the coast beyond it. They thought they could recognize bits of it, but the woods, which had grown up since their time, made everything look very different.

When they had come round into open sea on the east of the island, the Dwarf took to fishing. They had an excellent catch of pavenders, a beautiful rainbow-coloured fish which they all remembered eating in Cair Paravel in the old days. When they had caught enough they ran the boat up into a little creek and moored her to a tree. The Dwarf, who was a most capable person (and, indeed, though one meets bad Dwarfs, I never heard of a Dwarf who was a fool), cut the fish open, cleaned them, and said:

"Now, what we want next is some firewood."

"We've got some up at the castle," said Edmund.

The Dwarf gave a low whistle. "Beards and bedsteads!" he said. "So there really is a castle, after all?"

"It's only a ruin," said Lucy.

The Dwarf stared round at all four of them with a very curious expression on his face. "And who on earth — ?" he began, but then broke off and said, "No matter. Breakfast first. But one thing before we go on. Can you lay your hand on your hearts and tell me I'm really alive? Are you sure I wasn't drowned and we're not all ghosts together?"

When they had all reassured him, the next question was how to carry the fish. They had nothing to string them on and no basket. They had to use Edmund's hat in the end because no one else had a hat. He would have made much more fuss about this if he had not by now been so ravenously hungry.

At first the Dwarf did not seem very comfortable in the

castle. He kept looking round and sniffing and saying, "H'm. Looks a bit spooky after all. Smells like ghosts, too." But he cheered up when it came to lighting the fire and showing them how to roast the fresh pavenders in the embers. Eating hot fish with no forks, and one pocket knife between five people, is a messy business and there were several burnt fingers before the meal was ended; but, as it was now nine o'clock and they had been up since five, nobody minded the burns so much as you might have expected. When everyone had finished off with a drink from the well and an apple or so, the Dwarf produced a pipe about the size of his own arm, filled it, lit it, blew a great cloud of fragrant smoke, and said, "Now."

"You tell us your story first," said Peter. "And then we'll tell you ours."

"Well," said the Dwarf, "as you've saved my life it is only fair you should have your own way. But I hardly know where to begin. First of all I'm a messenger of King Caspian's."

"Who's he?" asked four voices all at once.

"Caspian the Tenth, King of Narnia, and long may he reign!" answered the Dwarf. "That is to say, he ought to be King of Narnia and we hope he will be. At present he is only King of us Old Narnians – "

"What do you mean by *old* Narnians, please?" asked Lucy.

"Why, that's us," said the Dwarf. "We're a kind of rebellion, I suppose."

"I see," said Peter. "And Caspian is the chief Old Narnian."

"Well, in a manner of speaking," said the Dwarf,

scratching his head. "But he's really a New Narnian himself, a Telmarine, if you follow me."

"I don't," said Edmund.

"It's worse than the Wars of the Roses," said Lucy.

"Oh dear," said the Dwarf. "I'm doing this very badly. Look here: I think I'll have to go right back to the beginning and tell you how Caspian grew up in his uncle's court and how he comes to be on our side at all. But it'll be a long story."

"All the better," said Lucy. "We love stories."

So the Dwarf settled down and told his tale. I shall not give it to you in his words, putting in all the children's questions and interruptions, because it would take too long and be confusing, and, even so, it would leave out some points that the children only heard later. But the gist of the story, as they knew it in the end, was as follows.

CHAPTER FOUR

THE DWARF TELLS OF PRINCE CASPIAN

PRINCE CASPIAN lived in a great castle in the centre of Narnia with his uncle, Miraz, the King of Narnia, and his aunt, who had red hair and was called Queen Prunaprismia. His father and mother were dead and the person whom Caspian loved best was his nurse, and though (being a prince) he had wonderful toys which would do almost anything but talk, he liked best the last hour of the day when the toys had all been put back in their cupboards and Nurse would tell him stories.

He did not care much for his uncle and aunt, but about twice a week his uncle would send for him and they would walk up and down together for half an hour on the terrace at the south side of the castle. One day, while they were doing this, the King said to him,

"Well, boy, we must soon teach you to ride and use a sword. You know that your aunt and I have no children, so it looks as if you might have to be King when I'm gone. How shall you like that, eh?"

"I don't know, Uncle," said Caspian.

"Don't know, eh?" said Miraz. "Why, I should like to know what more anyone could wish for!"

"All the same, I *do* wish," said Caspian.

"What do you wish?" asked the King.

"I wish – I wish – I wish I could have lived in the Old Days," said Caspian. (He was only a very little boy at the time.)

Up till now King Miraz had been talking in the tiresome way that some grown-ups have, which makes it quite clear that they are not really interested in what you are saying, but now he suddenly gave Caspian a very sharp look.

"Eh? What's that?" he said. "What old days do you mean?"

"Oh, don't you know, Uncle?" said Caspian. "When everything was quite different. When all the animals could talk, and there were nice people who lived in the streams and the trees. Naiads and Dryads they were called. And there were Dwarfs. And there were lovely little Fauns in all the woods. They had feet like goats. And —"

"That's all nonsense, for babies," said the King sternly. "Only fit for babies, do you hear? You're getting too old for that sort of stuff. At your age you ought to be thinking of battles and adventures, not fairy tales."

"Oh, but there *were* battles and adventures in those days," said Caspian. "Wonderful adventures. Once there was a White Witch and she made herself Queen of the whole country. And she made it so that it was always winter. And then two boys and two girls came from somewhere and so they killed the Witch and they were made Kings and Queens of Narnia, and their names were Peter and Susan and Edmund and Lucy. And so they reigned for ever so long and everyone had a lovely time, and it was all because of Aslan —"

"Who's he?" said Miraz. And if Caspian had been a very little older, the tone of his uncle's voice would have warned him that it would be wiser to shut up. But he babbled on,

"Oh, don't you know?" he said. "Aslan is the great Lion who comes from over the sea."

"Who has been telling you all this nonsense?" said the King in a voice of thunder. Caspian was frightened and said nothing.

"Your Royal Highness," said King Miraz, letting go of Caspian's hand, which he had been holding till now, "I insist upon being answered. Look me in the face. Who has been telling you this pack of lies?"

"N – Nurse," faltered Caspian, and burst into tears.

"Stop that noise," said his uncle, taking Caspian by the shoulders and giving him a shake. "Stop it. And never let me catch you talking – or *thinking* either – about all those silly stories again. There never were those Kings and Queens. How could there be two Kings at the same time? And there's no such person as Aslan. And there are no such things as lions. And there never was a time when animals could talk. Do you hear?"

"Yes, Uncle," sobbed Caspian.

"Then let's have no more of it," said the King. Then he called to one of the gentlemen-in-waiting who were standing at the far end of the terrace and said in a cold voice, "Conduct His Royal Highness to his apartments and send His Royal Highness's nurse to me AT ONCE."

Next day Caspian found what a terrible thing he had done, for Nurse had been sent away without even being allowed to say good-bye to him, and he was told he was to have a Tutor.

Caspian missed his nurse very much and shed many tears; and because he was so miserable, he thought about the old stories of Narnia far more than before. He dreamed of Dwarfs and Dryads every night and tried very hard to make the dogs and cats in the castle talk to him. But the dogs only wagged their tails and the cats only purred.

Caspian felt sure that he would hate the new Tutor, but when the new Tutor arrived about a week later he turned out to be the sort of person it is almost impossible not to like. He was the smallest, and also the fattest, man Caspian had ever seen. He had a long, silvery, pointed beard which came down to his waist, and his face, which was brown and covered with wrinkles, looked very wise, very ugly, and very kind. His voice was grave and his eyes were merry so that, until you got to know him really well, it was hard to know when he was joking and when he was serious. His name was Doctor Cornelius.

Of all his lessons with Doctor Cornelius the one that Caspian liked best was History. Up till now, except for Nurse's stories, he had known nothing about the History of Narnia, and he was very surprised to learn that the royal family were newcomers in the country.

"It was your Highness's ancestor, Caspian the First," said Doctor Cornelius, "who first conquered Narnia and made it his kingdom. It was he who brought all your nation into the country. You are not native Narnians at all. You are all Telmarines – that is, you all came from the Land of Telmar, far beyond the Western Mountains. That is why Caspian the First is called Caspian the Conqueror."

"Please, Doctor," asked Caspian one day, "who lived in Narnia before we all came here out of Telmar?"

"No men — or very few — lived in Narnia before the Telmarines took it," said Doctor Cornelius.

"Then who did my great-great-grandcesters conquer?"

"*Whom*, not *who*, your Highness," said Doctor Cornelius. "Perhaps it is time to turn from History to Grammar."

"Oh please, not yet," said Caspian. "I mean, wasn't

there a battle? Why is he called Caspian the Conqueror if there was nobody to fight with him?"

"I said there were very few *men* in Narnia," said the Doctor, looking at the little boy very strangely through his great spectacles.

For a moment Caspian was puzzled and then suddenly his heart gave a leap. "Do you mean," he gasped, "that there were other things? Do you mean it was like in the stories? Were there —?"

"Hush!" said Doctor Cornelius, laying his head very close to Caspian's. "Not a word more. Don't you know your Nurse was sent away for telling you about Old Narnia? The King doesn't like it. If he found me telling you secrets, you'd be whipped and I should have my head cut off."

"But why?" asked Caspian.

"It is high time we turned to Grammar now," said Doctor Cornelius in a loud voice. "Will your Royal Highness be pleased to open Pulverulentus Siccus at the fourth page of his *Grammatical garden or the Arbour of Accidence pleasantlie open'd to Tender Wits?*"

After that it was all nouns and verbs till lunchtime, but I don't think Caspian learned much. He was too excited. He felt sure that Doctor Cornelius would not have said so much unless he meant to tell him more sooner or later.

In this he was not disappointed. A few days later his Tutor said, "Tonight I am going to give you a lesson in Astronomy. At dead of night two noble planets, Tarva and Alambil, will pass within one degree of each other. Such a conjunction has not occurred for two hundred years, and your Highness will not live to see it again. It will be best if you go to bed a little earlier than usual. When the time of the conjunction draws near I will come and wake you."

This didn't seem to have anything to do with Old Narnia, which was what Caspian really wanted to hear about, but getting up in the middle of the night is always interesting and he was moderately pleased. When he went to bed that night, he thought at first that he would not be able to sleep; but he soon dropped off and it seemed only a few minutes before he felt someone gently shaking him.

He sat up in bed and saw that the room was full of moonlight. Doctor Cornelius, muffled in a hooded robe and holding a small lamp in his hand, stood by the bedside.

Caspian remembered at once what they were going to do. He got up and put on some clothes. Athough it was a summer night he felt colder than he had expected and was quite glad when the Doctor wrapped him in a robe like his own and gave him a pair of warm, soft buskins for his feet. A moment later, both muffled so that they could hardly be seen in the dark corridors, and both shod so that they made almost no noise, master and pupil left the room.

Caspian followed the Doctor through many passages and up several staircases, and at last, through a little door in a turret, they came out upon the leads. On one side were the battlements, on the other a steep roof; below them, all shadowy and shimmery, the castle gardens; above them, stars and moon. Presently they came to another door, which led into the great central tower of the whole castle: Doctor Cornelius unlocked it and they began to climb the dark winding stair of the tower. Caspian was becoming excited; he had never been allowed up this stair before.

It was long and steep, but when they came out on the roof of the tower and Caspian had got his breath, he felt that it had been well worth it. Away on his right he could see, rather indistinctly, the Western Mountains. On his left was the gleam of the Great River, and everything was so quiet that he could hear the sound of the waterfall at Beaversdam, a mile away. There was no difficulty in picking out the two stars they had come to see. They hung rather low in the southern sky, almost as bright as two little moons and very close together.

"Are they going to have a collision?" he asked in an awe-struck voice.

"Nay, dear Prince," said the Doctor (and he too spoke in a whisper). "The great lords of the upper sky know the steps of their dance too well for that. Look well upon them. Their meeting is fortunate and means some great good for the sad realm of Narnia. Tarva, the Lord of Victory, salutes Alambil, the Lady of Peace. They are just coming to their nearest."

"It's a pity that tree gets in the way," said Caspian. "We'd really see better from the West Tower, though it is not so high."

Doctor Cornelius said nothing for about two minutes, but stood still with his eyes fixed on Tarva and Alambil. Then he drew a deep breath and turned to Caspian.

"There," he said. "You have seen what no man now alive has seen, nor will see again. And you are right. We should have seen it even better from the smaller tower. I brought you here for another reason."

Caspian looked up at him, but the Doctor's hood concealed most of his face.

"The virtue of this tower," said Doctor Cornelius, "is that we have six empty rooms beneath us, and a long stair, and the door at the bottom of the stair is locked. We cannot be overheard."

"Are you going to tell me what you wouldn't tell me the other day?" said Caspian.

"I am," said the Doctor. "But remember. You and I must never talk about these things except here – on the very top of the Great Tower."

"No. That's a promise," said Caspian. "But do go on, please."

"Listen," said the Doctor. "All you have heard about Old Narnia is true. It is not the land of Men. It is the country of Aslan, the country of the Waking Trees and Visible Naiads, of Fauns and Satyrs, of Dwarfs and Giants, of the gods and the Centaurs, of Talking Beasts. It was against these that the first Caspian fought. It is you Telmarines who silenced the beasts and the trees and the fountains, and who killed and drove away the Dwarfs and Fauns, and are now trying to cover up even the memory of them. The King does not allow them to be spoken of."

"Oh, I do wish we hadn't," said Caspian. "And I *am* glad it was all true, even if it is all over."

"Many of your race wish that in secret," said Doctor Cornelius.

"But, Doctor," said Caspian, "why do you say *my* race? After all, I suppose you're a Telmarine too."

"Am I?" said the Doctor.

"Well, you're a Man anyway," said Caspian.

"Am I?" repeated the Doctor in a deeper voice, at the same moment throwing back his hood so that Caspian could see his face clearly in the moonlight.

All at once Caspian realized the truth and felt that he ought to have realized it long before. Doctor Cornelius was so small, and so fat, and had such a very long beard. Two thoughts came into his head at the same moment. One was a thought of terror – "He's not a real man, not a man at all, he's a *Dwarf*, and he's brought me up here to kill me." The other was sheer delight – "There are real Dwarfs still, and I've seen one at last."

"So you've guessed it in the end," said Doctor Cornelius. "Or guessed it nearly right. I'm not a pure Dwarf. I have human blood in me too. Many Dwarfs escaped in the great battles and lived on, shaving their beards and wearing high-heeled shoes and pretending to be men. They have mixed with your Telmarines. I am one of those, only a half-Dwarf, and if any of my kindred, the true Dwarfs, are still alive anywhere in the world, doubtless they would despise me and call me a traitor. But never in all these years have we forgotten our own people and all the other happy creatures of Narnia, and the long-lost days of freedom."

"I'm – I'm sorry, Doctor," said Caspian. "It wasn't my fault, you know."

"I am not saying these things in blame of you, dear Prince," answered the Doctor. "You may well ask why I say them at all. But I have two reasons. Firstly, because my old heart has carried these secret memories so long that it aches with them and would burst if I did not whisper them to you. But secondly, for this: that when you become King you may help us, for I know that you also, Telmarine though you are, love the Old Things."

"I do, I do," said Caspian. "But how can I help?"

"You can be kind to the poor remnants of the Dwarf people, like myself. You can gather learned magicians and try to find a way of awaking the trees once more. You can search through all the nooks and wild places of the land to see if any Fauns or Talking Beasts or Dwarfs are perhaps still alive in hiding."

"Do you think there are any?" asked Caspian eagerly.

"I don't know — I don't know," said the Doctor with a deep sigh. "Sometimes I am afraid there can't be. I have been looking for traces of them all my life. Sometimes I have thought I heard a Dwarf-drum in the mountains. Sometimes at night, in the woods, I thought I had caught a glimpse of Fauns and Satyrs dancing a long way off; but when I came to the place, there was never anything there. I have often despaired; but something always happens to start me hoping again. I don't know. But at least you can try to be a King like the High King Peter of old, and not like your uncle."

"Then it's true about the Kings and Queens too, and about the White Witch?" said Caspian.

"Certainly it is true," said Cornelius. "Their reign was the Golden Age in Narnia and the land has never forgotten them."

"Did they live in this castle, Doctor?"

"Nay, my dear," said the old man. "This castle is a thing of yesterday. Your great-great-grandfather built it. But when the two sons of Adam and the two daughters of Eve were made Kings and Queens of Narnia by Aslan himself, they lived in the castle of Cair Paravel. No man alive has seen that blessed place and perhaps even the ruins of it have now vanished. But we believe it was far from here, down at the mouth of the Great River, on the very shore of the sea."

"Ugh!" said Caspian with a shudder. "Do you mean in

the Black Woods? Where all the – the – you know, the ghosts live?"

"Your Highness speaks as you have been taught," said the Doctor. "But it is all lies. There are no ghosts there. That is a story invented by the Telmarines. Your Kings are in deadly fear of the sea because they can never quite forget that in all stories Aslan comes from over the sea. They don't want to go near it and they don't want anyone else to go near it. So they have let great woods grow up to cut their people off from the coast. But because they have quarrelled with the trees they are afraid of the woods. And because they are afraid of the woods they imagine that they are full of ghosts. And the Kings and great men, hating both the sea and the wood, partly believe these stories, and partly encourage them. They feel safer if no one in Narnia dares to go down to the coast and look out to sea – towards Aslan's land and the morning and the eastern end of the world."

There was a deep silence between them for a few minutes. Then Doctor Cornelius said, "Come. We have been here long enough. It is time to go down and to bed."

"Must we?" said Caspian. "I'd like to go on talking about these things for hours and hours and hours."

"Someone might begin looking for us, if we did that," said Doctor Cornelius.

CHAPTER FIVE

CASPIAN'S ADVENTURE IN
THE MOUNTAINS

AFTER this, Caspian and his Tutor had many more secret conversations on the top of the Great Tower, and at each conversation Caspian learned more about Old Narnia, so that thinking and dreaming about the old days, and longing that they might come back, filled nearly all his spare hours. But of course he had not many hours to spare, for now his education was beginning in earnest. He learned sword-fighting and riding, swimming and diving, how to shoot with the bow and play on the recorder and the theorbo, how to hunt the stag and cut him up when he was dead, besides Cosmography, Rhetoric, Heraldry, Versification, and of course History, with a little Law, Physic, Alchemy, and Astronomy. Of Magic he learned only the theory, for Doctor Cornelius said the practical part was not proper study for princes. "And I myself," he added, "am only a very imperfect magician and can do only the smallest experiments." Of Navigation ("Which is a noble and heroical art," said the Doctor) he was taught nothing, because King Miraz disapproved of ships and the sea.

He also learned a great deal by using his own eyes and ears. As a little boy he had often wondered why he disliked his aunt, Queen Prunaprismia; he now saw that it was because she disliked him. He also began to see that Narnia was an unhappy country. The taxes were high and the laws were stern and Miraz was a cruel man.

After some years there came a time when the Queen seemed to be ill and there was a great deal of bustle and pother about her in the castle and doctors came and the courtiers whispered. This was in early summertime. And one night, while all this fuss was going on, Caspian was unexpectedly wakened by Doctor Cornelius after he had been only a few hours in bed.

"Are we going to do a little Astronomy, Doctor?" said Caspian.

"Hush!" said the Doctor. "Trust me and do exactly as I tell you. Put on all your clothes; you have a long journey before you."

Caspian was very surprised, but he had learned to have confidence in his Tutor and he began doing what he was told at once. When he was dressed the Doctor said, "I have a wallet for you. We must go into the next room and fill it with victuals from your Highness's supper table."

"My gentlemen-in-waiting will be there," said Caspian.

"They are fast asleep and will not wake," said the Doctor. "I am a very minor magician but I *can* at least contrive a charmed sleep."

They went into the antechamber and there, sure enough, the two gentlemen-in-waiting were, sprawling on chairs and snoring hard. Doctor Cornelius quickly cut up the remains of a cold chicken and some slices of venison and put them, with bread and an apple or so and a little flask of good wine, into the wallet which he then gave to Caspian. It fitted on by a strap over Caspian's shoulder, like a satchel you would use for taking books to school.

"Have you your sword?" asked the Doctor.

"Yes," said Caspian.

"Then put this mantle over all to hide the sword and the wallet. That's right. And now we must go to the Great Tower and talk."

When they had reached the top of the Tower (it was a cloudy night, not at all like the night when they had seen the conjunction of Tarva and Alambil) Doctor Cornelius said,

"Dear Prince, you must leave this castle at once and go to seek your fortune in the wide world. Your life is in danger here."

"Why?" asked Caspian.

"Because you are the true King of Narnia: Caspian the Tenth, the true son and heir of Caspian the Ninth. Long life to your Majesty' – and suddenly, to Caspian's great surprise, the little man dropped down on one knee and kissed his hand.

"What does it all mean? I don't understand," said Caspian.

"I wonder you have never asked me before," said the Doctor, "why, being the son of King Caspian, you are not King Caspian yourself. Everyone except your Majesty knows that Miraz is a usurper. When he first began to rule he did not even pretend to be the King: he called himself Lord Protector. But then your royal mother died, the good Queen and the only Telmarine who was ever kind to me. And then, one by one, all the great lords, who had known your father, died or disappeared. Not by accident, either. Miraz weeded them out. Belisar and Uvilas were shot with arrows on a hunting party: by chance, it was pretended. All the great house of the Passarids he sent to fight giants on the northern frontier till one by one they fell. Arlian and Erimon and a dozen more he executed for treason on a false charge. The two brothers of Beaversdam he shut up as madmen. And finally he persuaded the seven noble lords, who alone among all the Telmarines did not fear the sea, to sail away and look for new lands beyond the Eastern Ocean, and, as he intended, they never came back. And when there was no one left who could speak a word for you, then his flatterers (as he had instructed them) begged him to become King. And of course he did."

"Do you mean he now wants to kill me too?" said Caspian.

"That is almost certain," said Doctor Cornelius.

"But why now?" said Caspian. "I mean, why didn't he do it long ago if he wanted to? And what harm have I done him?"

"He has changed his mind about you because of something that happened only two hours ago. The Queen has had a son."

"I don't see what that's got to do with it," said Caspian.

"Don't see!" exclaimed the Doctor. "Have all my lessons in History and Politics taught you no more than that? Listen. As long as he had no children of his own, he was willing enough that you should be King after he died. He may not have cared much about you, but he would rather you should have the throne than a stranger. Now that he has a son of his own he will want his own son to be the next King. You are in the way. He'll clear you out of the way."

"Is he really as bad as that?" said Caspian. "Would he really murder me?"

"He murdered your Father," said Doctor Cornelius.

Caspian felt very queer and said nothing.

"I can tell you the whole story," said the Doctor. "But not now. There is no time. You must fly at once."

"You'll come with me?" said Caspian.

"I dare not," said the Doctor. "It would make your

danger greater. Two are more easily tracked than one. Dear Prince, dear King Caspian, you must be very brave. You must go alone and at once. Try to get across the southern border to the court of King Nain of Archenland. He will be good to you."

"Shall I never see you again?" said Caspian in a quavering voice.

"I hope so, dear King," said the Doctor. "What friend have I in the wide world except your Majesty? And I have a little magic. But in the meantime, speed is everything. Here are two gifts before you go. This is a little purse of gold — alas, all the treasure in this castle should be your own by rights. And here is something far better."

He put in Caspian's hands something which he could hardly see but which he knew by the feel to be a horn.

"That," said Doctor Cornelius, "is the greatest and most sacred treasure of Narnia. Many terrors I endured, many spells did I utter, to find it, when I was still young. It is the magic horn of Queen Susan herself which she left behind her when she vanished from Narnia at the end of the Golden Age. It is said that whoever blows it shall have strange help — no one can say how strange. It may have the power to call Queen Lucy and King Edmund and Queen Susan and High King Peter back from the past, and they will set all to rights. It may be that it will call up Aslan himself. Take it, King Caspian: but do not use it except at your greatest need. And now, haste, haste, haste. The little door at the very bottom of the Tower, the door into the garden, is unlocked. There we must part."

"Can I get my horse Destrier?" said Caspian.

"He is already saddled and waiting for you just at the corner of the orchard."

During the long climb down the winding staircase Cornelius whispered many more words of direction and advice. Caspian's heart was sinking, but he tried to take it all in. Then came the fresh air in the garden, a fervent handclasp with the Doctor, a run across the lawn, a welcoming whinny from Destrier, and so King Caspian the Tenth left the castle of his fathers. Looking back, he saw fireworks going up to celebrate the birth of the new prince.

All night he rode southward, choosing by-ways and bridle paths through woods as long as he was in country that he knew; but afterwards he kept to the high road. Destrier was as excited as his master at this unusual journey, and Caspian, though tears had come into his eyes at saying good-bye to Doctor Cornelius, felt brave and, in a way, happy, to think that he was King Caspian riding to seek adventures, with his sword on his left hip and Queen Susan's magic horn on his right. But when day came, with a sprinkle of rain, and he looked about him and saw on every side unknown woods, wild heaths, and blue mountains, he thought how large and strange the world was and felt frightened and small.

As soon as it was full daylight he left the road and found an open grassy place amid a wood where he could rest. He took off Destrier's bridle and let him graze, ate some cold chicken and drank a little wine, and presently fell asleep. It was late afternoon when he awoke. He ate a morsel and continued his journey, still southward, by many unfrequented lanes. He was now in a land of hills, going up and down, but always more up than down. From every ridge he could see the mountains growing bigger and blacker ahead. As the evening closed in, he was riding their lower slopes. The wind rose. Soon rain fell in torrents.

Destrier became uneasy; there was thunder in the air. And now they entered a dark and seemingly endless pine forest, and all the stories Caspian had ever heard of trees being unfriendly to Man crowded into his mind. He remembered that he was, after all, a Telmarine, one of the race who cut down trees wherever they could and were at war with all wild things; and though he himself might be

unlike other Telmarines, the trees could not be expected to know this.

Nor did they. The wind became a tempest, the woods roared and creaked all round them. There came a crash. A tree fell right across the road just behind him. "Quiet, Destrier, quiet!" said Caspian, patting his horse's neck; but he was trembling himself and knew that he had escaped death by an inch. Lightning flashed and a great crack of thunder seemed to break the sky in two just overhead.

Destrier bolted in good earnest. Caspian was a good rider, but he had not the strength to hold him back. He kept his seat, but he knew that his life hung by a thread during the wild career that followed. Tree after tree rose up before them in the dusk and was only just avoided. Then, almost too suddenly to hurt (and yet it did hurt him too) something struck Caspian on the forehead and he knew no more.

When he came to himself he was lying in a firelit place with bruised limbs and a bad headache. Low voices were speaking close at hand.

"And now," said one, "before it wakes up we must decide what to do with it."

"Kill it," said another. "We can't let it live. It would betray us."

"We ought to have killed it at once, or eise let it alone," said a third voice. "We can't kill it now. Not after we've taken it in and bandaged its head and all. It would be murdering a guest."

"Gentlemen," said Caspian in a feeble voice, "whatever you do to me, I hope you will be kind to my poor horse."

"Your horse had taken flight long before we found you," said the first voice – a curiously husky, earthy voice, as Caspian now noticed.

"Now don't let it talk you round with its pretty words," said the second voice. "I still say –"

"Horns and halibuts!" exclaimed the third voice. "Of course we're not going to murder it. For shame, Nikabrik. What do you say, Trufflehunter? What shall we do with it?"

"I shall give it a drink," said the first voice, presumably

Trufflehunter's. A dark shape approached the bed. Caspian felt an arm slipped gently under his shoulders – if it was exactly an arm. The shape somehow seemed wrong. The face that bent towards him seemed wrong too. He got the impression that it was very hairy and very long nosed, and there were odd white patches on each side of it. "It's a mask of some sort," thought Caspian. "Or perhaps I'm in a fever and imagining it all." A cupful of something sweet and hot was set to his lips and he drank. At that moment one of the others poked the fire. A blaze sprang up and Caspian almost screamed with the shock as the sudden light revealed the face that was looking into his own. It was not a man's face but a badger's, though larger and friendlier and more intelligent than the face of any badger he had seen before. And it had certainly been talking. He saw, too, that he was on a bed of heather, in a cave. By the fire sat two little bearded men, so much wilder and shorter and hairier and thicker than Doctor Cornelius that he knew them at once for real Dwarfs, ancient Dwarfs with not a drop of human blood in their veins. And Caspian knew that he had found the Old Narnians at last. Then his head began to swim again.

In the next few days he learned to know them by names.

The Badger was called Trufflehunter; he was the oldest and kindest of the three. The Dwarf who had wanted to kill Caspian was a sour Black Dwarf (that is, his hair and beard were black, and thick and hard like horsehair). His name was Nikabrik. The other Dwarf was a Red Dwarf with hair rather like a Fox's and he was called Trumpkin.

"And now," said Nikabrik on the first evening when Caspian was well enough to sit up and talk, "we still have to decide what to do with this Human. You two think you've done it a great kindess by not letting me kill it. But I suppose the upshot is that we have to keep it a prisoner for life. I'm certainly not going to let it go alive – to go back to its own kind and betray us all."

"Bulbs and bolsters! Nikabrik," said Trumpkin. "Why need you talk so unhandsomely? It isn't the creature's fault that it bashed its head against a tree outside our hole. And I don't think it looks like a traitor."

"I say," said Caspian, "you haven't yet found out whether I *want* to go back. I don't. I want to stay with you – if you'll let me. I've been looking for people like you all my life."

"That's a likely story," growled Nikabrik. "You're a Telmarine and a Human, aren't you? Of course you want to go back to your own kind."

"Well, even if I did, I couldn't," said Caspian. "I was flying for my life when I had my accident. The King wants to kill me. If you'd killed me, you'd have done the very thing to please him."

"Well now," said Trufflehunter, "you don't say so!"

"Eh?" said Trumpkin. "What's that? What have you been doing, Human, to fall foul of Miraz at your age?"

"He's my uncle," began Caspian, when Nikabrik jumped up with his hand on his dagger.

"There you are!" he cried. "Not only a Telmarine but close kin and heir to our greatest enemy. Are you still mad enough to let this creature live?" He would have stabbed Caspian then and there, if the Badger and Trumpkin had not got in the way and forced him back to his seat and held him down.

"Now, once and for all, Nikabrik," said Trumpkin. "Will you contain yourself, or must Trufflehunter and I sit on your head?"

Nikabrik sulkily promised to behave, and the other two asked Caspian to tell his whole story. When he had done so there was a moment's silence.

"This is the queerest thing I ever heard," said Trumpkin.

"I don't like it," said Nikabrik. "I didn't know there were stories about us still told among the Humans. The less they know about us the better. That old nurse, now. She'd better have held her tongue. And it's all mixed up with that Tutor: a renegade Dwarf. I hate 'em. I hate 'em worse than the Humans. You mark my words – no good will come of it."

"Don't you go talking about things you don't understand, Nikabrik," said Trufflehunter. "You Dwarfs are as forgetful and changeable as the Humans themselves. I'm a beast, I am, and a Badger what's more. We don't change. We hold on. I say great good will come of it. This is the true King of Narnia we've got here: a true King, coming back to true Narnia. And we beasts remember, even if Dwarfs forget, that Narnia was never right except when a son of Adam was King."

"Whistles and whirligigs! Trufflehunter," said

Trumpkin. "You don't mean you want to give the country to Humans?"

"I said nothing about that," answered the Badger. "It's not Men's country (who should know that better than me?) but it's a country for a man to be King of. We badgers have long enough memories to know that. Why, bless us all, wasn't the High King Peter a Man?"

"Do you believe all those old stories?" asked Trumpkin.

"I tell you, we don't change, we beasts," said Trufflehunter. "We don't forget. I believe in the High King Peter and the rest that reigned at Cair Paravel, as firmly as I believe in Aslan himself."

"As firmly as *that*, I dare say," said Trumpkin. "But who believes in Aslan nowadays?"

"I do," said Caspian. "And if I hadn't believed in him before, I would now. Back there among the Humans the people who laughed at Aslan would have laughed at stories about Talking Beasts and Dwarfs. Sometimes I did wonder if there really was such a person as Aslan: but then sometimes I wondered if there were really people like you. Yet there you are."

"That's right," said Trufflehunter. "You're right, King Caspian. And as long as you will be true to Old Narnia you shall be *my* King, whatever they say. Long life to your Majesty."

"You make me sick, Badger," growled Nikabrik. "The High King Peter and the rest may have been Men, but they were a different sort of Men. This is one of the cursed Telmarines. He has *hunted* beasts for sport. Haven't you, now?" he added, rounding suddenly on Caspian.

"Well, to tell you the truth, I have," said Caspian. "But they weren't Talking Beasts."

"It's all the same thing," said Nikabrik.

"No, no, no," said Trufflehunter. "You know it isn't. You know very well that the beasts in Narnia nowadays are different and are no more than the poor dumb, witless creatures you'd find in Calormen or Telmar. They're smaller too. They're far more different from us than the half-Dwarfs are from you."

There was a great deal more talk, but it all ended with the agreement that Caspian should stay and even the promise that, as soon as he was able to go out, he should be taken to see what Trumpkin called "the Others"; for apparently in these wild parts all sorts of creatures from the Old Days of Narnia still lived on in hiding.

CHAPTER SIX

THE PEOPLE THAT LIVED IN HIDING

Now began the happiest times that Caspian had ever known. On a fine summer morning when the dew lay on the grass he set off with the Badger and the two Dwarfs, up through the forest to a high saddle in the mountains and down on to their sunny southern slopes where one looked across the green wolds of Archenland.

"We will go first to the Three Bulgy Bears," said Trumpkin.

They came in a glade to an old hollow oak tree covered with moss, and Trufflehunter tapped with his paw three times on the trunk and there was no answer. Then he tapped again and a woolly sort of voice from inside said, "Go away. It's not time to get up yet." But when he tapped the third time there was a noise like a small earthquake from inside and a sort of door opened and out came three brown bears, very bulgy indeed and blinking their little eyes. And when everything had been explained to them (which took a long time because they were so sleepy) they said, just as Trufflehunter had said, that a son of Adam ought to be King of Narnia and all kissed Caspian – very wet, snuffly kisses they were – and offered him some honey. Caspian did not really want honey, without bread, at that time in the morning, but he thought it polite to accept. It took him a long time afterwards to get unsticky.

After that they went on till they came among tall beech trees and Trufflehunter called out, "Pattertwig! Pattertwig! Pattertwig!" and almost at once, bounding down from branch to branch till he was just above their heads, came

the most magnificent red
squirrel that Caspian had
ever seen. He was far bigger
than the ordinary dumb squirrels
which he had sometimes seen
in the castle gardens; indeed he was nearly the size of
a terrier and the moment you looked in his face you
saw that he could talk. Indeed the difficulty was to
get him to stop talking, for, like all squirrels, he was
a chatterer. He welcomed Caspian at once and asked if he
would like a nut and Caspian said thanks, he would. But as
Pattertwig went bounding away to fetch it, Trufflehunter
whispered in Caspian's ear, "Don't look. Look the other
way. It's very bad manners among squirrels to watch
anyone going to his store or to look as if you wanted to
know where it was." Then Pattertwig came back with the
nut and Caspian ate it and after that Pattertwig asked if he
could take any messages to other friends. "For I can go
nearly everywhere without setting foot to ground," he said.
Trufflehunter and the Dwarfs thought this a very good idea
and gave Pattertwig messages to all sorts of people with
queer names telling them all to come to a feast and council
on Dancing Lawn at midnight three nights ahead. "And
you'd better tell the three Bulgies too," added Trumpkin.
"We forgot to mention it to them."

Their next visit was to the Seven Brothers of Shuddering

Wood. Trumpkin led the way back to the saddle and then down eastward on the northern slope of the mountains till they came to a very solemn place among rocks and fir trees. They went very quietly and presently Caspian could feel the ground shake under his feet as if someone were hammering down below. Trumpkin went to a flat stone about the size of the top of a water-butt, and stamped on it with his foot. After a long pause it was moved away by someone or something underneath, and there was a dark, round hole with a good deal of heat and steam coming out of it and in the middle of the hole the head of a Dwarf very like Trumpkin himself. There was a long talk here and the dwarf seemed more suspicious than the Squirrel or the Bulgy Bears had been, but in the end the whole party were invited to come down. Caspian found himself descending a dark stairway into the earth, but when he came to the bottom he saw firelight. It was the light of a furnace. The whole place was a smithy. A subterranean stream ran past on one side of it. Two Dwarfs were at the bellows, another was holding a piece of red-hot metal on the anvil with a pair of tongs, a fourth was hammering it, and two, wiping their horny little hands on a greasy cloth, were coming forward to meet the visitors. It took some time to satisfy them that Caspian was a friend and not an enemy, but when they did, they all cried, "Long live the King," and their gifts were noble – mail shirts and helmets and swords for Caspian and Trumpkin and Nikabrik. The Badger could have had the same if he had liked, but he said he was a beast, he was, and if his claws and teeth could not keep his skin whole, it wasn't worth keeping. The workmanship of the arms was far finer than any Caspian had ever seen, and he gladly accepted the Dwarf-made sword instead of his own, which looked, in comparison, as feeble as a toy and as clumsy as a stick. The seven brothers (who were all Red Dwarfs) promised to come to the feast at Dancing Lawn.

A little farther on, in a dry, rocky ravine they reached the cave of five Black Dwarfs. They looked suspiciously at Caspian, but in the end the eldest of them said, "If he is against Miraz, we'll have him for King." And the next oldest said, "Shall we go farther up for you, up to the crags? There's an Ogre or two and a Hag that we could introduce you to, up there."

"Certainly not," said Caspian.

"I should think not, indeed," said Trufflehunter. "We want none of that sort on our side." Nikabrik disagreed with this, but Trumpkin and the Badger overruled him. It gave Caspian a shock to realize that the horrible creatures out of the old stories, as well as the nice ones, had some descendants in Narnia still.

"We should not have Aslan for friend if we brought in *that* rabble," said Trufflehunter as they came away from the cave of the Black Dwarfs.

"Oh, Aslan!" said Trumpkin, cheerily but contemptuously. "What matters much more is that you wouldn't have me."

"Do *you* believe in Aslan?" said Caspian to Nikabrik.

"I'll believe in anyone or anything," said Nikabrik, "that'll batter these cursed Telmarine barbarians to pieces or drive them out of Narnia. Anyone or anything, Aslan *or* the White Witch, do you understand?"

"Silence, silence," said Trufflehunter. "You do not know what you are saying. She was a worse enemy than Miraz and all his race."

"Not to Dwarfs, she wasn't," said Nikabrik.

Their next visit was a pleasanter one. As they came lower down, the mountains opened out into a great glen or wooded gorge with a swift river running at the bottom. The open places near the river's edge were a mass of foxgloves and wild roses and the air was buzzing with bees. Here Trufflehunter called again, "Glenstorm! Glenstorm!" and after a pause Caspian heard the sound of hoofs. It grew louder till the valley trembled and at last, breaking and trampling the thickets, there came in sight the noblest creatures that Caspian had yet seen, the great Centaur Glenstorm and his three sons. His flanks were glossy chestnut and the beard that covered his broad chest was goldenred. He was a prophet and a star-gazer and knew what they had come about.

"Long live the King," he cried. "I and my sons are ready for war. When is the battle to be joined?"

Up till now neither Caspian nor the others had really been thinking of a war. They had some vague idea, perhaps, of an occasional raid on some Human farmstead or of attacking a party of hunters, if it ventured too far into these southern wilds. But, in the main, they had thought only of living to themselves in woods and caves and building up an attempt at Old Narnia in hiding. As soon as Glenstorm had spoken everyone felt much more serious.

"Do you mean a real war to drive Miraz out of Narnia?" asked Caspian.

"What else?" said the Centaur. "Why else does your Majesty go clad in mail and girt with sword?"

"Is it possible, Glenstorm?" said the Badger.

"The time is ripe," said Glenstorm. "I watch the skies,

Badger, for it is mine to watch, as it is yours to remember. Tarva and Alambil have met in the halls of high heaven, and on earth a son of Adam has once more arisen to rule and name the creatures. The hour has struck. Our council at the Dancing Lawn must be a council of war." He spoke in such a voice that neither Caspian nor the others hesitated for a moment: it now seemed to them quite possible that they might win a war and quite certain that they must wage one.

As it was now past the middle of the day, they rested with the Centaurs and ate such food as the centaurs provided – cakes of oaten meal, and apples, and herbs, and wine, and cheese.

The next place they were to visit was quite near at hand, but they had to go a long way round in order to avoid a region in which Men lived. It was well into the afternoon before they found themselves in level fields, warm between hedgerows. There Trufflehunter called at the mouth of a little hole in a green bank and out popped the last thing Caspian expected – a Talking Mouse. He was of course bigger than a common mouse, well over a foot high when he stood on his hind legs, and with ears nearly as long as (though broader than) a rabbit's. His name was Reepicheep and he was a gay and martial mouse. He wore a tiny little rapier at his side and twirled his long whiskers as if they were a moustache. "There are twelve of us, Sire," he said with a dashing and graceful bow, "and I place all the resources of my people unreservedly at your Majesty's disposal." Caspian tried hard (and successfully) not to laugh, but he couldn't help thinking that Reepicheep and all his people could very easily be put in a washing basket and carried home on one's back.

It would take too long to mention all the creatures whom Caspian met that day – Clodsley Shovel the Mole, the three Hardbiters (who were badgers like Trufflehunter), Camillo the Hare, and Hogglestock the Hedgehog. They rested at last beside a well at the edge of a wide and level circle of grass, bordered with tall elms which now threw long shadows across it, for the sun was setting, the daisies closing, and the rooks flying home to bed. Here they supped on food they had brought with them and Trumpkin lit his pipe (Nikabrik was not a smoker).

"Now," said the Badger, "if only we could wake the spirits of these trees and this well, we should have done a good day's work."

"Can't we?" said Caspian.

"No," said Trufflehunter. "We have no power over them. Since the Humans came into the land, felling forests and defiling streams, the Dryads and Naiads have sunk into a deep sleep. Who knows if ever they will stir again? And that is a great loss to our side. The Telmarines are horribly afraid of the woods, and once the Trees moved in anger, our enemies would go mad with fright and be chased out of Narnia as quick as their legs could carry them."

"What imaginations you Animals have!" said Trumpkin, who didn't believe in such things. "But why stop at Trees and Waters? Wouldn't it be even nicer if the stones started throwing themselves at old Miraz?"

The Badger only grunted at this, and after that there was such a silence that Caspian had nearly dropped off to sleep

when he thought he heard a faint musical sound from the depth of the woods at his back. Then he thought it was only a dream and turned over again; but as soon as his ear touched the ground he felt or heard (it was hard to tell which) a faint beating or drumming. He raised his head. The beating noise at once became fainter, but the music returned, clearer this time. It was like flutes. He saw that Trufflehunter was sitting up staring into the wood. The moon was bright; Caspian had been asleep longer than he thought. Nearer and nearer came the music, a tune wild and yet dreamy, and the noise of many light feet, till at last, out from the wood into the moonlight, came dancing shapes such as Caspian had been thinking of all his life. They were not much taller than dwarfs, but far slighter and more graceful. Their curly heads had little horns, the upper part of their bodies gleamed naked in the pale light, but their legs and feet were those of goats.

"Fauns!" cried Caspian, jumping up, and in a moment they were all round him. It took next to no time to explain the whole situation to them and they accepted Caspian at once. Before he knew what he was doing he found himself joining in the dance. Trumpkin, with heavier and jerkier movements, did likewise and even Trufflehunter hopped and lumbered about as best he could. Only Nikabrik stayed where he was, looking on in silence. The Fauns footed it all round Caspian to their reedy pipes. Their strange faces, which seemed mournful and merry all at once, looked into his; dozens of Fauns, Mentius and Obentinus and Dumnus, Voluns, Voltinus, Girbius, Nimienus, Nausus, and Oscuns. Pattertwig had sent them all.

When Caspian awoke next morning he could hardly believe that it had not all been a dream; but the grass was covered with little cloven hoof-marks.

CHAPTER SEVEN

OLD NARNIA IN DANGER

THE place where they had met the Fauns was, of course, Dancing Lawn itself, and here Caspian and his friends remained till the night of the great Council. To sleep under the stars, to drink nothing but well water and to live chiefly on nuts and wild fruit, was a strange experience for Caspian after his bed with silken sheets in a tapestried chamber at the castle, with meals laid out on gold and silver dishes in the anteroom, and attendants ready at his call. But he had never enjoyed himself more. Never had sleep been more refreshing nor food tasted more savoury, and he began already to harden and his face wore a kinglier look.

When the great night came, and his various strange subjects came stealing into the lawn by ones and twos and threes or by sixes and sevens – the moon then shining almost at her full – his heart swelled as he saw their numbers and heard their greetings. All whom he had met were there: Bulgy Bears and Red Dwarfs and Black Dwarfs, Moles and Badgers, Hares and Hedgehogs, and others whom he had not yet seen – five Satyrs as red as foxes, the whole contingent of Talking Mice, armed to the teeth and following a shrill trumpet, some Owls, the Old Raven of Ravenscaur. Last of all (and this took Caspian's breath away), with the Centaurs came a small but genuine Giant, Wimbleweather of Deadman's Hill, carrying on his back a basketful of rather sea-sick Dwarfs who had accepted his offer of a lift and were now wishing they had walked instead.

The Bulgy Bears were very anxious to have the feast first and leave the council till afterwards: perhaps till tomorrow. Reepicheep and his Mice said that councils and feasts could both wait, and proposed storming Miraz in his own castle that very night. Pattertwig and the other Squirrels said they could talk and eat at the same time, so why not have the council and feast all at once? The Moles proposed throwing up entrenchments round the Lawn before they did anything else. The Fauns thought it would be better to begin with a solemn dance. The Old Raven, while agreeing with the Bears that it would take too long to have a full council before supper, begged to be allowed to give a brief address to the whole company. But Caspian and the Centaurs and the Dwarfs overruled all these suggestions and insisted on holding a real council of war at once.

When all the other creatures had been persuaded to sit down quietly in a great circle, and when (with more difficulty) they had got Pattertwig to stop running to and fro and saying "Silence! Silence, everyone, for the King's speech", Caspian, feeling a little nervous, got up. "Narnians!" he began, but he never got any further, for at that very moment Camillo the Hare said, "Hush! There's a Man somewhere near."

They were all creatures of the wild, accustomed to being hunted, and they all became still as statues. The beasts all turned their noses in the direction which Camillo had indicated.

"Smells like Man and yet not quite like Man," whispered Trufflehunter.

"It's getting steadily nearer," said Camillo.

"Two badgers and you three Dwarfs, with your

bows at the ready, go softly off to meet it," said Caspian.

"We'll settle 'un," said a Black Dwarf grimly, fitting a shaft to his bowstring.

"Don't shoot if it is alone," said Caspian. "Catch it."

"Why?" asked the Dwarf.

"Do as you're told," said Glenstorm the Centaur.

Everyone waited in silence while the three Dwarfs and two Badgers trotted stealthily across to the trees on the north-west side of the Lawn. Then came a sharp dwarfish cry, "Stop! Who goes there?" and a sudden spring. A moment later a voice, which Caspian knew well, could he heard saying, "All right, all right, I'm unarmed. Take my wrists if you like, worthy Badgers, but don't bite right through them. I want to speak to the King."

"Doctor Cornelius!" cried Caspian with joy, and rushed forward to greet his old tutor. Everyone else crowded round.

"Pah!" said Nikabrik. "A renegade Dwarf. A half-and-halfer! Shall I pass my sword through its throat?"

"Be quiet, Nikabrik," said Trumpkin. "The creature can't help its ancestry."

"This is my greatest friend and the saviour of my life," said Caspian. "And anyone who doesn't like his company may leave my army: at once. Dearest doctor, I *am* glad to see you again. How ever did you find us out?"

"By a little use of simple magic, your Majesty," said the Doctor, who was still puffing and blowing from having walked so fast. "But there's no time to go into that now. We must all fly from this place at once. You are already betrayed and Miraz is on the move. Before midday to-morrow you will be surrounded."

"Betrayed!" said Caspian. "And by whom?"

"Another renegade Dwarf, no doubt," said Nikabrik.

"By your horse Destrier," said Doctor Cornelius. "The poor brute knew no better. When you were knocked off, of course, he went dawdling back to his stable in the castle. Then the secret of your flight was known. I made myself scarce, having no wish to be questioned about it in Miraz's torture chamber. I had a pretty good guess from my crystal as to where I should find you. But all day – that was the day before yesterday – I saw Miraz's tracking parties out in the woods. Yesterday I learned that his army is out. I don't think some of your – um – pure-blooded Dwarfs have as much woodcraft as might be expected. You've left tracks all over the place. Great carelessness. At any rate something has warned Miraz that Old Narnia is not so dead as he had hoped, and he is on the move."

"Hurrah!" said a very shrill and small voice from somewhere at the Doctor's feet. "Let them come! All I ask is that the King will put me and my people in the front."

"What on earth?" said Doctor Cornelius. "Has your Majesty got grasshoppers – or mosquitoes – in your army?" Then after stooping down and peering carefully through his spectacles, he broke into a laugh.

"By the Lion," he swore, "it's a mouse. Signior Mouse, I desire your better acquaintance. I am honoured by meeting so valiant a beast."

"My friendship you shall have, learned Man," piped Reepicheep. "And any Dwarf – or Giant – in the army who does not give you good language shall have my sword to reckon with."

"Is there time for this foolery?" asked Nikabrik. "What are our plans? Battle or flight?"

"Battle if need be," said Trumpkin. "But we are hardly ready for it yet, and this is no very defensible place."

"I don't like the idea of running away," said Caspian.

"Hear him! Hear him!" said the Bulgy Bears. "Whatever we do, don't let's have any *running*. Especially not before supper; and not too soon after it neither."

"Those who run first do not always run last," said the Centaur. "And why should we let the enemy choose our position instead of choosing it ourselves? Let us find a strong place."

"That's wise, your Majesty, that's wise," said Trufflehunter.

"But where are we to go?" asked several voices.

"Your Majesty," said Doctor Cornelius, "and all you variety of creatures, I think we must fly east and down the river to the great woods. The Telmarines hate that region. They have always been afraid of the sea and of something that may come over the sea. That is why they have let the great woods grow up. If traditions speak true, the ancient Cair Paravel was at the river-mouth. All that part is friendly to us and hateful to our enemies. We must go to Aslan's How."

"Aslan's How?" said several voices. "We do not know what it is."

"It lies within the skirts of the Great Woods and it is a huge mound which Narnians raised in very ancient times over a very magical place, where there stood — and perhaps still stands — a very magical Stone. The Mound is all hollowed out within into galleries and caves, and the Stone is in the central cave of all. There is room in the mound for all our stores, and those of us who have most need of cover and are most accustomed to underground life can be lodged in the caves. The rest of us can lie in the wood. At a pinch all of us (except this worthy Giant) could retreat into the Mound itself, and there we should be beyond the reach of every danger except famine."

"It is a good thing we have a learned man among us," said Trufflehunter; but Trumpkin muttered under his breath, "Soup and celery! I wish our leaders would think less about these old wives' tales and more about victuals and arms." But all approved of Cornelius's proposal and

that very night, half an hour later, they were on the march. Before sunrise they arrived at Aslan's How.

It was certainly an awesome place, a round green hill on top of another hill, long since grown over with trees, and one little, low doorway leading into it. The tunnels inside were a perfect maze till you got to know them, and they were lined and roofed with smooth stones, and on the stones, peering in the twilight, Caspian saw strange characters and snaky patterns, and pictures in which the form of a Lion was repeated again and again. It all seemed to belong to an even older Narnia than the Narnia of which his nurse had told him.

It was after they had taken up their quarters in and around the How that fortune began to turn against them. King Miraz's scouts soon found their new lair, and he and his army arrived on the edge of the woods. And as so often happens, the enemy turned out stronger than they had reckoned. Caspian's heart sank as he saw company after company arriving. And though Miraz's men may have been afraid of going into the wood, they were even more afraid of Miraz, and with him in command they carried battle deeply into it and sometimes almost to the How itself. Caspian and other captains of course made many sorties into the open country. Thus there was fighting on most days and sometimes by night as well; but Caspian's party had on the whole the worst of it.

At last there came a night when everything had gone as badly as possible, and the rain which had been falling heavily all day had ceased at nightfall only to give place to raw cold. That morning Caspian had arranged what was his biggest battle yet, and all had hung their hopes on it. He, with most of the Dwarfs, was to have fallen on the King's right wing at daybreak, and then, when they were heavily engaged, Giant Wimbleweather, with the Centaurs and some of the fiercest beasts, was to have broken out from another place and endeavoured to cut the King's right off from the rest of the army. But it had all failed. No one had warned Caspian (because no one in these later days of Narnia remembered) that Giants are not at all clever. Poor Wimbleweather, though as brave as a lion, was a true Giant in that respect. He had broken out at the wrong time and from the wrong place, and both his party and

Caspian's had suffered badly and done the enemy little harm. The best of the Bears had been hurt, a Centaur terribly wounded, and there were few in Caspian's party who had not lost blood. It was a gloomy company that huddled under the dripping trees to eat their scanty supper.

The gloomiest of all was Giant Wimbleweather. He knew it was all his fault. He sat in silence shedding big tears which collected on the end of his nose and then fell off with a huge splash on the whole bivouac of the Mice, who had just been beginning to get warm and drowsy. They all jumped up, shaking the water out of their ears and wringing their little blankets, and asked the Giant in shrill but forcible voices whether he thought they weren't wet enough without this sort of thing. And then other people woke up and told the Mice they had been enrolled as scouts and not as a concert party, and asked why they couldn't keep quiet. And Wimbleweather tiptoed away to find some place where he could be miserable in peace and stepped on somebody's tail and somebody (they said afterwards it was a fox) bit him. And so everyone was out of temper.

But in the secret and magical chamber at the heart of the How, King Caspian, with Cornelius and the Badger and Nikabrik and Trumpkin, were at council. Thick pillars of ancient workmanship supported the roof. In the centre was the Stone itself – a stone table, split right down the centre, and covered with what had once been writing of some kind: but ages of wind and rain and snow had almost worn them away in old times when the Stone Table had stood on the hilltop, and the Mound had not yet been built above it. They were not using the Table nor sitting round it: it was too magic a thing for any common use. They sat on logs a little way from it, and between them was a rough wooden table, on which stood a rude clay lamp lighting up their pale faces and throwing big shadows on the walls.

"If your Majesty is ever to use the Horn," said Trufflehunter, "I think the time has now come." Caspian had of course told them of his treasure several days ago.

"We are certainly in great need," answered Caspian. "But it is hard to be sure we are at our greatest. Supposing there came an even worse need and we had already used it?"

"By that argument," said Nikabrik, "your Majesty will never use it until it is too late."

"I agree with that," said Doctor Cornelius.

"And what do you think, Trumpkin?" asked Caspian.

"Oh, as for me," said the Red Dwarf, who had been listening with complete indifference, "your Majesty knows

I think the Horn — and that bit of broken stone over there — and your great King Peter — and your Lion Aslan — are all eggs in moonshine. It's all one to me when your Majesty blows the Horn. All I insist on is that the army is told nothing about it. There's no good raising hopes of magical help which (as I think) are sure to be disappointed."

"Then in the name of Aslan we will wind Queen Susan's Horn," said Caspian.

"There is one thing, Sire," said Doctor Cornelius, "that should perhaps be done first. We do not know what form the help will take. It might call Aslan himself from oversea. But I think it is more likely to call Peter the High King and his mighty consorts down from the high past. But in either case, I do not think we can be sure that the help will come to this very spot —"

"You never said a truer word," put in Trumpkin.

"I think," went on the learned man, "that they — or he — will come back to one or other of the Ancient Places of Narnia. This, where we now sit, is the most ancient and most deeply magical of all, and here, I think, the answer is likeliest to come. But there are two others. One is Lantern Waste, up-river, west of Beaversdam, where the Royal Children first appeared in Narnia, as the records tell. The other is down at the river-mouth, where their castle of Cair Paravel once stood. And if Aslan himself comes, that would be the best place for meeting him too, for every story says that he is the son of the great Emperor-over-the-Sea, and over the sea he will pass. I should like very much to send messengers to both places, to Lantern Waste and the river-mouth, to receive them — or him — or it."

"Just as I thought," muttered Trumpkin. "The first

result of all this foolery is not to bring us help but to lose us two fighters."

"Who would you think of sending, Doctor Cornelius?" asked Caspian.

"Squirrels are best for getting through enemy country without being caught," said Trufflehunter.

"All *our* squirrels (and we haven't many)," said Nikabrik, "are rather flighty. The only one I'd trust on a job like that would be Pattertwig."

"Let it be Pattertwig, then," said King Caspian. "And who for our other messenger? I know you'd go, Trufflehunter, but you haven't the speed. Nor you, Doctor Cornelius."

"I *won't* go," said Nikabrik. "With all these Humans and beasts about, there must be a Dwarf here to see that the Dwarfs are fairly treated."

"Thimbles and thunderstorms!" cried Trumpkin in a rage. "Is that how you speak to the King? Send me, Sire, I'll go."

"But I thought you didn't believe in the Horn, Trumpkin," said Caspian.

"No more I do, your Majesty. But what's that got to do with it? I might as well die on a wild goose chase as die here. You are my King. I know the difference between giving advice and taking orders. You've had my advice, and now it's the time for orders."

"I will never forget this, Trumpkin," said Caspian. "Send for Pattertwig, one of you. And when shall I blow the Horn?"

"I would wait for sunrise, your Majesty," said Doctor Cornelius. "That sometimes has an effect in operations of White Magic."

A few minutes later Pattertwig arrived and had his task explained to him. As he was, like many squirrels, full of courage and dash and energy and excitement and mischief (not to say conceit), he no sooner heard it than he was eager to be off. It was arranged that he should run for Lantern Waste while Trumpkin made the shorter journey to the river-mouth. After a hasty meal they both set off with the fervent thanks and good wishes of the King, the Badger, and Cornelius.

CHAPTER EIGHT

HOW THEY LEFT THE ISLAND

"AND SO," said Trumpkin (for, as you have realized, it was he who had been telling all this story to the four children, sitting on the grass in the ruined hall of Cair Paravel) – "and so I put a crust or two in my pocket, left behind all weapons but my dagger, and took to the woods in the grey of the morning. I'd been plugging away for many hours when there came a sound that I'd never heard the like of in my born days. Eh, I won't forget that. The whole air was full of it, loud as thunder but far longer, cool and sweet as music over water, but strong enough to shake the woods. And I said to myself, 'If that's not the Horn, call me a rabbit.' And a moment later I wondered why he hadn't blown it sooner –"

"What time was it?" asked Edmund.

"Between nine and ten of the clock," said Trumpkin.

"Just when we were at the railway station!" said all the children, and looked at one another with shining eyes.

"Please go on," said Lucy to the Dwarf.

"Well, as I was saying, I wondered, but I went on as hard as I could pelt. I kept on all night – and then, when it was half light this morning, as if I'd no more sense than a Giant, I risked a short cut across open country to cut off a big loop of the river, and was caught. Not by the army, but by a pompous old fool who has charge of a little castle which is Miraz's last stronghold towards the coast. I needn't tell you they got no true tale out of me, but I was a Dwarf and that was enough. But, lobsters and lollipops! it is a good thing the seneschal *was* a pompous fool. Anyone else would have run me through there and then. But nothing would do for him short of a grand execution: sending me down 'to the ghosts' in the full ceremonial way. And then this young lady" (he nodded at Susan) "does her bit of archery — and it was pretty shooting, let me tell you — and here we are. And without my armour, for of course they took that." He knocked out and refilled his pipe.

"Great Scott!" said Peter. "So it was the horn — your own horn, Su — that dragged us all off that seat on the platform yesterday morning! I can hardly believe it; yet it all fits in."

"I don't know why you shouldn't believe it," said Lucy, "if you believe in magic at all. Aren't there lots of stories about magic forcing people out of one place — out of one world — into another? I mean, when a magician in *The Arabian Nights* calls up a Jinn, it has to come. We had to come, just like that."

"Yes," said Peter, "I suppose what makes it feel so queer is that in the stories it's always someone in our world who does the calling. One doesn't really think about where the Jinn's coming *from*."

"And now we know what it feels like for the Jinn," said Edmund with a chuckle. "Golly! It's a bit uncomfortable to know that *we* can be whistled for like that. It's worse than what Father says about living at the mercy of the telephone."

"But we want to be here, don't we," said Lucy, "if Aslan wants us?"

"Meanwhile," said the Dwarf, "what are we to do? I suppose I'd better go back to King Caspian and tell him no help has come."

"No help?" said Susan. "But it *has* worked. And here we are."

"Um – um – yes, to be sure. I see that," said the Dwarf, whose pipe seemed to be blocked (at any rate he made himself very busy cleaning it). "But – well – I mean –"

"But don't you yet see who we are?" shouted Lucy. "You *are* stupid."

"I suppose you are the four children out of the old stories," said Trumpkin. "And I'm very glad to meet you of course. And it's very interesting, no doubt. But – no offence?' – and he hesitated again.

"Do get on and say whatever you're going to say," said Edmund.

"Well, then – no offence," said Trumpkin. "But, you know, the King and Trufflehunter and Doctor Cornelius were expecting – well, if you see what I mean, help. To put it in another way, I think they'd been imagining you as great warriors. As it is – we're awfully fond of children and all that, but just at the moment, in the middle of a war – but I'm sure you understand."

"You mean you think we're no good," said Edmund, getting red in the face.

"Now pray don't be offended," interrupted the Dwarf. "I assure you, my dear little friends – "

"*Little* from you is really a bit too much," said Edmund, jumping up. "I suppose you don't believe we won the Battle of Beruna? Well, you can say what you like about me because I know –"

"There's no good losing our tempers," said Peter. "Let's fit him out with fresh armour and fit ourselves out from the treasure chamber, and have a talk after that."

"I don't quite see the point –" began Edmund, but Lucy

whispered in his ear, "Hadn't we better do what Peter says? He is the High King, you know. And I think he has an idea." So Edmund agreed and by the aid of his torch they all, including Trumpkin, went down the steps again into the dark coldness and dusty splendour of the treasure house.

The Dwarf's eyes glistened as he saw the wealth that lay on the shelves (though he had to stand on tiptoes to do so) and he muttered to himself, "It would never do to let Nikabrik see this; never." They found easily enough a mail shirt for him, a sword, a helmet, a shield, a bow and quiverful of arrows, all of dwarfish size. The helmet was of copper, set with rubies, and there was gold on the hilt of the sword: Trumpkin had never seen, much less carried, so much wealth in all his life. The children also put on mail shirts and helmets; a sword and shield were found for Edmund and a bow for Lucy — Peter and Susan were of course already carrying their gifts. As they came back up the stairway, jingling in their mail, and already looking and feeling more like Narnians and less like schoolchildren, the two boys were behind, apparently making some plan. Lucy heard Edmund say, "No, let me do it. It will be more of a sucks for him if I win, and less of a let-down for us all if I fail."

"All right, Ed," said Peter.

When they came out into the daylight Edmund turned to the Dwarf very politely and said, "I've got something to ask you. Kids like us don't often have the chance of meeting a great warrior like you. Would you have a little fencing match with me? It would be frightfully decent."

"But, lad," said Trumpkin, "these swords are sharp."

"I know," said Edmund. "But I'll never get anywhere

near you and you'll be quite clever enough to disarm me without doing me any damage."

"It's a dangerous game," said Trumpkin. "But since you make such a point of it, I'll try a pass or two."

Both swords were out in a moment and the three others jumped off the dais and stood watching. It was well worth it. It was not like the silly fighting you see with broad swords on the stage. It was not even like the rapier fighting which you sometimes see rather better done. This was real broad-sword fighting. The great thing is to slash at your enemy's legs and feet because they are the part that have no armour. And when he slashes at yours you jump with both feet off the ground so that his blow goes under them. This gave the Dwarf an advantage because Edmund, being much taller, had to be always stooping. I don't think Edmund would have had a chance if he had fought Trumpkin twenty-four hours earlier. But the air of Narnia had been working upon him ever since they arrived on the island, and all his old battles came back to him, and his arms and fingers remembered their old skill. He was King Edmund once more. Round and round the two combatants circled, stroke after stroke they gave, and Susan (who never could learn to like this sort of thing) shouted out, "Oh, *do* be careful." And then, so quickly that no one (unless they knew, as Peter did) could quite see how it happened, Edmund flashed his sword round with a peculiar twist, the Dwarf's sword flew out of his grip, and Trumpkin was wringing his empty hand as you do after a "sting" from a cricket-bat.

"Not hurt, I hope, my dear little friend?" said Edmund, panting a little and returning his own sword to its sheath.

"I see the point," said Trumpkin drily. "You know a trick I never learned."

"That's quite true," put in Peter. "The best swordsman in the world may be disarmed by a trick that's new to him. I think it's only fair to give Trumpkin a chance at something else. Will you have a shooting match with my sister? There are no tricks in archery, you know."

"Ah, you're jokers, you are," said the Dwarf. "I begin to

see. As if I didn't know how she can shoot, after what happened this morning. All the same, I'll have a try." He spoke gruffly, but his eyes brightened, for he was a famous bowman among his own people.

All five of them came out into the courtyard.

"What's to be the target?" asked Peter.

"I think that apple hanging over the wall on the branch there would do," said Susan.

"That'll do nicely, lass,"
said Trumpkin. "You mean
the yellow one near the
middle of the arch?"

"No, not that," said
Susan. "The red one up above – over
the battlement."

The Dwarf's face fell. "Looks more
like a cherry than an apple," he muttered, but he said nothing out loud.

They tossed up for first shot (greatly to the interest of
Trumpkin, who had never seen a coin tossed before) and
Susan lost. They were to shoot from the top of the steps
that led from the hall into the courtyard. Everyone could
see from the way the Dwarf took his position and handled
his bow that he knew what he was about.

Twang went the string. It was an excellent shot. The tiny
apple shook as the arrow passed, and a leaf came fluttering
down. Then Susan went to the top of the steps and strung
her bow. She was not enjoying her match half so much as
Edmund had enjoyed his; not because she had any doubt
about hitting the apple but because Susan was so tender-
hearted that she almost hated to beat someone who had
been beaten already. The Dwarf watched her keenly as she
drew the shaft to her ear. A moment later, with a little soft
thump which they could all hear in that quiet place, the
apple fell to the grass with Susan's arrow in it.

"Oh, well done, Su," shouted the other children.

"It wasn't really any better than yours," said Susan to
the Dwarf. "I think there was a tiny breath of wind as you
shot."

"No, there wasn't," said Trumpkin. "Don't tell me. I

know when I am fairly beaten. I won't even say that the scar of my last wound catches me a bit when I get my arm well back –"

"Oh, are you wounded?" asked Lucy. "Do let me look."

"It's not a sight for little girls," began Trumpkin, but then he suddenly checked himself. "There I go talking like a fool again," he said. "I suppose you're as likely to be a great surgeon as your brother was to be a great swordsman or your sister to be a great archer." He sat down on the steps and took off his hauberk and slipped down his little shirt, showing an arm hairy and muscular (in proportion) as a sailor's though not much bigger than a child's. There was a clumsy bandage on the shoulder which Lucy proceeded to unroll. Underneath, the cut looked very nasty and there was a good deal of swelling. "Oh, poor Trumpkin," said Lucy. "How horrid." Then she carefully dripped on to it one single drop of the cordial from her flask.

"Hullo. Eh? What have you done?" said Trumpkin. But however he turned his head and squinted and whisked his beard to and fro, he couldn't quite see his own shoulder. Then he felt it as well as he could, getting his arms and fingers into very difficult positions as you do when you're trying to scratch a place that is just out of reach. Then he swung his arm and raised it and tried the muscles, and finally jumped to his feet crying, "Giants and junipers! It's cured! It's as good as new." After that he burst into a great laugh and said, "Well, I've made as big a fool of myself as ever a Dwarf did. No offence, I hope? My humble duty to your Majesties all – humble duty. And thanks for my life, my cure, my breakfast – and my lesson."

The children all said it was quite all right and not to mention it.

"And now," said Peter, "if you've really decided to believe in us —"

"I have," said the Dwarf.

"It's quite clear what we have to do. We must join King Caspian at once."

"The sooner the better," said Trumpkin. "My being such a fool has already wasted about an hour."

"It's about two days' journey, the way you came," said Peter. "For us, I mean. We can't walk all day and night like you Dwarfs." Then he turned to the others. "What Trumpkin calls Aslan's How is obviously the Stone Table itself. You remember it was about half a day's march, or a little less, from there down to the Fords of Beruna —"

"Beruna's Bridge, we call it," said Trumpkin.

"There was no bridge in our time," said Peter. "And then from Beruna down to here was another day and a bit. We used to get home about teatime on the second day, going easily. Going hard, we could do the whole thing in a day and a half perhaps."

"But remember it's all woods now," said Trumpkin, "and there are enemies to dodge."

"Look here," said Edmund, "need we go by the same way that Our Dear Little Friend came?"

"No more of that, your Majesty, if you love me," said the Dwarf.

"Very well," said Edmund. "May I say our D.L.F.?"

"Oh, Edmund," said Susan. "Don't keep *on* at him like that."

"That's all right, lass — I mean your Majesty," said

Trumpkin with a chuckle. "A jibe won't raise a blister." (And after that they often called him the D.L.F. till they'd almost forgotten what it meant.)

"As I was saying," continued Edmund, "we needn't go that way. Why shouldn't we row a little south till we come to Glasswater Creek and row up it? That brings us up behind the Hill of the Stone Table, and we'll be safe while we're at sea. If we start at once, we can be at the head of Glasswater before dark, get a few hours' sleep, and be with Caspian pretty early tomorrow."

"What a thing it is to know the coast," said Trumpkin. "None of us know anything about Glasswater."

"What about food?" asked Susan.

"Oh, we'll have to do with apples," said Lucy. "Do let's get on. We've done nothing yet, and we've been here nearly two days."

"And anyway, no one's going to have my hat for a fish-basket again," said Edmund.

They used one of the raincoats as a kind of bag and put a good many apples in it. Then they all had a good long drink at the well (for they would meet no more fresh water till they landed at the head of the Creek) and went down to the boat. The children were sorry to leave Cair Paravel, which, even in ruins, had begun to feel like home again.

"The D.L.F. had better steer," said Peter, "and Ed and I will take an oar each. Half a moment, though. We'd better take off our mail: we're going to be pretty warm before we're done. The girls had better be in the bows and shout directions to the D.L.F. because he doesn't know the way. You'd better get us a fair way out to sea till we've passed the island."

And soon the green, wooded coast of the island was
falling away behind them, and its little bays and headlands
were beginning to look flatter, and the boat was rising and
falling in the gentle swell. The sea began to grow bigger
around them and, in the distance, bluer, but close round
the boat it was green and bubbly. Everything smelled salt
and there was no noise except the swishing of water and
the clop-clop of water against the sides and the splash of
the oars and the jolting noise of the rowlocks. The sun
grew hot.

It was delightful for Lucy and Susan in the bows, bending over the edge and trying to get their hands in the sea
which they could never quite reach. The bottom, mostly
pure, pale sand but with occasional patches of purple
seaweed, could be seen beneath them.

"It's like old times," said Lucy. "Do you remember our
voyage to Terebinthia – and Galma – and Seven Isles – and
the Lone Islands?"

"Yes," said Susan, "and our great ship the *Splendour
Hyaline*, with the swan's head at her prow and the carved
swan's wings coming back almost to her waist?"

"And the silken sails, and the great stern lanterns?"

"And the feasts on the poop and the musicians."

"Do you remember when we had the musicians up in the
rigging playing flutes so that it sounded like music out of
the sky?"

Presently Susan took over Edmund's oar and he came
forward to join Lucy. They had passed the island now and
stood closer in to the shore – all wooded and deserted.
They would have thought it very pretty if they had not
remembered the time when it was open and breezy and full
of merry friends.

CHAPTER NINE

WHAT LUCY SAW

Susan and the two boys were bitterly tired with rowing before they rounded the last headland and began the final pull up Glasswater itself, and Lucy's head ached from the long hours of sun and the glare on the water. Even Trumpkin longed for the voyage to be over. The seat on which he sat to steer had been made for men, not Dwarfs, and his feet did not reach the floor-boards; and everyone knows how uncomfortable that is even for ten minutes. And as they all grew more tired, their spirits fell. Up till now the children had only been thinking of how to get to Caspian. Now they wondered what they would do when they found him, and how a handful of Dwarfs and woodland creatures could defeat an army of grown-up Humans.

Twilight was coming on as they rowed slowly up the windings of Glasswater Creek – a twilight which deepened as the banks drew closer together and the overhanging trees began almost to meet overhead. It was very quiet in here as the sound of the sea died away behind them; they could even hear the trickle of the little streams that poured down from the forest into Glasswater.

They went ashore at last, far too tired to attempt lighting a fire; and even a supper of apples (though most of them felt that they never wanted to see an apple again) seemed better than trying to catch or shoot anything. After a little silent munching they all huddled down together in the moss and dead leaves between four large beech trees.

Everyone   except Lucy went to sleep at once. Lucy, being far less tired, found it hard to get comfortable. Also, she had forgotten till now that all Dwarfs snore. She knew that one of the best ways of getting to sleep is to stop trying, so she opened her eyes. Through a gap in the bracken and branches she could just see a patch of water in the Creek and the sky above it. Then, with a thrill of memory, she saw again, after all those years, the bright Narnian stars. She had once known them better than the stars of our own world, because as a Queen in Narnia she had gone to bed much later than as a child in England. And there they were – at least, three of the summer constellations could be seen from where she lay: the Ship, the Hammer, and the Leopard. "Dear old Leopard," she murmured happily to herself.

Instead of getting drowsier she was getting more awake – with an odd, night-time, dreamish kind of wakefulness. The Creek was growing brighter. She knew now that the moon was on it, though she couldn't see the moon. And now she began to feel that the whole forest was coming awake like herself. Hardly knowing why she did it, she got up quickly and walked a little distance away from their bivouac.

"This is lovely," said Lucy to herself. It was cool and fresh; delicious smells were floating everywhere.

Somewhere close by she heard the twitter of a nightingale beginning to sing, then stopping, then beginning again. It was a little lighter ahead. She went towards the light and came to a place where there were fewer trees, and whole patches or pools of moonlight, but the moonlight and the shadows so mixed that you could hardly be sure where anything was or what it was. At the same moment the nightingale, satisfied at last with his tuning up, burst into full song.

Lucy's eyes began to grow accustomed to the light, and she saw the trees that were nearest her more distinctly. A great longing for the old days when the trees could talk in Narnia came over her. She knew exactly how each of these trees would talk if only she could wake them, and what sort of human form it would put on. She looked at a silver birch: it would have a soft, showery voice and would look like a slender girl, with hair blown all about her face, and fond of dancing. She looked at the oak: he would be a wizened, but hearty old man with a frizzled beard and warts on his face and hands, and hair growing out of the warts. She looked at the beech under which she was standing. Ah! – she would be the best of all. She would be a gracious goddess, smooth and stately, the lady of the wood.

"Oh, Trees, Trees, Trees," said Lucy (though she had not been intending to speak at all). "Oh, Trees, wake, wake, wake. Don't you remember it? Don't you remember *me*? Dryads and Hamadryads, come out, come to me."

Though there was not a breath of wind they all stirred about her. The rustling noise of the leaves was almost like words. The nightingale stopped singing as if to listen to it.

Lucy felt that at any moment she would begin to understand what the trees were trying to say. But the moment
did not come. The rustling died away. The nightingale
resumed its song. Even in the moonlight the wood looked
more ordinary again. Yet Lucy had the feeling (as you
sometimes have when you are trying to remember a name
or a date and almost get it, but it vanishes before you
really do) that she had just missed something: as if she

had spoken to the trees a split second too soon or a split
second too late, or used all the right words except one, or
put in one word that was just wrong.

Quite suddenly she began to feel tired. She went back
to the bivouac, snuggled down between Susan and Peter,
and was asleep in a few minutes.

It was a cold and cheerless waking for them all next
morning, with a grey twilight in the wood (for the sun
had not yet risen) and everything damp and dirty.

"Apples, heigh-ho," said Trumpkin with a rueful grin. "I must say you ancient kings and queens don't overfeed your courtiers!"

They stood up and shook themselves and looked about. The trees were thick and they could see no more than a few yards in any direction.

"I suppose your Majesties know the way all right?" said the Dwarf.

"I don't," said Susan. "I've never seen these woods in my life before. In fact I thought all along that we ought to have gone by the river."

"Then I think you might have said so at the time," answered Peter, with pardonable sharpness.

"Oh, don't take any notice of her," said Edmund. "She always is a wet blanket. You've got that pocket compass of yours, Peter, haven't you? Well, then, we're as right as rain. We've only got to keep on going north-west — cross that little river, the what-do-you-call-it? — the Rush —"

"I know," said Peter. "The one that joins the big river at the Fords of Beruna, or Beruna's Bridge, as the D.L.F. calls it."

"That's right. Cross it and strike uphill, and we'll be at the Stone Table (Aslan's How, I mean) by eight or nine o'clock. I hope King Caspian will give us a good breakfast!"

"I hope you're right," said Susan. "I can't remember all that at all."

"That's the worst of girls," said Edmund to Peter and the Dwarf. "They never carry a map in their heads."

"That's because our heads have something inside them," said Lucy.

At first things seemed to be going pretty well. They

even thought they had struck an old path; but if you know anything about woods, you will know that one is always finding imaginary paths. They disappear after about five minutes and then you think you have found another (and hope it is not another but more of the same one) and it also disappears, and after you have been well lured out of your right direction you realize that none of them were paths at all. The boys and the Dwarf, however, were used to woods and were not taken in for more than a few seconds.

They had plodded on for about half an hour (three of them very stiff from yesterday's rowing) when Trumpkin suddenly whispered, "Stop." They all stopped. "There's something following us," he said in a low voice. "Or rather, something keeping up with us: over there on the left." They all stood still, listening and staring till their ears and eyes ached. "You and I'd better each have an arrow on the string," said Susan to Trumpkin. The Dwarf nodded, and when both bows were ready for action the party went on again.

They went a few dozen yards through fairly open woodland, keeping a sharp look-out. Then they came to a place where the undergrowth thickened and they had to pass nearer to it. Just as they were passing the place, there came a sudden something that snarled and flashed, rising out from the breaking twigs like a thunderbolt. Lucy was knocked down and winded, hearing the twang of a bowstring as she fell. When she was able to take notice of things again, she saw a great grim-looking grey bear lying dead with Trumpkin's arrow in its side.

"The D.L.F. beat you in *that* shooting match, Su," said

Peter, with a slightly forced smile. Even he had been shaken by this adventure.

"I – I left it too late," said Susan, in an embarrassed voice. "I was so afraid it might be, you know – one of our kind of bears, a *talking* bear." She hated killing things.

"That's the trouble of it," said Trumpkin, "when most of the beasts have gone enemy and gone dumb, but there are still some of the other kind left. You never know, and you daren't wait to see."

"Poor old Bruin," said Susan. "You don't think he *was*?"

"Not he," said the Dwarf. "I saw the face and I heard the snarl. He only wanted Little Girl for his breakfast. And talking of breakfast, I didn't want to discourage your Majesties when you said you hoped King Caspian would give you a good one: but meat's precious scarce in camp. And there's good eating on a bear. It would be a shame to leave the carcass without taking a bit, and it won't delay us more than half an hour. I dare say you two youngsters – Kings, I should say – know how to skin a bear?"

"Let's go and sit down a fair way off," said Susan to Lucy. "I know what a horrid messy business *that* will be." Lucy shuddered and nodded. When they had sat down she said: "Such a horrible idea has come into my head, Su."

"What's that?"

"Wouldn't it be dreadful if some day, in our own world, at home, men started going wild inside, like the animals here, and still looked like men, so that you'd never know which were which?"

"We've got enough to bother about here and now in

Narnia," said the practical Susan, "without imagining things like that."

When they rejoined the boys and the Dwarf, as much as they thought they could carry of the best meat had been cut off. Raw meat is not a nice thing to fill one's pockets with, but they folded it up in fresh leaves and made the best of it. They were all experienced enough to know that they would feel quite differently about these squashy and unpleasant parcels when they had walked long enough to be really hungry.

On they trudged again (stopping to wash three pairs of hands that needed it in the first stream they passed) until the sun rose and the birds began to sing, and more flies than they wanted were buzzing in the bracken. The stiffness from yesterday's rowing began to wear off. Everybody's spirits rose. The sun grew warmer and they took their helmets off and carried them.

"I suppose we *are* going right?" said Edmund about an hour later.

"I don't see how we can go wrong as long as we don't bear too much to the left," said Peter. "If we bear too much to the right, the worst that can happen is wasting a little time by striking the great River too soon and not cutting off the corner."

And again they trudged on with no sound except the thud of their feet and the jingle of their chain shirts.

"Where's this bally Rush got to?" said Edmund a good deal later.

"I certainly thought we'd have struck it by now," said Peter. "But there's nothing to do but keep on." They both knew that the Dwarf was looking anxiously at them, but he said nothing.

And still they trudged on and their mail shirts began to feel very hot and heavy.

"What on earth?" said Peter suddenly.

They had come, without seeing it, almost to the edge of a small precipice from which they looked down into a gorge with a river at the bottom. On the far side the cliffs rose much higher. None of the party except Edmund (and perhaps Trumpkin) was a rock climber.

"I'm sorry," said Peter. "It's my fault for coming this way. We're lost. I've never seen this place in my life before."

The Dwarf gave a low whistle between his teeth.

"Oh, do let's go back and go the other way," said Susan. "I knew all along we'd get lost in these woods."

"Susan!" said Lucy, reproachfully, "don't nag at Peter like that. It's so rotten, and he's doing all he can."

"And don't you snap at Su like that, either," said Edmund. "I think she's quite right."

"Tubs and tortoiseshells!" exclaimed Trumpkin. "If we've got lost coming, what chance have we of finding our way back? And if we're to go back to the Island and begin all over again — even supposing we could — we might as well give the whole thing up. Miraz will have finished with Caspian before we get there at that rate."

"You think we ought to go on?" said Lucy.

"I'm not sure the High King *is* lost," said Trumpkin. "What's to hinder this river being the Rush?"

"Because the Rush is not in a gorge," said Peter, keeping his temper with some difficulty.

"Your Majesty says *is*," replied the Dwarf, "but oughtn't you to say *was*? You knew this country hundreds — it may be a thousand — years ago. Mayn't it have changed? A landslide might have pulled off half the side of that hill, leaving bare rock, and there are your precipices beyond the gorge. Then the Rush might go on deepening its course year after year till you get the little precipices this side. Or there might have been an earthquake, or anything."

"I never thought of that," said Peter.

"And anyway," continued Trumpkin, "even if this is not the Rush, it's flowing roughly north and so it must

fall into the Great River anyway. I think I passed something that might have been it, on my way down. So if we go downstream, to our right, we'll hit the Great River. Perhaps not so high as we'd hoped, but at least we'll be no worse off than if you'd come my way."

"Trumpkin, you're a brick," said Peter. "Come on, then. Down this side of the gorge."

"Look! Look! Look!" cried Lucy.

"Where? What?" said everyone.

"The Lion," said Lucy. "Aslan himself. Didn't you

see?" Her face had changed completely and her eyes shone.

"Do you really mean —?" began Peter.

"Where did you think you saw him?" asked Susan.

"Don't talk like a grown-up," said Lucy, stamping her foot. "I didn't *think* I saw him. I saw him."

"Where, Lu?" asked Peter.

"Right up there between those mountain ashes. No, this side of the gorge. And up, not down. Just the opposite of the way you want to go. And he wanted us to go where he was — up there."

"How do you know that was what he wanted?" asked Edmund.

"He — I — I just know," said Lucy, "by his face."

The others all looked at each other in puzzled silence.

"Her Majesty may well have seen a lion," put in Trumpkin. "There are lions in these woods, I've been told. But it needn't have been a friendly and talking lion any more than the bear was a friendly and talking bear."

"Oh, don't be so stupid," said Lucy. "Do you think I don't know Aslan when I see him?"

"He'd be a pretty elderly lion by now," said Trumpkin, "if he's one you knew when you were here before! And if it could be the same one, what's to prevent him having gone wild and witless like so many others?"

Lucy turned crimson and I think she would have flown at Trumpkin, if Peter had not laid his hand on her arm. "The D.L.F. doesn't understand. How could he? You must just take it, Trumpkin, that we do really know about Aslan; a little bit about him, I mean. And you mustn't talk about him like that again. It isn't lucky for one thing: and it's all nonsense for another. The only question is whether Aslan was really there."

"But I know he was," said Lucy, her eyes filling with tears.

"Yes, Lu, but we don't, you see," said Peter.

"There's nothing for it but a vote," said Edmund.

"All right," replied Peter. "You're the eldest, D.L.F. What do you vote for? Up or down?"

"Down," said the Dwarf. "I know nothing about Aslan. But I do know that if we turn left and follow the gorge up, it might lead us all day before we found a place where we could cross it. Whereas if we turn right and go down, we're bound to reach the Great River in about a couple of hours. And if there *are* any real lions about, we want to go away from them, not towards them."

"What do you say, Susan?"

"Don't be angry, Lu," said Susan, "but I do think we should go down. I'm dead tired. Do let's get out of this wretched wood into the open as quick as we can. And none of us except you saw *anything*."

"Edmund?" said Peter.

"Well, there's just this," said Edmund, speaking quickly and turning a little red. "When we first discovered Narnia a year ago – or a thousand years ago, whichever it is – it was Lucy who discovered it first and none of us would believe her. I was the worst of the lot, I know. Yet she was right after all. Wouldn't it be fair to believe her this time? I vote for going up."

"Oh, Ed!" said Lucy and seized his hand.

"And now it's your turn, Peter," said Susan, "and I do hope –"

"Oh, shut up, shut up and let a chap think,"

interrupted Peter. "I'd much rather not have to vote."

"You're the High King," said Trumpkin sternly.

"Down," said Peter after a long pause. "I know Lucy may be right after all, but I can't help it. We must do one or the other."

So they set off to their right along the edge, downstream. And Lucy came last of the party, crying bitterly.

CHAPTER TEN

THE RETURN OF THE LION

To keep along the edge of the gorge was not so easy as it had looked. Before they had gone many yards they were confronted with young fir woods growing on the very edge, and after they had tried to go through these, stooping and pushing for about ten minutes, they realized that, in there, it would take them an hour to do half a mile. So they came back and out again and decided to go round the fir wood. This took them much farther to their right than they wanted to go, far out of sight of the cliffs and out of sound of the river, till they began to be afraid they had lost it altogether. Nobody knew the time, but it was getting to the hottest part of the day.

When they were able at last to go back to the edge of the gorge (nearly a mile below the point from which they had started) they found the cliffs on their side of it a good deal lower and more broken. Soon they found a way down into the gorge and continued the journey at the river's edge. But first they had a rest and a long drink. No one was talking any more about breakfast, or even dinner, with Caspian.

They may have been wise to stick to the Rush instead of going along the top. It kept them sure of their direction: and ever since the fir wood they had all been afraid of being forced too far out of their course and losing themselves in the wood. It was an old and pathless forest, and you could not keep anything like a straight course in it. Patches of hopeless brambles, fallen trees, boggy places and dense undergrowth would be always getting in your way. But the gorge of the Rush was not at all a nice place

for travelling either. I mean, it was not a nice place for
people in a hurry. For an afternoon's ramble ending in a
picnic tea it would have been delightful. It had everything
you could want on an occasion of that sort – rumbling
waterfalls, silver cascades, deep, amber-coloured pools,
mossy rocks, and deep moss on the banks in which you
could sink over your ankles, every kind of fern, jewel-like
dragon flies, sometimes a hawk overhead and once (Peter
and Trumpkin both thought) an eagle. But of course what

the children and the Dwarf wanted to see as soon as possible was the Great River below them, and Beruna, and the
way to Aslan's How.

As they went on, the Rush began to fall more and more
steeply. Their journey became more and more of a climb
and less and less of a walk – in places even a dangerous
climb over slippery rock with a nasty drop into dark
chasms, and the river roaring angrily at the bottom.

You may be sure they watched the cliffs on their left
eagerly for any sign of a break or any place where they

could climb them; but those cliffs remained cruel. It was maddening, because everyone knew that if once they were out of the gorge on that side, they would have only a smooth slope and a fairly short walk to Caspian's headquarters.

The boys and the Dwarf were now in favour of lighting a fire and cooking their bear-meat. Susan didn't want this; she only wanted, as she said, "to get *on* and finish it and get out of these beastly woods". Lucy was far too tired and miserable to have any opinion about anything. But as there was no dry wood to be had, it mattered very little what anyone thought. The boys began to wonder if raw meat was really as nasty as they had always been told. Trumpkin assured them it was.

Of course, if the children had attempted a journey like this a few days ago in England, they would have been knocked up. I think I have explained before how Narnia was altering them. Even Lucy was by now, so to speak, only one-third of a little girl going to boarding school for the first time, and two-thirds of Queen Lucy of Narnia.

"At last!" said Susan.

"Oh, hurray!" said Peter.

The river gorge had just made a bend and the whole view spread out beneath them. They could see open country stretching before them to the horizon and, between it and them, the broad silver ribbon of the Great River. They could see the specially broad and shallow place which had once been the Fords of Beruna but was now spanned by a long, many-arched bridge. There was a little town at the far end of it.

"By Jove," said Edmund. "We fought the Battle of Beruna just where that town is!"

This cheered the boys more than anything. You can't help feeling stronger when you look at a place where you won a glorious victory not to mention a kingdom, hundreds of years ago. Peter and Edmund were soon so busy talking about the battle that they forgot their sore feet and the heavy drag of their mail shirts on their shoulders. The Dwarf was interested too.

They were all getting on at a quicker pace now. The going became easier. Though there were still sheer cliffs on their left, the ground was becoming lower on their right. Soon it was no longer a gorge at all, only a valley. There were no more waterfalls and presently they were in fairly thick woods again.

Then – all at once – *whizz*, and a sound rather like the stroke of a woodpecker. The children were still wondering where (ages ago) they had heard a sound just like that and why they disliked it so, when Trumpkin shouted, "Down', at the same moment forcing Lucy (who happened to be next to him) flat down into the bracken. Peter, who had been looking up to see if he could spot a squirrel, had seen what it was – a long cruel arrow had sunk into a tree trunk just above his head. As he pulled Susan down and dropped himself, another came rasping over his shoulder and struck the ground at his side.

"Quick! Quick! Get back! *Crawl*!" panted Trumpkin.

They turned and wriggled along uphill, under the

bracken amid clouds of horribly buzzing flies. Arrows whizzed round them. One struck Susan's helmet with a sharp ping and glanced off. They crawled quicker. Sweat poured off them. Then they ran, stooping nearly double. The boys held their swords in their hands for fear they would trip them up.

It was heart-breaking work — all uphill again, back over the ground they had already travelled. When they felt that they really couldn't run any more, even to save their lives,

they all dropped down in the damp moss beside a waterfall and behind a big boulder, panting. They were surprised to see how high they had already got.

They listened intently and heard no sound of pursuit.

"So *that's* all right," said Trumpkin, drawing a deep breath. "They're not searching the wood. Only sentries, I expect. But it means that Miraz has an outpost down there. Bottles and battledores! though, it was a near thing."

"I ought to have my head smacked for bringing us this way at all," said Peter.

"On the contrary, your Majesty," said the Dwarf. "For one thing it wasn't you, it was your royal brother, King Edmund, who first suggested going by Glasswater."

"I'm afraid the D.L.F.'s right," said Edmund, who had quite honestly forgotten this ever since things began going wrong.

"And for another," continued Trumpkin, "if we'd gone my way, we'd have walked straight into that new outpost, most likely; or at least had just the same trouble avoiding it. I think this Glasswater route has turned out for the best."

"A blessing in disguise," said Susan.

"Some disguise!" said Edmund.

"I suppose we'll have to go right up the gorge again now," said Lucy.

"Lu, you're a hero," said Peter. "That's the nearest you've got today to saying *I told you so*. Let's get on."

"And as soon as we're well up into the forest," said Trumpkin, "whatever anyone says, I'm going to light a fire and cook supper. But we must get well away from here."

There is no need to describe how they toiled back up the gorge. It was pretty hard work, but oddly enough everyone felt more cheerful. They were getting their second wind; and the word *supper* had had a wonderful effect.

They reached the fir wood which had caused them so much trouble while it was still daylight, and bivouacked in a hollow just above it. It was tedious gathering the firewood; but it was grand when the fire blazed up and they began producing the damp and smeary parcels of bear-meat which would have been so very unattractive to anyone who had spent the day indoors. The Dwarf had splendid ideas about cookery. Each apple (they still had a few of these) was wrapped up in bear's meat – as if it was to be apple dumpling with meat instead of pastry, only much thicker – and spiked on a sharp stick and then roasted. And the juice of the apple worked all through the meat, like apple sauce with roast pork. Bear that has lived too much on other animals is not very nice, but bear that has had plenty of honey and fruit is excellent, and this turned out to be that sort of bear. It was a truly glorious meal. And, of course, no washing up – only lying back and watching the smoke from Trumpkin's pipe and stretching one's tired legs and chatting. Everyone felt quite hopeful now about finding King Caspian tomorrow and defeating Miraz in a few days. It may not have been sensible of them to feel like this, but they did.

They dropped off to sleep one by one, but all pretty quickly.

Lucy woke out of the deepest sleep you can imagine, with the feeling that the voice she liked best in the world had been calling her name. She thought at first it was her father's voice, but that did not seem quite right. Then she thought it was Peter's voice, but that did not seem to fit either. She did not want to get up; not because she was still tired – on the contrary she was wonderfully rested and all the aches had gone from her bones – but because she felt so extremely happy and comfortable. She was looking straight up at the Narnian moon, which is larger than ours, and at the starry sky, for the place where they had bivouacked was comparatively open.

"Lucy," came the call again, neither her father's voice nor Peter's. She sat up, trembling with excitement but not with fear. The moon was so bright that the whole forest landscape around her was almost as clear as day, though it looked wilder. Behind her was the fir wood; away to her right the jagged cliff-tops on the far side of the gorge; straight ahead, open grass to where a glade of trees began about a bow-shot away. Lucy looked very hard at the trees of that glade.

"Why, I do believe they're moving," she said to herself. "They're walking about."

She got up, her heart beating wildly, and walked towards them. There was certainly a noise in the glade, a noise such as trees make in a high wind, though there was no wind tonight. Yet it was not exactly an ordinary tree-noise either. Lucy felt there was a tune in it, but she could not catch the tune any more than she had been able to catch the words when the trees had so nearly talked to her the night before. But there was, at least, a lilt; she felt her own feet wanting to dance as she got nearer. And now there was no doubt that the trees were really moving – moving in and out through one another as if in a complicated country dance. ("And I suppose," thought Lucy, "when trees dance, it must be a very, very country dance indeed.') She was almost among them now.

The first tree she looked at seemed at first glance to be not a tree at all but a huge man with a shaggy beard and great bushes of hair. She was not frightened: she had seen such things before. But when she looked again he was only a tree, though he was still moving. You couldn't see whether he had feet or roots, of course, because when trees move they don't walk on the surface of the earth; they wade in it as we do in water. The same thing happened with every tree she looked at. At one moment they seemed to be the friendly, lovely giant and giantess forms which the tree-people put on when some good magic has called them into full life: next moment they all looked like trees again. But when they looked like trees, it was like strangely human trees, and when they looked like people, it was like strangely branchy and leafy people – and all the time that queer lilting, rustling, cool, merry noise.

"They are almost awake, not quite," said Lucy. She knew she herself was wide awake, wider than anyone usually is.

She went fearlessly in among them, dancing herself as she leaped this way and that to avoid being run into by these huge partners. But she was only half interested in them. She wanted to get beyond them to something else; it was from beyond them that the dear voice had called.

She soon got through them (half wondering whether she had been using her arms to push branches aside, or to take hands in a Great Chain with big dancers who stooped to reach her) for they were really a ring of trees round a central open place. She stepped out from among their shifting confusion of lovely lights and shadows.

A circle of grass, smooth as a lawn, met her eyes, with dark trees dancing all round it. And then – oh joy! For *he* was there: the huge Lion, shining white in the moonlight, with his huge black shadow underneath him.

But for the movement of his tail he might have been a stone lion, but Lucy never thought of that. She never stopped to think whether he was a friendly lion or not. She rushed to him. She felt her heart would burst if she lost a moment. And the next thing she knew was that she was kissing him and putting her arms as far round his neck as

she could and burying her face in the beautiful rich silkiness of his mane.

"Aslan, Aslan. Dear Aslan," sobbed Lucy. "At last."

The great beast rolled over on his side so that Lucy fell, half sitting and half lying between his front paws. He bent forward and just touched her nose with his tongue. His warm breath came all round her. She gazed up into the large wise face.

"Welcome, child," he said.

"Aslan," said Lucy, "you're bigger."

"That is because you are older, little one," answered he.

"Not because you are?"

"I am not. But every year you grow, you will find me bigger."

For a time she was so happy that she did not want to speak. But Aslan spoke.

"Lucy," he said, "we must not lie here for long. You have work in hand, and much time has been lost today."

"Yes, wasn't it a shame?" said Lucy. "*I* saw you all right. They wouldn't believe me. They're all so —"

From somewhere deep inside Aslan's body there came the faintest suggestion of a growl.

"I'm sorry," said Lucy, who understood some of his moods. "I didn't mean to start slanging the others. But it wasn't my fault anyway, was it?"

The Lion looked straight into her eyes.

"Oh, Aslan," said Lucy. "You don't mean it was? How could I — I couldn't have left the others and come up to you alone, how could I? Don't look at me like that . . . oh well, I suppose I *could*. Yes, and it wouldn't have been alone, I know, not if I was with you. But what would have been the good?"

Aslan said nothing.

"You mean," said Lucy rather faintly, "that it would have turned out all right — somehow? But how? Please, Aslan! Am I not to know?"

"To know what *would* have happened, child?" said Aslan. "No. Nobody is ever told that."

"Oh dear," said Lucy.

"But anyone can find out what *will* happen," said Aslan. "If you go back to the others now, and wake them up; and tell them you have seen me again; and that you must all get up at once and follow me — what will happen? There is only one way of finding out."

"Do you mean that is what you want me to do?" gasped Lucy.

"Yes, little one," said Aslan.

"Will the others see you too?" asked Lucy.

"Certainly not at first," said Aslan. "Later on, it depends."

"But they won't believe me!" said Lucy.

"It doesn't matter," said Aslan.

"Oh dear, oh dear," said Lucy. "And I was so pleased at finding you again. And I thought you'd let me stay. And I thought you'd come roaring in and frighten all the enemies away — like last time. And now everything is going to be horrid."

"It is hard for you, little one," said Aslan. "But things never happen the same way twice. It has been hard for us all in Narnia before now."

Lucy buried her head in his mane to hide from his face. But there must have been magic in his mane. She could feel lion-strength going into her. Quite suddenly she sat up.

"I'm sorry, Aslan," she said. "I'm ready now."

"Now you are a lioness," said Aslan. "And now all Narnia will be renewed. But come. We have no time to lose."

He got up and walked with stately, noiseless paces back to the belt of dancing trees through which she had just come: and Lucy went with him, laying a rather tremulous hand on his mane. The trees parted to let them through and for one second assumed their human forms completely. Lucy had a glimpse of tall and lovely wood-gods and wood-goddesses all bowing to the Lion; next moment they were trees again, but still bowing, with such graceful sweeps of branch and trunk that their bowing was itself a kind of dance.

"Now, child," said Aslan, when they had left the trees behind them, "I will wait here. Go and wake the others and tell them to follow. If they will not, then you at least must follow me alone."

It is a terrible thing to have to wake four people, all older than yourself and all very tired, for the purpose of telling them something they probably won't believe and making them do something they certainly won't like. "I mustn't think about it, I must just do it," thought Lucy.

She went to Peter first and shook him. "Peter," she whispered in his ear, "wake up. Quick. Aslan is here. He says we've got to follow him at once."

"Certainly, Lu. Whatever you like," said Peter unexpectedly. This was encouraging, but as Peter instantly rolled round and went to sleep again it wasn't much use.

Then she tried Susan. Susan did really wake up, but only to say in her most annoying grown-up voice, "You've been dreaming, Lucy. Go to sleep again."

She tackled Edmund next. It was very difficult to wake

him, but when at last she had done it he was really awake
and sat up.

"Eh?" he said in a grumpy voice. "What are you talking
about?"

She said it all over again. This was one of the worst parts
of her job, for each time she said it, it sounded less
convincing.

"Aslan!" said Edmund, jumping up. "Hurray! Where?"

Lucy turned back to where she could see the Lion
waiting, his patient eyes fixed upon her. "There," she said,
pointing.

"Where?" asked Edmund again.

"There. There. Don't you see? Just this side of the trees."

Edmund stared hard for a while and then said, "No.
There's nothing there. You've got dazzled and muddled
with the moonlight. One does, you know. I thought I saw
something for a moment myself. It's only an optical
what-do-you-call-it."

"I can see him all the time," said Lucy. "He's looking
straight at us."

"Then why can't I see him?"

"He said you mightn't be able to."

"Why?"

"I don't know. That's what he said."

"Oh, bother it all," said Edmund. "I do wish you
wouldn't keep on seeing things. But I suppose we'll have to
wake the others."

CHAPTER ELEVEN

THE LION ROARS

WHEN the whole party was finally awake Lucy had to tell her story for the fourth time. The blank silence which followed it was as discouraging as anything could be.

"I can't see anything," said Peter after he had stared his eyes sore. "Can you, Susan?"

"No, of course I can't," snapped Susan. "Because there isn't anything to see. She's been dreaming. Do lie down and go to sleep, Lucy."

"And I do hope," said Lucy in a tremulous voice, "that you will all come with me. Because – because I'll have to go with him whether anyone else does or not."

"Don't talk nonsense, Lucy," said Susan. "Of course you can't go off on your own. Don't let her, Peter. She's being downright naughty."

"I'll go with her, if she *must* go," said Edmund. "She's been right before."

"I know she has," said Peter. "And she may have been right this morning. We certainly had no luck going down the gorge. Still – at this hour of the night. And why should Aslan be invisible to us? He never used to be. It's not like him. What does the D.L.F. say?"

"Oh, I say nothing at all," answered the Dwarf. "If you all go, of course, I'll go with you; and if your party splits up, I'll go with the High King. That's my duty to him and King Caspian. But, if you ask my private opinion, I'm a plain dwarf who doesn't think there's much chance of finding a road by night where you couldn't find one by day. And I have no use for magic lions which are talking lions and don't talk, and friendly lions though they don't do us any good, and whopping big lions though nobody can see them. It's all bilge and beanstalks as far as I can see."

"He's beating his paw on the ground for us to hurry," said Lucy. "We must go *now*. At least I must."

"You've no right to try to force the rest of us like that. It's four to one and you're the youngest," said Susan.

"Oh, come on," growled Edmund. "We've got to go. There'll be no peace till we do." He fully intended to back Lucy up, but he was annoyed at losing his night's sleep and was making up for it by doing everything as sulkily as possible.

"On the march, then," said Peter, wearily fitting his arm into his shield-strap and putting his helmet on. At any other time he would have said something nice to Lucy, who was his favourite sister, for he knew how wretched she must be feeling, and he knew that, whatever had happened, it was not her fault. But he couldn't help being a little annoyed with her all the same.

Susan was the worst. "Supposing *I* started behaving like Lucy," she said. "I might threaten to stay here whether the rest of you went on or not. I jolly well think I shall."

"Obey the High King, your Majesty," said Trumpkin, "and let's be off. If I'm not to be allowed to sleep, I'd as soon march as stand here talking."

And so at last they got on the move. Lucy went first, biting her lip and trying not to say all the things she thought of saying to Susan. But she forgot them when she fixed her eyes on Aslan. He turned and walked at a slow pace about thirty yards ahead of them. The others had only Lucy's directions to guide them, for Aslan was not only invisible to them but silent as well. His big cat-like paws made no noise on the grass.

He led them to the right of the dancing trees – whether they were still dancing nobody knew, for Lucy had her eyes on the Lion and the rest had their eyes on Lucy – and nearer the edge of the gorge. "Cobbles and kettledrums!" thought Trumpkin. "I hope this madness isn't going to end in a moonlight climb and broken necks."

For a long way Aslan went along the top of the precipices. Then they came to a place where some little trees grew right on the edge. He turned and disappeared among them. Lucy held her breath, for it looked as if he had plunged over the cliff; but she was too busy keeping him in sight to stop and think about this. She quickened her pace and was soon among the trees herself. Looking down, she could see a steep and narrow path going slantwise down into the gorge between rocks, and Aslan descending it. He turned and looked at her with his happy eyes. Lucy clapped her hands and began to scramble down after him. From behind her she heard the voices of the others shouting, "Hi! Lucy! Look out, for goodness' sake. You're right on the edge of the gorge. Come back – " and then, a moment later, Edmund's voice saying, "No, she's right. There *is* a way down."

Half-way down the path Edmund caught up with her.

"Look!" he said in great excitement. "Look! What's that shadow crawling down in front of us?"

"It's *his* shadow," said Lucy.

"I do believe you're right, Lu," said Edmund. "I can't think how I didn't see it before. But where is he?"

"With his shadow, of course. Can't you see him?"

"Well, I almost thought I did — for a moment. It's such a rum light."

"Get on, King Edmund, get on," came Trumpkin's voice from behind and above: and then, farther behind and still nearly at the top, Peter's voice saying, "Oh, buck up, Susan. Give me your hand. Why, a baby could get down here. And do stop grousing."

In a few minutes they were at the bottom and the roaring of water filled their ears. Treading delicately, like a cat, Aslan stepped from stone to stone across the stream. In the middle he stopped, bent down to drink, and as he raised his shaggy head, dripping from the water, he turned to face them again. This time Edmund saw him. "Oh, Aslan!" he cried, darting forward. But the Lion whisked round and began padding up the slope on the far side of the Rush.

"Peter, Peter," cried Edmund. "Did you see?"

"I saw something," said Peter. "But it's so tricky in this moonlight. On we go, though, and three cheers for Lucy. I don't feel half so tired now, either."

Aslan without hesitation led them to their left, farther up the gorge. The whole journey was odd and dream-like — the roaring stream, the wet grey grass, the glimmering cliffs which they were approaching, and always the glorious, silently pacing Beast ahead. Everyone except Susan and the Dwarf could see him now.

Presently they came to another steep path, up the face of the farther precipices. These were far higher than the ones they had just descended, and the journey up them was a long and tedious zig-zag. Fortunately the Moon shone right above the gorge so that neither side was in shadow.

Lucy was nearly blown when the tail and hind legs of Aslan disappeared over the top: but with one last effort she scrambled after him and came out, rather shaky-legged and breathless, on the hill they had been trying to reach ever since they left Glasswater. The long gentle slope (heather and grass and a few very big rocks that shone white in the moonlight) stretched up to where it vanished in a glimmer of trees about half a mile away. She knew it. It was the hill of the Stone Table.

With a jingling of mail the others climbed up behind her. Aslan glided on before them and they walked after him.

"Lucy," said Susan in a very small voice.

"Yes?" said Lucy.

"I see him now. I'm sorry."

"That's all right."

"But I've been far worse than you know. I really believed it was him — he, I mean — yesterday. When he warned us not to go down to the fir wood. And I really believed it was him tonight, when you woke us up. I mean, deep down inside. Or I could have, if I'd let myself. But I just wanted to get out of the woods and — and — oh, I don't know. And what ever am I to say to him?"

"Perhaps you won't need to say much," suggested Lucy.

Soon they reached the trees and through them the children could see the Great Mound, Aslan's How, which had been raised over the Table since their days.

"Our side don't keep very good watch," muttered Trumpkin. "We ought to have been challenged before now —"

"Hush!" said the other four, for now Aslan had stopped and turned and stood facing them, looking so majestic that they felt as glad as anyone can who feels afraid, and as afraid as anyone can who feels glad. The boys strode forward: Lucy made way for them: Susan and the Dwarf shrank back.

"Oh, Aslan," said King Peter, dropping on one knee and raising the Lion's heavy paw to his face, "I'm so glad. And I'm so sorry. I've been leading them wrong ever since we started and especially yesterday morning."

"My dear son," said Aslan.

Then he turned and welcomed Edmund. "Well done," were his words.

Then, after an awful pause, the deep voice said, "Susan." Susan made no answer but the others thought she was crying. "You have listened to fears, child," said Aslan. "Come, let me breathe on you. Forget them. Are you brave again?"

"A little, Aslan," said Susan.

"And now!" said Aslan in a much louder voice with just a hint of roar in it, while his tail lashed his flanks. "And now, where is this little Dwarf, this famous swordsman and archer, who doesn't believe in lions? Come here, son of Earth, come HERE!" — and the last word was no longer the hint of a roar but almost the real thing.

"Wraiths and wreckage!" gasped Trumpkin in the ghost of a voice. The children, who knew Aslan well enough to see that he liked the Dwarf very much, were not disturbed; but it was quite another thing for Trumpkin, who had never seen a lion before, let alone this Lion. He did the only sensible thing he could have done; that is, instead of bolting, he tottered towards Aslan.

Aslan pounced. Have you ever seen a very young kitten being carried in the mother cat's mouth? It was like that. The Dwarf, hunched up in a little, miserable ball, hung from Aslan's mouth. The Lion gave him one shake and all his armour rattled like a tinker's pack and then — hey-presto — the Dwarf flew up in the air. He was as safe as if he had been in bed, though he did not feel so. As he came down the huge velvety paws caught him as gently as a

mother's arms and set him (right way up, too) on the ground.

"Son of Earth, shall we be friends?" asked Aslan.

"Ye — he — he — hes," panted the Dwarf, for it had not yet got its breath back.

"Now," said Aslan. "The Moon is setting. Look behind you: there is the dawn beginning. We have no time to lose. You three, you sons of Adam and son of Earth, hasten into the Mound and deal with what you will find there."

The Dwarf was still speechless and neither of the boys dared to ask if Aslan would follow them. All three drew their swords and saluted, then turned and jingled away into the dusk. Lucy noticed that there was no sign of weariness in their faces: both the High King and King Edmund looked more like men than boys.

The girls watched them out of sight, standing close beside Aslan. The light was changing. Low down in the east, Aravir, the morning star of Narnia, gleamed like a little moon. Aslan, who seemed larger than before, lifted his head, shook his mane, and roared.

The sound, deep and throbbing at first like an organ beginning on a low note, rose and became louder, and then far louder again, till the earth and air were shaking with it. It rose up from that hill and floated across all Narnia. Down in Miraz's camp men woke, stared palely in one another's faces, and grasped their weapons. Down below that in the Great River, now at its coldest hour, the heads and shoulders of the nymphs, and the great weedy-bearded head of the river-god, rose from the water. Beyond it, in every field and wood, the alert ears of rabbits rose from their holes, the sleepy heads of birds came out from under wings, owls hooted, vixens barked, hedgehogs grunted, the trees stirred. In towns and villages mothers pressed babies close to their breasts, staring with wild eyes, dogs whimpered, and men leaped up groping for lights. Far away on the northern frontier the mountain giants peered from the dark gateways of their castles.

What Lucy and Susan saw was a dark something coming to them from almost every direction across the hills. It looked first like a black mist creeping on the ground, then

like the stormy waves of a black sea rising higher and
higher as it came on, and then, at last, like what it was —
woods on the move. All the trees of the world appeared to
be rushing towards Aslan. But as they drew nearer they
looked less like trees, and when the whole crowd, bowing
and curtsying and waving thin long arms to Aslan, were all
around Lucy, she saw that it was a crowd of human
shapes. Pale birch-girls were tossing their heads, willow-
women pushed back their hair from their brooding faces to
gaze on Aslan, the queenly beeches stood still and adored

him, shaggy oak-men, lean and melancholy elms, shock-
headed hollies (dark themselves, but their wives all bright
with berries) and gay rowans, all bowed and rose again,
shouting, "Aslan, Aslan!" in their various husky or
creaking or wave-like voices.

The crowd and the dance round Aslan (for it had
become a dance once more) grew so thick and rapid that
Lucy was confused. She never saw where certain other
people came from who were soon capering about among
the trees. One was a youth, dressed only in a fawn-skin,
with vine-leaves wreathed in his curly hair. His face would
have been almost too pretty for a boy's, if it had not looked

so extremely wild. You felt, as Edmund said when he saw him a few days later, "There's a chap who might do anything – absolutely anything." He seemed to have a great many names – Bromios, Bassareus, and the Ram were three of them. There were a lot of girls with him, as wild as he. There was even, unexpectedly, someone on a donkey. And everybody was laughing: and everybody was shouting out, "Euan, euan, eu-oi-oi-oi."

"Is it a Romp, Aslan?" cried the youth. And apparently it was. But nearly everyone seemed to have a different idea as to what they were playing. It may have been Tig, but Lucy never discovered who was It. It was rather like Blind Man's Buff, only everyone behaved as if they were blindfolded. It was not unlike Hunt the Slipper, but the slipper was never found. What made it more complicated was that the man on the donkey, who was old and enormously fat, began calling out at once, "Refreshments! Time for refreshments," and falling off his donkey and being bundled on to it again by the others, while the donkey was under the impression that the whole thing was a circus and tried to give a display of walking on its hind legs. And all the time there were more and more vine leaves everywhere. And soon not only leaves but vines. They were climbing up everything. They were running up the legs of the tree people and circling round their necks. Lucy put up her hands to push back her hair and found she was pushing back vine branches. The donkey was a mass of them. His tail was completely entangled and something dark was nodding between his ears. Lucy looked again and saw it was a bunch of grapes. After that it was mostly grapes – overhead and underfoot and all around.

"Refreshments! Refreshments," roared the old man.

Everyone began eating, and whatever hothouses your people may have, you have never tasted such grapes. Really good grapes, firm and tight on the outside, but bursting into cool sweetness when you put them into your mouth, were one of the things the girls had never had quite enough of before. Here, there were more than anyone could possibly want, and no table-manners at all. One saw sticky and stained fingers everywhere, and, though mouths were full, the laughter never ceased nor the yodelling cries of *Euan, euan, eu-oi-oi-oi-oi*, till all of a sudden everyone felt at the same moment that the game (whatever it was), and the feast, ought to be over, and everyone flopped down breathless on the ground and turned their faces to Aslan to hear what he would say next.

At that moment the sun was just rising and Lucy remembered something and whispered to Susan,

"I say, Su, I know who they are."

"Who?"

"The boy with the wild face is Bacchus and the old one on the donkey is Silenus. Don't you remember Mr Tumnus telling us about them long ago?"

"Yes, of course. But I say, Lu –"

"What?"

"I wouldn't have felt safe with Bacchus and all his wild girls if we'd met them without Aslan."

"I should think not," said Lucy.

CHAPTER TWELVE

SORCERY AND SUDDEN VENGEANCE

MEANWHILE Trumpkin and the two boys arrived at the dark little stone archway which led into the inside of the Mound, and two sentinel badgers (the white patches on their cheeks were all Edmund could see of them) leaped up with bared teeth and asked them in snarling voices, "Who goes there?"

"Trumpkin," said the Dwarf. "Bringing the High King of Narnia out of the far past."

The badgers nosed at the boys' hands. "At last," they said. "At last."

"Give us a light, friends," said Trumpkin.

The badgers found a torch just inside the arch and Peter lit it and handed it to Trumpkin. "The D.L.F. had better lead," he said. "We don't know our way about this place."

Trumpkin took the torch and went ahead into the dark tunnel. It was a cold, black, musty place, with an occasional bat fluttering in the torchlight, and plenty of cobwebs. The boys, who had been mostly in the open air since that morning at the railway station, felt as if they were going into a trap or a prison.

"I say, Peter," whispered Edmund. "Look at those carvings on the walls. Don't they look old? And yet we're older than that. When we were last here, they hadn't been made."

"Yes," said Peter. "That makes one think."

The Dwarf went on ahead and then turned to the right, and then to the left, and then down some steps, and then to the left again. Then at last they saw a light ahead — light from under a door. And now for the first time they heard voices, for they had come to the door of the central chamber. The voices inside were angry ones. Someone was talking so loudly that the approach of the boys and the Dwarf had not been heard.

"Don't like the sound of that," whispered Trumpkin to Peter. "Let's listen for a moment." All three stood perfectly still on the outside of the door.

"You know well enough," said a voice ("That's the

King," whispered Trumpkin), "why the Horn was not blown at sunrise this morning. Have you forgotten that Miraz fell upon us almost before Trumpkin had gone, and we were fighting for our lives for the space of three hours and more? I blew it when first I had a breathing space."

"I'm not likely to forgot it," came the angry voice, "when my Dwarfs bore the brunt of the attack and one in five of them fell." ("That's Nikabrik," whispered Trumpkin.)

"For shame, Dwarf," came a thick voice ("Truffle-hunter's," said Trumpkin). "We all did as much as the Dwarfs and none more than the King."

"Tell that tale your own way for all I care," answered

Nikabrik. "But whether it was that the Horn was blown too late, or whether there was no magic in it, no help has come. You, you great clerk, you master magician, you know-all; are you still asking us to hang our hopes on Aslan and King Peter and all the rest of it?"

"I must confess — I cannot deny it — that I am deeply disappointed in the result of the operation," came the answer. ("That'll be Doctor Cornelius," said Trumpkin.)

"To speak plainly," said Nikabrik, "your wallet's empty, your eggs addled, your fish uncaught, your promises broken. Stand aside then and let others work. And that is why —"

"The help will come," said Trufflehunter. "I stand by Aslan. Have patience, like us beasts. The help will come. It may be even now at the door."

"Pah!" snarled Nikabrik. "You badgers would have us wait till the sky falls and we can all catch larks. I tell you we *can't* wait. Food is running short; we lose more than we can afford at every encounter; our followers are slipping away."

"And why?" asked Trufflehunter. "I'll tell you why. Because it is noised among them that we have called on the Kings of old and the Kings of old have not answered. The last words Trumpkin spoke before he went (and went, most likely, to his death) were, 'If you must blow the Horn, do not let the army know why you blow it or what you hope from it.' But that same evening everyone seemed to know."

"You'd better have shoved your grey snout in a hornets' nest, Badger, than suggest that I am the blab," said Nikabrik. "Take it back, or —"

"Oh, stop it, both of you," said King Caspian. "I want

to know what it is that Nikabrik keeps on hinting we should do. But before that, I want to know who those two strangers are whom he has brought into our council and who stand there with their ears open and their mouths shut."

"They are friends of mine," said Nikabrik. "And what better right have you yourself to be here than that you are a friend of Trumpkin's and the Badger's? And what right has that old dotard in the black gown to be here except that he is your friend? Why am I to be the only one who can't bring in his friends?"

"His Majesty is the King to whom you have sworn allegiance," said Trufflehunter sternly.

"Court manners, court manners," sneered Nikabrik. "But in this hole we may talk plainly. You know – and he knows – that this Telmarine boy will be king of nowhere and nobody in a week unless we can help him out of the trap in which he sits."

"Perhaps," said Cornelius, "your new friends would like to speak for themselves? You there, who and what are you?"

"Worshipful Master Doctor," came a thin, whining voice. "So please you, I'm only a poor old woman, I am, and very obliged to his Worshipful Dwarfship for his friendship, I'm sure. His Majesty, bless his handsome face, has no need to be afraid of an old woman that's nearly doubled up with the rheumatics and hasn't two sticks to put under her kettle. I have some poor little skill – not like yours, Master Doctor, of course – in small spells and cantrips that I'd be glad to use against our enemies if it was agreeable to all concerned. For I hate 'em. Oh yes. No one hates better than me."

"That is all most interesting and — er — satisfactory," said Doctor Cornelius. "I think I now know what you are, Madam. Perhaps your other friend, Nikabrik, would give some account of himself?"

A dull, grey voice at which Peter's flesh crept replied, "I'm hunger. I'm thirst. Where I bite, I hold till I die, and even after death they must cut out my mouthful from my enemy's body and bury it with me. I can fast a hundred years and not die. I can lie a hundred nights on the ice and not freeze. I can drink a river of blood and not burst. Show me your enemies."

"And it is in the presence of these two that you wish to disclose your plan?" said Caspian.

"Yes," said Nikabrik. "And by their help that I mean to execute it."

There was a minute or two during which Trumpkin and the boys could hear Caspian and his two friends speaking in low voices but could not make out what they were saying. Then Caspian spoke aloud.

"Well, Nikabrik," he said, "we will hear your plan."

There was a pause so long that the boys began to wonder if Nikabrik was ever going to begin; when he did, it was in a lower voice, as if he himself did not much like what he was saying.

"All said and done," he muttered, "none of us knows the truth about the ancient days in Narnia. Trumpkin believed none of the stories. I was ready to put them to the trial. We tried first the Horn and it has failed. If there ever was a High King Peter and a Queen Susan and a King Edmund and a Queen Lucy, then either they have not heard us, or they cannot come, or they are our enemies —"

"Or they are on the way," put in Trufflehunter.

"You can go on saying that till Miraz has fed us all to his dogs. As I was saying, we have tried one link in the chain of old legends, and it has done us no good. Well. But when your sword breaks, you draw your dagger. The stories tell of other powers beside the ancient Kings and Queens. How if we could call *them* up?"

"If you mean Aslan," said Trufflehunter, "it's all one calling on him and on the Kings. They were his servants. If he will not send them (but I make no doubt he will), is he more likely to come himself?"

"No. You're right there," said Nikabrik. "Aslan and the Kings go together. Either Aslan is dead, or he is not on our side. Or else something stronger than himself keeps him back. And if he did come – how do we know he'd be our friend? He was not always a good friend to Dwarfs by all that's told. Not even to all beasts. Ask the Wolves. And anyway, he was in Narnia only once that I ever heard of, and he didn't stay long. You may drop Aslan out of the reckoning. I was thinking of someone else."

There was no answer, and for a few minutes it was so still that Edmund could hear the wheezy and snuffling breath of the Badger.

"Who do you mean?" said Caspian at last.

"I mean a power so much greater than Aslan's that it held Narnia spellbound for years and years, if the stories are true."

"The White Witch!" cried three voices all at once, and from the noise Peter guessed that three people had leaped to their feet.

"Yes," said Nikabrik very slowly and distinctly, "I mean the Witch. Sit down again. Don't all take fright at a name as if you were children. We want power: and we want a power that will be on our side. As for power, do not the stories say that the Witch defeated Aslan, and bound him, and killed him on that very stone which is over there, just beyond the light?"

"But they also say that he came to life again," said the Badger sharply.

"Yes, they *say*," answered Nikabrik, "but you'll notice that we hear precious little about anything he did afterwards. He just fades out of the story. How do you explain that, if he really came to life? Isn't it much more likely that he didn't, and that the stories say nothing more about him because there was nothing more to say?"

"He established the Kings and Queens," said Caspian.

"A King who has just won a great battle can usually establish himself without the help of a performing lion," said Nikabrik. There was a fierce growl, probably from Trufflehunter.

"And anyway," Nikabrik continued, "what came of the Kings and their reign? They faded too. But it's very different with the Witch. They say she ruled for a hundred years: a hundred years of winter. There's power, if you like. There's something practical."

"But, heaven and earth!" said the King, "haven't we always been told that she was the worst enemy of all? Wasn't she a tyrant ten times worse than Miraz?"

"Perhaps," said Nikabrik in a cold voice. "Perhaps she *was* for you humans, if there were any of you in those days. Perhaps she was for some of the beasts. She stamped out the Beavers, I dare say; at least there are none of them in Narnia now. But she got on all right with us Dwarfs. I'm a Dwarf and I stand by my own people. *We're* not afraid of the Witch."

"But you've joined with us," said Trufflehunter.

"Yes, and a lot of good it has done my people, so far," snapped Nikabrik. "Who is sent on all the dangerous raids? The Dwarfs. Who goes short when the rations fail? The Dwarfs. Who –?"

"Lies! All lies!" said the Badger.

"And so," said Nikabrik, whose voice now rose to a scream, "if you can't help my people, I'll go to someone who can."

"Is this open treason, Dwarf?" asked the King.

"Put that sword back in its sheath, Caspian," said Nikabrik. "Murder at council, eh? Is that your game? Don't be fool enough to try it. Do you think I'm afraid of you? There's three on my side, and three on yours."

"Come on, then," snarled Trufflehunter, but he was immediately interrupted.

"Stop, stop, stop," said Doctor Cornelius. "You go on too fast. The Witch is dead. All the stories agree on that. What does Nikabrik mean by calling on the Witch?"

That grey and terrible voice which had spoken only once before said, "Oh, *is* she?"

And then the shrill, whining voice began, "Oh, bless his heart, his dear little Majesty needn't mind about the White Lady – that's what *we* call her – being dead. The Worshipful Master Doctor is only making game of a poor old woman like me when he says that. Sweet Master Doctor, learned Master Doctor, who ever heard of a witch that really died? You can always get them back."

"Call her up," said the grey voice. "We are all ready. Draw the circle. Prepare the blue fire."

Above the steadily increasing growl of the Badger and

Cornelius's sharp "What?" rose the voice of King Caspian like thunder.

"So that is your plan, Nikabrik! Black sorcery and the calling up of an accursed ghost. And I see who your companions are – a Hag and a Wer-Wolf!"

The next minute or so was very confused. There was an animal roaring, a clash of steel; the boys and Trumpkin rushed in; Peter had a glimpse of a horrible, grey, gaunt creature, half man and half wolf, in the very act of leaping

upon a boy about his own age, and Edmund saw a badger and a Dwarf rolling on the floor in a sort of cat fight. Trumpkin found himself face to face with the Hag. Her nose and chin stuck out like a pair of nut-crackers, her dirty grey hair was flying about her face and she had just got Doctor Cornelius by the throat. At one slash of Trumpkin's sword her head rolled on the floor. Then the light was knocked over and it was all swords, teeth, claws, fists, and boots for about sixty seconds. Then silence.

"Are you all right, Ed?"

"I – I think so," panted Edmund. "I've got that brute Nikabrik, but he's still alive."

"Weights and water-bottles!" came an angry voice. "It's *me* you're sitting on. Get off. You're like a young elephant."

"Sorry, D.L.F.," said Edmund. "Is that better?"

"Ow! No!" bellowed Trumpkin. "You're putting your boot in my mouth. Go away."

"Is King Caspian anywhere?" asked Peter.

"I'm here," said a rather faint voice. "Something bit me."

They all heard the noise of someone striking a match. It was Edmund. The little flame showed his face, looking pale and dirty. He blundered about for a little, found the candle (they were no longer using the lamp, for they had run out of oil), set it on the table, and lit it. When the flame rose clear, several people scrambled to their feet. Six faces blinked at one another in the candlelight.

"We don't seem to have any enemies left," said Peter. "There's the Hag, dead." (He turned his eyes quickly away from her.) "And Nikabrik, dead too. And I suppose this thing is a Wer-Wolf. It's so long since I've seen one. Wolf's head and man's body. That means he was just turning from man into wolf at the moment he was killed. And you, I suppose, are King Caspian?"

"Yes," said the other boy. "But I've no idea who you are."

"It's the High King, King Peter," said Trumpkin.

"Your Majesty is very welcome," said Caspian.

"And so is *your* Majesty," said Peter. "I haven't come to take your place, you know, but to put you into it."

"Your Majesty," said another voice at Peter's elbow. He turned and found himself face to face with the Badger.

Peter leaned forward, put his arms round the beast and kissed the furry head: it wasn't a girlish thing for him to do, because he was the High King.

"Best of badgers," he said. "You never doubted us all through."

"No credit to me, your Majesty," said Trufflehunter. "I'm a beast and we don't change. I'm a badger, what's more, and we hold on."

"I am sorry for Nikabrik," said Caspian, "though he hated me from the first moment he saw me. He had gone sour inside from long suffering and hating. If we had won quickly he might have become a good Dwarf in the days of peace. I don't know which of us killed him. I'm glad of that."

"You're bleeding," said Peter.

"Yes, I'm bitten," said Caspian. "It was that – that wolf thing." Cleaning and bandaging the wound took a long time, and when it was done Trumpkin said, "Now. Before everything else we want some breakfast."

"But not here," said Peter.

"No," said Caspian with a shudder. "And we must send someone to take away the bodies."

"Let the vermin be flung into a pit," said Peter. "But the Dwarf we will give to his people to be buried in their own fashion."

They breakfasted at last in another of the dark cellars of Aslan's How. It was not such a breakfast as they would have chosen, for Caspian and Cornelius were thinking of venison pasties, and Peter and Edmund of buttered eggs and hot coffee, but what everyone got was a little bit of cold bear-meat (out of the boys' pockets), a lump of hard cheese, an onion, and a mug of water. But, from the way they fell to, anyone would have supposed it was delicious.

CHAPTER THIRTEEN

THE HIGH KING IN COMMAND

"Now," said Peter, as they finished their meal, "Aslan and the girls (that's Queen Susan and Queen Lucy, Caspian) are somewhere close. We don't know when he will act. In his time, no doubt, not ours. In the meantime he would like us to do what we can on our own. You say, Caspian, we are not strong enough to meet Miraz in pitched battle."

"I'm afraid not, High King," said Caspian. He was liking Peter very much, but was rather tongue-tied. It was much stranger for him to meet the great Kings out of the old stories than it was for them to meet him.

"Very well, then," said Peter, "I'll send him a challenge to single combat." No one had thought of this before.

"Please," said Caspian, "could it not be me? I want to avenge my father."

"You're wounded," said Peter. "And anyway, wouldn't he just laugh at a challenge from you? I mean, we have seen that you are a king and a warrior but he thinks of you as a kid."

"But, Sire," said the Badger, who sat very close to Peter and never took his eyes off him. "Will he accept a challenge even from you? He knows he has the stronger army."

"Very likely he won't," said Peter, "but there's always the chance. And even if he doesn't, we shall spend the best part of the day sending heralds to and fro and all that. By then Aslan may have done something. And at least I can inspect the army and strengthen the position. I will send the challenge. In fact I will write it at once. Have you pen and ink, Master Doctor?"

"A scholar is never without them, your Majesty," answered Doctor Cornelius.

"Very well, I will dictate," said Peter. And while the Doctor spread out a parchment and opened his ink-horn and sharpened his pen, Peter leant back with half-closed eyes and recalled to his mind the language in which he had written such things long ago in Narnia's golden age.

"Right," he said at last. "And now, if you are ready, Doctor?"

Doctor Cornelius dipped his pen and waited. Peter dictated as follows:

"Peter, by the gift of Aslan, by election, by prescription, and by conquest, High King over all Kings in Narnia, Emperor of the Lone Islands and Lord of Cair Paravel, Knight of the Most Noble Order of the Lion, to Miraz, Son of Caspian the Eighth, sometime Lord Protector of Narnia and now styling himself King of Narnia, Greeting. Have you got that?"

"Narnia, comma, greeting," muttered the Doctor. "Yes, Sire."

"Then begin a new paragraph," said Peter. *"For to prevent the effusion of blood, and for the avoiding all other inconveniences likely to grow from the wars now levied in our realm of Narnia, it is our pleasure to adventure our royal person on behalf of our trusty and well-beloved Caspian in clean wager of battle to prove upon your Lordship's body that the said Caspian is lawful King under us in Narnia both by our gift and by the laws of the Telmarines, and your Lordship twice guilty of treachery both in withholding the dominion of Narnia from the said*

Caspian and in the most abhominable, – don't forget to spell it with an H, Doctor – bloody, and unnatural murder of your kindly lord and brother King Caspian Ninth of that name. Wherefore we most heartily provoke, challenge, and defy your Lordship to the said combat and monomachy, and have sent these letters by the hand of our well beloved and royal brother Edmund, sometime King under us in Narnia, Duke of Lantern Waste and Count of the Western March, Knight of the Noble Order of the Table, to whom we have given full power of determining with your Lordship all the conditions of the said battle. Given at our lodging in Aslan's How this XII day of the month Greenroof in the first year of Caspian Tenth of Narnia.

"That ought to do," said Peter, drawing a deep breath. "And now we must send two others with King Edmund. I think the Giant ought to be one."

"He's – he's not very clever, you know," said Caspian.

"Of course not," said Peter. "But any giant looks impressive if only he will keep quiet. And it will cheer him up. But who for the other?"

"Upon my word," said Trumpkin, "if you want someone who can kill with looks, Reepicheep would be the best."

"He would indeed, from all I hear," said Peter with a laugh. "If only he wasn't so small. They wouldn't even see him till he was close!"

"Send Glenstorm, Sire," said Trufflehunter. "No one ever laughed at a Centaur."

An hour later two great lords in the army of Miraz, the Lord Glozelle and the Lord Sopespian, strolling along their lines and picking their teeth after breakfast, looked up and saw coming down to them from the wood the Centaur and Giant Wimbleweather, whom they had seen before in battle, and between them a figure they could not recognize. Nor indeed would the other boys at Edmund's school have recognized him if they could have seen him at that moment. For Aslan had breathed on him at their meeting and a kind of greatness hung about him.

"What's to do?" said the Lord Glozelle. "An attack?"

"A parley, rather," said Sopespian. "See, they carry green branches. They are coming to surrender most likely."

"He that is walking between the Centaur and the Giant has no look of surrender in his face," said Glozelle. "Who can he be? It is not the boy Caspian."

"No indeed," said Sopespian. "This is a fell warrior, I warrant you, wherever the rebels have got him from. He is (in your Lordship's private ear) a kinglier man than ever Miraz was. And what mail he wears! None of our smiths can make the like."

"I'll wager my dappled Pomely he brings a challenge, not a surrender," said Glozelle.

"How then?" said Sopespian. "We hold the enemy in our fist here. Miraz would never be so hair-brained as to throw away his advantage on a combat."

"He might be brought to it," said Glozelle in a much lower voice.

"Softly," said Sopespian. "Step a little aside here out of earshot of those sentries. Now. Have I taken your Lordship's meaning aright?"

"If the King undertook wager of battle," whispered Glozelle, "why, either he would kill or be killed."

"So," said Sopespian, nodding his head.

"And if he killed we should have won this war."

"Certainly. And if not?"

"Why, if not, we should be as able to win it without the King's grace as with him. For I need not tell your Lordship that Miraz is no very great captain. And after that, we should be both victorious and kingless."

"And it is your meaning, my Lord, that you and I could hold this land quite as conveniently without a King as with one?"

Glozelle's face grew ugly. "Not forgetting," said he, "that it was we who first put him on the throne. And in all the years that he has enjoyed it, what fruits have come our way? What gratitude has he shown us?"

"Say no more," answered Sopespian. "But look – here comes one to fetch us to the King's tent."

When they reached Miraz's tent they saw Edmund and his two companions seated outside it and being entertained with cakes and wine, having already delivered the challenge, and withdrawn while the King was considering it. When they saw them thus at close quarters the two Telmarine lords thought all three of them very alarming.

Inside, they found Miraz, unarmed and finishing his breakfast. His face was flushed and there was a scowl on his brow.

"There!" he growled, flinging the parchment across the table to them. "See what a pack of nursery tales our jackanapes of a nephew has sent us."

"By your leave, Sire," said Glozelle. "If the young warrior whom we have just seen outside is the King Edmund mentioned in the writing, then I would not call him a nursery tale but a very dangerous knight."

"King Edmund, pah!" said Miraz. "Does your Lordship believe those old wives' fables about Peter and Edmund and the rest?"

"I believe my eyes, your Majesty," said Glozelle.

"Well, this is to no purpose," said Miraz, "but as touching the challenge, I suppose there is only one opinion between us?"

"I suppose so, indeed, Sire," said Glozelle.

"And what is that?" asked the King.

"Most infallibly to refuse it," said Glozelle. "For though I have never been called a coward, I must plainly say that to meet that young man in battle is more than my heart would serve me for. And if (as is likely) his brother, the High King, is more dangerous than he – why, on your life, my Lord King, have nothing to do with him."

"Plague on you!" cried Miraz. "It was not that sort of council I wanted. Do you think I am asking you if I should be afraid to meet this Peter (if there is such a man)? Do you think I fear him? I wanted your counsel on the policy of the matter; whether we, having the advantage, should hazard it on a wager of battle."

"To which I can only answer, your Majesty," said Glozelle, "that for all reasons the challenge should be refused. There is death in the strange knight's face."

"There you are again!" said Miraz, now thoroughly angry. "Are you trying to make it appear that I am as great a coward as your Lordship?"

"Your Majesty may say your pleasure," said Glozelle sulkily.

"You talk like an old woman, Glozelle," said the King. "What say you, my Lord Sopespian?"

"Do not touch it, Sire," was the reply. "And what your Majesty says of the policy of the thing comes in very happily. It gives your Majesty excellent grounds for a refusal without any cause for questioning your Majesty's honour or courage."

"Great Heaven!" exclaimed Miraz, jumping to his feet. "Are *you* also bewitched today? Do you think I am *looking* for grounds to refuse it? You might as well call me coward to my face."

The conversation was going exactly as the two lords wished, so they said nothing.

"I see what it is," said Miraz, after staring at them as if his eyes would start out of his head, "you are as lily-livered as hares yourselves and have the effrontery to imagine my heart after the likeness of yours! Grounds for a refusal, indeed! Excuses for not fighting! Are you soldiers? Are you Telmarines? Are you men? And if I do refuse it (as all good reasons of captaincy and martial policy urge me to do) you will think, and teach others to think, I was afraid. Is it not so?"

"No man of your Majesty's age," said Glozelle, "would be called coward by any wise soldier for refusing the combat with a great warrior in the flower of his youth."

"So I'm to be a dotard with one foot in the grave, as well as a dastard," roared Miraz. "I'll tell you what it is, my Lords. With your womanish counsels (ever shying from the true point, which is one of policy) you have done the very opposite of your intent. I had meant to refuse it. But I'll accept it. Do you hear, accept it! I'll not be shamed because some witchcraft or treason has frozen both your bloods."

"We beseech your Majesty —" said Glozelle, but Miraz had flung out of the tent and they could hear him bawling out his acceptance to Edmund.

The two lords looked at one another and chuckled quietly.

"I knew he'd do it if he were properly chafed," said Glozelle. "But I'll not forget he called me coward. It shall be paid for."

There was a great stirring at Aslan's How when the news came back and was communicated to the various creatures. Edmund, with one of Miraz's captains, had already marked out the place for the combat, and ropes and stakes had been put round it. Two Telmarines were to stand at two of the corners, and one in the middle of one side, as marshals of the lists. Three marshals for the other two corners and the other side were to be furnished by the High King. Peter was just explaining to Caspian that he could not be one, because his right to the throne was what they were fighting about, when suddenly a thick, sleepy voice said, "Your Majesty, please." Peter turned and there stood the eldest of the Bulgy Bears.

"If you please, your Majesty," he said, "I'm a bear, I am."

"To be sure, so you are, and a good bear too, I don't doubt," said Peter.

"Yes," said the Bear. "But it was always a right of the bears to supply one marshal of the lists."

"Don't let him," whispered Trumpkin to Peter. "He's a good creature, but he'll shame us all. He'll go to sleep and he *will* suck his paws. In front of the enemy too."

"I can't help that," said Peter. "Because he's quite right. The Bears had that privilege. I can't imagine how it has been remembered all these years, when so many other things have been forgotten."

"Please, your Majesty," said the Bear.

"It is your right," said Peter. "And you shall be one of the marshals. But you *must* remember not to suck your paws."

"Of course not," said the Bear in a very shocked voice.

"Why, you're doing it this minute!" bellowed Trumpkin.

The Bear whipped his paw out of his mouth and pretended he hadn't heard.

"Sire!" came a shrill voice from near the ground.

"Ah – Reepicheep!" said Peter after looking up and down and round as people usually did when addressed by the Mouse.

"Sire," said Reepicheep. "My life is ever at your command, but my honour is my own. Sire, I have among my people the only trumpeter in your Majesty's army. I had thought, perhaps, we might have been sent with the challenge. Sire, my people are grieved. Perhaps if it were your pleasure that I should be a marshal of the lists, it would content them."

A noise not unlike thunder broke out from somewhere overhead at this point, as Giant Wimbleweather burst into one of those not very intelligent laughs to which the nicer sorts of Giant are so liable. He checked himself at once and looked as grave as a turnip by the time Reepicheep discovered where the noise came from.

"I am afraid it would not do," said Peter very gravely. "Some humans are afraid of mice –"

"I had observed it, Sire," said Reepicheep.

"And it would not be quite fair to Miraz," Peter continued, "to have in sight anything that might abate the edge of his courage."

"Your Majesty is the mirror of honour," said the Mouse with one of his admirable bows. "And on this matter we have but a single mind. . . . I thought I heard someone laughing just now. If anyone present wishes to make me the subject of his wit, I am very much at his service – with my sword – whenever he has leisure."

An awful silence followed this remark, which was

broken by Peter saying, "Giant Wimbleweather and the Bear and the Centaur Glenstorm shall be our marshals. The combat will be at two hours after noon. Dinner at noon precisely."

"I say," said Edmund as they walked away, "I suppose it *is* all right. I mean, I suppose you can beat him?"

"That's what I'm fighting him to find out," said Peter.

CHAPTER FOURTEEN

HOW ALL WERE VERY BUSY

A LITTLE before two o'clock Trumpkin and the Badger
sat with the rest of the creatures at the wood's edge looking
across at the gleaming line of Miraz's army which was
about two arrow-shots away. In between, a square space of
level grass had been staked for the combat. At the two far
corners stood Glozelle and Sopespian with drawn swords.
At the near corners were Giant Wimbleweather and the
Bulgy Bear, who in spite of all their warnings was sucking
his paws and looking, to tell the truth, uncommonly silly.
To make up for this, Glenstorm on the right of the lists,
stock-still except when he stamped a hind hoof occa-
sionally on the turf, looked much more imposing than the
Telmarine baron who faced him on the left. Peter had just
shaken hands with Edmund and the Doctor, and was now
walking down to the combat. It was like the moment
before the pistol goes at an important race, but very much
worse.

"I wish Aslan had turned up before it came to this," said
Trumpkin.

"So do I," said Trufflehunter. "But look behind you."

"Crows and crockery!" muttered the Dwarf as soon as
he had done so. "What are they? Huge people – beautiful
people – like gods and goddesses and giants. Hundreds
and thousands of them, closing in behind us. What are
they?"

"It's the Dryads and Hamadryads and Silvans," said
Trufflehunter. "Aslan has waked them."

"Humph!" said the Dwarf. "That'll be very useful if the

enemy try any treachery. But it won't help the High King very much if Miraz proves handier with his sword."

The Badger said nothing, for now Peter and Miraz were entering the lists from opposite ends, both on foot, both in chain shirts, with helmets and shields. They advanced till they were close together. Both bowed and seemed to speak, but it was impossible to hear what they said. Next moment the two swords flashed in the sunlight. For a second the clash could be heard but it was immediately drowned because both armies began shouting like crowds at a football match.

"Well done, Peter, oh, well done!" shouted Edmund as he saw Miraz reel back a whole pace and a half. "Follow it up, quick!" And Peter did, and for a few seconds it looked as if the fight might be won. But then Miraz pulled himself together – began to make real use of his height and weight. "Miraz! Miraz! The King! The King!" came the roar of the Telmarines. Caspian and Edmund grew white with sickening anxiety.

"Peter is taking some dreadful knocks," said Edmund.

"Hullo!" said Caspian. "What's happening now?"

"Both falling apart," said Edmund. "A bit blown, I expect. Watch. Ah, now they're beginning again, more scientifically this time. Circling round and round, feeling each other's defences."

"I'm afraid this Miraz knows his work," muttered the Doctor. But hardly had he said this when there was such a clapping and baying and throwing up of hoods among the Old Narnians that it was nearly deafening.

"What was it? What was it?" asked the Doctor. "My old eyes missed it."

"The High King has pricked him in the arm-pit," said

Caspian, still clapping. "Just where the arm-hole of the hauberk let the point through. First blood."

"It's looking ugly again now, though," said Edmund. "Peter's not using his shield properly. He must be hurt in the left arm."

It was only too true. Everyone could see that Peter's shield hung limp. The shouting of the Telmarines redoubled.

"You've seen more battles than I," said Caspian. "Is there any chance now?"

"Precious little," said Edmund. "I suppose he might *just* do it. With luck."

"Oh, why did we let it happen at all?" said Caspian.

Suddenly all the shouting on both sides died down. Edmund was puzzled for a moment. Then he said, "Oh, I see. They've both agreed to a rest. Come on, Doctor. You and I may be able to do something for the High King." They ran down to the lists and Peter came outside the ropes to meet them, his face red and sweaty, his chest heaving.

"Is your left arm wounded?" asked Edmund.

"It's not exactly a wound," Peter said. "I got the full weight of his shoulder on my shield — like a load of bricks — and the rim of the shield drove into my wrist. I don't think it's broken, but it might be a sprain. If you could tie it up very tight I think I could manage."

While they were doing this, Edmund asked anxiously, "What do you think of him, Peter?"

"Tough," said Peter. "Very tough. I have a chance if I can keep him on the hop till his weight and short wind come against him — in this hot sun too. To tell the truth, I haven't much chance else. Give my love to — to everyone at home, Ed, if he gets me. Here he comes into the lists again.

So long, old chap. Good-bye, Doctor. And I say, Ed, say something specially nice to Trumpkin. He's been a brick."

Edmund couldn't speak. He walked back with the Doctor to his own lines with a sick feeling in his stomach.

But the new bout went well. Peter now seemed to be able to make some use of his shield, and he certainly made good use of his feet. He was almost playing Tig with Miraz now, keeping out of range, shifting his ground, making the enemy work.

"Coward!" booed the Telmarines. "Why don't you stand up to him? Don't you like it, eh? Thought you'd come to fight, not dance. Yah!"

"Oh, I do hope he won't listen to them," said Caspian.

"Not he," said Edmund. "You don't know him – Oh!" – for Miraz had got in a blow at last, on Peter's helmet. Peter staggered, slipped sideways, and fell on one knee. The roar of the Telmarines rose like the noise of the sea. "Now, Miraz," they yelled. "Now. Quick! Quick! Kill him." But indeed there was no need to egg the usurper on. He was on top of Peter already. Edmund bit his lips till the blood came, as the sword flashed down on Peter. It looked as if it would slash off his head. Thank heavens! it had glanced down his right shoulder. The Dwarf-wrought mail was sound and did not break.

"Great Scott!" cried Edmund. "He's up again. Peter, go it, Peter."

"I couldn't see what happened," said the Doctor. "How did he do it?"

"Grabbed Miraz's arm as it came down," said Trumpkin, dancing with delight. "There's a man for you! Uses his enemy's arm as a ladder. The High King! The High King! Up, Old Narnia!"

"Look," said Trufflehunter. "Miraz is angry. It is good."

They were certainly at it hammer and tongs now: such a flurry of blows that it seemed impossible for either not to be killed. As the excitement grew, the shouting almost died away. The spectators were holding their breath. It was most horrible and most magnificent.

A great shout arose from the Old Narnians. Miraz was down – not struck by Peter, but face downwards, having tripped on a tussock. Peter stepped back, waiting for him to rise.

"Oh bother, bother, bother," said Edmund to himself. "Need he be as gentlemanly as all that? I suppose he must. Comes of being a Knight *and* a High King. I suppose it is what Aslan would like. But that brute will be up again in a minute and then –"

But "that brute" never rose. The Lords Glozelle and Sopespian had their own plans ready. As soon as they saw their King down they leaped into the lists crying, "Treachery! Treachery! The Narnian traitor has stabbed him in the back while he lay helpless. To arms! To arms, Telmar!"

Peter hardly understood what was happening. He saw two big men running towards him with drawn swords. Then the third Telmarine had leaped over the ropes on his left. "To arms, Narnia! Treachery!" Peter shouted. If all three had set upon him at once he would never have spoken again. But Glozelle stopped to stab his own King dead where he lay: "That's for your insult, this morning," he whispered as the blade went home. Peter swung to face Sopespian, slashed his legs from under him and, with the back-cut of the same stroke, walloped off his head. Edmund was now at his side crying, "Narnia, Narnia! The Lion!" The whole Telmarine army was rushing towards them. But now the Giant was stamping forward, stooping low and swinging his club. The Centaurs charged. *Twang, twang* behind and *hiss, hiss* overhead came the archery of Dwarfs. Trumpkin was fighting at his left. Full battle was joined.

"Come back, Reepicheep, you little ass!" shouted Peter. "You'll only be killed. This is no place for mice." But the ridiculous little creatures were dancing in and out among the feet of both armies, jabbing with their swords. Many a Telmarine warrior that day felt his foot suddenly pierced as if by a dozen skewers, hopped on one leg cursing the pain, and fell as often as not. If he fell, the mice finished him off; if he did not, someone else did.

But almost before the Old Narnians were really warmed to their work they found the enemy giving way. Tough-looking warriors turned white, gazed in terror not on the Old Narnians but on something behind them, and then flung down their weapons, shrieking, "The Wood! The Wood! The end of the world!"

But soon neither their cries nor the sound of weapons could be heard any more, for both were drowned in the ocean-like roar of the Awakened Trees as they plunged through the ranks of Peter's army, and then on, in pursuit of the Telmarines. Have you ever stood at the edge of a great wood on a high ridge when a wild south-wester broke over it in full fury on an autumn evening? Imagine that sound. And then imagine that the wood, instead of being fixed to one place, was rushing *at* you; and was no longer trees but huge people; yet still like trees because their long arms waved like branches and their heads tossed and leaves fell round them in showers. It was like that for the Telmarines. It was a little alarming even for the

Narnians. In a few minutes all Miraz's followers were running down to the Great River in the hope of crossing the bridge to the town of Beruna and there defending themselves behind ramparts and closed gates.

They reached the river, but there was no bridge. It had disappeared since yesterday. Then utter panic and horror fell upon them and they all surrendered.

But what had happened to the bridge?

Early that morning, after a few hours' sleep, the girls had

waked, to see Aslan standing over them and to hear his voice saying, "We will make holiday." They rubbed their eyes and looked round them. The trees had all gone but could still be seen moving away towards Aslan's How in a dark mass. Bacchus and the Maenads – his fierce, madcap girls – and Silenus were still with them. Lucy, fully rested, jumped up. Everyone was awake, everyone was laughing, flutes were playing, cymbals clashing. Animals, not Talking Animals, were crowding in upon them from every direction.

"What is it, Aslan?" said Lucy, her eyes dancing and her feet wanting to dance.

"Come, children," said he. "Ride on my back again today."

"Oh, lovely!" cried Lucy, and both girls climbed on to the warm golden back as they had done no one knew how many years before. Then the whole party moved off – Aslan leading, Bacchus and his Maenads leaping, rushing, and turning somersaults, the beasts frisking round them, and Silenus and his donkey bringing up the rear.

They turned a little to the right, raced down a steep hill, and found the long Bridge of Beruna in front of them. Before they had begun to cross it, however, up out of the water came a great wet, bearded head, larger than a man's, crowned with rushes. It looked at Aslan and out of its mouth a deep voice came.

"Hail, Lord," it said. "Loose my chains."

"Who on earth is *that*?" whispered Susan.

"I think it's the river-god, but hush," said Lucy.

"Bacchus," said Aslan. "Deliver him from his chains."

"That means the bridge, I expect," thought Lucy. And so it did. Bacchus and his people splashed forward into the shallow water, and a minute later the most curious things began happening. Great, strong trunks of ivy came curling up all the piers of the bridge, growing as quickly as a fire grows, wrapping the stones round, splitting, breaking, separating them. The walls of the bridge turned into hedges gay with hawthorn for a moment and then disappeared as the whole thing with a rush and a rumble collapsed into the swirling water. With much splashing, screaming, and laughter the revellers waded or swam or danced across the ford ("Hurrah! It's the Ford of Beruna again now!" cried the girls) and up the bank on the far side and into the town.

Everyone in the streets fled before their faces. The first house they came to was a school: a girls' school, where a lot of Narnian girls, with their hair done very tight and ugly tight collars round their necks and thick tickly stockings on their legs, were having a history lesson. The sort of "History" that was taught in Narnia under Miraz's rule was duller than the truest history you ever read and less true than the most exciting adventure story.

"If you don't attend, Gwendolen," said the mistress, "and stop looking out of the window, I shall have to give you an order-mark."

"But please, Miss Prizzle –" began Gwendolen.

"Did you hear what I said, Gwendolen?" asked Miss Prizzle.

"But please, Miss Prizzle," said Gwendolen, "there's a LION!"

"Take two order-marks for talking nonsense," said Miss Prizzle. "And now –" A roar interrupted her. Ivy came curling in at the windows of the classroom. The walls became a mass of shimmering green, and leafy branches arched overhead where the ceiling had been. Miss Prizzle found she was standing on grass in a forest glade. She clutched at her desk to steady herself, and found that the desk was a rose-bush. Wild people such as she had never even imagined were crowding round her. Then she saw the Lion, screamed and fled, and with her fled her class, who were mostly dumpy, prim little girls with fat legs. Gwendolen hesitated.

"You'll stay with us, sweetheart?" said Aslan.

"Oh, *may* I? Thank you, thank you," said Gwendolen. Instantly she joined hands with two of the Maenads, who whirled her round in a merry dance and helped her take off some of the unnecessary and uncomfortable clothes that she was wearing.

Wherever they went in the little town of Beruna it was the same. Most of the people fled, a few joined them. When they left the town they were a larger and a merrier company.

They swept on across the level fields on the north bank, or left bank, of the river. At every farm animals came out to join them. Sad old donkeys who had never known joy grew suddenly young again; chained dogs broke their chains; horses kicked their carts to pieces and came trotting along with them – clop-clop – kicking up the mud and whinnying.

At a well in a yard they met a man who was beating a boy. The stick burst into flower in the man's hand. He tried to drop it, but it stuck to his hand. His arm became a branch, his body the trunk of a tree, his feet took root. The boy, who had been crying a moment before, burst out laughing and joined them.

At a little town half-way to Beaversdam, where two rivers met, they came to another school, where a tired-looking girl was teaching arithmetic to a number of boys who looked very like pigs. She looked out of the window and saw the divine revellers singing up the street and a stab of joy went through her heart. Aslan stopped right under the window and looked up at her.

"Oh, don't, don't," she said. "I'd love to. But I mustn't. I

must stick to my work. And the children would be frightened if they saw you."

"Frightened?" said the most pig-like of the boys. "Who's she talking to out of the window? Let's tell the inspector she talks to people out of the window when she ought to be teaching us."

"Let's go and see who it is," said another boy, and they all came crowding to the window. But as soon as their mean little faces looked out, Bacchus gave a great cry of *Euan, euoi-oi-oi-oi* and the boys all began howling with fright and trampling one another down to get out of the door and jumping out of the windows. And it was said afterwards (whether truly or not) that those particular little boys were never seen again, but that there were a lot of very fine little pigs in that part of the country which had never been there before.

"Now, Dear Heart," said Aslan to the Mistress: and she jumped down and joined them.

At Beaversdam they re-crossed the river and came east again along the southern bank. They came to a little cottage where a child stood in the doorway crying. "Why are you crying, my love?" asked Aslan. The child, who had never seen a picture of a lion, was not afraid of him. "Auntie's very ill," she said. "She's going to die." Then Aslan went to go in at the door of the cottage, but it was too small for him. So, when he had got his head through, he pushed with his shoulders (Lucy and Susan fell off when he did this) and lifted the whole house up and it fell backwards and apart. And there, still in her bed, though the bed was now in the open air, lay a little old woman who looked as if she had Dwarf blood in her. She was at death's door, but when she opened her eyes and saw the bright, hairy head of the lion staring into her face, she did not scream or faint. She said, "Oh, Aslan! I knew it was true. I've been waiting for this all my life. Have you come to take me away?"

"Yes, Dearest," said Aslan. "But not the long journey yet." And as he spoke, like the flush creeping along the underside of a cloud at sunrise, the colour came back to her white face and her eyes grew bright and she sat up and said, "Why, I do declare I feel *that* better. I think I could take a little breakfast this morning."

"Here you are, mother," said Bacchus, dipping a pitcher in the cottage well and handing it to her. But what was in it now was not water but the richest wine, red as red-currant jelly, smooth as oil, strong as beef, warming as tea, cool as dew.

"Eh, you've done something to our well," said the old woman. "That makes a nice change, that does." And she jumped out of bed.

"Ride on me," said Aslan, and added to Susan and Lucy, "You two queens will have to run now."

"But we'd like that just as well," said Susan. And off they went again.

And so at last, with leaping and dancing and singing, with music and laughter and roaring and barking and neighing, they all came to the place where Miraz's army stood flinging down their swords and holding up their hands, and Peter's army, still holding their weapons and breathing hard, stood round them with stern and glad faces. And the first thing that happened was that the old woman slipped off Aslan's back and ran across to Caspian and they embraced one another; for she was his old nurse.

CHAPTER FIFTEEN

ASLAN MAKES A DOOR IN THE AIR

AT the sight of Aslan the cheeks of the Telmarine soldiers became the colour of cold gravy, their knees knocked together, and many fell on their faces. They had not believed in lions and this made their fear greater. Even the Red Dwarfs, who knew that he came as a friend, stood with open mouths and could not speak. Some of the Black Dwarfs, who had been of Nikabrik's party, began to edge away. But all the Talking Beasts surged round the Lion, with purrs and grunts and squeaks and whinneys of delight, fawning on him with their tails, rubbing against him, touching him reverently with their noses and going to and fro under his body and between his legs. If you have ever seen a little cat loving a big dog whom it knows and trusts, you will have a pretty good picture of their behaviour. Then Peter, leading Caspian, forced his way through the crowd of animals.

"This is Caspian, Sir," he said. And Caspian knelt and kissed the Lion's paw.

"Welcome, Prince," said Aslan. "Do you feel yourself sufficient to take up the Kingship of Narnia?"

"I – I don't think I do, Sir," said Caspian. "I'm only a kid."

"Good," said Aslan. "If you had felt yourself sufficient, it would have been a proof that you were not. Therefore, under us and under the High King, you shall be King of Narnia, Lord of Cair Paravel, and Emperor of the Lone Islands. You and your heirs while your race lasts. And your coronation – but what have we here?" For at that

moment a curious little procession was approaching –
eleven Mice, six of whom carried between them something on a litter made of branches, but the litter was no
bigger than a large atlas. No one has ever seen mice more
woebegone than these. They were plastered with mud –
some with blood too – and their ears were down and their
whiskers drooped and their tails dragged in the grass, and
their leader piped on his slender pipe a melancholy tune.
On the litter lay what seemed little better than a damp
heap of fur; all that was left of Reepicheep. He was still
breathing, but more dead than alive, gashed with
innumerable wounds, one paw crushed, and, where his
tail had been, a bandaged stump.

"Now, Lucy," said Aslan.

Lucy had her diamond bottle out in a moment. Though
only a drop was needed on each of Reepicheep's wounds,
the wounds were so many that there was a long and
anxious silence before she had finished and the Master
Mouse sprang from the litter. His hand went at once to
his sword hilt, with the other he twirled his whiskers. He
bowed.

"Hail, Aslan!" came his shrill voice. "I have the honour
–" But then he suddenly stopped.

The fact was that he still had no tail – whether that
Lucy had forgotten it or that her cordial, though it could
heal wounds, could not make things grow again. Reepicheep became aware of his loss as he made his bow; perhaps it altered something in his balance. He looked over
his right shoulder. Failing to see his tail, he strained his
neck further till he had to turn his shoulders and his
whole body followed. But by that time his hind-quarters
had turned too and were out of sight. Then he strained his

neck looking over his shoulder again, with the same result. Only after he had turned completely round three times did he realize the dreadful truth.

"I am confounded," said Reepicheep to Aslan. "I am completely out of countenance. I must crave your indulgence for appearing in this unseemly fashion."

"It becomes you very well, Small One," said Aslan.

"All the same," replied Reepicheep, "if anything could

be done . . . Perhaps her Majesty?" and here he bowed to Lucy.

"But what do you want with a tail?" asked Aslan.

"Sir," said the Mouse, "I can eat and sleep and die for my King without one. But a tail is the honour and glory of a Mouse."

"I have sometimes wondered, friend," said Aslan, "whether you do not think too much about your honour."

"Highest of all High Kings," said Reepicheep, "permit me to remind you that a very small size has been bestowed on us Mice, and if we did not guard our dignity, some (who weigh worth by inches) would allow themselves very unsuitable pleasantries at our expense. That is why I have been at some pains to make it known that no one who does not wish to feel this sword as near his heart as I can reach shall talk in my presence about Traps or Toasted Cheese or Candles: no, Sir – not the tallest fool in Narnia!" Here he glared very fiercely up at Wimbleweather, but the Giant, who was always a stage behind everyone else, had not yet discovered what was being talked about down at his feet, and so missed the point.

"Why have your followers all drawn *their* swords, may I ask?" said Aslan.

"May it please your High Majesty," said the second Mouse, whose name was Peepiceek, "we are all waiting to cut off our own tails if our Chief must go without his. We will not bear the shame of wearing an honour which is denied to the High Mouse."

"Ah!" roared Aslan. "You have conquered me. You have great hearts. Not for the sake of your dignity, Reepicheep, but for the love that is between you and your people, and still more for the kindness your people showed me long ago when you ate away the cords that bound me on the Stone Table (and it was then, though you have long forgotten it, that you began to be *Talking* Mice), you shall have your tail again."

Before Aslan had finished speaking the new tail was in its place. Then, at Aslan's command, Peter bestowed the Knighthood of the Order of the Lion on Caspian, and Caspian, as soon as he was knighted, himself bestowed it on Trufflehunter and Trumpkin and Reepicheep, and made Doctor Cornelius his Lord Chancellor, and confirmed the Bulgy Bear in his hereditary office of Marshal of the Lists. And there was great applause.

After this the Telmarine soldiers, firmly but without taunts or blows, were taken across the ford and all put under lock and key in the town of Beruna and given beef and beer. They made a great fuss about wading in the river, for they all hated and feared running water just as much as they hated and feared woods and animals. But in the end the nuisance was over: and then the nicest parts of that long day began.

Lucy, sitting close to Aslan and divinely comfortable, wondered what the trees were doing. At first she thought they were merely dancing; they were certainly going round slowly in two circles, one from left to right and the other from right to left. Then she noticed that they kept throwing something down in the centre of both circles. Sometimes she thought they were cutting off long strands of their hair; at other times it looked as if they were breaking off bits of their fingers – but, if so, they had plenty of fingers to spare and it did not hurt them. But whatever they were throwing down, when it reached the ground, it became brushwood or dry sticks. Then three or four of the Red Dwarfs came forward with their tinder boxes and set light to the pile, which first crackled, and then blazed, and finally roared as a woodland bonfire on midsummer night ought to do. And everyone sat down in a wide circle round it.

Then Bacchus and Silenus and the Maenads began a dance, far wilder than the dance of the trees; not merely a dance for fun and beauty (though it was that too) but a magic dance of plenty, and where their hands touched,

and where their feet fell, the feast came into existence —
sides of roasted meat that filled the grove with delicious
smell, and wheaten cakes and oaten cakes, honey and
many-coloured sugars and cream as thick as porridge and
as smooth as still water, peaches, nectarines, pome-
granates, pears, grapes, strawberries, raspberries —
pyramids and cataracts of fruit. Then, in great wooden
cups and bowls and mazers, wreathed with ivy, came the
wines; dark, thick ones like syrups of mulberry juice, and
clear red ones like red jellies liquefied, and yellow wines

and green wines and yellow-green and greenish-yellow.

But for the tree people different fare was provided.
When Lucy saw Clodsley Shovel and his moles scuffling
up the turf in various places (which Bacchus had pointed
out to them) and realized that the trees were going to eat
earth it gave her rather a shudder. But when she saw the
earths that were actually brought to them she felt quite
different. They began with a rich brown loam that looked
almost exactly like chocolate; so like chocolate, in fact,
that Edmund tried a piece of it, but he did not find it at
all nice. When the rich loam had taken the edge off their

hunger, the trees turned to an earth of the kind you see in Somerset, which is almost pink. They said it was lighter and sweeter. At the cheese stage they had a chalky soil, and then went on to delicate confections of the finest gravels powdered with choice silver sand. They drank very little wine, and it made the Hollies very talkative: for the most part they quenched their thirst with deep draughts of mingled dew and rain, flavoured with forest flowers and the airy taste of the thinnest clouds.

Thus Aslan feasted the Narnians till long after the

sunset had died away, and the stars had come out; and the great fire, now hotter but less noisy, shone like a beacon in the dark woods, and the frightened Telmarines saw it from far away and wondered what it might mean. The best thing of all about this feast was that there was no breaking up or going away, but as the talk grew quieter and slower, one after another would begin to nod and finally drop off to sleep with feet towards the fire and good friends on either side, till at last there was silence all round the circle, and the chattering of water over stone at the Ford of Beruna could be heard once more. But all night Aslan and the

Moon gazed upon each other with joyful and unblinking eyes.

Next day messengers (who were chiefly squirrels and birds) were sent all over the country with a proclamation to the scattered Telmarines — including, of course, the prisoners in Beruna. They were told that Caspian was now King and that Narnia would henceforth belong to the Talking Beasts and the Dwarfs and Dryads and Fauns and other creatures quite as much as to the men. Any who

chose to stay under the new conditions might do so; but for those who did not like the idea, Aslan would provide another home. Anyone who wished to go there must come to Aslan and the Kings at the Ford of Beruna by noon on the fifth day. You may imagine that this caused plenty of head-scratching among the Telmarines. Some of them, chiefly the young ones, had, like Caspian, heard stories of the Old Days and were delighted that they had come back. They were already making friends with the creatures. These all decided to stay in Narnia. But most of the older men, especially those who had been important under Miraz, were sulky and had no wish to live in a country where they could not rule the roost. "Live here with a lot of blooming performing animals! No fear," they said. "And ghosts too," some added with a shudder. "That's what those there Dryads really are. It's not canny." They were also suspicious. "I don't trust 'em," they said. "Not with that awful Lion and all. He won't keep his claws off us long, *you'll* see." But then they were equally suspicious of his offer to give them a new home. "Take us off to his den and eat us one by one most likely," they muttered. And the more they talked to one another the sulkier and more suspicious they became. But on the appointed day more than half of them turned up.

At one end of the glade Aslan had caused to be set up two stakes of wood, higher than a man's head and about three feet apart. A third, and lighter, piece of wood was bound across them at the top, uniting them, so that the whole thing looked like a doorway from nowhere into nowhere. In front of this stood Aslan himself with Peter on his right and Caspian on his left. Grouped round them were Susan and Lucy, Trumpkin and Trufflehunter, the Lord Cornelius, Glenstorm, Reepicheep, and others. The children and the Dwarfs had made good use of the royal wardrobes in what had been the castle of Miraz and was now the castle of Caspian, and what with silk and cloth of gold, with snowy linen glancing through slashed sleeves, with silver mail shirts and jewelled sword-hilts, with gilt helmets and feathered bonnets, they were almost too bright to look at. Even the beasts wore rich chains about their necks. Yet nobody's eyes were on them or the children. The living and strokable gold of Aslan's mane outshone them all. The rest of the Old Narnians stood down each side of the glade. At the far end stood the

Telmarines. The sun shone brightly and pennants fluttered in the light wind.

"Men of Telmar," said Aslan, "you who seek a new land, hear my words. I will send you all to your own country, which I know and you do not."

"We don't remember Telmar. We don't know where it is. We don't know what it is like," grumbled the Telmarines.

"You came into Narnia out of Telmar," said Aslan. "But you came into Telmar from another place. You do not belong to this world at all. You came hither, certain generations ago, out of that same world to which the High King Peter belongs."

At this, half the Telmarines began whimpering, "There you are. Told you so. He's going to kill us all, send us right out of the world," and the other half began throwing out their chests and slapping one another on the back and whispering, "There you are. Might have guessed we didn't belong to this place with all its queer, nasty, unnatural creatures. We're of royal blood, you'll see." And even Caspian and Cornelius and the children turned to Aslan with looks of amazement on their faces.

"Peace," said Aslan in the low voice which was nearest to his growl. The earth seemed to shake a little and every living thing in the grove became still as stone.

"You, Sir Caspian," said Aslan, "might have known that you could be no true King of Narnia unless, like the Kings of old, you were a son of Adam and came from the world of Adam's sons. And so you are. Many years ago in that world, in a deep sea of that world which is called the South Sea, a shipload of pirates were driven by storm on an island. And there they did as pirates would: killed the

natives and took the native women for wives, and made
palm wine, and drank and were drunk, and lay in the
shade of the palm trees, and woke up and quarrelled, and
sometimes killed one another. And in one of these frays
six were put to flight by the rest and fled with their
women into the centre of the island and up a mountain,
and went, as they thought, into a cave to hide. But it was
one of the magical places of that world, one of the chinks
or chasms between that world and this. There were many
chinks or chasms between worlds in old times, but they
have grown rarer. This was one of the last: I do not say
the last. And so they fell, or rose, or blundered, or
dropped right through, and found themselves in this
world, in the Land of Telmar which was then unpeopled.
But why it was unpeopled is a long story: I will not tell it
now. And in Telmar their descendants lived and became a
fierce and proud people; and after many generations there
was a famine in Telmar and they invaded Narnia, which
was then in some disorder (but that also would be a long
story), and conquered it and ruled it. Do you mark all this
well, King Caspian?"

"I do indeed, Sir," said Caspian. "I was wishing that I
came of a more honourable lineage."

"You come of the Lord Adam and the Lady Eve," said
Aslan. "And that is both honour enough to erect the head
of the poorest beggar, and shame enough to bow the
shoulders of the greatest emperor on earth. Be content."

Caspian bowed.

"And now," said Aslan, "you men and women of
Telmar, will you go back to that island in the world of
men from which your fathers first came? It is no bad
place. The race of those pirates who first found it has died

out, and it is without inhabitants. There are good wells of fresh water, and fruitful soil, and timber for building, and fish in the lagoons; and the other men of that world have not yet discovered it. The chasm is open for your return; but this I must warn you, that once you have gone through, it will close behind you for ever. There will be no more commerce between the worlds by that door."

There was silence for a moment. Then a burly, decent-looking fellow among the Telmarine soldiers pushed forward and said:

"Well, I'll take the offer."

"It is well chosen," said Aslan. "And because you have spoken first, strong magic is upon you. Your future in that world shall be good. Come forth."

The man, now a little pale, came forward. Aslan and his court drew aside, leaving him free access to the empty doorway of the stakes.

"Go through it, my son," said Aslan, bending towards him and touching the man's nose with his own. As soon as the Lion's breath came about him, a new look came into the man's eyes – startled, but not unhappy – as if he were trying to remember something. Then he squared his shoulders and walked into the Door.

Everyone's eyes were fixed on him. They saw the three pieces of wood, and through them the trees and grass and sky of Narnia. They saw the man between the doorposts: then, in one second, he had vanished utterly.

From the other end of the glade the remaining Telmarines set up a wailing. "Ugh! What's happened to him? Do you mean to murder us? We won't go that way." And then one of the clever Telmarines said:

"We don't see any other world through those sticks. If

you want us to believe in it, why doesn't one of *you* go? All your own friends are keeping well away from the sticks."

Instantly Reepicheep stood forward and bowed. "If *my* example can be of any service, Aslan," he said, "I will take eleven mice through that arch at your bidding without a moment's delay."

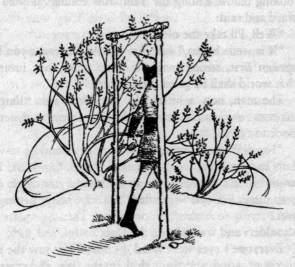

"Nay, little one," said Aslan, laying his velvety paw ever so lightly on Reepicheep's head. "They would do dreadful things to you in that world. They would show you at fairs. It is others who must lead."

"Come on," said Peter suddenly to Edmund and Lucy. "Our time's up."

"What do you mean?" said Edmund.

"This way," said Susan, who seemed to know all about it. "Back into the trees. We've got to change."

"Change what?" asked Lucy.

"Our clothes, of course," said Susan. "Nice fools we'd look on the platform of an English station in *these*."

"But our other things are at Caspian's castle," said Edmund.

"No, they're not," said Peter, still leading the way into the thickest wood. "They're all here. They were brought down in bundles this morning. It's all arranged."

"Was that what Aslan was talking to you and Susan about this morning?" asked Lucy.

"Yes – that and other things," said Peter, his face very solemn. "I can't tell it to you all. There were things he wanted to say to Su and me because we're not coming back to Narnia."

"Never?" cried Edmund and Lucy in dismay.

"Oh, you two are," answered Peter. "At least, from what he said, I'm pretty sure he means you to get back some day. But not Su and me. He says we're getting too old."

"Oh, Peter," said Lucy. "What awful bad luck. Can you bear it?"

"Well, I think I can," said Peter. "It's all rather different from what I thought. You'll understand when it comes to your last time. But, quick, here are our things."

It was odd, and not very nice, to take off their royal clothes and to come back in their school things (not very fresh now) into that great assembly. One or two of the nastier Telmarines jeered. But the other creatures all cheered and rose up in honour of Peter the High King, and Queen Susan of the Horn, and King Edmund, and Queen Lucy. There were affectionate and (on Lucy's part) tearful farewells with all their old friends – animal kisses, and hugs from Bulgy Bears, and hands wrung by Trumpkin, and a last tickly, whiskerish embrace with Trufflehunter. And of course Caspian offered the Horn back to Susan and of course Susan told him to keep it. And then, wonderfully and terribly, it was farewell to

Aslan himself, and Peter took his place with Susan's hands on his shoulders and Edmund's on hers and Lucy's on his and the first of the Telmarine's on Lucy's, and so in a long line they moved forward to the Door. After that came a moment which is hard to describe, for the children seemed to be seeing three things at once. One was the mouth of a cave opening into the glaring green and blue of an island in the Pacific, where all the Telmarines would find themselves the moment they were through the Door. The second was a glade in Narnia, the faces of Dwarfs and Beasts, the deep eyes of Aslan, and the white patches on the Badger's cheeks. But the third (which rapidly swallowed up the other two) was the grey, gravelly surface of a platform in a country station, and a seat with luggage round it, where they were all sitting as if they had never moved from it — a little flat and dreary for a moment after all they had been through, but also, unexpectedly, nice in its own way, what with the familiar railway smell and the English sky and the summer term before them.

"Well!" said Peter. "We *have* had a time."

"Bother!" said Edmund. "I've left my new torch in Narnia."

The Chronicles of Narnia
by C. S. Lewis

C. S. Lewis's wit and wisdom, his blend of excitement and adventure with fantasy, have made this magnificent series beloved of many generations of readers. The final book, *The Last Battle*, won the Carnegie Medal for 1956.

Each of the seven titles is a complete story in itself, but all take place in the magical land of Narnia. Guided by the noble Lion Aslan, the children learn that evil and treachery can only be overcome by courage, loyalty and great sacrifice.

The titles, in suggested reading order, are as follows:

The Magician's Nephew
The Lion, the Witch and the Wardrobe
The Horse and His Boy
Prince Caspian
The Voyage of the Dawn Treader
The Silver Chair
The Last Battle

The Chronicles of Narnia
C. S. Lewis

Each of the seven titles is a complete story in itself, but all take place in the magical land of Narnia. Guided by the noble Lion Aslan, the children learn that evil and treachery can only be overcome by courage, loyalty and great sacrifice.

In reading order:

The Magician's Nephew
The Lion, The Witch and the Wardrobe
The Horse and His Boy
Prince Caspian
The Voyage of the *Dawn Treader*
The Silver Chair
The Last Battle
Narnia Gift Pack
(all seven titles in a slipcase)

The Chronicles of Narnia are also available in larger format editions.